The Haunted Martyr

The Haunted Martyr

Kenneth Cameron

Felony & Mayhem Press • New York

All the characters and events portrayed in this work are fictitious.

THE HAUNTED MARTYR

A Felony & Mayhem mystery

PRINTING HISTORY
First UK edition (Orion): 2012
Felony & Mayhem edition (first US edition): 2019

Copyright © 2012 by Kenneth Cameron

ISBN: 978-1-63194-197-9

Manufactured in the United States of America

Library of Congress Cataloging-in-Publication Data

Names: Cameron, Kenneth M., 1931- author.
Title: The haunted martyr / Kenneth Cameron.
Description: First US edition. | New York : Felony & Mayhem Press, 2019. |
  Series: A Felony & Mayhem mystery
Identifiers: LCCN 2019011446| ISBN 9781631941979 (pbk.) |
  ISBN 9781631941993 (e-book)
Subjects: | GSAFD: Mystery fiction.
Classification: LCC PS3553.A4335 H38 2019 | DDC 813/.54--dc23
LC record available at https://lccn.loc.gov/2019011446

To
Vincenzo Amato
Teacher, friend

The icon above says you're holding a copy of a book in the Felony & Mayhem "Historical" category, which ranges from the ancient world up through the 1940s. If you enjoy this book, you may well like other "Historical" titles from Felony & Mayhem Press.

For more about these books, and other Felony & Mayhem titles, or to place an order, please visit our website at:

www.FelonyAndMayhem.com

Other "Historical" titles from

FELONY&MAYHEM

ANNAMARIA ALFIERI
City of Silver
Strange Gods

KENNETH CAMERON
The Frightened Man
The Bohemian Girl

FIDELIS MORGAN
Unnatural Fire
The Rival Queens

ALEX REEVE
Half Moon Street

KATE ROSS
Cut to the Quick
A Broken Vessel
Whom the Gods Love
The Devil in Music

CATHERINE SHAW
The Library Paradox
The Riddle of the River

LC TYLER
A Cruel Necessity
A Masterpiece of Corruption

LAURA WILSON
The Lover
The Innocent Spy
An Empty Death
The Wrong Man
A Willing Victim
The Riot

OLGA WOJTAS
Miss Blaine's Prefect and the
Golden Samovar

The Haunted Martyr

'Sunny Italy,' he said.

The rain was pelting down, hammering the high windows and the little walled terrace beyond.

She said, 'It's bound to change.'

He made a rude noise, something between a laugh and a spit. 'I dragged you here because you're supposed to have a warm climate. It's freezing!'

'If it were freezing, Denton, it wouldn't be raining.'

'Janet—!' He scowled at her. 'Don't quibble with me.'

She smiled at him, a hint of the adult smiling at a child. She had a face more intelligent than handsome, filling out now after an almost fatal bout of typhus but still with shadows under the violet eyes, the left side marked by a scar that ran from temple to jawbone. Her long hair was worn loose, pulled back a little with a tortoise-shell band over the top of her head, no effort made to hide the scar.

What was to be noticed first about her, however, were her clothes—bright-colored lavenders and turquoise today, vaguely medieval, flowing, as if she had stepped out of a Pre-Raphaelite painting, and with no corset on. She looked fifty years behind the fashion, or perhaps ahead of it. Either way, she looked unusual, probably eccentric, unsettling to the mass of women who wore the new corsets that pulled their spines into a concave curve and thrust their torsos forward so that they looked as if they might fall over on them. She said, 'I don't like you reminding me that it's my fault we're here.'

'It isn't your fault!' He rattled the paper of a letter he was reading and then leaned his head on his left hand. 'I should have taken you somewhere farther south. Greece. Egypt.'

'Oh, Egypt!' She made it sound as if Egypt couldn't be taken seriously. 'Your real trouble is you miss Atkins.'

'I don't anything of the kind.'

'You've had a letter from him and it's made you grumpy.'

'It hasn't made me grumpy!' Atkins—ex-Sergeant Atkins, British Army—had for years been his servant, the two of them an odd pairing: Denton, an American who had never before in his life had a servant, reluctant to have somebody wait on him; Atkins, a former soldier-servant, eager to move up. Atkins had dreams of independence; Denton had encouraged him; now Atkins had chosen to leave his service, stay in London and go into the wax recording business. He had, however, agreed to stay in his old quarters for the present to keep somebody in Denton's house. 'Atkins sounds happy,' Denton said miserably. 'He's sold almost a thousand recordings of his comic song.' The truth was, he did miss Atkins. The truth was, he'd hoped that 'I'm a Knut, the K-nuttiest One of All' wouldn't sell a single recording and Atkins would be begging to join him in Naples.

Denton looked at the remains of an Italian's notion of breakfast as if he were looking at the ruins of his hopes: a plate of hard bread cut into inch-thick slices; a pot of milky coffee, now empty; a large bowl of an orange jam that was supposed to be marmalade. He wanted fried eggs and bacon.

'He's your best friend,' she said.

'I paid him extra *not* to be my best friend.'

'And you miss him.'

'I don't! Well, of course I do, but it isn't—It's this goddam living out of a trunk. I'm sick of living in a *pensione* with a lot of females who treat me like a menace and you like a fallen woman. I can't work here!' He was supposed to be writing a book on the spooks and spirits of Naples. He seemed unable to start.

'I *am* a fallen woman. If it's so unsettling here, why don't you go out? Go see that man from the International Society of whatever it is.'

'Super-Normal Investigation. His letters make him sound like an idiot.'

'You've got to see him some time; you said he's *the* authority on mediums.' She was studying an Italian grammar. 'Sophie wrote down some "useful phrases" for me, and I can't find them in my book. How am I supposed to learn if they're not in my book? I'm not like you, Denton, able to learn Italian out of the air.' She looked at a slip of paper. 'What do you suppose "*va fa n'cula*" really means? Sophie said it's a kind of greeting, but I'd like to—Why are you laughing?'

'Because it means "in your arse".'

'It doesn't.'

'The Italians I knew in the West used to say "Vafangoola". Same thing. "Va" is go; "fa", do it; "n" I think is a kind of dialect for "in the"; "cula" is arse. Actually, I think it's ruder than "in your arse". "Do it in your arse". "Up your arse". One of those. And I don't learn Italian out of the air; I once spent a year running a rail gang of Italians, and I paid one of them an extra dollar a week to teach me their lingo.'

'Sophie's a naughty little bitch.' She slammed her dictionary shut. 'She was having a joke! I didn't think she knew what a joke is.' Sophie was a whore in a famous London house; Janet often visited her friend the madame, Mrs Castle, there, had in fact once worked there herself.

'Well, look on the bright side: now you know how to insult somebody. You might use it on Mrs Newcombe.' Mrs Sylvester

Newcombe, as she called herself, was a manufacturer's wife from Rochester, New York, who was staying in the same *pensione* and who, as Janet quoted, 'knew the price of everything and the value of nothing', and always in what she called 'daalars' in a hard, nasal voice: *This tea gown cost me seventy-nine daalars in Paris.* Now Denton said, 'Put on your best smile, sing out, "*Vafancoola,* Mrs Newcombe," when she gives you one of her looks.'

'Unfortunately, I don't think she'd know what it means, even if I translated for her. Mrs Newcombe believes that ignorance is the foundation of good society, which makes you wonder how she ever had that rather sweet daughter.'

'Whom she means to keep as ignorant as a newborn pup, which is why she has forbidden the daughter to see you. Also why she gives you those looks. I'm really sick of Mrs Newcombe. And this goddam *pensione*!'

'I wonder what she tells Lucy. That I'm a former whore? I wonder how she gets that into words.' Unusually for her, Janet slipped into an excruciatingly nasal American accent and a rather flutey voice, her idea of Mrs Newcombe. 'Oh, Lucy, that awful Mrs Striker used to be a lady of the night!'

'Maybe we ought to go back to bed and forget the rain.'

'Lucy's bringing her friend to look at my dresses once she's got rid of her mother. And you're supposed to see that man about a house.'

'Oh, cripes, Lucy and a pal, giggling and screaming. Is it the plump one who thinks she's a comedy soubrette?'

'Mmm, Harriet. Her mother's the very fat one with the eyeglass.'

'And her daughter too homely to attract some measly Italian *conte* to drag back to the States. I'd feel sorry for the girls if they weren't so silly.' He threw himself back in his chair, tilted the coffee pot over his cup to establish that it was still empty, and sighed. 'Frioni wants to show me more *palazzi* up on the Vomero hill where the swells live. I can't get it through his head that we don't want to live up there. He gives me a superior smile every time I tell him I want to live in *Naples*. The last time I said, "I know what I want, Frioni," he said, "No, signore, you don't.'" He made a face. 'One more week of it and we head for Egypt.'

'*You* may head for Egypt if you like.'

He started to speak, thought better of it. She had made it clear from the beginning that he could not tell her what to do. She would never be his wife, in good part for that reason. The truth was that he wanted her more than she wanted him, and manoeuvring around that truth had become part of their relationship, even a kind of conspiracy between them. 'You know what I mean,' he said, his voice suddenly gentle. She had had typhus; she had almost died; he had only to remember that to become gentle.

She said, 'I intend to stay in Naples and enjoy myself and study my Italian grammar and wait for better weather.'

He exhaled noisily. 'I can't work in this damned place, all the coming and going—stupid adolescent females—their damned mothers—'

'Are you having a tantrum, Denton? Let me know if you're going to throw things.'

He stared at her, got the top of her head. She had lowered her face over her book again. He wanted to be angry, angrier than he already was. He wanted, in fact, to throw something. That coffee pot would do—His hand actually started towards it, the movement a kind of jerk, and he thought, *I'm having a tantrum, am I?* And then, *She's right. I am.*

His hand dropped to his lap. He faced the truth: it wasn't the weather; it wasn't the girls; it wasn't their mothers. It was coming here with something wrong between them; it was having to stay in a place where they couldn't be themselves, as if they'd had to rent masks along with the rooms. And it was not being able to get started on the new book. He'd contracted to write two before he left London; one had seemed easy enough—*The Ghosts of Naples*, about hauntings and séances—but once on the spot he wondered what he'd been thinking of. The other, a novel, was in bits and snippets in his head, not yet come together.

Denton had lived for most of a decade in London; he wrote about Americans and America, but he liked the alienation of being an expatriate. He liked the writer's life and, so far, the successful writer's income, and he didn't want to go back to any of the things he had had to do before to make a living: soldier, farmer, lawman, drifter, prison guard, railroad honcho, Wild West show *pistolero*, vagrant, drunk. At fifty, he looked as if all those things had left their tracks on his face, but he had young, ferocious eyes; between them, a huge nose stuck out and hooked over a grey moustache that hung down both sides of his mouth.

'I'll get dressed,' he said. He was wearing an old quilted smoking jacket over corduroy rat-catchers, on his feet moccasins he had got someplace in the West; they had holes in the soles and were falling apart.

'I want to go to the university today,' she said. She was taking a degree in economics at London's University College; she had made an arrangement to study in Naples while she was recuperating.

'I'll go with you. If I finish with the house man in time.'

'You're supposed to see the man from the Society for what's-it.'

'Not yet. No—I can't concentrate.' Denton ran a hand over his bristly hair. 'Fiction's so much easier to write. You don't have to talk to people.'

'Meanwhile, you have to find us a house.'

'Not with Frioni. I may finish with him this morning. In fact, I may finish with him right off. I *will* finish with him right off. Tell him I'll find my own damned house. I'm sick of him. To hell with him.'

'And how shall we find a house?'

'"The weather will change, or the wood will come."'

'When I said something like that, you took my head off.'

He kissed her. 'Never. Never.' With his face still close to hers, he said, 'You *will* lie down and rest after you go to the university—hmm?'

She pulled his head down and whispered in his ear. 'You're not my mother.'

'You've been sick!' He looked at her with the helplessness of the one who loves too much. 'Oh, the hell with it.'

He went to his own room (they had separate bedrooms with a sitting room between, rather a mirror of their London arrangement, where they lived in separate houses with back gardens and a gate between) and dressed—a dark brown lounge suit that buttoned very high, waistcoated; a soft-collared shirt, contrary to fashion, no Atkins to scold him about it; a heavy silk tie he'd picked up here in Naples, far too thick and decorated to please Atkins; and a Naples-bought soft hat that would have appalled him. Dark brown brogues, London-made, just right for a downpour. When he came out of the dressing room, he could hear female voices: the girls had arrived. *Judas Priest*. He hesitated at the sitting-room door, trying to think of what he'd say to pretty Lucy and her overweight friend Harriet, daughter of Mrs Rufus Guttmann of Canandaigua, New York, Mr Guttmann being said to be 'in dry goods'.

Harriet Guttmann saved him by not giving him a chance to speak. 'And lo, the lord and master cometh!' she cried. Lucy giggled, and the plump one guffawed and said, 'Huzza and hello, she cried as she waved her wooden leg!'

Denton smiled and started to mutter something about going out. Janet said the young ladies had come to look at dresses. Lucy said, 'Oh, I adore your clothes, Mrs Striker! So French and so *au courant*! Is this one by Brulant? He's all flowing lines and colour now, you know, quite shocking to the stick-in-the-muds.'

'Like our sainted mothers,' the other one said. She added that she was so excited her breath was coming in long gasps and short pants. The two young women screamed with laughter. Denton fled.

He had brought a hooded ulster and the new Italian hat (to be protected by the hood if necessary) from the bedroom. Headed for the *pensione*'s door, he wondered if he needed an umbrella and veered towards the closet that served as reception. To his surprise, the middle-aged woman on duty there said, 'You have a visitor,' the words heavily accented—no *h* in 'have', the *-or* in visitor given pride of place. As he didn't know anybody in Naples except Frioni, he supposed the house agent had come to save him a walk in the rain; he tried to work his anger up again, preparing to fire the man. 'Where?' he said.

'In the lounge room.' *In de lounge-eh rum.* She pointed. The *pensione* took up two floors of a fairly sizeable building, had a history of satisfying English and American travellers of a certain kind, which had turned out not to include Denton. Thus, the place had local interpretations of certain English rooms—a lounge, a breakfast room, a writing room, a smoking room, even a boxroom. God knows what the Neapolitans actually called them.

The lounge looked like every other room in the place, no more suggesting lounging than it suggested gymnastics: dated, over-elaborate furniture; faded fabrics; lamps and flower stands of bronze or something that looked like bronze; a lot of classical reference in engravings and bric-a-brac. In one corner was a square chair made to fit against the walls, its arms ending in ferocious dogs' heads that looked as if they were protecting the seat. Perched on it was not Frioni the house agent but a little man in a soaking-wet brown garment that was lifted just far enough off the floor to show leather sandals and bare feet that hadn't been washed in so long they had a kind of brown varnish. The robe, if that's what it was, was cinched around his waist with what might once have been curtain cord.

As Denton went closer, he realised that the man smelled. And that he was old and bald except for long, greasy hair at the back that looked as if it had been glued on. Denton reviewed his scatty Italian and put together the words '*Sono Denton. Vo'mi parlare?*' That wasn't right, but close enough.

The little man, now standing, came only to Denton's shoulder. His face, although grubby and lined, was delicate, almost childlike. He said, 'You don't need to speak Italian, unless of course you want to, and it must be a burden, as you don't speak it at all well.' His voice was also old, rather husky, but the accent was of the most upper-crust and annoying British kind. 'I am Gerald Sommers. I wish to report that I am haunted.'

Oh, Lord, a lunatic. 'I'm afraid, um, Mr—'

'Brother. Or *Fra*. I am mostly called Fra Geraldo in Spagnuoli.'

'Fra.' That explained the robe and the sandals, although Denton didn't think anybody actually dressed that way any more except in cobbled-up paintings of boozing monks. 'Mmm, well, Fra, I don't deal in… I mean, are you sure you have the right man?'

'Are you not the person who is writing a book about Neapolitan hauntings?'

The local newspapers, glad for copy, had published articles about him and his planned book. And now, like one of the ghosts he hadn't located yet, it had come back to haunt him. Denton said, 'I'm *planning* something like that, yes, but…'

'Well, then: I am being haunted.'

'Mm, well, um, why don't we meet sometime and I can take notes. If it's useful for the book, I'd of course put it in.'

The little man's head quivered and he said, 'I don't give a rap for your book! I'm haunted and they're trying to *kill* me!' Denton was scrabbling for a way to get rid of him when the man went on, 'Are you Texas Jack or aren't you?'

Denton sighed.

Almost thirty years before, he had killed four men when he had been the marshal of a little Nebraska town. That story still rode his shoulders, an inescapable moment of notoriety that every newspaper had to mention. The urchins of Naples had turned it into 'Texas Jack,' although his name wasn't Jack and he had never been in Texas. He supposed they had got it from Wild Bill Cody's sometime pal, Texas Jack Omohundro. Now he couldn't walk the Naples streets without some kid's screaming the name at him. It said something for the grapevine that twisted through the city's meanest streets: the kids couldn't read, but they knew who he was and what he'd done. He said, 'That's a mistake. A misunderstanding.'

'Do you kill bad people with your six-guns or don't you?'

'I did, um, get rid of some bad men with a, mm, shotgun. Once upon a time. Long ago. I don't go around shooting people, Fra Renaldo.'

'Geraldo, my name is *Gerald*. Renaldo is *Spanish*.' For a monk—if that was what he was—he was decidedly testy; or didn't monasticism necessarily make people nicer? 'I've lived here for donkey's years, far longer than I ever I lived in England, and people call me Fra *Geraldo*.' His voice softened. 'Fifty years. England is like a child's dream to me now. Children dream sweet dreams, don't they. Dreams of innocence. That is my England, innocence and beauty, always summer and always sunshine. I shall never go back.' His eyes had filled with tears. 'You live in London, I suppose. Horrible place. It's hell. If I go to hell, it will be London. Don't you think?'

Denton liked London; he skipped the comparison with hell. 'Are you being haunted by actual ghosts—things you can see and hear, or...? How are they trying to kill you?'

'I hear them. Laughing. Singing. Cruel children. They shouldn't laugh at me. I try. I've tried for fifty years. No, forty-seven years. Atonement. If we atone...' His voice trailed off, then recovered. 'They put things in my way. So I shall fall and be hurt. They mean to kill me and send me to hell.' His left hand, surprisingly strong, gripped Denton's arm. 'They mustn't be let do it! I must not be haunted when I am atoning!'

Denton felt both disgust and pity. The hand that held him was wrinkled and had a bloom of dirt across the back; the robe or cassock or whatever it was had dribbles of what was probably food down the front; the smell was nasty; and the face, intense now, had creases like knife-cuts down the cheeks and around the mouth, all of them dark with old dirt as if they'd been drawn with a soft pencil.

People were always asking Denton for help—some residue of the dime novels about his long-ago killings, 'the man who saved a town'—and he always tried to resist them. And usually failed. He had a hard mind but sometimes a soft heart, at least for the weak and the victimised. If some rotten kids were tormenting this old man, with his foolish fantasies of hell and innocence and redemption, how, Denton thought, could he refuse at least moral support? Atkins, alas, was not there to tell him to use his head, write his book, make money, and tell the old man to hop it. He said, 'I'm meeting somebody now, but maybe we could get together later. In the afternoon?'

'I have my rounds to make. Then prayers. Then vespers. Why do you think I came to you now? I don't have all day to swan about like some, you know.'

Denton reclaimed his arm. 'This evening?'

'I do my flagellations in the evening. Oh, well, I suppose if it must be, so it must. You're quite thoughtless, however. Religious devotion is nothing to you, I suppose. Come about eight.'

Eight would be the middle of the *pensione*'s evening meal. 'I suppose we couldn't make it a little—'

'No we could not!'

Denton, impatient himself now, said, 'Where?'

'The Palazzo Minerva, of course! Ask anybody. Next to the little church they call the Vecchio Catedrale, though of course it isn't. It's old, very old, but never the cathedral; that's nonsense. Just walk up any of the streets in Spagnuoli and ask for the Palazzo Minerva; they'll direct you. I'm very well known. Please don't be late. I shall have to put off my scourgings until after, and I do dislike going to bed with my wounds fresh.'

The little man sniffed, then looked around the lounge. 'This is how your sort of people live when they come to Napoli, is it? It's terribly vulgar.' He gathered his skirts about himself and hurried out, his sandals flapping on the terrazzo floor. Denton waited until he was gone and then went out after him, hoping he was far enough behind not to run into him again. He was already regretting having listened to the man. It was always the way. *If Atkins were here, he'd say something acid. 'Going to be made a sap of again, is it?'* Denton sighed. Janet was right: he missed Atkins.

He pulled on the heavy ulster and put the hood up over his new hat. Without thinking, he patted a pocket to make sure his derringer was there, but of course it wasn't; this was Italy, and they wouldn't allow him to have a gun. Even before he'd left London, the Italian consul had said that his 'history with fire-arms' was well known; if he tried to take guns into Italy, he'd be stopped, the guns confiscated. He could of course apply for a permit; approval for a foreigner took about a year. Denton and Janet planned to stay five months.

When he stepped outside the *pensione*, he found that the sun was shining.

'Oh, dammit.'

He ran back upstairs and threw the ulster into the concierge's closet. When he got downstairs again, a light drizzle had started.

He believed that thirty years before, he had killed his wife, and he bore the guilt and had bad dreams. Not killed her with his hands, not held the jug while she swallowed the lye, but killed her with a love that was relentless and a morality that was unforgiving: killed her with too many children too soon, killed her with a refusal to deal gently with her drinking, killed her with his own despair. She had walked out into a field with the lye jug and drunk her belly full and lived for four days with no doctor, and now she was in his dreams and his thoughts, his ghost. He was thinking of her now as he came out of the *pensione*, thinking that loving Janet might put that old crime to rest, except that things were not quite right between Janet and him, and maybe again his love was relentless and he was doing it all over again.

His ghosts.

Despite the drizzle, the streets were bright: puddles lay along the gutters where quick little streams, blocked by trash, had widened; the pavement reflected brightness from above. The air smelled clean and watery. Ahead of him, where the Via Chiaia went through an arch, a patch of sunlight shone on the buildings like gilding. It was December, almost Christmas, but in London this would have been April weather.

He passed into the sunny stretch, felt the sun's warmth; beyond, heading down towards Gambrinus's café, he went again into shadow, but the drizzle stopped. One day, he thought, he would go into Gambrinus's; he'd avoided it so far only because he'd been told it was where artists and writers and the singers from the San Carlo Opera across the way all went. Denton missed the raffish Café Royal in London, which he'd made a kind of club. Gambrinus's might be a replacement, but it sounded to him—terrible thought—'arty'.

He turned into the Via Toledo and headed towards the Galleria, where he was to meet the house agent. This was Naples' busiest street, straight as a ruler's edge for almost a mile: on one side was the original city laid out by the Greeks, on the other Spagnuoli, the quarter of the sixteenth-century Spanish (and the smelly Fra Geraldo). The Via Toledo was where old and new, rich and poor, native and tourist met; it was a street of great dash and colour— wandering food vendors, musicians, thieves, and in this season men and boys hawking carved figures for the *presepe*, the manger scene; women shopping, some of them from the brothels in Spagnuoli on their hours off; men lounging, talking, smoking, arguing with animated faces and hands that sketched their words in the air. Denton had had his pocket picked on this street two days after they had arrived. Thinking of it still made him grind his teeth—robbed like any hick just in from the country. There had been two of them, one to bump him and the other to use that distraction to remove his wallet from his inside pocket. He could still feel that quick, slim hand going into the buttoned-up jacket. Texas Jack, indeed.

The Via Toledo was a street that Denton liked—but not today. He had spoiled his own day with stupid responsibilities.

Why hadn't he told Fra Renaldo—no, Geraldo—that he'd go with him now instead of tonight? He could have killed two birds with one stone, satisfied the old man and got rid of Frioni with the excuse. Now he had the worst of both, Frioni to be told to his face and the monk—

Coming towards him on the same side of the street were the two young men who had stolen his wallet. He had no question who they were; in the instant of the theft, he'd seen both faces, now stamped on his brain. Young, insolent, looking for prey and pleased with themselves. One, the shorter, slimmer one who had lifted the wallet, was the better dressed in a dark suit, a rather more aggressive cut than an English tailor or Atkins would have risked, a soft hat with the brim rolled up on one side. The other wore a suit, too, but one somehow less smart, less exuberant, and a white shirt buttoned but without collar or tie, his trilby broader brimmed. Denton saw all this at a glance and turned his eyes away, because the slender one had seen him and nudged his pal.

They would be laughing now, he thought. *There's the stupid old* frocio *we took for a hundred lire.* And then one of them would say, *Let's hit him again.* And they would argue the risk and then love the risk. Denton glanced at them again, now about thirty feet away, and he saw the small one push his shoulders forward and then pull his elbows against his sides and move his hands outward as he raised the elbows, as if he were pulling his trousers up with them. He was getting ready.

Rob me once, shame on you. Rob me twice, shame on me.

He had learned to dissemble from some pretty hard teachers. Now, he made himself the stupid stranger, the tourist, the rube. He made himself seem mindless.

They came at him ready to do exactly what they had done before—criminals are stupid, an old axiom—ready to separate when two strides away from him, the tall one to bump his shoulder on the left, the slim one to take the wallet on his right. Except that the wallet was not there this time, and Denton was himself ready with all the morning's irritations—Atkins, Janet, the old man in the robe. He let them take their step apart, let them take the step that would make contact, and as one tried to bump him he swayed slightly towards instead of away from the man and reached down and grabbed the crotch of his trousers, the end of his flies, his testicles, at the same time swinging his right arm out and back to put the elbow into the other one's right kidney.

Both men gasped. Then the taller one tried to knock Denton's hand away. The slim one turned aside and arched his back and put his right hand where the elbow had landed. Denton let him go for the moment, released his hold on the crotch and brought his knee up into it instead, then broke the young man's nose with his forehead. The man went down on his knees.

Denton turned back to the other one, grabbed his coat as he was trying to get away—so much for loyalty among thieves—and swung him around, shoving him hard over his own extended foot. The youth went face first into the wall of a building, his head hitting with a wooden sound. Both men started to scream.

Noise, Denton knew, was an essential of Neapolitan communication. The loudest pig got not only the slops here, but also the whey and the corn and a pat on the head.

Denton did his own roaring. *'Ladri! Aiuta-me! Ladri!'* A word surfaced from his long-ago Italian. *'Sporchezza!'* He snarled it at the two on the pavement. Filth. He remembered loving the word, the spitting feeling of the trilled r's turning into the explosive *che* and then the hissed 'ts' sound of the double z, and the lengthened, contemptuous final a. It felt so good that he said it again.

'Texas Jack!' a voice cried behind him. He turned. A fat-faced man was gaping at him. Other people were running towards them. A woman recoiled when she saw the two on the ground, the bloody faces, and she said, shuddering, *'Crudele!'*

He had expected applause. It was a little much, being called cruel. He tried to think of how to say that his pocket had been picked two weeks before—*quindici giornate fa* would do for part of it—and realised that nobody had actually picked his pocket today. He saw himself suddenly as they must: a big, loud

American who had beaten up two local kids who hadn't done anything to him.

He knew what Atkins would say and refused to listen.

'*Animale!*'

Denton began to point and shout and stammer. Italian flew out of his head. '*Le due—due ladri—quelle due sono brigandi—*'

It was no good. Now the crowd was shouting at *him*. Faces turned ugly. And a voice from the far edge of the crowd was shouting something about the *polizia*. The police. And how would the police see it?

Denton moved the fat-faced man out of his way and pushed towards the crowd. A hand came out; he brushed it off. The crowd parted, but more voices were shouting for the *polizia*.

Denton began to walk very fast.

Now you've gone and done it, Atkins said inside his head.

❊ ❊ ❊

The Galleria was a glorious innovation in the city, a glass-roofed building with wide entrances that seemed to bring the outdoors in rather than shut it out. Galleries rose on all sides, behind them offices and *pensiones* and, he was told, one rather good whore-house; the geometrically patterned marble floor made a kind of public plaza where people, mostly men, were smoking and talking and looking about, dressed as if for the street in hats and long coats, outdoors but indoors under the faraway glass ceiling.

Frioni was sitting at a little table for two, the farthest out into the plaza of those set out by a café. He waved and gave Denton a huge smile, a dapper little man with a very black moustache, a round head, and plump little hands with manicured nails.

'Ah, Signore Den-ton! *Come me piace, questa* rendezvous...'

He reached up to embrace Denton, or at least put his hands on his shoulders; two kisses followed, aimed more or less at Denton's cheeks. 'What pleasure! What pleasure!'

Denton looked behind him, half expecting to find that an angry crowd had followed him. 'I can't stay,' he said.

'No, no, we go at once. I have for you today a *perfect* house. Perfect! Sixteen rooms wit' all immunities, a view towards Capri and the bay, the beauties of Sorrento and the *azura* sea—'

'I don't want it.' He looked behind himself again.

'—in the most *elegantissimo* part of the hill of Posillipo, where are already many English, Germans, other races, intelligentsia, people of substance, taste, *le bon gout*—'

'I don't want it! You don't get it. You're no good to me. What did I say? I want to live in Naples. Not Posillipo. Not the hill of Vomero. Naples! Naples!'

'But, you don't understand—'

They were still standing. Denton had moved them a little into the groups of other idlers and talkers. Now, looking over his shoulder again, he saw a policeman—one of the *guardie*, yellow buttons, white helmet, high-necked coat—come into the Galleria's entrance and look around. Denton gripped Frioni's arm. 'I understand everything! You're through. *Finito.* You're no good. Don't bother me any more!' He swung away.

Now there were two *guardie* at the entrance; they separated and began to walk around the outside of the vast floor in opposite directions. As if by a thrown switch, the sun came out, flooding the interior with golden light.

A hand took Denton's right elbow. He tried to throw it off, thinking it Frioni's, but the hand slipped through the crook of the elbow and he found himself being steered among the idlers. Looking down, he saw a small grey-haired man, clean shaven two or three days before; he wore a white shirt, collared and buttoned, but no necktie; a frock coat once probably black, long unpressed, made for somebody stouter; on his legs dark blue trousers with a silver stripe, certainly once part of a suit, baggy and fallen into permanent, thick folds like the drapery in a Renaissance painting. On his feet, shoes carefully shined but with one sole separated almost to the arch of the foot. He was carrying a fedora, sweat stains around the band like hightide marks on a beach. Feeling Denton's look, he glanced up and gave him a glorious grin so abrupt and winning it was like the sun's appearance over the Galleria. 'Talk some like we was pals,' he said in American-accented English. 'I get you outa here.'

All Denton could think to say was, 'Ehhhhh—'

The man walked them slowly, really an amble, among the chatting, smoking men. He stopped and turned in to Denton and, as if making a point, tapped Denton's chest with a not quite clean finger and said, 'You don't got no idea who I am, which is hokay.' He began to move them again. 'I get nervous you maybe getting in a little trouble here.' He had an assertive accent that was both very American and very Neapolitan: 'nervous' was 'noivous'; the *a* sounds were flat, even nasal. 'Now we get the hell outa here,' the little man said.

The policemen had met by the far entrance and were now moving again around the perimeter, each retracing the other's path. Denton's guide steered him between them, then angled towards the older of the two, off to their right.

'Walk small,' Denton's guide said. When Denton didn't understand, he hissed, 'Bend your legs, be short!'

Denton thought, *Why am I letting him do this? He's going to hand me over to that cop!* Nonetheless, he tried to bend his knees, thought he must look like a music-hall comedian imitating a duck. At the same time, he felt oddly at peace with what was happening, going arm-in-arm with another man, which he'd never have done in London or America, seeming here right and proper, a kind of admission to the local life. At least he'd got rid of Frioni. What was travel, if not the embrace of the novel, the surprising? And the dangerous?

Denton felt the hand detach itself from his elbow, and his guide said, as if Denton were a dog, 'Stay.' The man waved his hat and approached the policeman. 'Eh, Ruggieri!' The cop looked at him with a sad, round, clownish face. He was a middle-aged man who looked as if he hoped he wouldn't find what he was looking for; any change in his life would surely be for the worse.

'Eh, Vincenzo.' The cop sounded as if all hope was lost. The man he had called Vincenzo rattled off something Denton couldn't follow; the cop glanced at Denton; something else was said, in which Denton thought he heard *New York*.

The cop looked around the Galleria. Denton heard him say 'Texas Jack' in an otherwise incomprehensible gabble of Neapolitan. Denton's guide bowed his legs and raised his hat and mimed riding a horse. He laughed. The cop muttered something unhappy and Vincenzo said, *'Arrivaderla,* Ruggieri.'

'Eh, Vincenzo.'

Moments later, Denton was being steered to the exit, and then they were on the pavement, looking at the San Carlo Opera across the street. On the far kerb, a man with an enormous camera on a heavy tripod waved, not at Denton but at his guide; something passed between the two and the small man with Denton shook his head. He looked at Denton and shrugged. 'Guy I know.'

Denton said, 'What the hell was that with the cop?'

'I tell him you my cousin from New York. He tell me he's looking for Texas Jack. I tell him Texas Jack's a guy walks like he's been on a horse too long, his legs look like two spoons back to back. Keep walking.'

'My name isn't Texas Jack.'

'I know, I know; you're Mist' Denton the famous author. You staying at the *pensione* up Via Chiaia. You looking for a house.'

'How do you know all that?'

'I know ever't'ing.' He pointed ahead and across the street. 'We cross over to Gambrinus's, we have a couple coffees, I tell you about this house is for rent I know you gonna love.' He gave Denton that same magnificent smile. 'An' it's in *Naples. Da vero Napoli.*' He pulled Denton towards the Caffè Gambrinus.

'Now wait a—'

'I t'ink I see a cop back there.' He pulled Denton off the kerb and into the flow of carriages, let a horse-drawn streetcar pass in front of them and then hurried to the other side. They were in elegant Naples now, rich Naples; people drove their carriages and the rarer motor car here, strolled up and down, saw and were seen. It was where tourists spent most of their time when not up the hill at the museum or down the coast at Pompeii; it was where Mrs Newcombe and the plump girl's mother probably were at that moment, trailed by a courier hired to direct them to the shops where he got the highest kickback. Denton, in his elegant Italian tie and hat, fit right in. The tattered man with his hand through the crook of Denton's arm did not.

Pulling Denton into calmer waters near the kerb, the man said, 'What happen, them cops after you?'

'Somebody tried to pick my pocket.'

'Again? Jeez, what a bunch a crooks. "Tried"? You caught them?'

'I, um, let them know who's boss.' As if to justify himself (but why did he need justifying?), he said, 'It was the same pair as before!'

'Oh, Jeez, the same ones? One of them little like me, a kid, snappy dresser—? Oh, Jeez.' He seemed suddenly worried. Still, he pointed at the door to Gambrinus's.

The café was known, even to tourists, for its elegance. Denton expected that the little man might be refused entrance. Yet all the waiter said was, 'Eh, Vincenzo,' and made up-and-down signs in front of his own shirt. He wagged a finger. '*La prossima volta, un' cravate.*' Next time, wear a necktie. He showed them to a table by a window.

The big room was filled with money, expressed in clothes and voice and manner. Several women looked at Denton; one even smiled. Her cloak had a fur collar; the man with her wore diamonds in his cuffs. Yet there were also some obvious 'artists', if wide hats and earrings and gypsy neckerchiefs identified them here as they did in London. Denton suspected that they were what Augustus John called 'playing-at artists'.

'You come here a lot?' Denton said.

'Never been here in my life.' He smiled. 'The troot is, I come here alone, they t'row me out on my cheeks.'

'The waiter knew you.'

'Not as a customer. You want *caffè*?' He raised a finger at a waiter. '*Due caffè.* You want a pastry? The pastry is very famous. You see how fat the customers are?' He waved the waiter away.

Denton looked around. The room was huge, made to seem several rooms by a long service bar and mirrors. The walls were the colour of dried tobacco; glass and metal gleamed everywhere. On the service bar, rows of one- and two-cup brass coffee pots shone, the two-tiered kind that seemed to have their spouts on upside down: water was heated to boiling in the lower pot, the pot was turned over, and the hot water dripped through the grounds into the spouted half, now angled the right way.

'My name is Vincenzo DiNapoli,' the small man said. 'I got a wonderful house for you.'

'You looked worried when I said I'd knocked around the kid who picked my pocket. Why?'

DiNapoli shrugged. 'Prob'ly not'ing. Don' worry about it. Lemme tell you about this house.'

'You're a rental agent?'

DiNapoli smiled that enchanting smile and chuckled. 'I'm all kinda t'ing. You want it, I do it. A couple minutes ago, I was a guardian angel, eh?'

'"Things" don't seem to pay too well.'

'Eh, well…' DiNapoli rocked his hand back and forth. 'In Napoli, you learn to do what you gotta.'

The coffees came. DiNapoli twisted a sliver of lemon peel over his cup and then gulped the coffee down in one swallow. 'You wanna hear about this house or not? You gonna love it.'

'Maybe *you'd* like a pastry,' Denton said. DiNapoli shook his head. It occurred to Denton that DiNapoli, obviously on his uppers, might intend to pay the bill and didn't want to run it up. 'I'm buying.'

'You my guest.'

'No, no—'

'Assolutamente, senza dubito—'

'Si, si, io pagare—'

'Jeez, you speak Italian. Sort of.'

'What'd I say wrong?'

'Io pagare don't mean nothing—"I to pay". You mean *pagaro.* "I will pay."'

DiNapoli's expression was fastidious, suddenly rather priestly; language, it seemed, was important to him. He said, *'I pay. You my guest because I bring you here, try to put you inta this house I know about. Don' talk about it no more.'*

'"Any more,"' Denton said with a smile.

'Yeah, what I said.' Correctness in English apparently was less important than in Italian. 'You wanna hear about this house or don' you?'

Denton sipped his coffee. It was intense, bitter, exotic. He tried the twist of lemon in it. 'What have I got to lose?'

'Hokay, there's this house in Spaccanapoli—you know Spaccanapoli—?'

Spaccanapoli was the old Naples. Denton knew what the term meant but had only the vaguest idea where it was—east of the Via Toledo somewhere. He nodded.

'Hokay, this house, w'ich is really a *palazzo* but not too big, because I heard you don't want no *palazzo*. So call it a house. Ever't'ing done new! Electric on the *piano nobile*, every room! Running water! Hot in the bat'room! Bee-yootiful chandeliers like you don' believe! Furniture all elegant, some very antique, some new. A house so perfect for you it oughta have "Denton" over the door instead of the coat of arms of the Conte da Pizzinelli e Marbella, w'ich you can't read because of them peoples don' exist no more and the stone gone all to crumbles.' He leaned forward over the tiny table. 'And what's just great, you get two months free!' He sat back, grinning.

Denton was instantly suspicious. 'What's wrong with it?'

'Not'ing! What could be wrong with it? I just tole you, it's perfect!' DiNapoli looked into his empty cup, shrugged. 'There's one little t'ing, maybe.'

'Ah.' Denton tried taking the rest of his coffee at a gulp, regretted it. 'I knew it.' His voice sounded strangled because of the coffee.

'It's not'ing, not'ing. Little thing, you do it, the next day you're living in paradise. And the first two months *free*.'

'What's the little thing?'

'The owner, he says anybody gotta spend one night in the house before he can move in. You spend the night, the place is yours.'

Denton stared at him. DiNapoli met his eyes for some seconds, then looked away, looked back, raised his eyebrows, looked away again. When again he looked back, he said, 'There's this old story. See, the peoples of Napoli, they superstitious. They believe anyt'ing! You tell them Fifth Avenue has the trolley tracks made of gold, they believe you. So, see, they believe this old story, and so they give this house a bad name. Which it don't deserve!'

Denton folded his arms. He looked severe. 'Tell me.'

DiNapoli sighed. 'Once upon a time, in the *Cinquecento*, there was this bee-yootiful young lady. See?' Denton had to count: *cinque* was five, so the *Cinquecento* was the fifteen-hundreds and what he called the sixteenth century. He nodded. 'So she got this old husband, he got a bad disposition. And the lady has this piano teacher who's young and handsome and sings like a bird, so one day the husband comes home and finds the lovely girl lying on her bed with the piano teacher on top of her and no clothes on. The husband pulls his stiletto. The piano teacher goes out the window. The husband stabs the lady right below her left, um, you know, which is as gorgeous as something on Venus, and she's dying. She says, *"Muoro per l'amore, io vivo!"* Nice, eh? "Dying for love, I live". Eh?'

'In the house you're telling me about.'

'Yeah, in the Casa Gialla. The Yellow House. What they call *la camera rossa*, the red room. And, uh—' He looked embarrassed. 'And now the simple peoples, they say she comes back sometimes and, uh, drips blood here and there and, uh, kills guys remind her of her husband.' He managed a weak smile. 'Crazy, eh?'

'You mean the house is haunted, and the owner can't rent it, so he'll give two months free to anybody who spends a night in it and comes out in one piece.'

'See, you got it right off.'

'How many have tried?'

'Only a couple. Hardly nobody.'

'And they didn't last the night?'

'Not really.'

'What happened?'

'Well, you know, there was some blood, and there was this lady, but guys like that they make things up! They was lying to make themselves look better, you follow me? You don't believe in ghosts?'

'Actually, no.'

'Well, see, that's why I thought you was perfect for it!'

'What does the owner think?' When DiNapoli looked away and didn't answer, Denton said, 'You are representing the owner, aren't you?'

'You could say that, yeah.'

'You're doing it on your own! Yes? This is all spit and buffalo chips! Right?'

The glorious smile came again. DiNapoli raised his shoulders in a shrug and kept them there, hands spread. 'I tole you, in Napoli you do what you gotta. I hear about the house, I read about you, I put two and two together, I think it's a marriage made *nel' cielo*. What ghost is gonna dare to haunt Texas Jack?'

Denton stared at him. Then he began to laugh. The laughter rolled out of him like barrels from a dray. He felt better than he had all morning. 'Mr DiNapoli,' he said, 'you have your nerve.'

'In Naples, everybody got nerve. You spend a night in this house, hokay?'

'What have I got to lose?'

'Well, one guy, he left wit'out his pants. You smarter than that, I know. You scare the pants off the *ghost*.'

'I'm not sure ladies wore pants in the *Cinquecento*. Or that ghosts do. Interesting question. Why are ghosts supposed to wear clothes at all? Did these guys say that the lady was dressed?'

'Like a queen in a painting, they said. But I dunno why she look like that, because the story is she was nood when she died. But you gonna do it? I talk to the owner today, I tell him I got a sure-fire tenant, I get the keys and I confirm wit' you. Yes?'

'And you'd expect a finder's fee from me.'

'That's up to you,' DiNapoli said with a gracious gesture of one hand, his face now that of a noble, and very high-class, Roman.

They arranged to meet in the Galleria next day.

❀ ❀ ❀

Denton walked back to the *pensione* smiling. The sky was silver; the still-wet streets shone. Naples suddenly looked rather glorious. A night in a supposedly haunted *palazzo*, he thought, might make a fine beginning for the new book. Or maybe the ending. He wondered what they would serve for lunch at the *pensione*. He wondered if he could entice Janet out for supper after he had visited the filthy old man in the monk's robe. He would tell her the story of the two pickpockets and then the story of Mr DiNapoli; thinking of him made Denton smile again. He wondered if Janet would smile as he did.

He was still smiling as he went up the stairs two at a time and opened the *pensione* door. He stopped smiling when he saw *la Signora*, the proprietor. She was a very large woman with an embonpoint like a sailing ship's figurehead, grey hair piled above her face like thunderclouds, threatening ugly weather. So did her frown.

'A representative of the *polizia* is awaiting you in the lounge,' she said. Even in heavily accented English, she was fearsome. 'He inform me you have given scandal to my *pensione* with public fighting. In the street! When you are complete with him, please come to the office to settle your final bill.'

That tears it, Atkins said inside his head.

Inspettatore Gianaculo, for some reason addressed as *Dottor*, was frog-like and placid and reminded Denton of several about-to-retire cops he had known in London. He sat with his legs apart and his belly filling the space between, a black bowler held on one knee and a cup of the *pensione*'s coffee, apparently untouched, next to him. He wore a rather tired Prince Albert— probably called something else here, Denton thought—and dark trousers and a waistcoat that didn't match either, across it a watch chain big enough to have anchored a small boat. Getting to his feet with the slowness and dignity of a fat man, he said in a deep but almost quacking voice, 'Dottor Gianaculo, *inspettatore poliziano Napolitano.*' His hand was plump, warm, strong.

A woman hurried in; Denton recognised her as one of the Signora's lieutenants. She had a distinct moustache, steel-rimmed glasses, and hair like the Signora's—perhaps the house style. In a heavily accented voice, she said, 'I beg to excuse for my lateness. I am very busy.' She shrilled something, perhaps the same thing, to the policeman in Italian. Turning back to Denton, she said, 'I am to transalate.' She closed the door. 'We do not want scandal.'

The policeman sat down, so Denton did, too. The policeman smiled. Denton smiled. The woman refused to sit, said something to the *dottore*, and he rattled Italian back at her. She said to Denton in English, 'You have committed outrage against two citizens of Naples. On the *street.*'

'The two citizens of Naples tried to rob me.'

She translated this, and the frog-like *dottore* chuckled and nodded his head and wiggled his eyebrows at Denton as if they were sharing a secret. He spoke; the woman said, 'You have done a bad thing. The police could prosecute. However, the two victims do not complain and so the police warn you against repeating the outrage.'

Denton, who was less angry than wearied, said, 'They stole my wallet a week ago. The same two.'

The policeman smiled and held up a finger, then opened all the fingers of his right hand and shook them up and down. That meant something: Denton had seen it on the street. He said, 'I want to complain against the two men.'

The message that came back was, 'Do not pull the tail of a sleeping cat.'

Denton shrugged. The policeman smiled and nodded. The woman asked him something in Italian, got her answer, and went out, telling Denton crisply that she 'had important things to do'.

Denton looked at the policeman. Their eyes held. The policeman smiled. Denton opened his hands to signal, Is that everything? The policeman beamed and nodded. They stood at the same time, but, as Denton gathered his hat to go, the policeman closed the door and came close to Denton and said, '*Signore.*'

Denton, staring down at him from his much greater height, stopped.

'*Signore*—' He took Denton's arm. 'Is nothing—*capisce?*' He pinched Denton's arm. 'Is me, I give you—*uno medaglio. Capisce?*'

'A medal?'

'*Si, si,* a medal. These two—*immondizia,* eh? *Cammoristi. Guappi.*' He shook his head. 'Next time—you...kill them. Yes?' He bellowed out a laugh in his peculiar deep voice, then produced a card and explained in Italian what it was and which line was his name and which the address. '*La questura. Stato ogni giornata alla questura.* Yes? All hours—yes? Anything—yes?' He patted Denton's shoulder and said something that sounded to Denton like 'good fellow' and waddled out.

❀ ❀ ❀

Denton threw his hat and the ulster on a sofa. 'I'm sorry, I'm sorry. It's all my fault.'

'No, no, it's mine.'

'I "gave scandal" by a cop coming here to talk to me.' He threw himself into a chair. 'In London, I'm a lawman; in Naples, I'm a criminal. Actually, the cop was quite decent about it, but the Signora's got the hump and is throwing us out on our backsides.'

'It wasn't you, Denton; it was me. Mrs Newcombe came back early and found her daughter here with me and dragged her away. I suppose she went straight to the Signora and made a lot of noise about morality.'

'The dragon gave us until Friday.'

'Oh, good. Mrs Newcombe wanted me thrown out at once.'

'I said I'd get a lawyer if she put us out today.'

'Ah.' She kissed him. 'My hero.' She scowled. 'Poor Lucy was in tears. She was trying on one of my dresses when her mother barged in. Mama tried to drag her off; Lucy said she couldn't steal my clothes; Mama had rather a fit; and poor Lucy had to undress with both of us watching her do it, blubbering all the while.'

'Where was the comedienne?'

'Oh, she skedaddled—that's the word isn't it, skedaddled?—as soon as her own ma put her large nose between the door and the jamb. I was tempted to close the door on it.'

Janet was dressing to go to the university, not in the gaudy draperies she wore in private but in a severe, rather mannish grey suit. 'Fasten me in back, please. You can tell me about the pick-pockets while you do it.'

He told her; he fastened her. He got as far as his telling off Frioni, but she had to go. She kissed him quickly, meaninglessly. 'You stay here and work.'

'At what? I'm not ready to work. I'll come with you.' He sounded grumpy again.

'No, you won't.'

'Oh, dammit.' He made himself grin. 'But I've got a funny story to tell you.' He was thinking of Fra Geraldo and DiNapoli. 'Two funny stories.'

'Tell me tonight.' She started out. 'Look—the weather's changed! For me.' The sun was brilliant.

The daylight had gone, but the night was not yet cold and the streets were filled with people. Denton, able to see over the heads of most of them, looked around for signs, familiar names, but found none. The streets were dark, the only light what spilled from windows and doorways and the candles of the little shrines that stood at every corner, set into niches in the buildings. If there were street signs in deepest Spagnuoli, he didn't know where to look for them. He was trying to hurry through whatever nonsense the old man in the monk's robe had in store for him—get it over with and take Janet to supper and then to bed, lose himself in her, try to find in her some still place where there were no books to be written, no houses to be found.

'*Il vecchio catedrale?*' he said to a pretty girl.

'*Sinistra, sinistra.*' She laughed at him. Because of his accent? His hat? His height? More of the traveller's curse.

Left, left. He turned left at the next corner, sending the candles below a Virgin dancing, hoping the girl hadn't been playing a Sophie-like joke on him, then left into an alley no wider than his outstretched arms. No, a bit wider than that; he tried it and found that he had to hold his hat in one hand so the brim would just touch the wall. Still, a very narrow little way. Buildings rose solidly on both sides, but doors were open at ground level and light spilled out. Inside, families stared out at him from several steps below street level: people eating, children and a man in shirtsleeves at a table, one or two women stopping in the serving, too. Everybody round eyed, as if he had been long awaited and was feared. He tried smiling and speaking and got no answer.

A hundred feet, a hundred and fifty feet along, a ruined church spired up on his right. Light from an open doorway showed him rotted stone, carving reduced to rounded bulges, closed double doors.

'*Il vecchio catedrale?*' he said to a man coming towards him. The man looked like all the others he had seen in Spagnuoli because of the darkness.

The man said something but Denton couldn't follow it. Somebody else squeezed behind the man, somebody younger, one of the young toughs of these alleys, perhaps. The man pointed, turned away, headed wherever he was going.

To the right. Denton muttered *Grazie, mille grazie,* backed away into the darkness. Why did he feel obligated to politeness, to this spreading of the hands as if embarrassed? A lot of it was language, language he didn't understand and language he couldn't use to explain himself. Some of it was his old guilt over having enough money to be here in this suit and this hat among people who lived in one room and looked out at him as if he were a myth come calling. *Have to get some different clothes. Look like the locals.* But he could never change his size.

To the right. There was the 'old cathedral', surely, then a pair of huge wooden doors, opened inward at an angle, beyond them a courtyard that must once have allowed a carriage to turn around. Galleries rose four storeys high, light spilling from open doors at every level. Voices trilled down like falling coins, raucous ones and treble ones, laughter and shouting and murmurs, a child weeping. A slap. The smell of twenty suppers mingling, onions recognisable, wine, coffee.

'*Eh!*'

The voice came from within the double doors. His eyes adjusted; he saw a door within the right-hand door, a pedestrian door for when the great ones were closed at night. The little door was open and a small man stood in it. Denton thought that the man could easily have come around the big door, but he had chosen to half conceal himself in the little one.

'*La pioggia no' continua,*' the man said. The rain has stopped. As indeed it had. Denton agreed that the rain had stopped and said he was looking for Fra Geraldo.

'*Eh, Fra Geraldo!*' Fra Geraldo seemed to depress the man. Denton went still closer, took a side step so that the light from behind him would spill over the other man. What he could now see of him was not impressive: a hunched body, thin hair that looked surprisingly light coloured for a Neapolitan's, a rat's face.

'*Cerco Fra Geraldo. Palazzo Minerva.*'

'*Si, si, Palazzo Minerva. D'accordo, Palazzo Minerva.*' The man disappeared, reappeared immediately around the big door. He gestured for Denton to follow, then stood looking into the courtyard, shoulders rounded, as if the thought of crossing it—it couldn't be more than fifty feet deep, Denton thought—was too much for him. At last, he sighed mightily and set out, fetching up on the far side at a doorway that had once been magnificently carved and looked now like wet sugar. Even in the bad light, Denton could see the remains of a heraldic shield, the hind-quarters of some sort of animal, several heads without noses. A crudely painted board had been hung from a couple of the heads: *Fratelli di Santo Simeone Stilites.*

'*Palazzo Minerva,*' Denton's guide said. He sighed again, then hit an arched wooden door with the side of his left fist. The noise was thunderous, but nobody in the courtyard seemed to notice. The thunder went on—four, five, six blows. The man tapped his right ear. *'Sordo.'* Deaf. Denton hadn't thought Fra Geraldo deaf at all. Maybe deaf when he wanted to be.

They stood looking at the door for perhaps thirty seconds. The small man shrugged. *'Non c'e.'*

Denton had prepared his next speech with a dictionary before he had left the pension. *'O fatto un appuntamento per le otto.'* I made an appointment for eight.

'Eh. Lui dicii. Un americano, dicii, molto grande.' Denton got most of it—the Fra had apparently told the doorkeeper that a big American was coming.

The man nodded sadly as if it were the inevitable fate of appointments to go wrong, a shrug and a glance at the door suggesting that Fra Geraldo was not to be trusted. Still, he hit the door again with the side of his fist, the noise astonishing. *Fit to wake the dead*, Denton thought.

Denton looked around the courtyard as if Fra Geraldo might appear there, but there were only the lights spilling from doorways, the flitting passage of children running in the darkness. Something smelled delicious. He remembered he was missing his supper; there was some consolation in knowing it wouldn't have been as good as what he was smelling—the pension made much ado of its authentically English food, which the other guests seemed to like.

Denton turned back to his guide. *'Alora...'* The all-purpose word, like 'well'.

'Aspet', aspet'—' His face, half in darkness, was trying to look either pathetic or sly, Denton couldn't tell which. *'Sono il portiere. O le chiave...'* He jangled a bunch of oversized keys as if to suggest that he could use them if he had a reason to.

Denton figured that this was a time to offer money. He produced a coin, handed it over. The *portiere* shuffled closer to the door. He muttered again, something about Fra Geraldo and deafness. The key clattered in the lock and the door swung open a few inches and stuck against the stone floor. The *portiere* put his scrawny shoulder to it and pushed, and the door scraped and groaned inward. He muttered something about *sempre*, always, and gave up when there was just enough space for them to squeeze through.

'Fra Geraldo! Fra Gera-a-a-ldo!'

A candle burned in a candlestick on a table against a wall. Otherwise, the space beyond the door was in darkness. Denton got no hint of size or shape or colour. A smell, mostly damp, as if they had entered a cellar, asserted itself.

'Hello! Fra Geraldo? It's Mr Denton!'

'Personna.' The *portiere* hung back in the doorway. He rattled off something that Denton didn't catch, a gesture seeming to suggest that he was talking about getting out of there. Instead, Denton took out his electric flash-light (so called because it gave only a few seconds of light at a time) and shone it about, catching dull brown walls, a beamed ceiling overhead. His nostrils widened as he encountered another smell: cooking. Fish, unquestionably fish.

'Maybe,' he said in his limping Italian, 'maybe—eating.' He knew he hadn't got it right, but close enough. He raised his voice. 'Fra Geraldo?'

Ahead another fifteen feet was a second door, less massive but sturdy, also panelled. Oak. He went to it and pounded. Behind him the *portiere* shuffled partway in, now speaking incomprehensible words whose tone was perfectly clear: You're going to get me into trouble and my supper's getting cold.

Denton opened the door.

Beyond was a bigger space that vanished overhead in more darkness. To right and left, he had a sense of architectural bits picked out very dimly—a door frame, the edge of a panel—but he was focused on what lay ahead and was better lighted. A staircase ran up the wall to his left and then took a turn to the right and went up again; a massive oak newel stood at the bottom, its carved shape replicated in the spindles that marched up under an oak banister almost a foot broad. Two gaslights flared against the wall above the stairway. It was not, however, the architecture of the *Seicento* that held his eye.

A figure was sprawled on its back over the three lowest steps. One arm was flung up the stairs as if pointing or appealing for help in that direction; the legs were splayed; the head was rolled almost to its left shoulder, held only by the edge of the stair, it seemed, from rolling the rest of the way by itself.

The figure was nude from the waist down.

Denton knew it was the old man before he ever got to it. He could smell him; he could see the wrinkles in the skin of the thin old arms, the sagging leg muscles; he recognised the childlike face, even with its mouth open and its eyes bulging.

'O Dio!' the *portiere* whispered. 'E lui?'

But Denton was shining his flash-light on the old man's crotch, where there was nothing male except a thin tuft of grey hair. Denton's first shocked thought had been that the body was a woman's: the deep shadow between the skinny thighs was relieved by nothing to reflect the gaslight. He moved his own light and saw, however, a stump of tissue, below it an old and puckered scar that ran to the pubic synthesis. Some time long ago, Fra Geraldo had had both his penis and his testicles cut off.

The *portiere* looked down where Denton's light was shining. 'O Dio,' he whispered, 'no cazzo,' and with a sigh he fainted. No cock.

Denton pulled him away from the old man, one of whose feet had cushioned the *portiere*'s fall; he shook him, slapped his cheeks gently, moved his arms back and forth. The eyes opened, saw nothing they recognised; then he remembered and said, 'No cazzo!'

'Forget about his *cazzo*. Can you stand?' He realised he was speaking English, tried to think of the Italian, gave it up, and dragged the little man to his feet. 'Polizia,' he said. 'Get the *polizia*.' He shook him, pulled his head back when he tried to look again at the body on the stairs. 'Guardie, capisce? Eh? Polizia?'

The little man nodded. Denton shoved him towards the door. 'Get the *polizia*.' He shoved him again and the man started to trot. After he'd gone through the door, Denton shouted, 'And a doctor! *Medico! Dottore!*' Or did *dottore* mean only somebody like Inspector Gianaculo? What the hell. He shouted *'Medico!'* again and gave it up.

He went back to the stair. The old man's robe had caught up under his back, leaving his legs and groin bare. Denton put his hand on the old man's throat. There was no pulse in the neck, but the skin was warm to his touch. He looked again at the groin. The stump of the penis was visible when he held the light close, the old wound healed but looking somehow ugly and unfinished, while the scar where the testicles had been removed looked quite neat and rather unsurprising. Denton shone his light over the rest of the body, then the head. Blood had run from the nose and was still wet; a gash on the top of the bald head had bled a little and swelled very slightly, but the amount of blood seemed slight for what must have been a terrible fall.

Denton went up the stairs, shining his light back and forth at each step. Uncarpeted, the stairs were thick with dust except in the middle where Fra Geraldo must have gone up and down. The landing, however, twelve steps up, was clean. A twig broom lay at an angle a few steps above the body. Denton looked down at the next step below the landing, saw where dust from the landing had been swept over, probably broadcast over several of the lower steps. Had Fra Geraldo fallen while he was sweeping his stairs for his visitor?

Despite the sign outside that said that this was a monastery, Denton thought the place was empty. Above, there was nothing but silence; nobody had come to their loud knocking or their calls. Was Fra Geraldo the last brother in this order? Or was the brotherhood of Saint Simeon Stylites a fiction?

That Fra Geraldo might have been mad hardly surprised Denton. Upper-class Englishmen who turned up in Naples filthy and stinking weren't likely to be entirely sane. Or was this English eccentricity?

He went around the turn in the stairs and up the next half-flight to the floor above. Six steps. All had been swept. The corridor above had not. A path down the middle showed where Fra Geraldo's skirts had done the sweeping.

Alone? If there were any other brothers, they were deaf to the calls that Denton now made.

He went down again. Half a dozen men were crowded near the door, staring at the corpse. A couple of women stood behind, kerchiefs over their hair, trying to see over the men.

Denton put his flash-light off and stopped three steps above the body. In the silence, he said, '*E morto.*' Not so brilliant: He's dead.

The men murmured. One said something that was a question and involved the *cazzo*.

Denton tried to summon up words. 'Uunnh—*Aspetare—Aspeta—il medico. Dottore.*' *Aspetare* meant 'wait', he was fairly sure of that.

One of the men took a step forward. He seemed to accept that Denton was in charge. He said something that started with '*permesso*', which Denton thought meant 'permission', and ended with a question, the man gesturing and leaning forward. Denton risked it and said, 'No. *Aspetare la polizia. E il medico.*' He'd no idea what Neapolitan police procedure was like. He knew pretty well what the London police would have done, but in this city, which seemed to lurch constantly from the Middle Ages to the nineteenth century and back again, anything was possible. 'Don't touch anything!' he said in English. He risked another word. '*No tocca!*' Or did *toccare* have sexual overtones?

Nobody sniggered and nobody tried to touch the corpse. The man who had come closer stepped back; the women tried to squeeze through the doorway; and behind them lights and sounds announced newcomers. The crowd parted as a uniformed policeman came through, pushing people out of his way as if they were pieces of furniture. He stopped when he saw Denton on the stairs and saluted. His eyes, however, were already on the old man's crotch.

Denton came down two steps but maintained his advantage and what seemed to be his possession of the body. '*Sono americano,*' he said. '*Me chiama Denton.*' He recited again the sentence he'd prepared at the pension. '*O un appuntamento a le otto.*' Then he had to invent. Badly. *'Con il—uomo—'* He gestured to the dead man below him. *'Con questa uomo.'*

The cop was middle aged and apparently not used to corpses: Naples might be a hive of petty crime and tricks and scams, but it was not big on violent death. The policeman stared at Denton, gestured with sudden ferocity at the crowd, chased them out and slammed the door, then came back and beckoned Denton down from his eminence. Putting his head close to Denton's chest, he muttered a question whose only word Denton recognized was *'cazzo'*. The *portiere* must have spilled the goriest detail as the first words out of his mouth. *There's a dead man with no cock in the Palazzo Minerva!*

Denton's answer was to shine his flash-light on the old man's groin. The cop slapped his hand to his mouth and spun around, took a quick walk to the far wall and back, and presented a greyer face to Denton. Clearly, *cazzos—cazzi*—were taken seriously in Naples.

Before Denton could stop him, and while he was struggling to find the Italian words for *Don't move the body*, the cop had moved the dead man's legs together and put the left hand over the groin, suggesting something in classical art; as if to emphasise that connection, he tried to pull the old man's robe down, but it was caught, and so he pulled a large handkerchief, not entirely clean, from a pocket and draped it over the hand, the finished composition suggesting Lazarus or a deposition from the cross, minus the supporting players.

'Obscenita publica,' the cop said.

Denton looked him in the eye, saw only stolid propriety, shrugged.

The cop looked up the stairs. *'A caduta.'* He fell. He made looping motions with his right hand. *'Ba', ba', ba'—'* His gestures indicated that the old man had bounced down the stairs like a ball.

Denton gave up. *'Ascendo,'* he said, and without waiting for permission went back up the stairs. The cop said nothing, accepting Denton's authority. *I should collect a finder's fee.*

He walked quickly along the upper corridor, flashing his light into rooms, seeing only dust and cobwebs, ancient furniture and fallen plaster. At the far end, he found a room that was apparently the old man's; a gas light burned there, and the source of the cooking smell sat on a gas ring—a cast-iron pot with fish soup in it. He saw no sign of actual food preparation—no knife, no board, no spices or herbs—and wondered if Fra Geraldo had been a monk who begged his food, or even bought it. But with what?

Going back, he saw again the clean track down the middle of the corridor, the dirt on each side. Passing the top of the stairs, he went on, looked into more unused rooms, came to another stairway going up, blocked now with furniture that looked as if it had been purposely piled there. The old man's attempt to keep out his ghosts?

A voice shouted at him from below. He looked over the broad banister and saw more policemen and two men in civilian clothes. One of them was looking up at him, his face angry. Foreshortened by Denton's elevation, he looked toad-like, his gut seeming to swell and drop all the way to the floor. It was Inspector Gianaculo.

He shouted again. He sounded angry and therefore to Denton perhaps fearful. He certainly didn't seem to want to give Denton a medal this time. What was he afraid of? Was it because both the dead man and the man who had found him were foreigners? Would that bring in other forces the man feared—the national government? The hated *Carabinieri*?

Denton trotted down the stairs, stepping over the broom, then the body, which now lay stretched across the bottom tread. As he neared the bottom, he saw that another man in civilian clothes was down there as well. Tall, cadaverous, he wore evening clothes and looked furious. *Somebody pulled out of somewhere he'd rather be to come here. A bigwig.*

Denton reminded Gianaculo that he didn't understand Italian. The *portiere*, who was cowering next to a young policeman as if under his protection, murmured something that Denton took to mean that Denton was the man who had found the body. The young policeman slapped him. The tall one in evening clothes said something in a harsh, guttural tone, and the policeman pushed the *portiere* out the door.

The second man in civilian clothes, who had been on his knees beside the body, the first policeman's handkerchief now protecting his trousers from the floor, stood, his joints cracking, and groaned as he straightened his back. He bent again to pick up his hat from the corpse's groin, where it had replaced the handkerchief, and rather fussed over putting the handkerchief back over the offending nudity. Denton took him to be a doctor. He was in his fifties, overweight, his hair perhaps black more by design than nature. He folded silver-rimmed eyeglasses, then spoke to the man in evening clothes, as if they were the only two in the place. Denton heard the word *magistrato*. What the hell did that mean? In London, a magistrate presided in the police court, the first level the arrested person encountered. Was it the same here? So far as Denton could tell, this magistrate swung a lot of weight: everybody deferred to him, even Gianaculo.

Denton got nothing from the rest of the gabble, but the pantomime was clear: the old man had broken his neck. All three men looked up the staircase. The doctor pantomimed sweeping, a sudden loss of balance, then used the same gesture the policeman had—the bouncing ball.

Like he was made of rubber, Denton thought.

Dottor Gianaculo indicated Denton and said something. All three men looked at him.

'*Non parla italiano,*' Gianaculo said. The magistrate shook his head in disgust. They all looked severe. What sort of fool didn't speak Italian?

❀ ❀ ❀

'We're eating in our rooms,' Janet said. 'The Signora doesn't want us endangering the morals of the other customers. It's late now, anyway.' A table had been set up in the sitting room, a rolling cart next to it with serving dishes under imitation-silver covers.

'I waited for you.' She had a glass of wine in her hand. An open bottle stood on the table—the rich red from Vesuvius. 'I waited for you to eat, anyway.' She laughed, more like a man's laugh than a woman's, a laugh he loved; she drank again, said, 'Let's get tiddly and commit particularly exotic kinds of sex all over the apartment.' Her eyes were a little too wide. Rebellion against propriety excited her, made her imaginative, ironic.

'Eat first?'

'I suppose, but it was bad English food to start with, and now it's cold.' She threw herself down on a sofa. 'How was your monk?'

'He was dead.'

She stared, then broke into laughter again, then began to undo her dress. 'To hell with eating.'

❋ ❋ ❋

She was unabashed by her own naked body: eating in the nude or with only a Liberty shawl for cover seemed to extend her mood of rebelliousness. She was forty but had kept a fine, tight body, small breasted, lean. She was sipping the wine and eating a blood orange. He was eating boiled potatoes with cold gravy.

She said, 'One of the girls at Ruth's used to keep berry conserves so her clients could lick them off. I've often wondered if it's where the expression "She's the berries" came from. She was very popular. I couldn't do it. I'd giggle.'

He lifted the gravy boat. 'All I can offer is cold gravy.'

'I can't imagine you doing *gamahuche* with strawberry conserve, much less cold gravy. It's your gravitas.' She thought about it. 'Gravitas with gravy?'

He said, 'We're all low comedians when it comes to sex. But I couldn't do it with cold gravy, no.' He looked under another cover and found *zuppa inglese*, a sort of sweet custard. He dipped a finger in and held it up.

She put a hand over her pubis and shook her head. 'It isn't quite us, I think. And English soup doesn't sound very attractive, does it?' She ate a bit of orange and some of the juice, like watered blood, ran down from the corner of her mouth. She wiped it away with a finger. 'Tell me about your dead man.'

'Gloomy *palazzo*, like something out of an East End melodrama. He was lying at the bottom of the stairs. The police think he fell and broke his neck.'

'You don't?' She was starting on another orange, cutting a line of longitude around it with a fruit knife.

'I don't know. There was a broom on the stairs, and signs of sweeping. A man that old could have fallen—swept the landing with his back to the stairs, missed the step.' He dribbled more of the wine into their glasses. 'But there wasn't much blood for somebody who'd taken that kind of fall. And none on the stairs, which I would have expected. I told the police; they shrugged. The police work wasn't very good, in fact—a magistrate took over—that's the way they do it here—and he made it clear he wanted to get back to his dinner.'

'Suspicious?'

'You mean, was he hiding something? I don't think so. I think he just jumped at the obvious to get it over with—old man, broken neck, stairs. Gianaculo didn't want to move so fast.' Denton had pulled on his trousers and his shirt without its collar. He stretched his long legs, looked at his big, rather root-like feet. 'The monk came to me because he was haunted, he said, ghosts trying to kill him. Well, he was loony, of course. But when somebody says something's trying to kill him and then he turns up dead—'

'Denton the Deadeye Detective.'

He grunted. 'What really bothered the cops was that his privates were missing. Done long ago, I mean.'

'No testicles?'

'No anything.'

'Oh, dear. But that's nothing to do with his death, is it?'

'I don't see how.'

After more wine, and as much of the cold stodge as they could stand, and the *zuppa inglese* in its proper place, and more sex, they lay together on an imitation Aubusson and she said, 'Whatever shall we do?'

'Now or after we're thrown out?'

'After.'

'Go to a hotel. Go back to London.' He laughed. 'Move into a haunted house.'

'What?' She was using his belly for a pillow; now she raised her head with difficulty and stared at him.

'It's my funny story. You didn't give me the chance to tell you this morning. A local slicker told me he has the perfect house for us. Except that it's haunted. A man I met after I fired Frioni. In the Galleria. The police were looking for me—because I'd beaten up the two pickpockets—and this Neapolitan flim-flam man got me out of there and over to Gambrinus's. He's got a haunted house for us. Kind of wonderful character. Maybe a finagler, but—' Denton said, as if surprised, 'I kind of liked him.'

'You're not making much sense. Have I drunk too much wine or have you?'

Denton looked at the remaining bottle, still half full. 'Neither of us, I'd say. But he was there, as if he'd materialised from a séance—I'm going to have to go to one of those for my book—and he saved me from the coppers, and he told me this wild tale, so it's hard to tell it sensibly. It may all be some kind of joke. He knew me. My face, my name. Apparently everybody knows me. "Texas Jack". I knew the kids say that, but even the cops were looking for "Texas Jack".'

'Does that make me Texas Jack's fancy woman?'

'Mrs Jack.'

'I'd sooner you *gamahuched* me with the cold gravy. I wonder whatever happened to that girl who used the preserves. I wonder that a lot—what happened to girls I knew. All middle aged and fat or dead now. It's shocking what happens to whores. But no more shocking than what happens to all women.' She hooked her right hand behind his neck. She was looking at the ceiling. 'I feel bad about Lucy. I worry about her. That mother.'

'Seeing yourself?'

'Because my mother sold me, you mean? Yes, maybe it's that. But mine did it for, she thought, my own good—money, position, a husband—not that it turned it out that way. Mrs Newcombe wants a son-in-law with a title she can show off in Rochester, New York; it isn't for Lucy at all. She's only seventeen; she'll be married off and she won't know what men are or what a cheat marriage is or—' She moved impatiently against his chest. 'At least I suppose she won't end up in St Ives.' Janet had spent four years in the St Ives Prison for the Criminally Insane. Her husband had put her there because she was 'defiant'.

She stood, snatched the Liberty shawl from the sofa and draped it over her shoulders. Holding out a hand, she said, 'Sleep in my room tonight.' He got up, pleased. She opened her mouth to say something that he hoped would please him even more, but what she said was, 'Poor Lucy.' She took his hand, shook her head without looking at him and said, 'A night in a haunted house sounds a wonderful idea. It will clear our brains.'

CHAPTER

4

Midway through the next morning, Lucy flitted in, terrified that her mother would find her, bursting into tears as soon as she saw Janet.

'It's awful!' she cried. 'It's just awful! Ma's found a man for me!'

Denton was banished; he lingered only long enough to learn that Mrs Newcombe was enchanted with a genuine *marchese* who had happened to sit next to them at the opera. He was young; he was good looking; he had a title; he was unmarried. Lucy was terrified.

Denton used the smoking room for its supposed purpose, going through three cigarettes and contemplating a cigar to go with his fourth coffee while drafting an advertisement for the Naples newspapers: 'Author seeks authentic stories of ghosts, spirits, rappings, and supernatural phenomena for use in book'.

He would get somebody to translate it for him. He would get a postal box, or whatever they used here, or he'd have every nut in Naples at his door—witness the now dead Fra Geraldo. He was thinking about the old man's death and the night before when the Signora herself appeared and announced that there was a man. Denton, who had stood, was a foot taller than she but still felt as if he were on his knees. 'For me?'

'Another policeman. *Scandalo!*'

'We're trying as hard as—' She was gone.

The man, who followed her by only a few seconds, was young and stylish: not Denton's sort. He had a walking stick with a gold top, and a remarkably pale grey hat that he was carrying curled back against his left hip as if it were a dragoon's helmet. His black hair was combed very flat from a central parting and held down with some mixture that made it shine. He had a black moustache that came to two points, undoubtedly waxed, a scant half-inch beyond the ends of his thin lips. His eyes were clear and very bright behind *pince-nez* that Denton thought had plain glass in them. His skin was almost delicate, his cheeks rosy, his nails buffed. He wore a lounge suit cut to make the best of his slenderness, nipped in at the waist and padded aggressively at the chest. He was, Denton thought, a young man who was mostly vanity and the rest water.

'I,' the young man said in English, 'am *Capitano* Donati of the *Carabinieri*.' He smiled with self-satisfaction.

Denton said, 'From the *questura*?'

'The *questura*!' The young man laughed. 'What have I to do with the *questura*?' He was posed, right hand forward resting on the walking-stick, left hand (and hat) on hip. 'The *questura* is the police post.'

'And you're the police.'

'I am the *Carabinieri*!' He laughed again. 'My dear sir.' He cocked his head, swung the tip of the walking-stick towards a chair, and raised his eyebrows in a question. Denton said yes, apologised, said it was remiss of him, put out his hand, waited while the other sat, then stood again, removed a dove-grey glove and they shook hands. 'Sit down,' Denton said.

When he had sat and arranged himself becomingly, the young man said, 'My dear sir—the *Carabinieri* are the *national* police. The *military* police. Not the local *coppers*.' And laughed.

'Your English is very good.'

'The reason I am laden with this case.' He laid his hat and stick on another chair and dropped the gloves on top of them. 'I am a student of languages. English, French, German. It is the next step in police work—an international organisation dedicated to law enforcement across Europe. I am ahead of my time.' He took out a gold cigarette case, offered one to Denton and took one for himself. Like him, it was slim. He lit it with a Crown Vespa from the *pensione's* box, drew on it, and exhaled a stream that seemed to have all his attention until he said, 'I am spending six months in Newcastle-upon-Tyne two years ago, studying English methods.' He laughed. 'I had thought to be at Scotland Yard, but they got rid of me.' He guffawed—not, apparently, at his humiliation but at Scotland yard's stupidity—stopped abruptly and looked at Denton. 'I am here about the late Lord Easleigh.'

'Afraid that doesn't ring a bell with me.'

'Lord Easleigh? What is mysterious in Lord Easleigh?' He inhaled again, blew out the stream, then looked sideways at Denton. 'I am told you found his body.'

It seemed like a long time ago. Denton had to struggle with it before he got it. 'Fra Geraldo?'

'Is that what they call him? How very *Nnapulitan'*.' He smiled. *Nnapulitan'* was the local dialect, object of ridicule and contempt in the north. 'I am from Torino. I am educated at Bologna. The South is not my *cup of tea*.' The English cliché seemed to delight him. Then: 'Forgive me if I offend your *amour propre*.'

'I've only been here a week. I don't have an *amour propre*.' Denton's excruciating accent with the French words made Donati smile.

'Ah, then you know nothing of the place. You will learn.' He cackled softly. He flicked ash into a metal stand. '*Revenons à nos moutons*. You found Lord Easleigh's body, yes?'

'If he was Fra Geraldo, yes.'

'There have been inquiries from HM's consulate. A peer of the realm, dead under circumstances, if not mysterious, then not gin-clear, either. A desire for clarification. We are meeting an emissary from the consulate and will go on from there.'

'I'm seeing somebody about a new house today.'

'This takes precedence. I must be back in Roma tonight.' Denton started to object, but before he could speak the young man said, 'It is only a matter of an hour. I wish to see the site, hear your account of it, perhaps have a look-see myself at the physical surround. It is a matter of satisfying the British Crown that all has been done properly—*not* an automatic assumption in the case of the *Nnapulitan'* police.' He smiled without parting his lips. 'They are not quite Scotland Yard. They are not even Newcastle-on-Tyne CID. If I may say, they are given to dotting their t's and crossing their i's.' He tittered.

'Surely it can wait.'

'Surely I cannot. We need only the addition of the representative of the British consulate.' He looked at a watch worn on his wrist, to Denton and most of masculine London an effeminate affectation. 'He is late.'

'Is something wrong? I mean, is there doubt about the old man's death?'

'No, no doubt at all—he is very dead! Ha-ha!' Donati laughed happily at his joke. 'Well, to be serious for a moment, I believe that the consulate wishes to be sure its copybook is unblotted before a peerage changes hands. Lord Easleigh seems to have had no children and perhaps there is a question of succession. Or of a family fortune. Who knows? I am only the chosen agent of the Italian government, helping a friendly state.' He cocked his head and looked at the doorway. 'Ah. This will be our Englishman, from the heavy tread.'

My God, a Sherlock Holmes come to judgement, Denton thought. However, Donati was right: a maid was showing in a beefy young man—almost a boy, in fact—in English brogues that sounded like clogs on the terrazzo floors. He was of the physical type the English called a 'hearty', built for a rugby scrum, rather red faced, with a baby's cheeks and slugger whiskers that tried to hide them, ear to cleft of chin, no moustache. He had a plump mouth, sandy hair already going a little thin on top, although he could hardly have been far into his twenties. He stood looking at them as if it were every Englishman's right to look at foreigners as curiosities, then chose Denton to speak to. 'Frederick Maltby, His Majesty's consulate. You must be Denton.'

'I must.' Denton felt dislike, thought, *John Bull in nappies*. The name Frederick didn't suit him; he should have been a George or even a Buster. And then Denton was ashamed of himself because he saw, too, that this very young man was rude because he was sick at heart with insecurity. Maltby, he guessed, was what his late friend Hench-Rose had once called a 'manufactured gentleman, cobbled up from middle-class materials to help us run the empire—can't do without them, though you wouldn't want to take one home to Mother'. Products of grammar schools and the lowest rung of public schools, their patriotism a slurry boiled down from *Boy's Own* and Cicero, they were crammed and scholarshipped and pushed through the Foreign Office examinations like iffy meats through a sausage grinder. The result was Maltby—and his bully's lack of confidence. Denton wished he could like him, to offset his dislike of Donati's vanity.

Maltby had turned to Donati. 'You're the police chappie.'

'Donati, *Capitano, Carabinieri*.'

'Right.' Maltby sat in a slender chair and hitched it along the floor until the three men made the apexes of an isosceles triangle. 'Bit late, profuse apologies, press of work always terrific at the shop. I do hope you aren't going to make any trouble for us.'

'What trouble could we possibly make?' Donati raised an eyebrow and posed himself rather languidly. He lifted down his *pince-nez* as if they were heavy and stared at Maltby.

'Exactly. Don't want any trouble. Pro forma this—satisfying the old men in London.' Maltby gave a braying laugh that he couldn't have meant, as the moment he was done his mouth fell into a rather petulant baby's pout. Donati continued to stare at him. Maltby looked back and curled one of his lips. 'No suspicion of anything off, I hope. I speak for the consul when I say that.'

'I have seen nothing to suggest anything "off". I speak for myself.'

'Well, I don't want to be stuck with a lot of police gibberish that will cause some private sec to the under-sec to write a memo. We're here to tell London that the old fellow died the natural, no suspicions, everything above board. Right?'

'I trust you do not mean to imply that proper police procedure should make way for your dislike of complication.'

Maltby looked at him for long enough to show that he was English and Donati, after all, was *Italian* and said to Denton, 'You're the man found the old boy.'

Denton nodded.

'You see anything off about it?'

Denton had some views on what might have looked off, but he didn't see any point in sharing them with these two. 'I leave that for the police.'

Donati laughed, replaced his *pince-nez* and said, 'Signore Denton is too modest! He is a famous gentleman detective—the terror of Scotland Yard!' He turned to Denton and waggled a finger at him. 'I was in Newcastle-upon-Tyne when you at last caught Satterlee. Ver-r-r-y lucky!'

Maltby now stared at Denton. It was clear that he didn't like Donati and didn't like what he'd just heard about Denton, either; Denton didn't like him or Donati; and Donati surely was too taken up with himself to like anybody. The isosceles triangle expressed the three of them nicely. Denton stood. 'If we have to do this, let's get on with it.'

Donati got up and arranged himself into a posture. 'We shall visit the scene of death, and we shall have a look at the corpse.'

Maltby frowned. 'What's that?'

'The corpse first, I think. It is on our route.'

'My instructions don't include a corpse.'

'You may wait in the carriage, then. Shall we?' Donati rose, draped his overcoat across his shoulders, pointed with his walking-stick, and went out.

'Got a lot of brass, these Italians,' Maltby muttered. He turned to Denton. 'I asked to be posted to the Raj, I get this. I ought by rights to be an ADC in the Punjab—top ten in the examination.' He came closer and lowered his voice. 'Can't say I like these poofy Mediterranean types.'

'He's doing his job, as I'm sure you are.' Denton went off to get his hat and coat, tell Janet he had to go out. She was still comforting Lucy Newcombe and hardly glanced at him. He went out, feeling much put upon, and had started up the long, carpeted central corridor of the *pensione* towards Maltby's distant bulk when another shape materialised from a doorway and clutched at his arm. 'Aha!' it cried.

Christ, what now? Denton almost said it aloud, caught himself and stepped back. The figure turned into an attenuated man in his sixties, unquestionably English, who was red with exertion or embarrassment and who now hissed, 'I had to come! I know it's early, but *I had to come.*' He pulled his hand away. 'I'm Fanning, International Society of Super-Normal Investigation. *Ronald* Fanning.' The emphasis suggested that Denton ought to recognise the name.

'I'm afraid I don't—' Denton looked up towards Maltby and waved his hat in that direction. 'Somebody's waiting for—'

'An absolutely fascinating case.' Fanning, oblivious to Maltby, had his hand on Denton's arm again. 'The old man, Lord Easleigh, the late Lord Easleigh—you found him, isn't that right? I had to come at once. Has he come through? Sometimes they come through immediately after passing over, perhaps some reluctance to, mm, as if perhaps regret—Did he come through?'

'Come through what?'

Fanning stepped back. 'My dear fellow! You *are* a psychic investigator, are you not?'

'Not, um, really.'

'You're writing a book.' It sounded like an accusation.

'If I'm ever allowed to get to work, yes. Right now—' He waved the hat again towards Maltby.

'I'm dreadfully let down that Easleigh didn't come through. He had definite psychical affinities. I spoke with him several times—said he was haunted, spirits tormenting him, things of enormous scientific interest. I'd pencilled him in for a formal investigation. Now he's passed over and you say he didn't come through.' Fanning shook his head as if he were deeply disappointed in Denton.

'I really have to go.'

'Perhaps he *will* come through, however. You must stay alert—attentive, open. Have you had spirit messages before? Perhaps he needs time to accommodate to his new surroundings. I think the services of a trustworthy medium might be productive. You know of Signora Palladino?'

Denton was moving up the corridor; Fanning trailed half a step behind, head bent forward, one hand at Denton's sleeve as if he were making a touch. He gabbled on, his voice urgent, assured: they could go together to the medium, Signora Palladino; time was of the essence, before the ether lost the impression of the death.

When Denton reached Maltby, he said, 'Let's go.'

'And about time, too.'

Fanning held Denton's arm. 'We must see her *soon. Today.*'

Denton detached himself. 'Why don't you leave your card.'

'But this is so vitally—'

'Your card,' Denton said over his shoulder, letting Maltby shove him through the door. Fanning tried to come right behind him, but Maltby threw a kind of American football block and came next, and Fanning was left to patter down the stairs behind them, trying to sound urgent and important. Donati was waiting at the kerb with a carriage; he surprised Denton by grasping the situation at once and letting Denton and Maltby pass and then stepping in front of Fanning and saying in a surprisingly authoritative voice, 'Capitano Donati, *Carabinieri*! Official business, signore! Stand back.' And he leapt into the carriage and told the driver to go.

They went up the Via Toledo, Donati amused, Maltby glowering. Halfway along that broad, busy street, Denton thought suddenly, *Ronald Fanning, oh hell!* He remembered who Fanning was: he had a letter of introduction to him. An authority on all things super-normal. And Denton had brushed him off. *Oh, hell!*

Their destination was a rather frivolous-looking building near the museum that proved to be the morgue, a small *palazzo* with a lot of scrolls and cupids somewhat the worse for soot. The upper floors seemed to belong, if Denton's crude translation was right, to a Division of Non-Edible Marine Products of the Office of Industry and Labour; the basement and, as it turned out, a floor below were the morgue's. Donati seemed to know exactly where to go, and he led the way, his stick tapping, his overcoat billowing behind him like a cape. Maltby's heavy tread came right behind. Denton, leaving it to the two of them to make a race of it, came more slowly. He was still tired, not at all eager to spend the morning looking at death with two much younger men he didn't like. They went through a *portiere's* door, then down a corridor, past a guard who insisted that they sign a register, and so to a stairway, down whose steps the smell of death's formulary was first met—carbolic, formalin, ammonia, decay.

The morgue's premises surprised Denton by being as modern as any he'd seen in England, certainly more so than London's police morgue. The air was cold, like the interior of a closed house; the ammonia smell came from a rather efficient cooling system. He wondered what he had expected instead—medieval vaults? Catacombs?

'You wish to remain outside?' Donati was saying to Maltby.

'In for a penny, in for a pound.'

'You have looked at a corpse before?'

'Of course I have!'

Donati shrugged, cocked an eyebrow at Denton, twitched his moustache to one side.

An old man in a dark smock and grey trousers, carpet slippers worn against the cold of the stone floors, led them through double doors into a long chamber with a low, slightly vaulted ceiling, the walls painted grey-green to shoulder height, tan above. Wooden tables lined the sides, most with mounded shapes under slightly, probably permanently, grubby sheets, the effect that of a medium's apparition: suggestive bulges—feet, nose—and a lot of cloth. Electric lights hung by cloth-covered wires from the ceiling, their frosted tulip globes hurtful to the eye.

A balding man in a black cutaway was standing at the far end of the aisle between the rows of feet; he now came towards them and murmured with Donati in Italian, turned to Denton and Maltby and said, 'I have little bit English only. I am Dottor Vinciani. I am physician of the *polizia*.'

He beckoned with his whole hand, the fingers folding into the palm, opening, folding. He had prepared, apparently; there was no fumbling under sheets or looking at records. He took them directly to a table well along the room and pulled the stained grey covering down to the breastbone underneath.

'*L'inglese,*' he said to Donati. 'I know nutting 'bout a milord; *questo uomo qui se chiama "Fra Geraldo".*'

Denton got the last, also '*inglese*', 'English'. He said, 'He called himself Fra Geraldo. He was some sort of monk.'

'Certainly not,' Maltby said.

'Well, he dressed like one. In a robe. He told me to call him Fra Geraldo.'

Donati sniffed. 'I think this was a fragment of his imagining.'

'Figment,' Maltby said. 'Figment, old boy—you said "fragment".' He winked at Denton.

Donati frowned. '*Touché, man ami!*' He murmured something to the police doctor, who gave Maltby a severe look. Denton was leaning over the corpse's head to study the injury to the right side of the forehead. Still bending, he looked up at the doctor. 'What's the cause of death?'

'He fell!' Maltby snarled.

The doctor was tapping his own neck. 'Broken, ah—?'

'Neck? How did he break it?' The doctor looked puzzled; Denton appealed to Donati, who translated. The doctor spewed a stream of rapid Italian and Donati said, 'He thinks the fall down the stairs.'

'What I said!' Maltby cried.

Denton was frowning. He looked at the doctor, found that he, too, was frowning. Denton said, 'He told you more than that, didn't he?'

'Merely technical matter. Which vertebrae were affected, the result, et cetera, et cetera.'

'Ask him *how* in his fall down the stairs he broke his neck. I mean, exactly what motion broke the neck—hitting the head? Or hitting his neck? Or what?'

Maltby said he really had to be back at his shop soon, but Donati spoke to the doctor, who, instead of being annoyed, seemed to warm to Denton and began to lecture him. Most of it was in Italian, but where he knew the words he repeated himself in English, with demonstrations—the twisting of the head, the sideways blow that had left the contusion on the forehead, a head-over-heels tumble symbolised by spinning his hands one around the other. He finished by touching Denton's chin and the back of his head and pantomiming a quick twist. 'So, he turns—*così*—the head right, the body left—*crik-crak*—broke, eh?'

'And you have—mmm, *Lei a...aperti...*the neck?' Denton used his finger as a scalpel to mime cutting into his own neck.

'*Ah, sì, sì! Vogliete vederla? Guarda*—' The doctor rolled the head and the torso, indicating to Denton to help him lift the right shoulder; a long cut at the back of the neck appeared, the severed edge of skin surprisingly thick, bloodless, grey. The doctor took a wooden pencil from his breast pocket and used it as both probe and pointer to show things that Denton didn't see even when they were pointed out. Maltby turned away with an impatient hiss, but Donati, too, bent in close, then sidled around the table to the doctor's side.

'I don't know what he's showing me,' Denton said.

'A twisting of the spinal, mmm, chimney—'

'Column.'

'Ah. Yes, the—do you say spinal nerve? Ah, it is "cord"? Yes, twisting—see, he says, the colouring. With a glass, he sees torn fibres. He says it is definitive.'

'But it's *twisting*—that's definite? Twisting, not a blow right on the spine or something like that?'

'He says twisting.'

'And that's common in falls?'

Donati and the doctor talked. Donati's eyebrows went up. 'He says it is possible.'

'But not common?'

More talk. 'Possible.'

They let the body back down on the table; the doctor moved the head back to its position so that the incision was hidden. Denton pointed to the contusion on the forehead. *'E questa?'*

The doctor touched his own forehead. 'A stair.' He slapped his forehead. *'Cosi.'*

'There wasn't much blood.' The doctor looked puzzled. Denton, Donati and the doctor all talked; Denton finally got through the fact that he'd found the body and there'd been almost no blood from the wound. The doctor pushed out his lips, raised his eyebrows. *'Possibile.'* He said something to Donati.

'The police did not tell him this. They said there was blood. When the corpse came here, there was some little blood and they cleaned it. He wants to know what you are asking.'

Denton looked at the doctor. 'Was the old man already dead when he got that wound?'

Donati translated; the doctor shrugged. 'Dead, maybe—the—' He tapped his neck. '—broke already, dies, falls more—' He whacked his forehead with his hand.

'But not that quick.'

'Comè?'

'He fell down one flight of stairs. If he broke his neck halfway down, wouldn't he still bleed a lot at the bottom? Wouldn't his heart still be pumping for a few seconds?'

The doctor pursed his lips. *'Possibile.'*

'This is getting us nowhere!' Maltby growled.

Donati twisted one end of his moustache. 'To the contrary.' He eyed Denton. 'You raise a perhaps significant point.' He said something to the doctor, who nodded as if agreeing. Donati touched Denton's shoulder. 'He will think about this.'

'May we please in the name of God go!' Maltby was already partly up the long room and pointing at the doors.

Denton held his hand out to stop the doctor from covering the body. He searched his brain for the word the *portiere* had used. *'Il cazzo,'* he said. 'I want to see the *cazzo.*'

Donati sniggered and punched Denton's arm. 'Naughty boy,' he said.

The doctor, unfazed, was pulling the sheet down the body as far as the knees. The twin sadnesses of old age and death were revealed: bloodless skin the colour of putty, wrinkles, bones poking flaccid skin like wave-washed timbers emerging from sand. Denton heard an intake of breath from Donati, and Maltby, who had come back down the room in a rage, muttered, 'Oh, dear God,' and spun around and ran for the doors.

'What happened there?' Denton said to the doctor. *'Cosa...a succede—succedi?'* He couldn't get the past of the verb for 'happen'.

The doctor used his pencil to point. He spread the loose, rubbery flesh of the upper thighs with his other hand and pointed to the long-healed, slightly lighter-coloured seam where the remains of the scrotum had been sewn together. 'Here, the, mmm, sack, the—ah—'

'Scrotum.'

'Si, the testicles—taken off and mmm—' He made a gesture, palm to palm. 'Closed, eh? By a physician. Very nice, very good.'

Donati murmured something; the doctor answered; Donati said, 'He thinks this was a surgical removal. Maybe cancer or other medical explanation. Nothing to do with the death.'

'How long ago?'

'Long. Years. Maybe—twenty. More.'

'And the *cazzo?*'

The doctor made a tutting sound with his tongue, unclear whether he meant Denton's Italian or the injury.

'Very, mmm, rude. *Con violenza*—violent.'

'Knife—*coltello*?'

'*Si, coltello, forse.* Maybe.' He pointed at the stump of the penis; all three heads were low over the corpse, the smell of death and chemicals stronger in Denton's nostrils than the lingering odour, despite washing, of Fra Geraldo. '*Guarda.*' Denton knew that the word meant 'look', but he didn't know what he was to look at. Several sentences followed in Italian. Donati said, 'He says this old man had his organ removed nastily. He shows us these bumps? lumps?—which he says are left from sewing together the remains with something coarse. Thread or string, maybe. But also he points to this flat place—see?—which he says may be from a burn. As if there was some trying to—I do not know the word, to—'

'Cauterize? Close the wound with fire?'

'"Cauterize", what a fine word! Yes. To cauterize.'

'Painful.'

'Yes, he says agony.'

'Who would do such a thing? An enemy? Punishment? Is this something Neapolitan?'

Donati almost whispered. 'The criminals here will do *anything.*'

Denton looked at the doctor. 'How long ago?'

The doctor shook his head. 'Long—long.'

'Before or after the testicles?'

Another shrug, a shaking of the head. Donati, straightening, touched the knot of his necktie, started to touch his moustache, then thought better of it and began to wipe his fingers on the sheet. 'This is not, however, germane to our quest, Signore Denton. The state of his masculinity has nothing to do with his fall down the stairs, eh?'

'How do we know?'

Donati signalled to the doctor to cover the body. 'It is intuitively obvious.'

'I don't much trust intuition.'

But Donati was waggling his fingers at the doctor to indicate that he wanted to wash them; the old man was summoned, and he led Donati away through a door at the end of the room. The doctor, who had been tucking the corpse in, walked down along the table, head bent, the knuckle of one hand rubbing his upper lip, suggesting to Denton that he was less fastidious than Donati, and came around to Denton and took his arm. He stood there for three or four seconds and said, '*E* detective, *signore?*' He used the English word. He meant, Was Denton a detective?

'Unnhh—not—'

'This *corpo* is…interesting. Eh? The…back, woundings. Eh? Old woundings, what do you say—?'

'Scars?'

'*Ecco.*'

'He whipped himself.' Denton pantomimed using a cat-o'-nine-tails on his own back. 'Flagellation.'

'*Ah, flagellante. Eh, d'accordo.*' The doctor tutted and shook the open fingers of his right hand up and down. He gripped Denton's arm tighter. 'About the blood. Interesting. I think—' He cocked his head and frowned. 'I look some more. Open the—' He waved his fingers back and forth over his own head.

'Skull.'

'Eh. *Lei a ragione.* There must be—must was—more blood. Why no blood?' He let go of Denton's arm. 'I do some things. You…come back. Eh? Seven days.'

Donati came in rubbing his hands together; the doctor stepped away from Denton as if they had been caught planning an assignation. A minute later, Donati and Denton were out in the cold December air.

'That was quite unnecessary.' Maltby, his eyes red, was scolding Denton. 'Not only did you take up the time of a Crown official, but you also confused the issue of what we're about. I shall have no end of explaining to do at the consulate.'

'You could blackball me from the Empire Club. If I'd applied to be a member.'

'Don't be uncivil, Mr Denton! I don't let a difference in ages keep me from speaking out. What you did was most objectionable. I'm sure that you artists think us government wallahs stiff-necked, but I find looking at a dead man's—you know—a display of prurience. I don't know what I'll say to my superiors.' He leaned towards Denton. 'All Britain is judged by what we do in places like this, and your looking at—you know—invites the worst kind of low laughter.'

'"American Novelist Studies Severed Johnson". I doubt it'll make *The Times*.'

They were swaying along the Via Toledo in their carriage again. Donati, sitting next to Maltby and across from Denton, laughed. 'Where did you learn that very interesting bit of Italian, Mr Denton?'

'*Cazzo?*'

Donati nudged Maltby. 'Mr Denton uses a vulgar term for the male organ.'

Maltby set his jaw.

'*Va fan' cula,*' Denton muttered. Donati roared. The driver coughed and might have been trying to cover a laugh.

'I suppose that was meant for me,' Maltby said, 'and is also some sort of Italian vulgarism. I'm happy to say I've no idea what it means.'

They rode in silence. The air was cold, thin winter sunlight casting unsure shadows on the pavements. The street was crowded with horse-drawn trams and carriages; on the pavements, middle-class men and women moved with what seemed to be purpose, while hawkers moved along more slowly—young women with silk flowers; men with cheap coral jewellery, probably the apprentice work of the coral factories; sandwich men with advertising boards; *presepe* sellers with trays of figures, animals, moss and stones and barked sticks for making the manger; here and there a breadman with breads and rolls carried head high on a board; girls with bits of lace and ribbon—many of them calling out or singing. It was both a spectacle and a symphony—but one given its downbeat by that harsh conductor, poverty.

'The young ladies are very pretty,' Donati said. He chuckled. 'Until they reach five and twenty.'

'Use a bath, most of them,' Maltby said.

'Ah, well, my friend, after all, it is the *South*.'

They turned at Piazza Dante, a vast square with an impressive colonnade around the far side; after several small streets, each meaner than the one before, the people shabbier and their numbers greater—Denton was trying to recognise landmarks from the night before and failing—they stopped and the driver pointed with his whip and said, 'Palazzo Minerva.'

Denton wouldn't have recognised it. The sense of distance was different in the daylight: the gateway and the courtyard beyond it looked smaller, scruffier. However, the same rat-like *portiere* now appeared and, when he saw Denton, nodded like a Chinese doll, not stopping until Donati said crisply, '*Carabinieri. Le chiave al Palazzo Minerva!*' He stepped down and put out a hand, not even bothering to look at the *portiere*. Denton followed, then Maltby; by then, Donati had the keys and was saying something brusque to the little man, who shrank back into his lodge.

Maltby looked around; he put his head back and turned a complete circle, holding his hat on with one hand. 'Damned slum,' he muttered. 'Peer of the realm, living in a place like this.'

'Naples,' Donati said. 'The great families sink or die out; their palaces become like the nests of ants—five to a room, ten to a room! The poor of Naples are like rats, waiting to run in and out.' He had led them to the big door of the Palazzo Minerva. He looked up to read the hand-painted sign. 'What is the brotherhood of Santo Simeone Stilites?'

'Roman Catholic,' Maltby offered.

'Without doubt.' Donati laughed. 'This is Italy, after all.' He smiled. 'Barely.'

Denton, who had actually read Gibbon, said, 'Saint Simeon Stylites was an early hermit. Lived on a pillar, I think. Bowed all the time.'

Maltby snorted. Donati said, 'I hope we do not find that Lord Easleigh bowed himself to death.' He opened the door.

The entrance hall seemed hardly less dark than it had the night before; the windows were shuttered, and Denton's eyes were accustomed to the brighter outside light. He saw for the first time, however, that the room was hardly furnished, the floor bare except for a trail of dirt left by the police and the gawkers. He pointed ahead and they stepped into the *palazzo*'s central hall, the two-storey space down whose staircase Fra Geraldo had plunged. Denton gestured at the stairs, then went ahead and showed the other two precisely where he had found the old man's body. He sketched briefly what the first policeman had done, rearranging the legs and hiding the groin.

'Quite right, too,' Maltby said.

'Bad police procedure,' Donati murmured.

'But absolutely justified,' Maltby replied. 'Admirable to find that sort of tactfulness in an other-ranks. The first bright spot I've seen in this sad affair.'

'No blood on the stairs,' Denton said.

'No, no, 'course not.' Maltby, like a tourist being shown the spot Where Our Gallant Captain Fell, had made short work of staring at a couple of boards. 'Anything else we need to see?'

'No blood?' Donati said. 'You expected blood on the stairs, too, Mr Denton?'

'If I fell down a flight of stairs hard enough to break my neck, I'd expect to leave some blood behind.'

'Ah. Hmm. Inevitably?'

Denton mentioned the contusion on the old man's forehead. Donati put his hands behind his back and went slowly up the stairs and down again, staring at the treads. 'The broom was where?'

Before Denton could answer, Maltby said, 'Now see here.' They looked at him. 'I've important work waiting for me at the consulate. If we're through here, I must move along. Seems quite straightforward to me, exactly as the local police made it. He was old; he took a wrong step; down he came. *Finito.* Medical boffin at the morgue bears it out—broken neck.'

'You don't want to see his rooms?' Donati said. 'Interview the other monks—?'

'There are no other monks,' Denton said. 'I think that's an invention.'

'He wasn't a real monk?'

'You'd have to ask the Church.'

Maltby said rather angrily, 'He was a member of the Church of England! It's neither here nor there what the monk stuff meant. My charge is to confirm the police report and get on with the Crown's business.'

Donati, one step above him, removed his eyeglasses and stared down. 'Inventing his own brotherhood might be interpreted as a sign of questionable sanity.'

'His sanity wasn't in my charge.'

'No question of inheritance—being of right mind, et cetera, et cetera—?'

'I don't know anything about that. That would be for his heirs, surely. Not His Majesty's responsibility. Leave that for the lawyers, if it's ever an issue.' He pulled a watch from his waistcoat. 'I really *must* go!'

'Then take the carriage, friend Maltby. We shall find another.' Donati counted out some *soldi*. 'The Italian share of the carriage ride.' He held it out.

Maltby was perplexed. The protocol of transportation costs hadn't been taught him. He grappled with some inner anguish, at last said that he'd pay it himself, and rushed out. Donati smiled at Denton. 'I daresay he would be happier in Africa, ordering black men about. Of course, he is very young.'

Denton went back to explaining about the blood, the injury, the false notion of 'instant death'. Donati, however, twisted the end of his moustache and lamented 'the lack of evidence to the contrary'. He stared at the spot where Fra Geraldo had lain. 'Evidence, evidence…' He raised his head. 'You are saying foul play?'

'I'm not saying anything.'

Donati prowled about the hall, now and then saying, 'Mmmm,' and staring into unswept, dark corners as if evidence might have washed up there. He opened the doors of an armoire, found it empty, pulled out the drawers of a sideboard, found them the same. 'The brotherhood of Santo Simeone were not very clean,' he said. He stood in the centre of the hall and looked up and down, looked at the stairs, looked at the bottom step. 'I see no evidence,' he said. 'Let us look elsewhere.'

Denton was thinking that his usefulness to Donati was ended; he was also bored. He suggested that he could leave.

'No, no—you are the man on the spot! You are the authority, Mr Denton!'

'You know everything I know.'

Donati put the tip of a finger just below the left side of Denton's collarbone. 'You are the man who found the murderer, Satterlee. You pursued him and you found him and you shot him. You are, signore, very lucky, and perhaps rather clever. I will accept the contribution of either.'

'But isn't Maltby right? Even with my carping, isn't the police version probably correct?'

'"Probably". Yes.' Donati probed with the end of his stick in the angle where the bottom stair met the floor; when he had got a good purchase, he leaned on the stick. 'But it is the *Nnapulitan'* police, remember. First, they are not all of them very good—some yes, some no. Second, they are not all of them very trustworthy. There is a criminal entity here, the Camorra, who sometimes buy policemen the way other people buy *biscotti*. A false finding of accidental death would be quite cheap in Napoli, I am sure. And third, as you say, there are questions.'

'But you don't really think that the old man was connected with some criminal lot, do you?'

'I think nothing. I ask, "What is the evidence?" Just now, I see no evidence. But we have not been exhaustive. Nor have the some-what pathetic Neapolitan police.' Donati straightened and lifted the end of the stick to point up the stairs. 'Let us seek for evidence.'

Denton shrugged and took it in good grace. There was still time before Janet would be ready to go out to meet the peculiar man, DiNapoli, at the Galleria. She had insisted on going with him. He said, 'I can give you another fifteen minutes.'

Donati flashed a smile. 'Then we shall walk very quickly,' and he bounded up the steps two at a time, suddenly boyish.

Denton came more slowly, and then they strode along the corridor that Denton had walked the night before. They looked into the same rooms, found nothing that Donati seemed to consider evidence. The fish stew or whatever it had been intended to be was still there, starting to go bad. They agreed that it had been a monastery of one, only one room seeming occupied.

The same was true on the next floor, which they reached by unpiling the furniture that blocked the lowest steps. The storeys above the ground had all been built to the same pattern: a corridor running the width of the house, which was wider than it was deep, with rooms along the rear house wall and, along the front, larger rooms or suites separated by short corridors that each ended in a floor-to-ceiling window. Despite these windows, the main corridor was gloomy.

Most of the rooms were locked. Donati had the keys, found quickly that one key opened most of the doors, behind which were dust, cobwebs, rotted curtains, and apparently random pieces of furniture set here and there as if they had been merely dropped. They found no sign of recent use, no footprints on the dusty carpets.

'No fingerprints,' Donati said. 'I adore fingerprints. I look towards the day when everyone on earth will have his finger-prints taken at birth. *Then* we shall have evidence!'

'If the theory is correct.'

'Oh, the theory is correct. I have made a study of it.' Donati was leading the way to another stair upwards. 'Above will be more of the same; however, we shall be able to say that we exam-ined it.'

They turned left from the stairs and found more of the same, indeed, minus the furniture, for up there the rooms were small and mostly bare, except for one that had a chair abandoned against a wall. Through their filthy windows, Denton could see over rooftops to the dome of a church, and beyond it the bulk of the hill below the Castel Sant' Elmo. 'A good view,' he said to say something.

'This is where they put the servants and the crazy aunties. The view was their consolation.' Donati gestured with his stick at a flaking chromo of the Virgin that had survived whatever had emptied the rooms. 'And of course the Holy Mother. Imagine creeping down all those stairs to eat and creeping back up three times a day because the great ones didn't want to see you or listen to you. Holy Mother would be a consolation.'

'Imagine creeping down three times a night to piss.'

They had found primitive WC's on the lower floors but none up here. Donati led him back to the stairs. 'I must in fact creep down the stairs for the purpose just mentioned.' He tittered.

'There's only four more doors up here.'

Donati handed over the keys with a smile. 'My need is urgent.' He ran down the stairs.

Denton opened three of the rooms and found nothing more sensational than a dead mouse, its odour long since absorbed into that of the dust. The fourth door resisted the key; this had happened at a couple of other doors, which, for some reason, needed another of the keys from the ring. He tried five before he got the right one, noted that it was brass, not iron, and that it had a good deal of wear. But the opened door showed him nothing any different from all the other rooms, except for an almost ceiling-high armoire that stood to his right. He opened it. It was empty, except for a wood shaving, which he studied and dropped back to where it had been lying. He closed it, went out, closed and locked the door.

Something was not quite right.

He opened the door again and looked at the armoire, then leaned out the door and looked along the wall, which ran to the end of the corridor and the outer wall of the house. No window gave him a view: the buildings here stood shoulder to shoulder, held each other up, shared this solid wall.

He went back to the room and looked in. Something was off about the proportions—

Donati was shouting from below. 'Signore Detective, what have you found up there—another corpse?' Donati's voice was delighted with the joking use of 'detective'. His footsteps rang on the bare boards as he ran up the stairs.

'Nothing.' Denton was annoyed by the mockery of 'detective'. He held out the keys. 'See for yourself.'

Donati curled his upper lip in a bad-smell expression. 'Now, I am more interested in looking at the *primo piano*, where so far I have seen only the staircase. Down we go.' He tripped down, very light on his feet. Denton came more heavily.

Only four spaces, it turned out, filled the ground floor, the largest a kitchen, the others two storerooms and what had once been perhaps an office. Whatever family life had gone on had been lived on the floors above; down here was, except for the stairway and the anteroom, utilitarian.

Standing in the huge doorway of the house, the keys in his hand as he was about to lock up, Donati said, 'You insist the old man should have bled more?'

'I didn't insist; I said it was possible. Likely.'

Donati slammed the door. 'Detection is based on objectivity. We must not bring preconceptions. You, I believe, want there to have been a crime.'

'The old man told me somebody was trying to kill him.'

'You told the Neapolitan police he said *ghosts* were trying to kill him.'

'Oh, for God's sake—!'

'We must be accurate, Mr Denton.' Donati put out his hand. 'We shall not meet again, barring the discovery of some new evidence. I shall not say I am satisfied—only a minute examination of the scene of crime would give us that, and we have not the resource—but I see no reason to return.' He touched his moustache. 'Will you share a carriage? No?'

No prolonged parting followed. Seconds later, Donati was gone and Denton, pausing to make sure he went in a different direction, was on his way to the *pensione*.

He said to Janet, 'Nobody wants it to have been a crime. *I* don't want it to be a crime, although that highfalutin ass from the *Carabinieri* accused me of it. But damn it! It *could* have been a crime.'

'Is "could have been" worth getting worked up about?'

He was sprawled in an easy chair, his hands pushed low in his trouser pockets. 'It gravels me.'

'It's the old fellow's "ghosts", isn't it.'

'He comes to me and complains he's being haunted or something, and then he's dead. Donati says there's no evidence, and I agree, but all Donati knows is evidence. He doesn't have...a nose.'

'And you do, and it smells evil deeds, and you're just delighted.'

'I'm not delighted; I'm in a funk. There *isn't* any evidence; what there is, is a lack of evidence. There was blood on his head. There ought to be blood on the damned stairs! Without it—' He wriggled still lower on the chair, his spine almost at the edge of the seat cushion.

'He could have been pushed?'

He shook his head. 'The only way it works is if he didn't land until he hit the bottom step. That's why there'd be no blood except at the bottom.'

'But you said he didn't bleed.'

'I said he didn't bleed *enough*.'

'Well?'

'I think he could have been already dead when somebody threw him down the stairs.' He curled his upper lips and glared at his boots. 'And they weren't ghosts!'

CHAPTER

5

They met DiNapoli in the Galleria soon after. DiNapoli was dressed in the same clothes and the same old hat; his cheeks now had a faint glimmer of silver stubble. He was distressed by Janet's being there, and when Denton introduced them, DiNapoli seemed as embarrassed as a small boy. He mumbled, '*Piacere...*' and left the rest of the conventional greeting unsaid. It occurred to Denton that DiNapoli might think that a haunted house was no place for a lady—some curious personal code of chivalry. Even when the ghost was herself a lady.

They sat at a table out on the great marble floor of the Galleria. The same people as yesterday seemed to be standing and sitting around them, doing the same things, as if they were a permanent display of the business life of Naples, as if they had been here all night and would be here all day. The sun was shining again and the glass cupola sent down golden light. Janet looked around her with what seemed to him honest delight. On the table next to her, Denton saw a newspaper open to the brief article that announced Fra Geraldo's death: *Incidente Tragico a Spagnuoli. Un Inglese Famoso è Morto.* Denton tried to puzzle it out—*'tragico'* was clear enough; Spagnuoli was the area where the old man had lived. But *'inglese famoso'*—famous Englishman? Had he been famous? But for what, except an obvious eccentricity?

'You want *caffè*, *caffè latte*, or *cappuccino?*' Recovered, DiNapoli was mediating between them and the waiter, whose rapid Italian Denton couldn't follow.

'We had *caffè latte* for breakfast. What's *cappuccino?*'

'Coffee wit' milk.'

'That's *caffè latte.*'

'They sort of stir the milk up. Give it a head.'

'That's why it's thirty *centésimi* more?'

DiNapoli said something to the waiter, listened to the answer. 'He says they put some cinnamon on the milk. See, *caffè latte* comes mixed together. Wit' *cappuccino*, they bring you a *caffè* and a jug of milk, you mix your own.'

'For thirty *centésimi* extra.'

'It's a thing, you know? Like going first class when it's the same train as third class.'

'I'll have the *caffè.*' He glanced at Janet, who said, '*Cappuccino*, by all means.' She was laughing over DiNapoli, not at him but from pleasure in him. Denton was pleased because she looked healthy and happy. When the waiter had gone, she said to DiNapoli, 'So, what about this haunted house?'

DiNapoli glanced at her as if her being there had changed everything and he no longer believed in what he was doing. He jerked his shoulders and looked at his hands and began to mumble. 'The owner ask me if maybe Mist' Denton was a journalist just doing this for a story. I told him he was a man of honor and he want the house.' He looked at Janet again and she smiled back at him.

'We haven't seen the house; we don't know if we want it,' Denton said.

DiNapoli recovered his confidence. 'You gonna love it.' This to Janet. Then, to Denton, 'He says any night you wanta spend, good.' He turned back to Janet, his voice suddenly apologetic. 'He gotta stay all night and he gotta stay in the red room. It isn't *my* idea.'

She smiled. 'We,' she said. '*We* must stay in the red room.' Denton thought she was going to pat DiNapoli's hand. She was starting to include him in her collection of waifs and strays, Denton thought, of which she had several in London but none as yet in Naples. She said, 'How will the owner know if we spend the whole night?'

'The *portiere* locks you in. But, signora, you can't—'

Denton frowned. 'What if there's a fire?'

'She lets you out. Or you go out the window, like the guy lost his pants. *Scusi*, signora.'

'She lets *us* out,' Janet said. Now she did pat DiNapoli's hand. 'All three of us.'

DiNapoli's face lost expression. '*I* ain't going.'

'Oh, you must. I want you to.'

'I don't want to rent no house!'

'But Mr DiNapoli, suppose the ghost speaks to us in Italian?'

'There ain't no ghost.'

'Surely you wouldn't abandon us.'

DiNapoli scowled and looked very much as if abandoning them looked fine to him. Their coffee came; he drank his at a gulp. Denton watched a ragged boy of ten or twelve making his way among the people in the Galleria, the boy offering something—a *presepe* figure, Denton saw now—and getting abrupt, now and then rough, refusals. He said, 'One of the street kids.'

'Which? Him? Yeah—a *scugnizzo*.' DiNapoli chuckled without amusement. 'Me, forty years ago.' The *scugnizzi* were Naples' street boys, ragged, barefoot, tough, living by their wits, often criminal. What the British called 'street Arabs', God knew why. Denton continued to watch this one. A waiter ran from a café and shook a towel one-handed at the boy as if he were a heifer that had got loose; the boy dodged aside, shouted, '*Bacc' mi minchia!*' and put his free hand over his crotch.

Janet said, 'Does that mean what I think it means? *Baccia* is "kiss", isn't it?'

DiNapoli was shaking his head. '*Scugnizz*', they grow up quick, who can keep up?'

Janet studied the boy. 'Do they have families?'

'They got born, signora, but after that... These kids, they really live on the street.' DiNapoli gestured to the boy, and, when he came close, to Denton's surprise gave him a coin and said something that sounded gentle. The boy gave Janet and Denton a big grin and held up the *presepe* figure and said in a high voice, '*Fatto da Fra Geraldo! A l'originale! Genuino!*'

'What's he saying about Fra Geraldo?'

The boy thrust the carved figure, a fisherman, into Denton's face. '*Fra Geraldo! E morto, questo è l'ultima! Non più!*'

DiNapoli said something to him, his voice sharp now; the boy pulled the figure back a little but turned to DiNapoli, one hand on a hip, his posture and expression deliberately both effeminate and mocking. DiNapoli pointed a finger, said something. The boy shrugged and backed away a couple of feet, and DiNapoli said, 'He says the carving is by Fra Geraldo, he's an old guy dressed up like a monk and carved dese t'ings for Christmas. Every year, he carve t'ree, he gives them to poor peoples to sell. They very famous. Every year he makes t'ree, every year the *scugnizzi* sell t'irty.' He grinned. 'I show you a place in Porto, they make Fra Geraldos better than Fra Geraldo.'

The boy thrust the figure at them again. '*A l'originale! E morto!*'

'He says Fra Geraldo's dead. It's the troot, he died last night, peoples say he got murdered by the rich peoples and the cops cover it up. I hear the story all over the place—it's the Camorra, it's the landlords, it's the archbishop. But I don' t'ink this kid got a real Fra Geraldo; he says "*a l'originale*", which means it's the real t'ing, but it isn't.' He jerked his head at the boy. '*Va via, scugnizz*'.' The boy let out a torrent of words; his head came forward; his lip curled; his free hand made a cone of fingers and twirled around the wrist.

Denton was thinking of the wood shaving he had found in the armoire in the dead man's house. 'Tell him I'm interested in buying a *real* Fra Geraldo.'

DiNapoli spoke, listened, and said, 'He says this one is real, I tell him he's making wool wit'out sheep, he says he can get a real one for hundred *lire*. He's dreaming.' Denton did the figures in his head: a hundred *lire* was almost four pounds.

'Can you tell if it's a real one?'

'Well—I know a guy makes them, he says he can always tell. He'd want a few *lire* to say.'

'Tell the *scugnizzo* I'll pay thirty *lire* for a real one—but I'll get it checked first.'

DiNapoli said something and the boy ran off, shouting something back as he headed for the Galleria's entrance. 'He says he see me tomorrow. He don't say where or when. Them kids are no good,' DiNapoli said.

Janet smiled. 'Then why did you give him money?'

DiNapoli shrugged. 'You give everybody a *soldo*. The kid's hungry. I been in that place.'

'But then he insulted you—didn't he?'

'That's just the way they are.'

Denton wanted to know more about Fra Geraldo's carving. He had seen nothing in the old man's house to suggest any talent of that sort, and only now did the shaving suggest that some sort of woodworking might have gone on at Palazzo Minerva. The figure the boy had held out to him had been brilliantly detailed, the work of a craftsman. Even if it had not been '*a l'originale*', it had been meant to imitate quality work. He tried now to ask DiNapoli about it, but Janet got in ahead of him and said, 'Mr DiNapoli, you *will* come with us to this house, won't you!'

DiNapoli screwed up his face. 'When you wanta go?'

'Tonight.'

DiNapoli looked bleak. 'You don't lose no time!' He turned to Denton. 'You bringing your guns?'

'They won't let me have guns in Italy. But Mrs Striker is better than a gun.'

DiNapoli bent lower over the table. 'Maybe you better forget it.'

Janet touched him again and held his eyes. 'We have to be out of our *pensione* the day after tomorrow. If we don't find a place to live, we'll be wretched. Denton won't be able to write. And I shall be terribly unhappy.' She put her hand over his and squeezed. 'Please.'

DiNapoli pulled down one side of his mouth. 'Maybe if I brung some holy water—'

'We'll bring wine. Also a cold supper. What time? Nine? Midnight? Three in the morning?'

DiNapoli was shaking his head. 'I didn't figure for a lady, signora. I mean, somet'ing gonna happen, has to, otherwise why those peoples run away? It ain't right you should be there.'

'Mr DiNapoli, when you know me better, you'll know I was meant to be there. I wouldn't miss the chance to meet a woman who wants to kill men who remind her of her husband. I've often wanted to do the same thing.' She smiled.

DiNapoli felt the impact of her. He shook his head. He looked into the middle distance of the Galleria. 'I t'ink I got into something over my head here.'

Denton got up and patted his shoulder. 'It'll make a fine story to tell your grandchildren.'

Janet stood. 'And you can tell us all about yourself while we wait for the ghost.'

DiNapoli looked at her and then at Denton. He stood, put his awful hat on his head. 'I meet you at your *pensione* at ten o'clock.' He looked sombre. 'Only for you, signora.'

As they walked away, her hand through Denton's arm, she said, 'One of us had better take a chamber pot.'

'Three, if the ghost shows up.'

'I like your confidence man.'

'I could tell.'

'He's the first *nice* person I've met since we got to Naples. Except for Lucy. And Lucy's only a child. Although I think he's a child, too. Don't you? Something completely innocent about him, for all you say he's some sort of crook. Isn't he? I saw a few like him in prison—utterly baffled, sweet, trying so hard to be as awful as the rest of us...' And so talking, they made their way up the Via Toledo.

❀ ❀ ❀

Heat lightning flashed across the low lid of clouds as they came out of the *pensione* to the waiting cab. Building fronts were fitfully lighted, as if a yellow blush had passed across them; the murmur of thunder started seconds later and echoed back from the Vomero hill and Posillipo. Denton said, 'I'd have preferred a completely dark and stormy night. Meeting ghosts calls for clichés by the bucket.'

DiNapoli was waiting for them at the carriage, the door held open. He hadn't come into the *pensione* but had sent in a message that he was there, a gesture that told Denton that he was tactful, knew he might cause them trouble by appearing— but what would a confidence man be but tactful? Janet sensed it, too; she whispered, 'A nice consideration he has. This is a rare bird, Denton.'

Denton grunted.

DiNapoli started to get up with the driver, but Janet made him get into the carriage with them. 'You're not a courier,' she said sharply. 'You're not a servant.'

His grin was visible in a slow gleam of lightning, as if a match had been struck and burned and gone out. '*Signor Nessuno,*' he said.

'What does that mean?'

'Mr Nobody.'

'I want you to teach me Italian, Mr DiNapoli. I have a book, but I'm no good at it. Where are we? Oh, there's the Galleria; we were there this morning. Now where are we going?'

DiNapoli began to point out landmarks in the sporadic light—the Castel Nuovo, a black presence blotting out the clouds; the Gesu Nuovo church. Denton let him and Janet talk. He had a picnic basket between his feet, another beside him, a china chamber pot in his lap, wrapped in one of his overcoats.

Late as it was, the streets were crowded. The cafés were open, warm-looking places that attracted him. He smelled the bitter smoke of roasting chestnuts; horses and urine; cooking (a people who ate late)—not much of meat, but nonetheless promising good tastes. They passed a street that had been turned into a *presepe* market, the sense of imminent Christmas strong despite an unseasonal warmth. He felt a low excitement, the beginning of an adventure—whatever 'adventure' meant at his age. Perhaps only the first step towards a book.

DiNapoli leaned towards Janet, opposite whom he was sitting. When she smiled at him, he said, 'I teach you how to cook Italian, if you like.'

'Oh, Mr DiNapoli, I can't cook English!'

Even in the near-darkness, Denton could see him make a face. 'English cooking ain't food. Italian food is *food*. I teach you. You love it.'

Janet laughed. Denton wondered if DiNapoli was in fact the innocent she thought, or if he was working an elaborate finagle that would end with their being robbed.

The carriage turned right into a narrower street. DiNapoli pointed into the darkness and said it was Sant'Angelo del Nilo. It could have been the Tower of London for all Denton could tell. 'Not long now,' DiNapoli said. He sighed.

They were headed towards the water. Denton could smell the sea, or thought he could, a salty presence under the other odours. Maybe it had been there all along. The streets were darker now and narrower, fewer people moving. Passing a lighted doorway, he heard a burst of laughter; a pretty woman looked out, met his eyes for an instant. They left the light behind and passed into near-darkness.

The carriage pulled up in front of a blackness with a deeper blackness beyond it. Denton thought he could see, after staring into it for some seconds, a shallow area, perhaps once a courtyard, with unknowable shapes at its back. Looking up, he saw the sky, yellow, turbid, silhouetted against it the bulk of a building. 'This is it?' he said.

DiNapoli grunted.

'They don't seem to be expecting us,' Janet said. 'Help me down, Denton.'

He got down, held up a hand. DiNapoli followed, handing various bundles to Denton, who was fumbling in his overcoat pocket for his flash-light. 'I put in a new battery,' he said. He turned it on. Janet was paying the carriage driver. The carriage rolled away and disappeared into the darkness, reappearing in the pale, scummy green of a gas light and then fading for good.

Janet looked into the black space. 'I wish I'd had the sense to look at it in daylight.'

Denton tried to shine the flash-light on it, but the light was too feeble. 'Maybe we'll get a bolt of lightning.' A low growl of thunder sounded far away beyond the Vomero hill.

DiNapoli said. 'They don't give the peoples in this part of town much light.' He picked up the picnic baskets and walked towards the deepest dark. 'I go knock.' But before he had gone a dozen feet, a rectangle of light opened ahead of him, bright only because it was set in absolute blackness. A point of light moved into it. A candle, Denton guessed, and, holding it, a figure too dim to be defined.

'I expect the signature music for the ghost at any moment,' Janet whispered. She pressed against him, squeezing his left arm. He started after DiNapoli and she said, 'Don't forget the chamber pot.'

DiNapoli began to speak as he approached the doorway, his voice too low to hear. His tone suggested a question; no answer came. He said something else. Denton thought he must be speaking dialect, which was enough unlike Italian as to be incomprehensible—if he could have understood Italian. The holder of the candle became visible when they got close, an elderly woman in a black dress from some style that might have gone back to the sixties. She was gaunt, hard looking, middling tall; she wore a black shawl over her head and shoulders. When all three were lined up in front of her as if they were going to sing her a carol, she said, *'Entrate.'*

Going in the wide doorway, DiNapoli said the requisite *'Permesso'*, and, to Denton's surprise, so did Janet. The old woman said nothing, but slammed the door behind them with a sound that might have meant that all hope was to be abandoned. She turned a huge key and put it in a pocket, shot two big bolts, the second with so much difficulty that Denton reached forward to help her. She snarled something and leaned into the bolt and drove it home.

'Sono la portiere,' she said to them. I am the porter. That much was obvious. She lifted her chin. *'Sopra.'* Up.

'Come se chiama, signora?' Janet said, her accent atrocious. Maybe the old woman was deaf, or maybe she had too much contempt for them to be bothered to tell them her name. She pushed past them and led them to a flight of stone stairs and started up, carrying the candle a little higher as a nominal concession to her visitors.

'I thought there was electricity,' Denton said. DiNapoli mumbled something to the old woman and got a single-word answer. He turned back to Denton, who was coming last, and said, 'It ain't turned on.'

Denton tried to add to the candle with his flash-light. Even then, little was to be seen, that little not reassuring. He could smell fresh paint, and a finger dragged along the wall told him that it was slick and probably shiny; a close look with his feeble light told him it was pink. At the top of the stairs, the colour changed to robin's-egg blue. The space seemed cavernous. A wall sconce, lightless as they passed, suggested the glorious decor that DiNapoli had described: pink, yellow and green glass shaped into flowers around the light bulb that didn't work. A little island of bad taste in the darkness.

They walked a long corridor, their footfalls loud on bare marble floors. He was aware of a mirror, of his flash-light's shining at him in it, his own shape behind. The fresh-paint smell mingled up here with mildew. Janet whispered, 'I feel that I've had my money's worth already.'

Something gave repeated blows on something else, a slow thudding.

'The wind's coming up. Maybe it'll storm after all.' He stopped to listen, and a satisfactory roll of thunder sounded, followed by a crash as if a bomb had gone off in the street. Behind them, lightning sprang through windows he hadn't known existed as he had passed them, flashed and vanished.

They turned to the right. No windows here—they were moving from somewhere near the front of the house to the back, on their right rooms with closed doors, on their left an outer wall, windowless because it must abut another building.

They turned right again, now apparently moving parallel to the building's front. The old woman led them another thirty feet and stopped. Behind her, a narrow staircase went upward and disappeared. Between her and the three of them was an open door on their left.

'*La camera rossa,*' she said. The red room of song and story. Her nostrils dilated with contempt; her lips gave the faintest of smiles. '*Dormite bene.*' Sleep well.

DiNapoli said in Italian, but Denton got it, 'And you, signora?'

She pointed up with her free hand. '*Sopra.*' Above. She said something more to DiNapoli and jingled a ring of keys at her belt.

'She gonna lock us in,' DiNapoli said, as if he expected Denton to stop her.

'Oh, lovely!' Janet said and passed into the red room.

'In, in,' Denton said. He shepherded DiNapoli towards the doorway, nudging him with the chamber pot. Passing the old woman, Denton smiled and thanked her. She hissed at him.

As soon as he was through the door, it closed and he heard the lock turn. He tried it; it was indeed locked.

Minutes later, Janet had lit two candles in a heavy silver candelabra and, holding it above her, was moving around the room, crying, 'Wonderful! Wonderful!' The room was at least thirty feet on a side; opposite the door, two tall windows rose from the floor almost to the heavy cornice, and as he looked the lightning came again and illuminated the room. DiNapoli jumped; Janet laughed.

A fireplace took up much of one side wall. Denton bent to look up into the chimney.

'Ghosts?' she said.

'Bird lime.'

Janet went on exploring. She found another door, which led into what might have been a dressing room ('It's where she left the clothes she wasn't wearing while she took her piano lesson') and, she reported, a water closet that had once, she thought, been a long-drop privy. 'Very authentic. All the comforts of the *Cinquecento*. Mr DiNapoli, you're not getting into the spirit of things! Don't look so glum! Come, let's set out the picnic and we'll eat something.'

'This ain't my idea of a good time.'

'I know, but it's only a few hours. We shall sit on the floor and eat and drink, and you can tell us the story of your life. Come along, come—!'

DiNapoli protested, but not too much.

'Chamber pot in the WC?' Denton said.

'It's that or the fireplace, which is big enough but not very private.' She was lighting more candles, of which there were many, as well another dozen she'd brought. 'When we've eaten, we must put some of these out so we'll have enough for the night. I doubt the ghost will be thoughtful enough to bring her own. Mr DiNapoli, did you bring a blanket? This room is cold, and I dare say it will get colder.' She was opening a huge chest that stood next to the dressing-room door. 'You'd think they'd have put some blankets in here, but it's as empty as Mother Hubbard's. That old woman wouldn't give you the hairs from her nose if you needed to make a paintbrush.'

When she was done making light, the room was revealed to be red because of a moire-like wallpaper, stained in one corner with water in the shape of India but otherwise sound. Red velvet curtains hung beside the windows, tattered at the bottom and sun-bleached in their folds. The upholstery of several chairs was a slightly bloodier red, the nap worn from many human behinds. 'Well, somebody had the grit to sit in here,' Janet said. 'Has it always been red, do you suppose, or only since the bloodshed?' DiNapoli groaned.

❀ ❀ ❀

They sat on the red chairs with the feast laid out on the floor. The *pensione* had done them well, no thanks to the Signora but to the cook, whom Janet had bribed. The food was for once not English but, DiNapoli said, 'real Neapolitan stuff', pretty much unrecognisable to Denton. DiNapoli explained each dish— roasted red bell pepper in olive oil and garlic; cold *osso bucco*, a slice of meat rolled around herbs and roasted, then sliced into rounds; grilled eggplant pickled in wine vinegar and anchovies; fresh-caught sardines, grilled and sauced; a kind of fresh bacon with tomatoes and a cheese he called *mozzarella*; three other cheeses, one of them a redolent ('stinky', in Denton's silent view) Gorgonzola; two loaves of crackly-crusted bread, only slightly the worse for having been baked that morning; blood oranges; a separate box of pastries; and two bottles of Vesuvian red wine and one of *Est! Est! Est!* white.

'I think we'll survive,' Denton said. He was pouring glasses of the white to start.

Janet said, 'Mr DiNapoli, which is the garlic?' She was looking into the roasted peppers. Her English guidebook had warned her against garlic and she was eager to eat some.

He pointed to the chopped white bits but told her that English people didn't eat garlic. Instead, she took a large piece of the pepper, making sure to get some of the minced garlic with it, then insisted that Denton eat some, too. 'I'd rather we stink together,' she said. 'Anyway, it's delicious. Wonderful.' She was using the garlic, he thought, to drive away a monster, propriety.

DiNapoli had got more cheerful. Janet's attention both embarrassed and pleased him; wine and food gave him back his confidence, and he ate as if he seldom saw a proper meal—not too far from the facts, Denton suspected. When Janet was done eating and was sipping a second glass of the red wine, she said, 'And now, Mr DiNapoli, the story of your life!'

'Aw, no.' He glanced at the window as thunder sounded. It was raining, too. She said, 'It's only a little past midnight. I'd give the ghost a couple of hours yet. Mr DiNapoli?'

'I ain't done not'ing very interesting.'

'I don't believe it. Come—tell us to start how you learned to speak English.'

He glanced at Denton. 'I went to America for a while.'

'But you've come back.'

'After a while.'

'Why?'

He grinned at Denton, the expression wry, then as the grin vanished sombre. 'Well, I tell you the troot. They t'rew me out.' He gave them each a smile, not the radiant one but an embarrassed, sad after-glimmer. 'I was a crook. I dint t'ink I was a crook, but they said I was. And I guess they was right.'

The lightning flashed above the city again; he flinched; rain slashed at the windows; something banged on the wall.

Denton poured more red wine for DiNapoli and himself. 'Go on.'

'It's a long story.'

'It'll be a long night.'

DiNapoli sprawled in his armchair and gazed towards the fireplace as if it held glowing coals. His ancient frock coat was buttoned all the way up, and he had pulled the overcoat that had held the chamber pot over himself like a blanket. 'Well,' he said, 'it was like this:

'I was born near here, down by the Porto, poor like ever'body. I go to work when I was nine, running messages, like that, then other things, then I get a job in a restaurant, in the kitchen. I gonna be a chef, I t'ink. Then, I'm almost twenty, they want me in the army. I dint want to go fight Savoia or somebody I never seen; let Garibaldi do it! So I go to the *picciotto*, that's like a little sort of big frog in the puddle, which is my neighbourhood. I tell him my problem, he says go and see the *compare.*' He looked at Janet. 'You know the Camorra?' He rolled the r's with extra precision. 'They're like a sort of lodge. They sort of take care of peoples. The *compare* is the big boss.'

'I heard the Camorra's a criminal gang,' Denton said.

'Well, yeah, that too.' DiNapoli grinned. 'But down where I lived, there's not many *cammoristi,* but everybody knows who to go to with a problem. So I go to the *compare,* he says, "We send you to America." I say I don' wanta go to America; he says that or the army. "We send you to somebody we know," he says.' The lightning flashed again; DiNapoli winced and drummed his fingers on the chair arm. 'So pretty soon I'm on a ship. Last t'ing before we sail, this guy shows up, he gives me a package like a fat letter, he says, "The capo wants you to take this to New York, 17 Bleecker Street, tell them you looking for Rafi." That's it.'

Janet said, 'Smuggling?'

'I don' know, and I never looked, because I figure maybe this is a test, the *cammoristi* want to find out can they trust me.' He looked around the candlelit room. 'This place is giving me the creeps. Maybe we oughta do this another time. Eh? No?' He slid farther down, pulled the overcoat up around his ears. He sighed. 'So I put the package in my coat pocket; when we get to New York, all these guys in uniforms come on board, ask questions, open our boxes, all like that, but nobody looks in my pocket. So I get off, I'm carrying my box on my shoulder and I ask somebody, where's Bleecker Street. They don't speak Italian; I don't speak English. Finally, I find a guy speaks Italian, I ask, he says, "I dunno, I just got off that ship over there." The same one I come on. So I walk and walk—'

A sound keened through the room, faint and high pitched.

'Only the wind,' Janet said.

DiNapoli was sitting upright. 'Some wind.' He sank back. 'We all gonna be killed. Where was I? Phhh, I was lost. So I keep saying, "Bleecker Street, Bleecker Street," and people point or they push me that way and I come to Brooklyn Bridge. I'm in

Brooklyn! I never heard of Brooklyn; I don't understand it's not New York. I t'ink I got off the ship at the wrong place, but no, people point over the bridge. I tell you, I walk about twenny miles that day, this box on my shoulder, I'm *tired*.

'Finally, I come to Bleecker Street. Number seventeen. It's a little place they sell food over a board on the windowsill. *Little*, I mean I seen bigger closets. So I say, "I'm looking for Rafi," he points up. Don't say not'ing, just points. I t'ink, well, either Rafi died and gone to heaven, or he's upstairs.' He stopped, raised his head to listen. All three listened. Only the wind and the rain.

'I find a doorway and these stairs. At the top is a guy, pretty young, strong. I seen hundreds like him in Naples. He holds out his hand—don't say nothing. I give him the envelope, he opens it, looks inside, says I done good. That's it. He says sleep over there, eat this, have a coffee, put the box there.'

'Now you were a *cammoristi*,' Denton said.

'No, no, nothing like that. You mean *cammoristo*—one is *cammoristo*, two is *cammoristi*. No, I wasn't a *cammoristo*, only a guy.'

'Was Rafi a *cammoristo*?' Janet said.

'His name wasn't Rafi; that was just something I was supposed to say. Yeah, I suppose he was Camorra. But he never said nothing about it. No, his name was Ettore.' He listened again. The banging on the walls started again and he muttered, 'Maybe a shutter.' He looked at Janet. 'How about I do this some other time?'

She smiled and shook her head. He sighed.

'Ettore give me a job in a kitchen, a restaurant over on Fifth Avenue. Couple of other Italians there, too, but there wasn't so many Italians in America then. We was, what's the word—the first ones to go—?'

'Pioneers?' Denton said.

'That's it! We was pioneers. So I spend a couple years in the restaurant, and then Ettore sends for me, he says, you gonna run a smoke shop. I tell him I want to stay in the restaurant, I like it; he says I'm gonna run a smoke shop. You know a smoke shop?'

Janet shook her head.

'They sell cigars, cigarettes, tobacco, candy, little t'ings. But we also sell numbers on the Napoli lottery and the Irish sweepstakes, plus a little thing, square, got holes all over it, a penny a go. You take a match, you push on one of the holes, it pushes out a little rolled-up paper and you read it, maybe it says, "Win five cents" or "Win a dime". Mostly it says you lose. Nobody don't tell me it's illegal; in Naples, all that stuff you can do.' The overcoat heaved as if he had belched: he was laughing at himself. 'After I run the smoke shop for a couple years, Ettore sends a guy to run a card game in the back room. I also got some stuff to sell I don't like, French postcards and photographs, I won't say of what, which I keep under the counter and I don't mention, except some guy ask me particularly for one I sell it to him. Otherwise, I pretend they ain't there.' He looked at Janet and shrugged. 'I ain't proud of this.'

'We've all done things we aren't proud of, Mr DiNapoli. Go on.'

'Well—' He stopped, listened. Denton heard only the rain and an echo of thunder so far away it was more felt than heard. DiNapoli looked again at Janet. 'You ain't scared, are you.'

'Not of the dead. Of the living, sometimes.'

He shrugged himself deeper into his overcoat. 'Well—' Again he stopped to listen, shook his head. 'I run the smoke shop for nine years. Ettore give me two more to run, too, so I'm making pretty good money. I never steal from him; I t'ink, I do a good job here, they move me up. Maybe I get to run a restaurant. Nine years. I get married, I got three kids, things go good. Then Ettore sends for me—' The high keening came again; it seemed louder. DiNapoli cleared his throat and spoke louder. 'He says I want you should have dinner with me; he names a fancy place. I t'ink, *Madonna mia*, he gonna tell me I'm moving up. This is something really good. So we have this great meal, he says, "Oh, Vincenzo what a good job you doing, oh, Vincenzo, I know I can count on you." Then we're drinking a *caffè*, he says, "We want you to do something for us." I t'ink, oh boy, here it comes, I'm made. He says the city got a new police commissioner, he trying to make a splash, there gotta be some arrests. So, he says, "I'm gonna give them the smoke shops, Vincenzo. We gonna give them you, too.'"

He smiled sadly. For the first time, Denton saw him as he thought Janet did, his naivete, his innocence. 'You went to prison,' he said.

DiNapoli said, *'Dio mio*, did I! Ettore says it'll be only a year. Seven years! Hard labour! They get me for public nuisance, operating a gambling establishment, possession of obscene materials, offence to public morals, and procuring for prostitution, which I swear on my mother's grave I never done. There was some girls upstairs from the smoke shop, Ettore put them there, if some guy asked me, how do I meet a girl—excuse me, signora, I don't know how else to say it—I say, "Try upstairs." That's all. So I'm procuring. I'm—*scusi*, signora—a pimp! Me!'

'And you went to prison for it.'

'Ettore says, we send a salary every month to your wife, don't worry. Everything taken care of. You be out in no time. Seven years. First two, I'm in the laundry, about killed me. Then they move me to the kitchen. Better.'

'And did they send your wife the money?'

'Oh, sure. That's the Camorra way. They got a guy, he don't do nothing but carry the money around to give the wives and the widows and the mothers. They take care of people. Look how they take care of me.' He smiled again, listened. 'My wife, the first year she has somebody write me a couple letters—we're fine, we miss you, come home soon. The second year, one letter. Then nothing. Then one day—I hear a woman's voice out there!'

They all listened. DiNapoli whispered, 'She's *singing*. *She's coming for us!*'

Janet looked at Denton. There was no question that it was a woman's voice or that she was singing. She sounded far away, perhaps under them somewhere, but she was singing. Janet said to DiNapoli, 'And then what?'

'And then what, what d'you mean? And then she comes to get us!'

'Your story, Mr DiNapoli. Tell your story.'

'We just gonna sit here, telling *stories? Dio mio*, you two got hearts of stone! She's a *ghost!* '

'There are no ghosts, Mr DiNapoli. Go on with your story. You were saying that you got no letters from your wife, and then one day—?'

DiNapoli sank down into the coat. '*Dio mio*. Then one day, another guy in the prison, he's *cammoristo*, he says, I got a message for you, your wife's annulled you. I says annulled me, what the hell is that? He says you ain't married to her no more. I was married Cat'lic, my wife was Irish, I say Cat'lics can't end marriages. But she got two brothers are priests, some kinda in with the bishop, he annuls us. Three kids, and we're annulled. I coudn' believe it.' He stopped, and in the silence they could hear the singing, a rather thin, high voice.

'And she married somebody else,' Janet said relentlessly.

DiNapoli groaned. 'Yeah, when I get out finally, they tell me she married somebody else and left the city. Her family wouldn't tell me nothing. She was gone, my kids was gone. I couldn't do nothing because I was on the run then, see? When my time was up, they didn't let me go, they took me and three other guys to a ship was anchored out in the port; we was supposed to go straight to Naples. I says no to that, I wanta see my wife and kids, so at night I jump off. I could swim good; I used to dive for *lire* here when I was little, it was nothing. So I swim to land, I t'ink now I'm in New York again! I find out I'm someplace called the Sandy Hook. I can see New York, but to get there I got to walk back around this hook of land, miles and miles, and then I'm in New Jersey! Finally I get to New York, they tell me my wife is gone away with a new husband and the kids, don't look for her. I go look for Ettore, he's gone back to It'ly. Ever'ting's changed. So I go on the run, here, there, living like a bum, doing this and that. Then the bulls pick me up again and send me back to prison for excaping and violating something, and when I come out they don't let me jump overboard this time. They put me on a ship and they guard me and I come right back—'

A bang like the first crash of a close-by strike of lightning rang through the room. Even Denton jumped. Janet gasped. DiNapoli scrambled upright and said, 'I told you!'

The sound came again, now recognisably from the door. The three of them waited, all leaning forward for another crash; when it came, Denton stood. DiNapoli looked at them and then he, too, stood and came to stand between them. The flame of the candles, which had burned down during his story, seemed to bend and attenuate themselves as cold air gusted into the room. Three of the candles went out; the other flames thinned, drawing their light back into themselves, and when the wind abated and they straightened, they were small and cold.

Denton felt his scalp prickle. He knew better; he told himself that he knew better; but it was a fact that the door was locked and now it was open, and in the dim light of the diminished candles, a woman was standing where the locked door had been. She was wearing a long dress, the skirt bell shaped; her long neck rose from a square-topped bodice that plunged down over flattened breasts into a V below her waist. Denton didn't know what period the dress came from; he was aware only that the style was old: he had no sense of such things, couldn't have told *Cinquecento* from Etruscan, but he thought in the near-darkness that if this was the unhappy wife who had been murdered five centuries before, she looked the part as far as he was concerned.

CHAPTER

6

'*Oh, dio,*' DiNapoli was whispering. '*Oh, dio!*' The woman in the doorway said something. Denton couldn't follow it, but DiNapoli must have got it because he groaned. Then she said, '*Morto,*' which Denton did understand, and '*Morto!*' again, and then she raised her arms—puffed sleeves above the elbow, tight as gloves below—and showed them long-fingered hands that dripped dark liquid.

And then the arms began to lengthen. They were like separate creatures, things obscene. They lengthened and lengthened, reaching for them, coming at their faces—

And Denton roared and charged the doorway. He ducked under the groping hands and went straight for the woman's midriff, his own arms out and spread so that he grazed his right knuckles on the doorway. His head was slightly aside to the left so he could drive ahead with his right shoulder. When he made contact, he felt the hardness of what could have been bone, and he heard a grunt and a cry of anger or pain, and he drove on, pushing the thing from the room, crushing it in his arms and feeling the belled skirt collapse. The woman, such as she was, came down on top of him, the arms crashing down on his back and then his legs as he drove on, falling, sprawling almost the whole width of the corridor beyond the doorway.

He fell full length with his hands and arms full of cloth and things hard and round and long, and under him a squirming something that shouted in Italian and sounded surprisingly like a live male and not a female ghost.

Janet was laughing.

DiNapoli was moaning.

And a pair of feet were pounding away down the corridor.

Denton tried to wrap the wriggling something in the fabric of the ghost's dress, pushing his hands together along the stone floor until he could join the fingers, then rolling on his back to grasp it, but there were hard surfaces in the way, long things like insect legs that interfered, and then he felt a blow to the side of his head that made tears come, and then another. The wriggling thing, which smelled like onions, hit him again and struggled and was gone, and Denton, stunned, was holding in his arms an inert armature and a great amount of fabric.

Somebody was calling to him from somewhere. It was Janet, perhaps in her own garden and calling up to him, her voice shrill and not at all like her. He thought that Atkins should run out and ask her what she wanted, and he tried to shout for Atkins and made a sound like a dog's being sick.

'Denton!' she shouted again, closer to him now. He tried to raise his head. 'Denton, you're bleeding!'

'Not my fault.' His voice felt as thick as his tongue did. 'Where's Atkins when I need him?'

'Denton, you're not in London! You've been hurt.'

She was standing over him with a candelabrum, which he saw as two fuzzy balls of light. He tried to move and encountered the dress and things like bones, which proved to be not bones but sticks, and he remembered the ghost. 'Dammit!' He kicked the thing off him, pulled the fabric away, finding he was wound up in it and in thin cords like bootlaces. 'They've tied me up!' he shouted. 'Help me!'

She tried and made things worse. Denton tore at the stuff and felt the fabric rip; he kicked and tore and thrashed, and it flew away from him and he was free. 'He got away,' he said. 'Smelled of onions.'

'There were two of them! Down the corridor—to the left—I heard them on the stairs—'

'Two?'

'There were two.'

He remembered. 'So there were.' He tried to stand, swayed, got his weight on one hand on the floor and felt something hard under it. He lifted it, expecting another stick, found a metal rod a couple of feet long. 'It was a sort of puppet,' he said. He wielded the rod. 'Maybe this held it together or something.'

'We should go after them.'

Denton growled. '"We."' He had his flash-light out and was shining it down the corridor, the light so thin that it made things visible only a dozen feet ahead before it went to rest its battery. He saw the narrow staircase where the *portiere* had gone up and, moving closer, a blackness beyond that became a staircase going down. Janet stayed behind him, calling over her shoulder for DiNapoli, whom Denton remembered only when she spoke the name. She said again, 'You're bleeding.'

'He hit me with this rod, the little bastard.' He stopped at the top of the stairs. 'You go back to the room. Send DiNapoli after me.'

'I'll do nothing of the kind; I'm coming with you. Mr DiNapoli's beside himself.'

'You've been ill.'

'Oh, and you haven't been hit in the head and aren't spurting blood everywhere, I suppose! You'll probably faint.'

He growled again and turned away as the first spasm of pain went across his forehead and bored in on the left side. 'He was right handed,' he said as if it mattered. 'Mr DiNapoli, take care of the signora.' He launched himself down the stairs.

Later, he would suppose that the stairs had been for servants to go up and down in the middle of the house without offending their betters by being seen. They were hardly wide enough for two people to pass and had no rail. He wanted one to lean on and settled for putting the knuckles of the hand that held the iron rod on one plaster wall; it guided him around the turns where the stairs doubled back on themselves and then plunged down into darkness. He thought of somebody's waiting for him down there and of traps they could have laid—more of those sticks across the stairs, perhaps, or a wire stretched at one of the turnings. Nonetheless, he went on as if he were tripping down his own stairs at home, his feet fast and whispery on the stones, flashing his light on and off, ignoring his headache and his cut forehead, feeling grit under his shoes, smelling mildew and closed-up air and then coolness and earth, as if a door had been opened.

The red room was on the first floor—second floor to him, American style (Italians couldn't count, was his conclusion: first floor for second floor, *Cinquecento* for sixteenth century)—and so the first door he passed must have opened into the ground floor. He swayed to that side and put his shoulder against the door but nothing happened, and he bounced away and went on down, the smell of cool earth stronger now as, he thought, he was headed for cellars below the house. Would the two men have gone only to the ground floor and then got out of the house from there? If so, they must have had keys. Or the help of the *portiere*. And if they did, they would be long gone.

The stairs ended in a few feet of flagstone, like a landing, and then a doorway wider than the stairs themselves. He saw its rectangle, another rectangle of perfect blackness within it, just the edge of the door hinged there, the door open now into the cellarage. He put his hand up on the wooden frame. It felt porous, deeply textured, damp. He shone his flash-light where his hand lay. The wood was pitted and ridged with rot.

Above him, Janet and DiNapoli were coming more slowly, their feet scuffing and clicking. It occurred to him that she hadn't the sense she'd been born with, still weak from typhus, running about in the middle of the night when she needed to be sleeping. Wisely, it occurred to him not to say so.

He pushed the flash-light ahead of him through the opening as if he expected it to be resisted—as if a sheet of glass or perhaps cobweb waited there. On the other side, the flash-light showed nothing, not even the dimmest of shapes.

He followed it. The stone under his feet was smoother. He shone the light down. He was standing on tufa, the soft stone that underlay the city and that many of its buildings were made of. It would be yellow if he could get enough light on it; as it was, it looked grey-brown, perhaps simply less black than his shoes and his trouser cuffs. He was standing on the base rock, then; the cellar had been dug into it.

He took a few steps in the dark and flashed the light, wiping spider webs from his face. A mass bulked ahead on his left: the base of a chimney. There would be several of those, he thought. Yes, another off to the right. He moved forward again, then far enough to stand close to the left-hand chimney. Where was he? He tried to picture the house, the turns they had taken getting to the red room. Then how many turns had he made coming down the stairs? It didn't matter; it made no sense that he would be under the carriage courtyard at the front; he must be under the mass of the house, looking towards the back.

'Denton?'

He swung around and directed the light towards her. Wound up tight, he was glad to know she was there now, the two candles she held mere points of light from, he thought, the doorway; despite himself, he was thinking, *How shall I write this part? How shall I describe my relief when I heard her call even though I couldn't see her, as if it was her voice that gave light?* He flashed the light at her and turned back and went ahead and to his left, wanting to find a wall, wondering at himself for thinking about writing and then realising that the writing was the reason he was here: everything was writing.

And heard a sound. A scraping—furtive, metallic. Not a rat; people make too much of rats, he thought. Rats go where food is—corn cribs, in his experience—not empty cellars of empty houses. And they don't use metal.

He moved to the left. He held the iron bar up, one end touching his right shoulder, ready to strike. His left hand found the wall.

'Denton?' Her voice was farther away. Ghostly. He smiled. Ahead of him, the scraping became a thudding, as if somebody were using a hammer muffled with layers of felt. He went forward, holding the iron bar in front of him now. He realised again that his head ached, the pain coming in waves. He transferred the flash-light to the hand with the iron bar and, keeping one hand on the wall, moved ahead again. Now, he could hear breathing.

He stopped. Waited. He touched the places on his head where he thought he had been hit; there was a wet swelling in his hair, but no trickle of blood below it. A wound that would look worse than it was.

Ahead, the breathing had become almost panting. Under it, he could hear a kind of groan, the sound of desperation. He went forward three small steps and turned the light on. The panting stopped.

A very small man was standing with his back to Denton, his arms raised and spread in a V as if he might have been hung up there, and his torso leaning so far into the darkness that Denton was looking at the underside of his crotch. He seemed to be trying to lift the wall but was really trying to move an iron bar that held something closed and was jammed in its slots. On each side of him, heavy wooden doors stood open. Timbers a foot thick framed them at sides and bottom; vertical boards filled the openings on their far sides, studded every foot with iron.

'If you move, I'll kill you.' Denton didn't really mean that, and he'd said it in English, anyway. The little man made a sound like a sheep and tried to climb backwards towards Denton; one foot moved down towards the cellar floor, then the other, then his whole body bent forward. Denton grabbed an ankle and twisted him over on his back and shone the flash-light and saw that the man had been partway up an incline that ended half a dozen feet above him at metal double doors with the jammed bar across them—an old means of getting supplies down into the cellar from outside. Denton could imagine barrels rolling down it, or sacks of coal.

He put the iron bar, not entirely gently, on the top of the little man's head. The man bleated again. He was on his back now on the tufa. He blinked in the weak glow of the flash-light. Denton shouted, 'Janet, over here!' and the man tried to wriggle loose and a dark stain began to spread down his trousers.

Denton put the centre of the light on his face. It was middle aged, pinched, of a type with that of the *portiere* at Fra Geraldo's. *Not the one who was in charge of the ghost business*, Denton thought. *A man on the bottom. A man other men pushed around.*

Denton put the tip of the rod on the man's larynx. 'Janet!'

The man wailed.

'We're here, here—' He could hear her well now, off to his right and behind him. 'Where are you? Oh, there you are. I see you—'

'Do you have DiNapoli?'

'Yes, yes, with me—'

'I need a translator!'

Seconds later, she was standing next to him, her candles shedding only a little more light than his fading flash. 'Well, you got one of them, anyway,' she said. 'He is one of them, isn't he?'

'DiNapoli! Ask him what the hell he was doing with that puppet.'

There was a gabble of Neapolitan, contemptuous from DiNapoli, quivering from the man, and DiNapoli told them that the little man was a puppeteer and he didn't know why he had made the 'ghost', but he had been paid to do it and to come here with another man and work the puppet. His name was Beppe. 'I know this guy a little,' DiNapoli said. 'I seen him sometimes. He goes around, he's got this t'ing like a the-ayt-er on his back, he does Pulcinella puppets in the street.'

'Ask him how he got in here.'

'He says they come in this gate. Him and another guy.'

Denton hadn't been able to understand anything they'd said to each other. He thought he was tired, coming down off the excitement of the ghost. And his head hurt. He said, 'How did they get in here if that thing he was trying to open was locked?'

Jabber. 'The old woman, he says. She leave it open for them.'

'Where's the other guy?'

'He got away.'

Denton put his face close to the little man's. 'Tell him I know the other man came this way, too. Is he down here someplace or isn't he?'

Jabber, jabber. 'He got away.'

'How?'

Jabber. Silence. Jabber. Bleat. 'He says he kill him if he tells.'

'Tell him I'll kill him if he doesn't. Tell him I'm Texas Jack.'

Jabber. 'He says you ain't as bad as the other guy.'

Janet said, 'I don't follow. Why would somebody kill him over a haunted house?'

'Or a *not* haunted house that he wants to *seem* haunted. Eh, Beppe?' Denton put the tip of the iron rod on Beppe's throat again. The little man's eyes appealed to DiNapoli, who said something and then murmured to Denton, 'I t'ink he ain't the bad guy, Mist' Denton. I t'ink he's just some poor *pescelino* picking up a few *lire*, you know?' *Like me*, he meant. Denton had to think about *pescelino*. Maybe little fish?

Denton relaxed the pressure on the iron rod. He straightened and tried to stretch his back. 'Would he tell us anything if I pay him?'

'I t'ink money don't do it.'

Denton squatted. His flash-light was fading again; in a few seconds, he thought, he'd have to put the fresh battery into it. He looked into the little man's eyes. 'Tell him that the other man didn't go out this way. Tell him he must have another way out. Where is it?'

Jabber. The little man's eyes slid off to his left and snapped back to meet Denton's. 'He don't know. The guy was already gone when he got down here.'

Denton stood. His knees cracked. 'He's no good to us.' He jerked his head at Beppe. 'Tell him he can go.'

'Where?'

'Wherever he wants.'

'He says he don't know no way out except this one right here, and it don't work.'

'Tell him to go back up through the house and hide there until morning. The *portiere* will unlock the door and he can slip out.'

'He says he's afraid of the ghost.'

Denton was fumbling with the fresh battery. 'That takes the pickle dish,' he said. He dropped the fresh battery into the flashlight, turned it on and then off. 'Tell him to scoot before I change my mind.' He walked Janet away from the chute where the little man lay and murmured to her, 'He looked over this way when DiNapoli asked him how the other one got out.'

'Does it matter?'

'It matters to me.' He started into the blackness of the far side of the cellar, then said over his shoulder, 'This is a funny business. I don't like funny business.'

She came after him with her candles. They found the far wall and began to search along it. Her candles were low, one of them starting to gutter, and she replaced them with two from a pocket. He told her she was wonderful and she said she was only practical, and she'd lived with candles for a long time. DiNapoli stayed within the glow of her light. The little puppeteer was somewhere back in the void, for a little time a faint sob, then a whispered prayer, then silence.

That side of the cellar had rubbish from the centuries stacked and pushed against the wall. They found old barrels and kegs, a few pieces of furniture rotting into dust; broken glass, most of it once bottles; crockery, broken and whole, most of it thick, heavy stuff; broken tools, many for digging; indeterminate objects of wood, one perhaps a coffin but probably not. Denton went once the length of the wall and then started back. Two-thirds of the way along, he thought he heard a sound and stopped. Teetered on his toes, listening: a sound like a cat. He aimed his light down. Under his feet, a thin arc was scratched in the soft tufa floor.

He shone his light on the wall. There was a ceiling-high set of shelves loaded with wine bottles there, dust and cobwebs thick on them. Still, the arc started at the right-hand side of the shelves. And the sound came again—maybe, now that he saw the shelves, from behind them.

'What do you see?' Janet said.

Denton pulled at the shelves. Nothing happened. He pulled harder.

'Watch the bottles.'

'To hell with the bottles.' He tried to see past them to the wall behind, then took the necks of two in one hand and made as if to lift them. They stayed where they were. 'The bastards are glued down!' He tried others, then bottles up and down the whole rank of shelves. 'All of them!' He moved his light up and down the shelves. 'Hell of a lot of work somebody went to.' He tried the bottom shelf again. Something gave.

'Mmmp.'

He bent his knees, took a bottle in each hand and lifted. The shelf pivoted on its left-hand end, and the right-hand end rose eight inches and stopped. DiNapoli said that maybe they should let things be.

'If you let things be, you never get anywhere.' He pulled on the right-hand side of the set of shelves and it swung outward to follow the scratched arc in the cellar floor. 'See?' Behind the shelves was new wood framing a doorway and, within it, a solid door with a U-shaped handle. He laid his ear against the heavy door, listened, and said, 'Uh-huh.' When Denton put his hand into the handle, it opened a few inches.

The Haunted Martyr

'*Oh, Dio,*' DiNapoli said. 'We better stop.'

'Stop my arse.'

Denton pulled the door wide, the scraping on the floor like an angry hiss. Cooler, mustier air swept out, and with it a sound that went from soprano to baritone, part of it like something a cat might make, all of it like an emptying drain with the gurgle at the end. All three froze; the sound came again, then a rasping breath and then silence.

'*La mal'ombra!*' Di Napoli whispered. '*La donna morta!*'

Denton aimed the flash-light into the abyss beyond the open door. Feeble as the light was, it picked out the gleam of glass rising from the tufa floor to the faint lines of brickwork in a vaulted ceiling, and, on the floor, a crouching animal with horrified eyes that reflected the light like brilliants.

Denton's first thought was that it was some kind of reptile, its posture was so grotesque; then that it was rearing up at him, and he swayed back; then, as Janet lifted the candles, the thing resolved itself into the head of a human being, eyes wide, below it the torso but no arms or legs. The mouth was open, the tongue out. The sound came again, the gurgle, then some attempt at words. The tongue moved.

Janet said, 'My God—' and stepped back. DiNapoli sucked his breath in and backed into the cellar. Denton leaned forward and poked the thing with the iron rod and it wailed.

Denton went through the doorway and got close and saw arms and legs then, pulled behind and bent so that the ankles met the pulled-back elbows. Wire glittered in the light as it passed from the ankles up around the throat and back again so that the more the creature tried to move, the tighter became the garrotte. The wire was tight now.

It was a man. A young man. The eyes appealed for release. The mouth tried to make words. Denton shone the light full on the face, and he and DiNapoli recognised it at the same time.

It was the flash kid who'd tried to steal Denton's wallet.

'*Oh, Dio!*' DiNapoli wailed.

'The wire, we've got to cut the wire,' Denton shouted. He was scrabbling in a pocket for his own knife, but it was too small and too polite. Janet produced a heavy clasp knife from the Army and Navy Stores, military in its size and practicality, a conglomeration of cleverly nested tools on a single handle. The blade was thick at its spine and looked strong enough to cut through nails.

'Roll him on his side—his side, so we can cut the wire—'

DiNapoli was shocked. 'Leave him—just close the door and leave him—'

Denton was out the door into the cellar, then back with a half-rotten piece of board and a forearm-thick log that might once have been intended for firewood. He slipped the board under the wire. 'Tip him more—more, more, goddamit, don't be squeamish! It's better to hurt him than let him choke to death!' He pulled on the wire. The young man groaned and gurgled; Janet was panting, trying to roll him into position; DiNapoli, not sure what Denton was doing, was pushing when she pulled, pulling when she pushed. Denton put a knee on the boy's hip, rolling him still farther, then pushed down on the wire with the knife blade to force it against the board and swung the log. Three blows, and there was a low-pitched vibration and the wire snapped, and the bent legs tried to straighten and the boy screamed.

'Going to hurt like hell for a while,' Denton was saying. 'Get me some light over here—!' He was trying to pull the wire away from the young man's throat, where it had cut into the flesh. 'Now down here—no, on the hands—good!'

The hands were purple with backed-up blood. The wire had bitten deeply into the wrists; blood oozed. Denton shook his head at the deliberate cruelty. He unwrapped the wire, following its path around a wrist and an ankle and back, then the other wrist and around, then the ankle. When he got it all off and the young man was free, he lay and wept, unable yet to straighten his legs or move his hands.

'Must hurt like hell,' Denton said.

Janet bent and signalled DiNapoli to help her turn the man on his back, his knees bent. She raised his arms above his torso, and he screamed.

Denton said, 'It's one of the kids I licked for trying to take my wallet.'

Janet, trying to massage the man's arms, said, 'It can't be.'

'It's worse,' DiNapoli said. 'He's the grandson of Doro Scuttini, the *compare*. They call him Doro *o bufalo*. He's big. He ain't nice!'

Denton tried to straighten one of the legs and the young man screamed again. Denton began to massage the thigh and the calf, squeezing the muscles and then relaxing. He motioned to DiNapoli to do the other leg. 'You acted funny when I described him after we'd been in the Galleria. You knew who it was then, didn't you.'

'I t'ought maybe it don't matter, maybe the *capo* don't care if you push the kid around some, because he's a punk, what you call a *guappo*, he behaves like he isn't part of the *compare*'s family but he's some kind of show-off, some little street shit, pardon me, signora. But this—!' DiNapoli shook his head. '*Dio mio*, they don't forget this. For this, they *kill* people!'

'But not us,' Janet said. She was moving one of the *guappo*'s arms like the handle of a pump. 'We're the ones who found him; we didn't put him here or tie him up.'

'You t'ink they gonna believe that, signora?'

'We'll find out.' Denton stood. 'Grab his legs. We'll carry him out.'

'Mist' Denton, take my advice, leave him here.'

'If we do, it's murder. That's what this was, attempted murder. And the other one who was with the puppeteer, he's part of it, because he knew how to get out of the cellar this way. Do as I tell you.'

Janet was already lifting one leg. Denton took the shoulders; DiNapoli, protesting, took the other leg near the hip, and, grunting, they carried the young man into the cellar, Denton's flash-light, pressed between his left arm and his ribs, the only light. DiNapoli would have put him down but Denton kept on, scuttling forward with little steps, until they'd returned to the chute where they'd left the little man. He was gone.

Denton climbed into the opening and shone his light upward, then passed it to Janet and whacked the jammed bar. It was bigger around than a broom handle. Rust, he thought, old rust made the jam worse. He leaned on the metal doors and felt them bulge outward and the bar came free and he lifted it out of its supports. When he pushed again on the doors, they swung a little outward and the rain-washed air of the night swept in.

'Oh, my God,' Janet said, 'I'd forgotten how stuffy it is in here. You get used to anything, don't you.'

'Get used to hanging if you hang long enough, my grandmother used to say.' He stepped down into the cellar. 'DiNapoli, get a carriage.'

DiNapoli stared at him. His eyes seemed to be bulging from his head. 'Where do I get a carriage? It's two, t'ree in the morning!'

Denton put a hand on his chest. 'We're going to take this kid to his grandfather. Go get a carriage.'

'You crazy!'

'Yes or no? You don't want to be part of it—' He jerked his head towards the source of the sweet night air. 'Go. No hard feelings. But don't come back.'

'Aw, jeez—signora, tell him he's crazy.'

'There's no telling him, Mr DiNapoli. And usually, he's right.'

'Aw, jeez—' DiNapoli sagged. 'Well—' He sighed. 'You don' know what these peoples are like.' He put a foot on the chute. 'I do. So who's crazy, you or me?' He climbed another step up the chute. 'I be a while.' He sighed. 'But I come back. For you, signora. And you, too, o' course, Mist' Denton.' He disappeared into the darkness.

Denton and Janet looked at each other in the watery light. 'Will he really come back?' he said.

'If he doesn't—' She shrugged. 'It's almost morning.' She looked down at the young man on the floor. He was breathing more evenly but he was still groaning, his limbs moving slowly as if he were trying to swim. 'We might be better to go for a doctor.'

'No. DiNapoli's half right—if we don't get him to the *compare* right quick, we're the ones it will come down on. I'll get some wine for him. You stay here. You don't mind? I'll be quick.'

He crossed the cellar, more sure of its layout now, barking his shins only twice on ancient objects in the dark. The flashlight had gone out again; he thought he might have one more battery in his overcoat. Surely it wasn't yet morning, more like half past one. He was tired, though. How much wine had he drunk? Something made him feel used up—maybe the hits to the head. Still, it was only a matter of going on.

He came out on the *piano nobile* and made his way to the red room. Something moved in the corridor; he flashed his light, which went out at once but showed the little puppeteer like a rabbit frozen by an owl's shriek. Denton said, 'Good morning,' and the man howled. It must be hell for him up here in the dark, he thought. Very much like a rabbit. But he was surviving it; the light of morning would come.

Denton went back down with several candles and the remaining bottle of red wine and a glass and held it to the young man's mouth. He tried to drink but let most of it go down his neck. He tried to speak, managed only a rattle and a growl and sank back down.

'We don't want him to die on us,' Janet said. She massaged his legs.

Denton lit the new candles and glued them to the floor with their own melted wax, then took one and went back to the doorway through which they'd carried the young man. Holding the light high, he went in and examined the space. It was simple curiosity, yes; Janet would say so. But he did these things for the excitement of them, too: the idea of the Camorra, of the *capo*, titillated him. And there was writing about it later, too, for surely he would write about this, use it to cap the opening chapter of the book, and a different excitement would come with the writing. In Maine they said that the man who cuts his own firewood is warmed twice; well, the writer who seeks out experience is excited twice over. *If he does both things right*, he thought, and smiled at himself.

The chamber was less than twenty feet long, only half as wide. Shelves on each side had shallow cut-outs to keep bottles from rolling: it was a wine cellar. Empty bottles lay in the racks near the door—the glass that had glinted when he had first opened the door. Where the young man had lain, the stone floor was clear, but beyond was a raised stone square with a wood platform capping it, and beyond that boxes of dark bottles that proved to be Scotch whisky. *Bell's Best 12 Years Old*, the labels said. He counted twenty-two boxes, none dusty. Not something that had been put in here years ago and forgotten. And not something that had passed through the customs and picked up a revenue stamp, either.

He walked around the raised platform, no more than three feet on a side, and saw big strap hinges. He raised the opposite edge: it was a trapdoor, the wood new, like that of the doorway. Under it was darkness. Denton leaned down, then got to his knees and lowered the candle through and put his head as low as he dared. He smelled damp and earth and the sea. He could see the underside of a curved ceiling carved from the rock. He dropped a bit of broken stone; it seemed to hit almost immediately. He squirmed to his side and got his flash-light from his pocket and leaned down again, and below he could see a stone floor and a wooden ladder laid on its side, and in each direction a tunnel vanishing into blackness. This was the way the other man had got out.

When he rejoined Janet, he said, 'Somebody's smuggling whisky.'

She was rubbing the young man's arms and his neck. 'Take a turn, will you? We need to get his blood going, then get him on his feet.' She stood and stretched. 'Smuggling. One isn't precisely surprised.' Nor did she sound it. 'Smuggling, a sham ghost, a boy trussed up to die—what does Hawkshaw the Detective say?'

'Hawkshaw says he's too tired to think just now.'

DiNapoli showed up at half past two. They heard him first as the slow clop of horse hooves and the rolling, grinding sound of wheels. When Denton put his head out of the doors at the top of the chute, he saw that he was in a cul-de-sac, a carriage just visible where it opened on a narrow street. DiNapoli came towards him warily and whispered, 'I done the best I could. I had to go to the Rettifilo.'

'Let's get him into the carriage.'

The driver looked down as they put the boy on one of the seats. DiNapoli said, 'I tole him he's a drunk.' They tucked the boy's feet in. DiNapoli said, 'I tell you where you gotta go. I t'ink it's better you go to the neighbourhood guy under the *compare*, let him break the news. Maybe the *compare* decides to hit the messenger with whatever he got in his hand. Better the neighbourhood guy than you.'

'Than you, you mean.'

'Me!'

'And me,' Janet said. She was looking up at the sky, at a star caught between the buildings of the narrow street. 'I'll go as your bona fides. We'll go together, Mr DiNapoli.' She and Denton had talked it over as they had walked the boy around the cellar. Denton had started outlining his objections—she had been ill; she was a woman; it was his responsibility—but she had said simply that she would go, and she didn't think an irate grandfather would take his revenge on a woman, probably a foreign woman least of all. 'It's an errand of mercy, after all.'

'Mercy's not a regular caller on the Camorra.'

'All the more reason for me to go, then. I'll go, and I'll drag Mr DiNapoli along to translate for me, and you'll sit up with the ghost and prove to that dreadful old woman who let us in that you're still here.'

'As if it mattered now,' he said.

'To the contrary, it matters a great deal! I like the house. I quite love the *camera rossa*, which I shall make my own. I want the house, and I want you to be here at dawn to tell the old harridan so.'

He had reminded her again that she'd been ill, and she had told him to shut up.

Now, Denton told them both to come back as quickly as they could to tell him that they had delivered the young man. He was whispering, he wasn't sure why.

'If the old woman finds out you know a way out of the cellar, she'll say the ghost frightened you and you ran out of the house.'

'Then I'll come back again tonight. Or is it tomorrow night?' He kissed her. 'For God's sake, be careful.' She made an impatient sound and he helped her into the carriage. To DiNapoli he said, 'Take care of her.'

'I t'ink I got in over my head wit' you two peoples, is what I t'ink.'

'We'll make it up to you.' He held on to DiNapoli's arm. 'What's the word you used for "ghost"? In case I see the old woman—how do I say we saw the ghost?'

'Mal'ombra. La mal'ombra. Just say that a few times and say "finito". She get the message you not scared away. Laugh when you say it. "La mal'ombra e finita.'" He got into the carriage. 'What a night.'

Denton went back through the iron doors and down the chute into the cellar, where he rooted around until he came up with a splinter of board that would hold the doors closed but could be easily broken from the outside. He closed the door to the wine cellar but first piled cases of the Scotch on top of the trapdoor, hoping it was enough to keep anyone from climbing in from the tunnel below. Propping a decayed piece of heavy furniture against the door, he turned away and again made his way up through the house. He was saying to himself, mal'ombra, mal'ombra. Bad something-or-other. Shadow? Or was ombra like hombre? Out West they'd said 'a bad hombre', a badman. No, he liked 'bad shadow' for ghost. An expression that was a picture of itself.

He had the beginning of his book—and the title of chapter one.

He went up to the red room. This time, he did not meet the puppeteer, who must have found a refuge somewhere in the dark.

He lit more candles and then pulled the 'ghost' inside and draped her over the massive chest. In the light, it was clearer that most of the illusion was in the dress and a dead-white mask. A wood frame supported the dress; the arms were jointed constructions like the accordion racks that could be expanded or contracted to fit a space. The whole thing was ingenious and surprisingly well made. Denton thought of DiNapoli's tale of the fake Fra Geraldo figures, the level of craftsmanship that the city harboured. Naples was a city of artisans, even when their art was dedicated to sham.

He slept for two hours and woke when first light made the room's tall windows visible. The room, so striking in its red shabbiness by candlelight, now seemed merely dull, light was without colour. Empty plates and bottles stood everywhere. He wondered why he had woken, looked around him: the old woman stood in the doorway, her single candle a pale halo in the morning gloom.

'*Buon' matino,*' Denton said. He stood, grinning. He pointed at the windows. '*E matino.*'

She stared at him. If she hated him, she had the expression for it. She hissed something. Denton picked the ghost up from the chest where he had laid her and held her up. '*La mal'ombra.*' He shook the puppet and the head lolled forward. '*La mal'ombra e finita.*' He knew *finita*. Always a useful word. He said it again. '*Finita.*' He draped the puppet over the huge chest again. '*E matino. Sono—*' He searched for the word for 'here'. What was it? '*Qui. Sono qui.*' He wanted to say 'I'm still here' but didn't know the word for 'still'. Nonetheless, she got the message. She sniffed, looked more full of hate than ever, and turned away. Denton shouted after her, '*La porta! La porta, signora!*' The door, so the puppeteer could get out.

He found some bread among the wreck of the night, wanted coffee, found that the tall windows opened like doors and stepped gingerly to the shallow balcony outside.

The rain had stopped. The smell of air freshly washed struck him. He shivered because it was cold now, too; he pulled his jacket collar up. A bird was calling softly from above him somewhere; turning, he looked up and saw a ragged line of sticks and grass along the eaves of the house. *A nest up there.* He thought of a city of rooftops, whole lives lived up there. As if to confirm this idea, the first of the morning sun touched the roof of the tallest of the houses opposite, gilding it.

Turning again, he looked down. The balcony looked into a vast open space; directly below was a shallow garden the width of the house, now weeds ending in a stone wall. Beyond that were other gardens, several with arbours on which vines—grapes?—hung. Colours were indistinct, but he thought that the gardens here were given to vegetables and fruits, not flowers—a few trees, even, perhaps lemons but with no fruit this time of year. The open space was enclosed by buildings, the oldest ones once rather grand: pediments over windows, balconies of wrought iron or even stone, one doorway flanked by caryatids. The newer buildings were lighter coloured, rather pedestrian.

The old walls showed cracks and fallen-away stucco, the effect that of age and decay but not ruin; with the gardens, this was a living place. Rugs and clothing hung on balcony railings; lines had been strung between windows, even across the corners between buildings, to support laundry, most of them empty now because of the rain. A brown cat minced across the top of the garden wall, stopping to stare at him with yellow eyes and then sit and, after licking a paw once, begin to examine its anus.

He went back inside and found the card that the frog-like police inspector, Dottor Gianaculo, had given him. On a page torn from his notebook, he wrote, '*Dottore*, I have found in the cellar of a house twenty-two cases of whisky without customs stamps. Perhaps the police would like to seize it.' He drew a crude map of the cellar and the hidden wine vault. He signed his name and folded the paper, wondering how best to get it to the *questura*: this time, he thought, he wanted the police on his side. If Gianaculo could find somebody to translate, of course. And if they could figure out his sketch. And if they'd bother.

He went out again and leaned on the balcony railing. The light was brighter now, more of the housetops turned golden by the sun, the brown cat now a blazing orange. Birds were chirping, some of them flying between the houses. A woman carrying a bucket came out of a house across the way and, seeing him, put a hand over her eyes and stared at him.

Life, he thought. *Hundreds live here. All this life.* Could he use this? Could he somehow pose the darkness, the deadness of this house, against all this life? Or was the story really one of visible life and hidden life, gardens and families and trees above, tunnels and hidden doors and garrotted men below? Or was it a story about a rapturous embrace of life that also included, even caused, a dark love of death?

He heard the familiar sound of a horse's hooves and turned his head to the left, his forearms on the stone railing. He looked between two houses, one next to his own, one across a narrow cul-de-sac and at right angles to his own; he felt a start of recognition as he saw that the cul-de-sac had to be the one to which DiNapoli had brought the carriage before. As he watched, a carriage stopped across the little alley's mouth and DiNapoli, after being woken by the driver, oozed out. Denton called to him, then ran down to the front door. It was unlocked, as he had demanded. The puppeteer had, he supposed, slipped away.

'Where's Mrs Striker?'

'She's there with the *compare*. She's all right, no problem, they love her. I tell you, she made some swell impression. Like some queen, which she is, but I t'ought they was gonna kiss her feet.'

'She's safe? Really?'

'*O bufalo*, he took a shine to her. She stands there like a queen, she says—I was translating—she says, "Honoured signore, I bring you your beloved grandson, who has been saved from vile assassins by the famous American, Signore Denton! He is pleased and honoured to return to you this offspring of your great family." No kidding, she talks like that, I don't have to fix it up or not'ing. What a lady!'

'She's been ill.' Denton sounded to himself disapproving.

'They take care of her. They love her, I'm telling you. We gotta go. Scuttini wants you should come out there. The sooner we go, the sooner she comes back.'

'He threatened her?'

'No, no, it's just the way he is. You gotta be a little nice, listen to him make a speech, say t'ank you.'

Denton was feeling his lack of sleep and the blows he had taken. He had thought she would come back with DiNapoli, they would return to the *pensione* and sleep. 'How far?'

'Out beyond Porta Capuana. The capo's farm. A couple miles.'

They set off, the driver grumbling but mollified by the money that Denton passed to him. They clopped through almost silent streets, the city barely waking. Denton made him go by the *questura*, where he sent DiNapoli in, despite his unwillingness, to leave the note for Gianaculo. At Porta Capuana, DiNapoli pointed ahead at the arch that had been the city gate in the medieval wall. 'That's the *porta*. When I was kid, you looked through it, you saw green. Every't'ing green. Out there was all gardens, little farms, they grew everyt'ing green that peoples ate in Naples. Now, they build a new town out there.' They passed through the gateway, the hoofbeats and the grinding of the wheels echoing from the stone walls. On the other side were industrial buildings and smokestacks.

'Vasto,' DiNapoli said. 'They call it Vasto. Real ugly.'

'How much farther?'

'Little bit. The *compare* got a farm, it was like a big estate, one of the old families. They go broke, he buys it. Now he's the *patrone*, it's like he owns the peoples there. They come wit' the land. He bought them like the cows.'

This sounded like some crazy bit of Italian history to Denton, something medieval or worse. He had seen slavery in America; he had fought in a war that had been supposed to end it. This was the twentieth century, after all—how could people be bought and sold in the land that Garibaldi and Mazzini had made free?

Men and women were already on the road beyond Vasto. They must have got up in the dark. The traffic was going into Naples— donkey carts loaded with vegetables; women with bundles or big baskets on their heads, green leaves poking out the ends; a few men wheeling barrows. Denton said, 'What's that stink?'

'They put stuff from the sewers on the fields. It makes the vegetables grow.' DiNapoli waved an arm at the people coming towards them. 'They go to the Central Market to sell. Lot of them from Scuttini's farm.'

They turned off the road between tall stone gateposts, connecting the posts a wrought-iron arch with a place for a central medallion that had been removed. DiNapoli smiled at it. 'Coat of arms of the Milliciani. 'They still got the title, Scuttini got the farm.'

The 'farm' was a vast landscape of small fields as far as Denton could see on three sides. It included a small village that had its own church and its own shop—owned, DiNapoli said, by the *patrone*. 'No school?' Denton said. DiNapoli laughed.

Tiny houses surrounded the single street. Other houses, no bigger, were dotted among the fields. Denton saw men working behind donkeys, women and children working with their hands to glean some root crop that had already been harvested. He thought he knew what he was looking at: tenant farming, the system that had replaced slavery in the American South. Perpetual indebtedness to the *patrone*, perpetual ignorance, perpetual bondage to a piece of land whose products belonged half to the master.

DiNapoli pointed ahead. 'Palazzo Scuttini.' He chuckled, then ducked his head as if Doro *o bufalo* had ears everywhere.

It looked like a cluster of institutional buildings, perhaps a hospital or a college. None was more than three storeys, but the principal one had an austere grandeur about it, less a palace than a fortress, with narrow windows and a look of turning inward. Behind it, other buildings—stone barns, granaries, dairies, stables—formed two large squares; above one, a bell tower stood like an overseer. Donkey carts were going through an arched entrance into one square; the other, towards which the carriage was headed, lay behind one of the fortress-like buildings and was partly filled with long tables where women were putting out food and big pitchers.

'Breakfast,' DiNapoli said. 'First they work two hours, then they eat. Then really they go to work.'

As the carriage pulled into the open square, the women stopped to watch it. Some signal was given, and men came running from the other buildings and put themselves into ragged lines. Denton realised that he was looking at fifty or more people. The carriage stopped at a place the driver seemed to have had selected for him. Two of the men, dressed like the others in white collarless shirts, trousers with suspenders and soft caps, came to help Denton down. Shrugging them off, Denton stood in the carriage and looked around the square. All the men had their caps in their hands now. A door opened in the big building and two women came out, curtsying, and then came Janet, and then one of the largest men Denton had ever seen.

O bufalo. Doro Scuttini, the *compare.*

Denton thought that he should have been standing on the ground when the Camorra bigwig appeared, as a sign of respect—that was the plan, at any rate, as the two now anguished men standing by the carriage indicated. Denton jumped down and thanked them with a smile; they looked at the *compare.* DiNapoli scuttled behind. Scuttini waited at the edge of a low terrace that ran the length of the house, Janet a few feet from him. Denton allowed himself a long, frowning look at her: Was she all right? Was she a guest or a hostage? He went forward and stood below the man. Not removing his hat, he said, 'I am Denton.' Over Scuttini's shoulder, Janet winked at him.

Scuttini was at least sixty and had an enormous belly, but he was one of those fat men who look as if they could pick up a horse or knock it down with a blow. To Denton's surprise, he was dressed like his men—collarless shirt, trousers, a hat—and the size of his arms swelled the fabric of his sleeves. His face was severe, his eyes like stones, the face of a hundred Renaissance paintings of greedy, vulpine men, once the face of aristocrats that had now jumped to this boss from the bottom—or perhaps the face had come with the farm.

He came down the single step from the terrace to Denton and stood in front of him. He was inches shorter than Denton but probably weighed half again as much. His look was so severe that Denton wondered if he was going to lash out at him for beating up his grandson on the Via Toledo. They looked at each other, both men's look appraising, sceptical, giving nothing. Then Scuttini moved close and grabbed both of Denton's arms just above the elbow, his belly pressed against Denton's flat gut; the embrace was almost overtly sexual, male organ to organ. Scuttini squeezed Denton's upper arms and pushed his head forward on Denton's right shoulder, then on the left. When his head went back again, actual tears shone in his eyes. *'Grazie.'* His voice was husky. *'Mille grazie.'* Without taking his eyes from Denton's, he shouted, 'DiNapoli!'

DiNapoli trotted forward and put himself next to the two men, his face turned up to the *compare*. Denton was impressed both by DiNapoli's obedience and by Scuttini's command of his name.

'Signore Scuttini says you have saved the honour of his family,' DiNapoli translated. 'He says you have saved him grief and saved his daughter grief over her son. He says he owes you a life.' DiNapoli looked pained, as if he feared getting a word wrong.

'Tell Signor Scuttini that I'm happy to have been of service to him and to his family, and I am grateful for the hospitality he has shown to the lady who brought the boy here.' He looked at Janet and she smiled.

Scuttini continued to hold on to Denton while he listened to the translation. Then he smiled, put his cheek against Denton's again on each side, and then, still holding one of Denton's arms, stepped back up on the terrace and led him to Janet. *'Una donna dei mille! Dei millione!'* Scuttini took Janet's arm with his free hand and, now between them, led them along the terrace to a table that had been set up overlooking the square below. Seating them one on each side of him, he began to explain what they were seeing—his vassals coming in to be fed—and what they would be eating themselves—the same food. He seemed proud of this. He was a man of the people, he said. It wasn't like the old days.

There was no coffee. Denton had hoped for coffee.

Janet was the only woman sitting down. The rest, in long skirts and dark blouses, many bare headed but some in scarves and a few in broad straw hats, served the long tables. They came and went like ants from a kitchen somewhere at the far end of the house. The workmen were small and dark, many of them looking old. They wore their hats to eat.

Even at the *compare's* table on the terrace, the men kept their hats on. Besides Denton and Scuttini, there were a dozen others, two of them introduced as Scuttini sons-in-law, the others perhaps cousins or allies. DiNapoli stood behind Scuttini's chair at the *compare*'s command to translate for him. Mostly, it was not conversation but monosyllabic monologue.

The food was abundant, simple, strange: a kind of corn mush with a tomato sauce over it; a pie of a sort, of which a dozen appeared on the tables below them, bitter greens baked into layers of bread dough; baked root vegetables; abundant fresh bread; cheeses like millwheels, from which one of the women cut slices as thick as books; apples, now a little wrinkled because their season was past. It was all from the estate, they were told; the harsh red wine was their own, the previous year's; they didn't play around with vintages or fancy grapes.

The Scuttinis, Denton saw, had taken over the aristocracy's lands without taking over its manners: the men around him, including the *compare*, ate as if an enemy threatened to take the food away—an arm hooked around the plate, the head low so that the trip from plate to mouth would be as short as possible. Little was said: eating was serious business. Denton picked at the food, trying a bit of everything put before him. Bending his head, he looked past Scuttini at Janet, who raised her eyebrows at him. She looked exhausted but radiant, as if she had triumphed over herself to be there. He winked at her.

A bell rang, sonorous and carrying. The *compare* pushed his chair back and stood, his great belly pressed against the table edge. Below them, there was a surge as if the earth had erupted, pushing the little men ahead of it. Some were still chewing, some cramming food into their mouths, many grabbing bread and cheese and putting it in their trouser pockets. They converged in a line from the tables and hurried past the Scuttinis, each removing his hat as he passed and keeping it in his hand until he had turned down past the tables and headed across the square to a carriage-wide archway at the back. The fields lay beyond.

The women removed the last dishes from the tables, then dismantled the tables themselves and carried them away. Some of the women were very handsome, but only a few looked really young. The old ones, Denton guessed, were not in fact very old.

When their own table had been cleared, coffee at last appeared. The other men bolted theirs and then, in another version of the parade past the *compare*, walked behind them, hat against heart, each bowing awkwardly to Janet, murmuring a word (what word?) to Scuttini, and muttering some form of thanks to Denton before hurrying away.

'Is it like this every morning?' Denton said.

Scuttini stared at him while DiNapoli translated.

'No. This was for you and the great lady.'

'I was born on a farm. It was like this only at harvest time, when we helped each other and everybody ate together.'

'At harvest, we do this, too. This was the harvest of my grandson's life.'

Scuttini pushed his chair back so he could talk to both of them. He looked at Janet; the scarred left side of her face was towards him. Scuttini drew his forefinger down the side of his own face and looked at her. She said, *'Coltello.'* Knife. She pointed at Denton and made a gun of her fingers. *'Lui—'* She jerked her hand and made sound like a gunshot.

The *compare* turned to Denton. *'Morto?'*

Denton nodded. *'Morto.'*

'Bravo. Bravo-bravo.' He rattled off something that Denton couldn't follow. DiNapoli said, 'He says it's the best t'ing to kill your enemies right away.'

'And take care of your friends.'

DiNapoli translated that and Scuttini nodded and smiled like a big toy, slapped his huge hands on the stuffed thighs of his trousers and made an expansive gesture with his arms that seemed to be meant to include all of Italy, at least all that they could see. *All of this will take care of you*, it meant. Then he said it in so many words, said it in several ways, a particular warmth given to Janet. He seemed to mean it, seemed almost to mean a familial embrace, as if he were something far more primitive than he was (although Denton privately thought him primitive enough), an aborigine making them members of his family, perhaps, to replace ones who had died. He would be, Denton thought, a good companion if he liked you. For so long as he liked you.

When their carriage had been called and they were standing below the terrace by a mounting block that must have been useful to the now supplanted, horse-borne aristocrats, Denton started to say something about the second man who had run into the cellar but had got away.

'He will be taken care of.'

'You know who it was?'

'My grandson is a stupid kid. He thinks he will be a *guappo*, a tough guy, his own way, and not coming to me like he should have. He ran with the wrong people. This guy was one of those.'

Denton had wondered how he would handle the business of the street fight and the pocket-picking. He said, 'I had a little wrangle with them on the Via Toledo. I didn't know he was your grandson.'

The *compare*'s look was cold, ungiving; it might have been meant to say, *Under other circumstances, I would feel disrespected, and that would be the worse for you.* He said only, 'I heard of such things from other people. He was misbehaving.'

But Denton wanted it to be entirely clear. 'That was the second time. The first time, they picked my pocket. They took my purse. I owed them a beating.'

Scuttini's expression did not change. He said only, 'Now he owes you his life. We will take care of the other one.'

The carriage came. Denton saw Janet in and climbed in beside her. Scuttini removed his hat and kissed her hand. He said to her—not to Denton—'Anything you need, signora… anything…'

They rattled away. The sun was warm now. In the fields, men and women worked.

CHAPTER

They went back to the *pensione* and slept, but Denton was woken, groaning, after an hour because he had a visitor. The Signora herself came to their door with one of the maids and told him he was causing scandal and she wanted him out, and although the latest caller was a milord and a gentleman, she was fed up with Denton's visitors. He dressed, groggy and out of sorts, and dragged himself to the smoking room and found Ronald Fanning of the International Society for Super-Normal Investigations. Denton, who wanted only to sleep, had to apologise for rushing away yesterday: he had had to go to the morgue with the police. He even found it expedient to crawl a bit, remembering that Fanning was one of the important people he had thought he wanted to see when he had got the idea for a book on Naples and its ghosts.

Fanning had a handsome, sensitive face marred only by the near-absence of a chin, for which he'd compensated with an iron-grey moustache and terrific eyebrows. He was perhaps sixty, thin, tall, bespoke-dressed in a morning coat and striped trousers, in general a stylishness spoiled only by rather dirty-looking grey hair left long and combed straight back so that it lay against his skull. He waved away Denton's apologies with 'Of course, of course' and again clutched Denton's arm and said, 'Have you heard from him? Has he come through? No? No, of course.' He was breathing heavily, almost panting. 'Are you going with me to the medium or are you not? Much as I dislike being forthright with someone I hardly know, Mr Denton, but I must say it: it seems to me that my rigorous scientific interest in Fra Geraldo's attempt to reach us from the Other Side is to you...' He searched for a metaphor and spluttered, 'It is caviar to the general! You are writing a book about things that say "Boo", and I am doing a scientific investigation!' He broke away to stride up and down the rather small room.

Denton decided to ignore the insult, if that was what it was, and said, 'I didn't know we were talking about science.'

'Exactly what I mean! You are a...a writer of *romances*. I suppose that is what drew you to Naples. Romances are so without rigour!'

'It's one of the things I like about them.'

'We, on the other hand—we of the Society—are trying to bring to the investigation of the super-normal the sort of rigour that a chemist would bring to the study of a gas, or a physicist to a particle. We've no more tolerance for popular superstition than a chap at the Clarendon Laboratory would have for the belief in phlogiston.'

'You don't believe in ghosts and things.'

'It isn't a question of *belief*. Science doesn't operate in the realm of *belief*. It's a matter of *acceptance* of the demonstrably true. Only if a phenomenon can be *scientifically* verified do we accept it. Of course, there's *something* in the popular idea of ghosts and all that, but it isn't scientifically *proven*. It isn't *analysed*. It's gossip and myth and...and...superstition. Now, we grant, of course, that there is a dimension beyond our own, else from where would the mediums be receiving their spirit emanations? And what is death? One must accept the existence of the Other Side.'

Denton, wanting revenge for having been woken, said, 'And the "Other Side" is scientifically verified?'

Fanning put a hand on his arm. 'No, no, of course not. It's an *assumption*. Rather like the geometry, you know—there must be a few assumptions, as, were we in a laboratory, we would assume the existence of the atom, although we have never seen one and never could. Because of *logic*. Do you understand?'

Denton backed away from the hand and took a turn to a window. 'But even though atoms aren't proven, aren't they sort of accepted notions that work because they meet the requirements, but they're nonetheless hypothetical and are really waiting to be disproven?'

'Just so.'

'So the Other Side is also hypothetical and waiting to be disproven?'

'No, no, that isn't quite right. We have a body of evidence. Plus, of course, the logical argument that it *must* exist.'

'Why?'

'Oh, because if it did not, what would death be but—oblivion?'

Denton couldn't help smiling. 'And?'

'Not possible. We have far too many indications of its existence. Instances of contacts, of strivings to reach us, of—'

'Ghosts?'

Fanning looked severe. 'Do you believe in God?'

Denton folded his arms. 'Why does it matter?'

'My dear fellow! How can one be a Christian and not believe in the hereafter?'

'You said it wasn't a matter of belief.'

Fanning stared at him. He looked severe again, even more so. 'We were discussing something altogether different.' He frowned and pursed his lips. 'Let me go at it another way. If we had never seen an elephant but we had *proven* accounts of people touching, smelling, hearing, and seeing elephants, we would accept the hypothesis of the elephant—eh?'

'Sounds right.'

'Well, you see, we have verified instances of messages and returns from the Other Side—*scientifically*—and so we accept its existence as we accept the atom and the elephant. You see?'

Denton had his doubts about how well verified such messages might be, but all he said was 'Mmm,' and he nodded and stayed silent, hoping Fanning would go away. When he didn't, Denton tried to move him along, by saying, 'You mentioned that you want to make an appointment with a medium. To let the old man come through. From the Other Side.'

'The sooner the better, yes.'

The fact was, Fanning would be useful when his book did get to the subject of the city's mediums. Mediums were popular stuff, both here and in England; readers would want to read about them. Reluctantly, he said, 'How about in a couple of weeks?'

'Time is of the essence!'

'They keep time on the Other Side?'

Fanning said it was too technical to explain, and then he grumbled that he supposed he could accept two weeks' delay. Denton realised that the urgency was really in Fanning's character, something childish that wanted things while the desire was hot. He said gently, 'I'm sure that Fra Geraldo will still be over there in a couple of weeks.'

Fanning looked pained. But he did go away. Denton saw the outer door close on the thin figure with exhausted relief, and he tottered back to bed.

Janet woke him at two to eat. He stared at her over the cold lunch and said, 'The world is full of fools, and I'm one of them. My idea for a book on ghosts was a mistake. I didn't see what was involved.'

'But you'll do it anyway, because you need the money, and it will be quite good. Are you too exhausted to make love?'

'What a question.'

In the bed, he said, 'DiNapoli's coming by at five,' and she said she didn't expect to be that long, and in fact they were both asleep when DiNapoli rang the *pensione*'s bell.

❀ ❀ ❀

Denton and DiNapoli walked down to Chiaia, the neighbourhood along the seafront west of the Via Toledo. The Piazza dei Martiri was there and the Anglican church, and around it the houses and apartments of English residents and other people with money. There, too, was the apartment of *Avocato* Spinoso, the owner of the Casa Gialla and its sham ghost.

'He speaks English?'

'Pretty near as good as me.'

'Is he *camorristo*?'

'More like he gets hired by one of the families.'

'Not the Scuttini.'

'No, I t'ink he's in wit' the Mallardi.' DiNapoli looked around as if they were surrounded by eavesdroppers. 'They was saying out at the farm that the guy that got away in the cellar was Mallardi. It's about the whisky—the Mallardi are horning in on Scuttini business.'

'Smuggling—by way of the house I'm going to rent.'

'It don't pay to know too much.'

'Except I wasn't supposed to rent it. I was supposed to get scared off.' He and Janet had talked it over, decided that the house's owner didn't want to rent the Casa Gialla at all; he simply wanted to pretend to rent it with a wild tale that would keep it— and its cellar—empty.

DiNapoli led him to *Avocato* Spinoso's building. It was new, very handsome, a style for which Denton had no name but thought of as 'fancy'. Looking up at the decorated façade, he said, 'What's he like?'

'He's a lawyer.'

'And therefore a crook.' Denton shook himself, as if he could shake his fatigue away. 'Did you get your money from him?' For finding them, he meant, to spend the night in the Casa Gialla and then rent it.

'Not yet.'

'We'll see. You stay here.' Denton crossed the broad street, stepping back for an already out-of-date Panhard that came banging along. A *portiere* sold him a flat disc for the elevator, then got in with him and operated the elevator to the third floor. It was one of those incomprehensible Neapolitan systems.

Lawyer Spinoso was gaunt faced, almost cadaverous, his skin pocked with smallpox craters. He was in his forties but made himself look older with an expression of boundless pain. His frock-coated suit, on the other hand, was incomparable, as were his polished boots. He managed a smile for Denton. The smile suggested deep pools of hidden suffering, great forbearance. He introduced Denton to Signora Spinoso, a fat but severe-looking woman who was working on a needlepoint of the Bleeding Heart of Jesus, the reds particularly gaudy. After a curtsy that almost bent her knees, she sailed out, speaking Italian that Denton couldn't understand.

'My wife is very pious,' the lawyer said. In fact, his English was far better than DiNapoli's, accented but fluent, even nuanced. He led Denton to a cluster of hard chairs near a window. The room—presumably a drawing room, certainly too big to be much else—was chock-a-block with furniture, as if it were a showroom. Denton was aware of a lot of carving and dark varnish. The walls, like Signora Spinoso, were very pious: huge canvases of martyrdoms and miracles in a feeble style that suggested that the saints and apostles were maidens in disguise, the beards all rented somewhere.

The lawyer offered refreshment—his word—and Denton declined. A silence followed; at last the lawyer said, 'You have come about the Casa Gialla.' He sighed. 'I am desolated. You have shown courage and fortitude and have, I understand, spent the night there. All Naples talks of it.' He sighed again. 'Unhappily, the house is not ready to be occupied.'

'We have to move out of our *pensione* tomorrow.'

'Oh, there are other *pensione*. I can find you a place at one quite close by. This is the English quarter. Very nice.'

'We've set our hearts on moving into the Casa Gialla tomorrow.'

'Ah, it desolates me to say it, but such cannot be.'

'As I was saying this morning to my friend Doro Scuttini, we will move in tomorrow.' Denton smiled. The smile was not a good one, involved no teeth. 'My friend Signore Scuttini was thanking me for bringing his grandson to him, after I had found the boy tied up and strangling in the cellar of the Casa Gialla. The boy would have been dead in another hour. What an embarrassment for you, *Avocato*! If not worse.'

'I am shocked.'

'As I was. I also found twenty-two cases of whisky, without the customs stamps. You have been abused, *Avocato*—your house has been used as storage by smugglers! If not worse.' Denton gave him the smile again. 'It could be the Mallardi.'

'The Mallardi.'

'Signore Scuttini is, as I think you know, concerned about the Mallardi. The Casa Gialla is, after all, in a Scuttini neighbourhood. It looks bad to have somebody else using a house there for such purposes. You wouldn't want your name associated with it.'

'I had nothing to do with it.'

'Just what I told the police. I stopped at the *questura* earlier; the police should be at the house now, removing the illegal whisky. I told them about the so-called "ghost". A crude attempt to keep the house from being occupied, don't you think? I told them that I didn't see how you could have anything to do with it—after all, you're the owner and you want the rent. Don't you?'

'How could I have anything to do with such an outrage?'

'Just what I said. I told them you were eager to rent the place. Couldn't wait. Just wanted to get over the ghost business and get on with it. I told them that I'd be moving in tomorrow. Of course, it might look awkward for you if I *don't* move in tomorrow.'

'I have many friends in the police.'

'Just so. Now, we shall need a set of keys. *All* the keys. The old woman, by the way—the *portiere*—she'll have to go. A question of temperament. I'm sure you'll understand, a man of the world like you. I'd like her gone today, in fact.'

'She is my wife's auntie!'

'All the more reason to put her someplace where she's wanted. Not good for an old woman to be in a hostile atmosphere. Oh, and the WC in the red room—there isn't one. We'll want one installed immediately.'

'*Impossibile. Impossibile,* I mean, with you there. Well, you will not be there! It does not suit me. And the old woman, she stays.'

Denton looked at him. Denton sighed. 'I hate to tell that to the police.' He shook his head. 'I really hate to tell it to Compare Scuttini.'

The lawyer pushed his mouth out, lowered his head and stared at Denton as if he were trying to imitate a bull. If he was trying to be terrifically menacing, it didn't work. He said, 'I will have the WC installed…in good time. That is exactly what I was thinking of when I said a month. Maybe six weeks.'

'Tomorrow.'

'It is *impossibile!*'

Denton shook his head. 'Let me explain how it looks, *Avocato.*' He held up a finger, took its tip in the fingers of the other hand. 'One, you own a house that you say you want to rent, but there is a tale of a ghost and you require that prospective tenants spend a night there. Two—' He added another finger. 'The ghost is a hoax, and it looks bad for you because it is your wife's auntie who lets the men into the house to frighten off the prospective tenants. Three—' Another finger. 'You spread the tale that you have done extensive work on the house, but in fact the work is slapdash and slipshod, and what was really done was done in the cellar and the wine vault, a new door and a new trapdoor into the tunnel underneath.' Denton leaned forward, putting out his right hand, its three fingers very near the lawyer's nose. 'Taken together, it might look like you didn't want to rent the house at all, but wanted to scare people away. Anybody who heard this might think *you* were the smuggler and *you* had almost murdered Scuttini's grandson.' He shook his head. 'Bad.'

'This is a slander! I have a reputation! I have my honour!'

'Mmm. If I were you, I'd bung somebody into that house faster'n you can say Jack Robinson, show people you want the house occupied so the smugglers can't use it. It's like I told them at the *questura*—*Avocato* Spinoso will prove his innocence by helping me move in *today*.'

The lawyer's thin mouth turned downwards; the eyes narrowed. 'I am not a sissy boy, signore. I have friends. I have resources.'

'So have I.'

Spinoso stared at him, but his fingers were moving over the carved heads at the ends of his chair-arms. He licked his narrow lips. 'Two weeks.'

'Tomorrow.'

'I want a ten-year lease.'

'No, month by month. And the first two months free, of course. As you promised.' Denton stood. 'Please have the old woman leave the keys at my *pensione* this evening.' He glanced out the window. 'You have a nice view.' He turned back to the lawyer. 'This is for the best, signore. The Scuttini are likely to go pretty hard with the Mallardi and anybody connected with abusing the grandson. If we move into the house tomorrow, we're your bona fides. Mmm?'

The lawyer's face was wooden, the eyes seemingly almost closed. With his head tipped a little back, he seemed to be studying Denton but was perhaps studying his situation. A shrug suggested that he had found the situation not worth fighting. 'I will have papers made for the notary. The limit on your occupation to be one year.'

Denton put out his hand. 'That's a deal.'

'And now if you will forgive me—' Spinoso held out his left arm towards the door. 'I am desolated, but it is the time to lead my family in evening prayer.'

❀ ❀ ❀

Inspector Gianaculo was, to Denton's and the Signora's disgust—
a response shared for different reasons—waiting for him at
the *pensione*. Denton had no idea why he was waiting; to be
sure, Denton had sent the note about the whisky in the Casa
Gialla's cellar, but that was hardly worth a visit. Nonetheless, the
Inspector looked calm, patient, as if he could easily wait all night.
Again, he needed a translator and said, through the same austere
woman, 'I am pursuing the matter of Fra Geraldo.'

Denton remembered, as if it had been years ago, that
Gianaculo had been one of those who had been at Fra Geraldo's
house—the second wave, as it were, after the neighbours and the
policeman. In fact, Gianaculo had been there with the doctor
and the magistrate. Denton said, 'I thought the *magistrato* was
pursuing it now.' He wanted to say that Gianaculo should team
up with Ronald Fanning and talk to Fra Geraldo's ghost. What
he really wanted was to get rid of him and talk to Janet about his
visit to *Avocato* Spinoso.

Gianaculo said through the translator, 'You have doubts
about the manner of the death, Signore Denton. You visited the
corpse in the morgue.'

'Not because I wanted to.' Why did he have to go through
it again? The blood, the ghosts, the apparent accident. He
wondered why Gianaculo was bothering him, then remembered
that the local police and the *Carabinieri* were different creatures,
perhaps rivals; Donati had probably gone back to Rome without
even speaking to him. Maybe Gianaculo wanted to know what
Donati had said. 'Fra Geraldo was certainly frightened when he
talked to me. Did he have enemies?'

'Basically, he was a man of God. He took food and medicine
to the poor. During the cholera in eighty-four, he was down in
the Old City before the White Cross got there. The people in the
bassi believe he was a saint. They're already praying to him. Why
would he have enemies?'

'He was—' Denton told the woman to step into the corridor and wait until he called her. She was offended but went, anyway. Denton said, trying to dredge up the Italian he had once known, 'He was *castrato.*'

Gianaculo rapped out something, added, '*E il suo cazzo anche.* So?'

Denton tried to say in Italian, *You don't think some enemy did that to him?* but it came out as *You think not maybe enemy how do you say did for it—?* He was unable to fit the pronoun in and so couldn't refer back to the castration. He called the woman back and she translated in a frosty voice. 'I thought maybe somebody had done that to him. There's something called the Camorra. They do that kind of thing, don't they?'

Gianaculo grunted. 'The Camorra would have stuck—' He looked at the woman, hesitated, and said, '—them in his mouth and strangled him. Why would the Camorra care about Fra Geraldo?'

Denton shrugged. 'They're bad actors, aren't they?' The woman looked bewildered; it was the word 'actors,' an Americanism. He corrected himself, 'Bad people.'

'Yes, but—no… Yes, he told people not to waste their money on the *Piccolo Giocco,* the illegal lottery. And the Camorra take a slice of that, but nobody listened to him. And he told the people not to borrow money from the *usurie* but to come to him, and the Camorra take their slice from the usury business. And he preached against the *Risanamento,* the urban renewal after the cholera, and the Camorra had a slice of that. But who listened to him? A couple of city councillors who might as well have shouted down a drainpipe as make the speeches they made. Nobody else listened. Of course, they were right—all that the *Risanamento* did was move money from the treasury to some Northern bankers and the landlords and the builders—from which the Camorra got its slice—and the poor got nothing, but what's that got to do with Fra Geraldo?'

'Well, he thought *somebody* was trying to kill him.'

Gianaculo shrugged. 'He was old.' He asked more questions, got nothing from Denton he hadn't got the night before.

When he stood up to leave, he again sent the woman away, this time for good. He stood in front of Denton, a solid block of a man on strong legs, and said in his bad English, 'Very good you send me this morning...the message, ummm...to describe the whisky. The...under the house. Smugglering...very bad.' He tapped Denton's chest with the brim of his hat. '*Attenzione, signore*. That Scuttini—very bad. You understand?'

'Yes, of course.'

'*Very* bad.' He made a gesture, closing his fist tight. 'He... break you, like...like...*un' fiammiferro*.'

'A wooden match.'

'Eh.' He tapped his hat again. 'You have care. You eat his food, he...hope...he drink your blood.' He put the hat on. '*Buona note, signore.*'

And *that* was why he had been waiting.

CHAPTER

10

They moved into the Casa Gialla in a thump and clatter of trunks and boxes and suitcases. Janet was not vain, but she had two sets of clothes for two kinds of lives, one lived out in the world, the other in her own private spaces, for which she had the wardrobe of flowing, colourful gowns that Lucy Newcombe so admired. Nor was Denton a clothes horse, but Atkins, still his servant when he left London, had insisted on clothes formal and informal, on suits for casual wear and for what he had called 'society', and on clothes for 'at home', which to Denton meant a scabrous smoking jacket and an old pair of ratcatchers; plus he had brought three overcoats and a mackintosh and four hats and six pairs of gloves and sixteen shirts and... They had not travelled light.

The servants at the *pensione* had lined up for their departure, the youngest ones looking shamefaced, the more hardened ones brazen. They were waiting for their tips. Janet took charge. She had strict ideas about who had done well and who hadn't; still, like DiNapoli, she believed that in a city of the poor, everybody deserved something. She parcelled out her *lire* by individuals, astonishing some of them by how much she gave, angering others by how little. The Signora, overseeing the process, was scandalised all over again and flew into a rage when Janet offered her one *centésimo*, the smallest bit of money that was made.

When she had refused it, Janet said, 'But it is what you deserve, signora,' and with that they were gone.

The Casa Gialla was empty. The old woman was gone; her room on the second floor, which they reached in their first cursory sweep through their new house, was empty and clean. 'You'd never know she'd been here,' Janet said. 'I suppose we'll run into *her* ghost one night. Sheer hatred that glows in the dark.'

That afternoon, a woman named Assunta Morello walked in from the Scuttini farm. Janet said that they had become 'friends' while she was Scuttini's guest. Assunta would walk back that day and every day that Janet hired her, she said. Scuttini and her husband would allow her to come three days a week, would that do? Janet embraced her, rather to Denton's surprise, and put her to work unpacking a trunk. Assunta was an impressive woman, too strongly featured to be pretty—big hooked nose, full mouth, heavy eyebrows—but she had a ferocious attractiveness in her big-breasted, big-hipped body. Black hair tumbled from her head. Denton wondered what sort of husband she must have who could give or withhold permission to come into Naples, and Janet said, 'He's a pipsqueak. She could break him in two pieces. But he's *all* men. And he's Scuttini's tenant, so she's Scuttini's, too. She's a slave to both of them.' And, Denton thought, perhaps a spy—if Scuttini was as untrustworthy as Gianaculo said, he would want to keep an eye on them.

DiNapoli came a few minutes later with the *scugnizzo* they'd seen in the Galleria, who was supposed to find Denton a genuine Fra Geraldo carving. Denton met them in a little parlour near the stairs. The boy had a different *presepe* figure; he and DiNapoli had already been to DiNapoli's friend, who had reported that the piece was in fact genuine—Fra Geraldo had indeed made it. The boy had it wrapped in a smelly cloth; he unwrapped it and, with a strange care that looked almost like reverence, placed it in the centre of a marble-topped table. 'A l'originale,' he said. 'Michele 'l ubriacon'.' He held out his hand for money.

DiNapoli gave the hand a light slap. He said to Denton, 'These kids is greedy. He says he's starving; I buy him a piece of pizz' on the way here, he eats like a pig and asks for more. He'd go on eating all day. If you buy it, he takes the money and runs to the nearest *pizzaiulo* and buys five slices, gets himself a big glass of wine, then buys for all his pals. Tonight, he have nothing left.' He shrugged.

'What did he say—something about lubricating?'

'Lubricating? Lubricating? Oh, he says, *il ubriacone*, it means a guy who's drunk all the time. That's the statue—he's Michael the Drunk, *Michele 'l ubriacon'*.'

'A drunk—for the *presepe*?'

'Oh, yeah, he's very famous. Peoples put him close to the manger. It's good luck. Some years, Fra Geraldo carves him sleeping, they put him in the straw wit' the cows. Every year, like I tole you, Fra Geraldo makes t'ree figures for the *presepe*. One is always *Michele 'l ubriacon'*.'

'Why?'

'Nobody knows. It's part of the—what you call it?—the, you know, the sort of holy stuff around *Michele 'l ubriacon'*. People see him on the street, they touch him for luck. Did I say he's a real guy? No? Well, he is. You see him in Mercato, Spagnuoli, Porto, he's always someplace, falling down, singing, acting stupid. Fra Geraldo preaches that if you do it to him, you do it to me, you unnerstand?'

'"Inasmuch as ye have done it unto the least of these my brethren, ye have done it unto me."'

'Yeah, exactly. You got it. So every year, he makes two figures, they're always different, but they're real people you see in Napoli—a shepherd, a fisherman, a *pizzaiulo*, a girl wit' roses, the guy sells puppies. But he also makes Michele, because he's the least of them my brothers.'

Denton picked up the figure. It was not new, the paint a little dark where it had been handled; one finger—both hands completely carved, the fingers separate—broken off. But it was beautiful work. The face was booze-reddened, lined, almost toothless; an expression caught brilliantly between appeal and despair illuminated it. He wore an old overcoat, tattered; trousers that were too tight and too short; a trilby with a drooping gull's feather stuck in it. His feet were bare. Denton thought, *I'd know him from this if I saw him.* He said, 'Fra Geraldo was an artist.'

'The peoples say he was a artist oncet, but he stop to serve the Virgin.'

The boy made a sound, a kind of wail, the noise a dog makes. His hand was out again. He spat *Nnapulitan'* at Denton. Denton glanced at DiNapoli, looked again at the figure, and gave the boy thirty *lire* in notes. He was going to say something about saving some until tomorrow, but the boy screamed with triumph and shot off. Denton heard his feet on the stairs and then the slam of the downstairs door.

Denton raised his eyebrows. 'Does he have a name?'

'He gimme a name, he prolly makes it up just then.' He shook his head. 'You give him too much. He'd of taken half.'

'You didn't tell me.'

'I forgot, you don' know how they do t'ings here. Everyt'ing, you bargain. A Napolitan', he gets to Hell, he bargains wit' the Devil how long he gotta spend in the fire. But you like the figure, eh? It's good?'

'I like it very much.'

'That's good, then.'

'What do I owe you?'

'You don't owe me not'ing.'

'But you—Did you get your finder's fee from that lawyer?'

DiNapoli laughed. 'For putting you in this place? Yeah, he gimme fifty *lire*, then he tell me he never want to see me again in his life.' DiNapoli raised his eyebrows. 'I'm gonna buy a suit. Next time you see me, I look pretty swell.'

'A new suit!'

'Well, new on me. I buy it from the guy sells dead men's clothes near Santa Chiara. He got a dark suit, little stripe in it, fits me like it was made custom. Beautiful. Maybe a hat, too—I tole him, I buy a whole suit, vest, everyt'ing, he oughta t'row in a hat for not'ing. So we bargain.'

'And a necktie.'

'A necktie, I need a collar; I ain't got a collar. You know what they say, Rome don't get built overnight.'

'Buy yourself a new shirt and a necktie and three collars, Mr DiNapoli! You want to look swell, you have to have the whole outfit!'

DiNapoli scowled. He ran a finger under his nose. He said, 'I tell you the troot. I been paying money every week to the *cravattaro*—the what you call the *usuraio*—I don't know the English—'

'Usurer?'

'In New York, we called them the sharks. Yeah, "usurer". So I hand over a few *lire* every week, all I'm paying is the interest. So today, I go to the woman, I tell her, here's your money, every *soldo*, I'm paid, I'm finished, you never see me again! You know what? She laughs. She gives me a glass of wine, she says everybody says that, everybody comes back. Well.' He shrugged. 'So I got enough left for the suit and that's it.' He laughed. 'Unless you want I should go back to her and borrow the money for a shirt.'

Denton counted out fifty *lire* on the table. 'Buy a shirt—that's for a necktie—that's for three collars. Don't say no! The signora wants you to take her around Naples; she wants your help to hire a couple of housemaids; she says we need a cook. You can't go around without a necktie and a collar. Do it for her!'

DiNapoli stared down at the money. 'We didn't have no arrangement.'

'Now we have.'

DiNapoli chewed his lower lip. His eyes met Denton's. 'Twelve years I been here, living rough. I never took not'ing I hadn't arranged first, and I never begged. I tell you the troot, I done some bad things, but I earned my way.'

Denton understood. He'd lived rough, too. He said. 'A loan, then. No interest.'

DiNapoli hesitated and then, his lips moving as if he were calculating, he went through the notes that Denton had laid out and began putting most of them in a pile that he pushed towards Denton. He made a further calculation, counted the money he'd kept—Denton thought it was about five *lire*—and said, 'I buy a couple dead guys' shirts and their collars.' He shook his head. 'The more money you got, the more you gotta spend.' But suddenly he smiled. 'In New York, before I go to prison, I used to say to myself, "How am I gonna know when I make it? I'm always one step from it, and then I make the step, and I'm still one step from it." And look at me now.'

Then Janet came in and whisked him off to translate for her, and Denton was left to study the figure of Michael the Drunk and to think about Fra Geraldo, who was now a more complicated character than he had seemed: before the loony old man, there had been a young artist, perhaps one who had renounced art for—what? What had the old man been talking about? *Atonement?* For what? Not, Denton thought, for the Virgin; there was no sign of the Virgin in the Palazzo Minerva except for the one chipped chromo. A suffering Christ wouldn't have surprised him, or one of the penitents like Simeon Stylites, icons of whom would have jibed with atonement and flagellation. Although the style would have had to be more forceful than the piety that decked the walls of the *famiglia* Spinoso.

❀ ❀ ❀

Janet and DiNapoli found a kitchen on the ground floor of the Casa Gialla. DiNapoli was like a child, showing it to Denton. It was huge, abysmally dark; across one wall, an enormous fireplace had been closed in with iron to take the smoke from a twelve-foot-long stove that must have been assembled *in situ* before gas had arrived. It had three separate fireboxes for different heats, plus a place for warming serving dishes and an upper tank for water. DiNapoli said you could cook for fifty people on it. The challenge would be to cook for two.

There was no icebox. There were pantries like caves, small rooms with shelves to the ceiling that felt damp and had a light frost of mould. There were cupboards for dishes and racks with hooks for pots and pans and, perhaps, meats and fowl and cheeses.

'I t'ink,' DiNapoli said, 'if I was the cook, I could do better wit' one gas ring and a box o' matches.'

Janet demanded that he eat with them that first night in their new house, but Denton said there was no food. DiNapoli asked if they could eat *pizza*. Janet had heard of *pizza*, been warned against it by her guidebook; she clapped her hands. DiNapoli went away; it was a little after five, and he didn't come back until seven, resplendent in a new suit, hat, shirt, collar and tie, followed by a *pizzaiulo* with an entire tray of that strange dish, *pizza*, still hot from the oven two streets away. DiNapoli was carrying a basket in which he had wine from an *enoteca* around the corner, glasses from a used-everything shop near the Duomo, a loaf of crusted bread, and three small plates of *baccala*—dried cod in tomato sauce.

'I got fruit coming, a *scugnizz'*, I told him I'd kill him if he din't come wit' it. Then there'll be *pastierra*, which is a Naples pastry, you buy it on the street but I went to the bakery, they know me, the guy's gonna bring it on his way home.'

Janet rarely knew joy, or so Denton feared. That night, he thought, she did. DiNapoli delighted her; the *pizza* enchanted her; the dried cod tickled her; the wine got her slightly drunk. They ate in a large, dank room with an electric chandelier that cast its feeble, pasty light entirely on the ceiling, until Janet got candles and turned it off and the three of them sat at the great table and ate and drank and told stories.

Including Denton's killings and Janet's four years in prison.

They were halfway through their feast when there was a knocking at the downstairs door. DiNapoli ran down and almost immediately ran back, his face tense, voice unsteady. 'It's the Scuttini! Wit' guns—I saw one!'

Denton rushed downstairs, Janet a step behind him. Four large men were staring around the entrance hall. Even in the gaslight, Denton recognised the bulge at one man's tightly suited waist. All four of them wore trousers and lounge jackets, three of them mismatched, as if they'd taken trousers from one pile and coats from another; only one wore a necktie. All had on soft hats, all stylishly rolled at one side. The one in the matching trousers and coat and the necktie said in Italian, 'From the *compariello*.' He glanced at Denton, then bowed to Janet.

Denton understood but looked at DiNapoli anyway. DiNapoli said, '*Compariello*'s the same as *compare*—sort of friendlier.' The other man spoke; DiNapoli translated. 'They come to guard the cellar. They t'ink the bad guy coming back.' The other man said something and DiNapoli said, 'They *know* the bad guy's coming back.' He spread his hands and looked sheepish. 'They got spies.'

'What are they going to do in the cellar?'

'He says they going to protect you. When the bad guy comes, they fix him.'

'"Fix?" He said "fix"?'

'More like "deal wit", maybe.'

The leader of the four said something more, all the time looking at Denton.

'He says the *compariello* knows you gave the whisky to the *polizia*, but he don't hold it against you. Anyway, he bought it back from them cheap.'

Denton started to ask how he knew about the whisky, but he remembered the grandson, who must have been put into the wine vault when the whisky was there—maybe put into the vault at the same time as the whisky. And the police? The Camorra had its hands in the *questura,* too? Of course they did.

'I don't want any killing here.'

The leader looked shocked. DiNapoli translated his response as, 'Not *here*. The *compariello* respects you, Mist' Denton. And he got admiration for the signora. T'ank God.'

Denton sighed. 'Indeed.' He weighed his instinctive lawfulness against the cynical realities of Naples—criminal organisations, corrupt police—and decided to be pragmatic. He led the way to the cellar, opened the wine vault and pointed out the trapdoor into the tunnels. When he left, the four men were finding themselves comfortable places to sit.

In the darkest hours of the morning, Denton thought he heard noises. Only a minute or two later, the iron doors that the puppeteer had been unable to open clanged somewhere outside. And that was that. It was like hearing a mousetrap snap in the night, but without the discomfort of knowing you would have to remove the mouse in the morning.

But what was the price of letting the Camorra clean your mousetraps?

❉ ❉ ❉

They added two housemaids over the next several days, one fifteen and one who said she was seventeen but looked at least three years younger, both hired by Janet from an agency on the Via Toledo. She chose neophytes because she wanted them to be more employable when they left her. The immediate results were strain and pother: one was, as Denton said, as dumb as a stump; the other was shy and terrified of everything.

Janet had taken, as she had promised, the red room. Denton took the next two rooms along, one to sleep in and one for work. Rosa and Sirena, the two maids, were put at the farthest corner of the house away from them, meaning that they were in the front of the house and shared a bigger room than either Denton or Janet had. Denton didn't care; he liked to look into the backs of the houses outside his windows, the now dead gardens, the lives of women who hung from their own windows and gossiped and of children who played under the leafless trees and, seeing him, screamed, 'Texas Jack! Texas Jack!'

Fanning came once and left a card, but Denton told Sirena, the stupider of the maids (a major challenge to his Italian), that he wasn't at home. They spent two days moving furniture out of the *piano nobile* and up to the second floor and replacing it with much older and better things from up there. Janet found a carved and curtained bed, which they brought down in pieces; reassembled and with new curtains, it became her island, and his when he was invited. In this way, they furnished their own rooms and a sitting room and a small one where they could eat; they abandoned the oversized dining room and the public rooms at the front.

'The place suits me,' Janet said. 'It's very odd, but it suits me. Because I'm very odd.'

DiNapoli brought them a cook, an old man who insisted he had worked for '*gli inglese*' but promised, through DiNapoli, to cook Italian food. He lived somewhere else and came in only in the late afternoon to cook their evening meal.

On his fourth day, Denton looked down into the weedy garden and saw a line of women curving from a supposedly locked gate into his garden and up to a beehive-shaped brick structure that he had thought was a defunct privy.

'It's a oven,' DiNapoli said. 'That cook, he takes one look at it, he gotta clean it out and build a fire. Next t'ing, he's charging five *soldi* a shot to bake in it. He got women coming from all over Spaccanapoli!'

Janet said, 'Why?'

'It's Christmas! They all making *pizza ripiena* for Christmas.'

'But why don't they bake at home?'

DiNapoli laughed. 'Them peoples, they don't got ovens at home. They lucky if they got a stove. In Naples, you wanta bake somet'ing, you go to the baker, you pay him ten *soldi*. This guy's charging half.'

Janet thought they should let the women use the oven for free; the cook said it was his perk; the neighbourhood bakers said it was unfair competition, and Janet and Denton were already rich and shouldn't go into business against them. In the end, Scuttini—to Denton's dismay—got the complaints from the bakers and decreed that the cook had to charge the same as the bakers, and anyway the cook owed the Scuttini one *centésimo* in every twenty, just like the bakers, so the cook gave up, and Janet told some of the women whose rooms opened on the courtyard that they could use the oven during holidays if they provided their own wood. This seemed to satisfy everybody and resulted in a regular trickle of *pizza ripiena* and *pannetone* to their table until after *Epifania,* the Feast of the Epiphany. Denton groused that the Scuttini fingers were in every pie, including those baked in his own oven.

Without asking him, Janet invited DiNapoli to come and live with them. To Denton's relief, DiNapoli said he couldn't.

'But why? We've lots of room.'

'There's a lady.'

'Well, bring her to live here too!'

'Yeah, but there's her husband. You wouldn't like him.'

Denton looked at Janet with an expression that said that sometimes it was wise to know when to quit.

She said, 'I worry about you, Mr DiNapoli. You don't eat enough and you have a cough.'

'I eat fine! I'm healt'y as a horse!'

'You don't have much money.'

'I get along.' When she looked dubious, he said, 'Little here, little there, you be surprised how good I do! Peoples in Naples, we do lotsa t'ings, add them together, we get along.'

'What sort of things?'

'I write letters. That's my main profession.'

'Letters?'

'Mostly for the sailors and the girls at the *porto.*' The major European fleets, including the British, made stops in Naples. 'The girls are *putane*, sure, but they're mostly nice girls and they gonna get married and live in the *bassi* one day, but they can't read or write mostly, so is it wrong to write letters for them?'

'You write love letters, Mr DiNapoli?'

'Love? You making a joke? Look, a French sailor comes to me, he says, "Hey, Vince, I met this swell girl"—he don't mention she's a *putana*, he don't have to—"I want you should write a letter, you say for me, 'I had a great time, I like your charlies. See you soon.' And tell her I'm crazy for her." So I write, "O my darling Gelsomina, As my ship disappears over the horizon, my thoughts are all of you. My heart is sinking into sadness like the sun sinks into the Bay of Naples. I dream of your skin which is like cream, your eyes like wild flowers, your hair like the darkness shaken from the night sky by dawn. Oh, my dear one, how shall I live wit'out you—"'

'Mr DiNapoli, you're a poet!'

He grinned. 'In Naples, you do what you gotta do to live.'

❊ ❊ ❊

Fra Geraldo's death faded, eclipsed by the more immediate and, it seemed, more important. Denton remembered to go back to the morgue two days late because he had forgotten. The doctor had examined Fra Geraldo's head, as he had promised, and he agreed that there didn't seem to be enough bleeding, either externally or internally. But the old man's body had been released for burial because there was, as Donati might have said, 'no evidence'. Denton supposed that Inspector Gianaculo had agreed, perhaps found it easier, even politic, to agree; he hadn't come to visit again. Denton didn't doubt that Gianaculo could have found him if he had wanted to; everybody in Naples seemed to know that Texas Jack had taken the Casa Gialla.

Denton was one of the few foreigners at the English church for the brief funeral of Gerald Hackby John Edward Sommers, fifth Lord Easleigh. Maltby was there for the consulate. However, if Fra Geraldo had been famous, as the newspaper had said, he had not been so among the English colony; the church was almost empty. On the other hand, the streets of Spagnuoli had been filled as the over-decorated hearse had rolled past. Denton saw women weeping, and at one corner three men were singing a sad song that was some sort of farewell.

Denton, never pious, passed his time during the service looking at the church's decorations. Many were plaques set into the walls; one, readable from where he sat, said, 'Blessed by Our Maker, We Have Heard the Music of the Spheres, Thanks to Those Who Have Led our Choristers in His Praise'. Below was a list of choirmasters, and to his surprise, the dead man had been one of them. Most of them had done their work for twenty years or more, but the late Lord Easleigh for only two: 'Gerald Sommers, 1857–59'. How long had Fra Geraldo said he had lived in Naples? Fifty years, perhaps an approximation. Meaning that he must have led the choir in his first years there. Denton, idling through the service, stared at the plaque as if it would speak to him. Why had the young Sommers, not yet Fra Geraldo, stayed so short a time? Was it that leading a choir couldn't satisfy the desire—or madness, or obsession—that had then led him to become an imitation of a monk? Or had it been simply one of those things we try on and give up, a seemingly good idea that turned out to be bad?

After the ceremony, Denton and Maltby collided at the church door, both rushing to get out. On the steps outside, both paused. It was a brilliant day, not at all a day for a funeral, a slight chill along the edges of the wind but bright with sunshine. Maltby said, 'I'm representing the consulate. Of course. I'm the resident dogsbody, as I'm sure you've noticed.' Denton could find nothing to say to that. Maltby sniffed and, touching his arm, moved him out of the way of the few people now coming from the church. He lowered his voice. 'I'm glad that poof from the *Carabinieri* didn't show his face. I really took a dislike to him. I shouldn't say that, but you're practically British, so it's all right. I was a bit severe with you about something that happened at the morgue—my apologies. Not my place, you an older man. But we must remember we represent the Crown in this awful city.' Maltby pulled himself deeper into his black overcoat. 'I suppose the mutilation done to the old chap is typical of the sorts of things they do to each other here. Degenerate race. But that they should do it to an Englishman! I didn't tell anybody at the consulate. Too awful. Some things better left unsaid. Didn't put it in my report, either. Summarised what the police and you and that

Italian said—accidental death, you not quite convinced of it. Shot it off to London—intended for the family. Not the worst thing in the world, putting one's name on a report the new peer is to see.' He cleared his throat. 'I rather caught a rocket for not having looked the old man's house over with a fine-toothed comb. I was thoroughly upset at the time—you'd vouch for that. They don't appreciate that at the consulate, of course. Some remarkably coarse types there, between you and me. I suppose a few years in this place do that to you. At any rate, I've to go back and pore over the entire house. Marching orders from the consul himself, because now the old man's buried, the heir wants the place put to rights and sold. Of course, it's *my* job to do it. New boy at school. Everybody's fag.' His eyes forced themselves on Denton. 'I don't suppose you'd care to go with me? You're a bit of a gentleman detective, I understand—an eye for things, and so on. In case there's something off. Rather leery of going alone, I must admit. It was seeing the old man...that way.'

Denton said what was true: he had no wish any longer to go into Fra Geraldo's house; he didn't say that he had about given up on Fra Geraldo. Pressed by Maltby, however, surprising himself by feeling sorry for the young man, at the same time marvelling at the human ability to dislike somebody and feel sorry for him at the same time, he said he supposed he might go along if he was really needed—but not in the mornings; that was when he worked, the time inviolate, and not in the next week or two, as he *had* to get to work. And he was still, after all, moving into a new house.

Maltby shook his hand with what seemed like gratitude and said he'd come by one afternoon very soon. He seemed relieved that it wasn't going to be right away.

CHAPTER

11

The first two weeks in the Casa Gialla were thick with new experiences, new places, new sights. Both the old man and the Scuttini, smuggled whisky and trussed-up young men, lost their immediacy.

They got through Christmas—no gifts; Janet couldn't stand to get them. Denton, child of a cheerless household, loved the notion of a Dickensian Christmas but did as she wished—and the sensational Neapolitan New Year's Eve, raucous with fireworks, dangerous with old furniture and pans and trash being thrown into the street from windows high above. They allowed themselves to be tourists: they had been to see the solidified blood of San Gennaro in the Duomo, which twice a year for centuries had liquefied in answer to fervent prayers; this miracle assured the city of another half-year of the saint's protection and provided Denton with a metaphor for the new book—the city washed in blood. They had been to a coral factory in Torre del Greco; they had been to the Solfatara and had sniffed the odours of Hell and seen their guide throw a puppy into the pool of invisible gas, from which Denton had saved it—usually, the puppy died within seconds—by rushing in, coughing, snatching up the animal, rushing out, and knocking the guide down. The puppy was now Janet's, named Sophie after the whore who had taught her to say *Va fan' cula*, and much prized because it had been housebroken in three days. The guide, on the other hand, had screamed that he was being murdered; there had been unpleasantness with a local policeman, as throwing puppies to their deaths was respected as honest work. Denton had said, 'Maybe I should just let them throw me in the hoosegow. I'm a hardened criminal.'

Then the university started its session and Janet spent three days a week learning Italian from Mr DiNapoli and meeting a tutor to discuss David Ricardi, of whose monetary policy she was already weary. She was now engrossed by the economics of the poor, she had found a gang of socialists and (she said) communists who were more to her liking than the tutor; soon, she was having a dozen of them to lunch every Wednesday.

Denton wrote every morning in his room, but he was still forced to be a tourist. He visited haunted palaces that were listed in the guidebooks, spent a night in the catacombs, searched in old books for accounts of ghosts and apparitions and miraculous coincidences, sat in on theatrical but clearly fake séances. He envied Janet her communists.

✿ ✿ ✿

Every morning, women in black walked two by two with slow steps to the churches, their bodies heavy with age and bad diet. The sun cast their long shadows as it gilded the domes and spires and threw the narrow *vicoli* of the old city into a blue shadow that seemed deeper than the night that had just faded. On the pavements along the bay, fishermen mended nets, the light coming unimpeded across the water from Capri and Sorrento to brighten the colours of their shirts and their caps, their boats. On the roof-tops, the cats came home from their nocturnal prowls and curled in pools of light to sleep.

Denton, up since five, walked behind the women in black, overtaking them with his long stride and going around until he reached his now favourite café in a small *piazza*. Already, they knew him there: he was greeted, smiled at. He took a table near the front or even outside if Naples was to have one of its warm winter days, which came in threes or fours to separate the days of cloud and wind. Denton drank coffee—he would already have made one pot in his workroom at the Casa Gialla, where he had installed a spirit stove—and ate a *pastiera*, a chunk of slightly sweet bread, baked only minutes before nearby. The bar would be crowded with working men. At first, they had eyed him, laughed among themselves, but after two weeks his novelty was gone and some of them nodded when he came in.

He had given up the idea of trying to join the artists and writers of the Caffè Gambrinus. This neighbourhood place in the little *piazza* had become his local.

He would sit until the working men had finished their quick gulps of coffee and their morning gossip; the place would empty, the owner standing by the door as if to study the square outside for possible flaws while his wife wiped the bar-top with a wet cloth and piled dirty cups into a vast tin pan to be carried somewhere in the back. Now the girls who worked in the tobacco factories behind Castello Capuana would be crossing the square, seeking the sunny side and pulling their cotton shawls tighter. They were barely into their teens, some of them; they would smell, Denton knew, of tobacco if he walked among them; their hands were stained like heavy smokers'. Many already looked tired, and the day was only starting. They were mostly thin, dark skinned but pasty fleshed, too long indoors, too little fed. DiNapoli had told Denton that as a boy he had been given for breakfast the end of yesterday's loaf of bread with his father's coffee grounds on it. Denton wondered what these girls had eaten—nothing? Bread? Janet's socialists would tell him.

On the far side of the square, the market booths would already be opening. The awnings would extend in front like the bills of caps, orange and faded red and the natural near-white of the canvas, stained now with rain and soot but glaring like snow in the sunlight. The handcarts and the donkey carts would be there from the farms beyond Porta Capuana, being unloaded by wiry men and strong women like Assunta. Denton would get up and stroll across the square, the factory girls now gone, and walk among the stalls, admiring the best and greenest produce in Europe, the finest oranges, the blackest olives, the creamiest wheels of the local white cheese—and the highest prices, thanks to the Camorra, which set them. He balanced the stalls against the factory girls, their underfed faces against this abundance of food. The difference was money. Without money, what the working poor got was not the best and the greenest and the whitest, but the overripe and the spoiled and the rotten. He didn't need Janet's Wednesday lunch to learn this.

Walking home, he, too, took the sunny side, always the same route, nodded to by men now opening the shops, the *portiere* standing smoking by their doorways. He wondered, *How many of them pay Scuttini protection and know that I'm a Scuttini protégé, too?* Such children as went to school were out now, always apparently late, running, their *Scusi, scusi, scusi, signore* as much part of the morning chorus as the songs of the birds. Always from somewhere near, an adult voice would be singing 'Aprile' or 'Funiculi, Funiculà' or the song about the sun. Once, at a distance he had spotted a singer and, coming closer, had realised that he was *Michele 'l ubriacon'*, recognizable from the *presepe* figure by Fra Geraldo. Denton had tried to get closer but the man vanished. Reminded, Denton remembered then that he had told Maltby he would go with him to Fra Geraldo's *palazzo*. Maybe Maltby had forgotten. Or given up on him. Either was fine with Denton.

❀ ❀ ❀

Home every morning from his café by eight o'clock, Denton went immediately to his room to read and make notes. At noon, he stopped and went to the red room; if the door was open, he went in; if it was closed, he knocked. *Like a guest*, he thought. He felt a stab of resentment, then guilt at feeling it. Today, the door was open. He felt a stab of gratitude, then resentment again at feeling grateful.

She kissed him. The puppy, who seemed to remember being saved from the Solfatara, wiggled energetically in her arms. 'I've had a note from Lucy Newcombe. She wants to "come by".'

Dear God, Lucy Newcombe, the American girl with the awful mother from the pensione*! And the awful friend!* 'I thought you were forbidden fruit. With the soubrette?'

'Oh, she's the duenna, yes. They've given Mrs Newcombe their solemn word that they won't leave the "proper" part of the city, which is to say the few blocks around the *pensione*. Of course they lied. Lucy wants to try eating *pizza*.'

'Daring of her.' Denton was sorting his mail, which had finally begun to reach him at the Casa Gialla. 'She could do that on her own, couldn't she?'

'She thinks she'll be laughed at—the great horror when you're seventeen.'

'I doubt that the factory girls would think so. Tell Lucy to try going hungry. Or living in one room with a dozen other people.'

'She isn't like you and me, Denton. And she's still a child. Not like girls who work. Is that very American, to be still a child at seventeen?'

'If you've a rich papa, you can be a child at eighty.'

'Ah, just like England.'

He threw himself into an upholstered armchair—rusty green, not red, rescued from upstairs—and tore open an envelope.

'I meant to tell you, you've a letter from Atkins.'

'Bit late. Ah, "business is booming". Oh, well. "Two new comic songs recorded this week." I suppose he's going to realise his life's dream and become a music-hall star. Or a millionaire. I'll have to start calling him "Mr Atkins".' He put the letter down. 'Well, he sounds busy and happy.'

'And you sound heartbroken because of it.' She patted his shoulder.

He laughed. 'You know me too well. Rotten of me, not wishing him well. Selfish.'

'If you'd simply admit he's your best friend, there'd be no problem.'

She put her nose into the puppy's fur and laughed.

Denton thought, *This is where we should live. We're different people here. If she doesn't quite love me, she accepts my loving her. We belong here. We will stay here.*

❀ ❀ ❀

DiNapoli was his for two hours in the afternoon, when they mostly walked the city—Denton's way of learning a new place. He was a voracious walker, long legged and indefatigable; DiNapoli sometimes had to trot to keep up, but he had great stamina and could walk as far, if not as fast, as Denton. They talked. DiNapoli pointed things out, gave their Italian names; Denton asked, What is that, what is this, how do you say go, stay, come, listen, wait, send? The expression *come se dice?*, roughly 'how do you say?', was used a lot. They walked as far to the west as Piedigrotta, the entrance to the now closed tunnel that the Romans had cut through the Posillipo hill; they walked east past Piazza del Mercato and the old railway station; they climbed to the hills that circled the lower city; they visited the churches, where Denton saw his first frescoes by Giotto and was captivated by this different vision of reality with its green flesh and its skewed perspective. At Denton's insistence, they dawdled in shops that sold old prints and older books and paintings and sculptures that DiNapoli insisted were fakes, and Denton bought himself a sword-cane because he couldn't have his derringer.

❀ ❀ ❀

Letters piled up in answer to his newspaper advertisements. DiNapoli translated them, often laughing as he did so because the letters were barely literate. 'These are fake ghosts, not the real ghosts. Naples peoples, they do anyt'ing for a few *soldi*. I t'ink you got peoples all over town inventing ghosts for you. Here's one, they got the ghost of a cat comes in at night to kill ghost mice. There's another says the walls go knock-knock all night long and they let you listen for ten *lire*. Then one, they live over the old catacombs, they can hear the dead bodies scratching their fingernails on the walls. You can listen for twenty *lire*.'

'That doesn't sound too bad. Good local feel to it.'

'What d'you t'ink of a guy says he saw a ghost ship sail up to the *porto* and the whole crew is skeletons in Spanish clothes and they come ashore for a good time?' DiNapoli frowned at the letter. 'He says he seen ghost *putane* giving them the eye. This guy oughta be writing for the *scenegiatta*.'

They sorted the letters into useless, possible and worth pursuing. Denton found only a dozen that seemed as if they might give him usable material. He was disappointed that all the apparitions were post-medieval Italians—no Romans, no Greeks—and they all seemed to be from a period that started in a hazy, undefined Renaissance and ended in the eighteenth century, the dating always done by the clothes the ghost wore—except for one woman (he assumed it was a woman) who said that she had had 'love encounters' with a naked spectre who was 'very pleasurable, but cold'. She said she was using a false name and would communicate only through a third party to protect her reputation, and she wanted a hundred *lire* for her story.

'It's a pretty good story,' he said to Janet. 'I'm not sure I can use it in a book that my editor would agree to publish, though.'

'Some old maid having fantasies.'

'But interesting ones. Maybe I could do a chapter on ghost stories people have made up. The ghost ship, for example.'

'But then it wouldn't be your book.'

'What must it be like to have sex with a spectre? Kind of a contradiction in terms, isn't it? Maybe there's a new genre there—ghost pornography.'

'A man came to Ruth Castle's house while I was there who wanted a girl to spend the day in an icehouse and then pretend to be dead while he rogered her. Ruth drew the line at that.'

'But at least she would have had substance. I mean, the essence of sex is physical feeling, isn't it? And how do you feel a spectre?'

'I always thought the essence of sex was mental. In which case a spectre would do fine.'

'Not for me.'

❧ ❧ ❧

One afternoon DiNapoli took him to see the six-hundred-year-old mummies in the Castel Nuovo. He led Denton by way of the port, which Denton complained wasn't the shortest way. Then Denton saw ahead of them on the pavement a large device on legs, behind it a wiry, small man of DiNapoli's sort. He remembered that he had seen him that first day when DiNapoli had led him out of the Galleria. 'The photographer,' he said.

'Yeah, Spina.' DiNapoli stopped him with a hand. 'Smile. He takes your pitcher.' Denton scowled as he realised that this was why DiNapoli had brought him this way—the tourist as pigeon to be plucked. Some seconds later, DiNapoli let Denton walk forward. They reached the camera, a box as big as an armchair on splayed, squat legs. A lens in an ancient brass tube jutted out the front. At the rear, Spina's legs connected the pavement to a black cloth, under which he was making slow, arcane movements. Two minutes after he had taken their picture, he emerged with a wet photograph of an unsmiling Denton and a debonair DiNapoli, who grinned as if he were the tourist and Denton the guide.

DiNapoli introduced them. In fact, DiNapoli explained, when he guided tourists, he always came this way and Spina paid him ten *soldi* per subject, assuming they bought a photograph. Most did—the photograph was remarkably clear and showed the Castel del Ovo in the background, proof that you had visited Naples. 'Still,' Denton said, his better mood restored by DiNapoli's candour, 'it's a risky business, isn't it?' Spina takes the picture on spec?' DiNapoli translated. Spina shrugged. He gestured at the boards behind him, on which he had pinned a couple of dozen of the photographs that tourists hadn't bought. Why did he keep them? Spina shrugged again. 'Maybe somebody buys, who knows?'

As they walked on, Denton holding his damp photo, he said, 'You have many ways of earning money, DiNapoli.'

'Little here, little there.'

They had reached the Castel Nuovo, an enormous stone structure that had been new six hundred years before.

'Why do you call it *nuovo* if it isn't new any more?' Denton said.

'Well, the peoples, they call it the Maschio Angioino. "Angioino", that's the Angevins, they took over here a long time ago. Back then, it was new.'

'What's Maschio? "Mask"?'

'No, *maschio,* you know—like men and boys.' He cupped his hand over his crotch.

'Oh—like "masculine".' Denton looked up at the assertive, looming stone bulk. The rounded tower that bulged from the middle of one wall did, indeed, remind him of things masculine. 'It probably made more sense when men wore codpieces,' he said.

They went inside and for a few *soldi* were led down to the dank room where four of the Angevins' enemies lay in their coffins, mummies long since rendered unrecognisable by time but still datable by their clothes, like the local ghosts.

'Strange, keeping your enemies' corpses downstairs. Do they come back as ghosts and say "Boo" to the watchmen?'

'Don' make jokes. It's bad luck.' DiNapoli, who never went to church, crossed himself.

Denton bent close to the mummified faces. 'I suppose I'll describe them in the book. Readers like a good shudder.'

DiNapoli shuddered.

One day Denton, fresh from the shouting of a Wednesday lunch, the arguments translated for him by a sympathetic anarcho-syndicalist, asked DiNapoli to show him the wretched streets of the Mercato district—according to the socialists, Naples' worst.

'You don' wanna go there.'

'Yes, I do.'

'Tourist peoples don' go there.'

'I'm trying to get out of the tourist parts of town.'

'We get robbed down there.'

Denton brandished the sword cane. 'You're safe with me, DiNapoli.' DiNapoli sighed and gave in.

The terrible tenements called *fondaci* rose six storeys and more along alleys so narrow that vehicles couldn't penetrate them. The buildings, DiNapoli said, were without running water or gas or heat or electricity. The occupants lived six or eight to a windowless room—lived out their lives there, called 'cave-dwellers' by the better off. DiNapoli's tone was both patronising and pitying: even at his worst, he meant, he hadn't had to live like this.

One of the Wednesday guests, had told Denton that forty per cent of the city were unemployed; down here, the figure was higher. Even if he could find a job, a labourer made only three or four *lire* a day. Bread alone cost a family four or five *lire* a week.

'How do they survive?'

DiNapoli shrugged. 'It's Naples.'

Denton heard singing. At his insistence, they turned towards it, followed it down towards the shore, then left up a *vico* so narrow he and DiNapoli could hardly walk side by side. There was no paving. The earth underfoot had turned to slimy mud from the water and worse that always ran down it. The smell of urine was strong: men, women and children used the alley as a latrine, men standing by the dark walls; women squatting with their skirts slightly hoisted, as a puddle formed at their feet. Children, held by both hands, pissed into air.

Overhead, the buildings almost met; the sky was a narrow gash. The sun never penetrated to the bottom.

Michele 'l ubriacon' was leaning at a corner, singing 'O sole mio' in a roughened voice that might once have been a tenor but had dropped. He was entirely recognisable from Fra Geraldo's carving, although as Denton got close enough he could see that the real Michele was even older than the carving made him seem. The open mouth had no teeth. Michele's bare feet were scaly with filth; his overcoat, too big for him, was ragged; he wore a waist-coat but no shirt, filthy trousers, and the crown of a felt hat from which the brim had been cut or torn.

'*Soldi, signore—soldi!*' The terrible figure finished singing and rattled a wooden box that held a couple of stones and a coin. '*Soldi per la musica!*'

Denton dropped in twenty *centésimi*. '*Lei è Michele.*'

'*Eh!*' He gave Denton a horrible grin. His tongue lolled out of his mouth and hung there, then wagged.

He had to ask DiNapoli how to say it, then said in Italian, 'Do you remember Fra Geraldo, Michele?'

'Aa-a-h-h-h—*morto!*' The tongue waggled and the reddened eyes rolled back. He began to sing something that sounded sad but whose words Denton couldn't understand. As he sang, Michele seemed to grow agitated; he rattled the box and stamped his feet, almost dancing to the lugubrious tune. He stopped and shouted, '*Morto! Morto!*' The tongue stuck an inch out of the mouth and seemed to test the air like a snake's.

'He's stinking drunk, Mist' Denton. Don't waste your time.' DiNapoli pulled at his arm.

'I want to ask him about the carvings the old man did of him.'

'He's too drunk. I find him for you another time.' DiNapoli was trying to drag him along the *vico*.

'*Soldi,*' Michele said. '*Soldi per la—la—*' The tongue went from side to side of the toothless mouth in the same rhythm as the shaking box. He tried to push away from the building and almost fell.

Denton was looking back, stopped. 'He should be in a hospital.'

'So should half the peoples down here.' DiNapoli dragged him away. 'He got no brains left in his head. Peoples say his brains is wit' God—that's why they touch him for luck. What's God want wit' his brains?'

Denton shook his head. He looked down at his feet. He had stepped in human shit.

CHAPTER

12

To his surprise, Maltby sent a note saying that he had been ordered again to inspect the Palazzo Minerva *at once* and could Denton please go with him that day, as he had promised. When Maltby showed up at the Casa Gialla, he looked so woebegone that Denton couldn't refuse him. In fact, it was only a few days longer than two weeks since he had seen Maltby at the funeral.

They went out and found a carriage and went along the Corso and cut through to the Via Toledo, then up to Fra Geraldo's part of Spagnuoli. Maltby was mostly silent, perhaps nursing his many grievances. Denton tried conversation a couple of times, thought it hopeless, but got some interest when he mentioned his return visit to the morgue.

'That corpse!' Maltby growled. 'I was physically ill, you know. Not the manliest thing to have done, but I was very upset by the...the—you know.'

Denton told him about the first policeman's reaction to the missing *cazzo*, trying to make it humorous.

'I actually wanted to be a policeman once,' Maltby said gloomily. 'And I suppose it would have brought me to the same point—looking at an old man's mutilations in a morgue. I suppose I'm a prude. It's ironic, me being so much younger than you.'

'The missing *cazzo* might actually be relevant. To his death, I mean.'

'I don't think we should be making insinuations that are really more appropriate to some contemptible form of reading matter.'

'You said you wanted to be a policeman.'

'That was when I was a boy. What's that to do with it?'

'Policemen have to think of all sorts of possibilities.'

'You know policemen, I suppose.' He made it seem like an accusation.

'I have a fairly good friend at New Scotland Yard.'

'I'm glad now I'm not a policeman.' Maltby barked out a single laugh. 'Like that Italian poof.'

'At least he wasn't sick.'

'Oh, well, if you're going to throw that up at me—' And then they were both laughing at the 'throw up', Denton surprised by Maltby's sudden change, which he guessed was part of his youngness, even boyishness, and the irresistible subject of sicking up. When they were done laughing, Denton said, 'It's no disgrace to be sick at seeing a corpse, Maltby. Lots of coppers are, at least at first. And Donati wasn't as bad as you think. He was intelligent and he had some notion of evidence.'

'He's a *capitano* because his father's a big noise in the Catholic Liberty Party. I checked. It's like me being made a detective inspector at Scotland Yard if my pa was an MP. Of course, I'm not elevated enough for that. Some people have all the luck.'

'Look.' Denton had turned to him and stuck out a finger. 'If we're going to spend time together, for God's sake stop thinking that life's supposed to be fair. It isn't! About nine parts in ten of it is chance. That *scugnizzo* over there on the pavement looks at you going by in the carriage and says, "Some people have all the luck." If Donati got where he is because his father's a bigwig, it doesn't change the fact he's smart and he knows police work.'

'You don't have to get your back up about it.'

'I'm an older man trying to pass on some wisdom to a younger one.'

'Oh? Oh. Wish somebody'd do that at my shop—job might be more bearable. Well, mm, thanks. Much appreciated.'

'Oh, right.'

'What's a *scoo-neat-something*?'

'*Scugnizzo*. A kid who lives on the streets.'

'Oh, those rotten street arabs.'

'My God, you make yourself difficult to deal with. They're starving kids who live on their wits and probably do it a damn sight better than you or I would in their place. For Christ's sake stop being a narrow-minded English ass.'

'I don't like you insulting England like that.'

'Oh, good God.'

'I'm a moral chap.'

'You're a damned prig. Come on, we're there; let's look at this *palazzo*. If we're quick about it, I won't have time to insult you again before we're done.' Denton climbed down, wondering why he was being so direct with this rather oafish kid. Something parental, maybe, but Maltby wasn't anything like his two sons, and he hadn't raised them since they had been five and seven, anyway. Still, he looked at Maltby as he climbed out of the carriage, and wondered who he—red-faced, narrow-minded, deeply unsure—reminded him of. With a feeling as if a loud cracker had been banged just behind him, he thought, *It's me. It's me at twenty.*

Not that Maltby was really like him: Denton at twenty had been through a war, was married, had had a farm. But he, too, had been something of a bully because unsure; he, too, had thought the world too much for him. And he, too, had had a great deal of learning to do before he knew which side his bread was buttered on. His even younger wife had tried to smooth his rough edges and had infuriated him by doing so. She had tried to teach him table manners and he had got angry and shouted, *Why? Why the hell should I?* and she had said, *Because you eat like a pig*, and that had been the first time he had hit her.

'I'm sorry,' he said to Maltby. 'I was rude to you.'

'Oh...' Maltby was standing by the *portiere*'s lodge, waiting for the keys to the Palazzo Minerva. 'Well. I suppose you were doing it for my own good.'

'I was, yes. But why?'

'Well. I flatter myself that you see something in me.' Maltby got redder. 'Hope so, anyway.'

The rodent face of the *portiere* appeared, then the keys. The little man nodded to Denton and gave him something like a bow that didn't go below the breastbone. Maltby gave him money, apparently too much, because he got a bow that went to the waist.

'I never give them the right amount,' Maltby grumbled as they went towards the door. 'Some fellows always know exactly what to give. They learn it in the cradle or someplace.' He had the biggest key ready and put it in the lock.

The air in the lobby smelled stale and mousy. The big hall where the stairs stood was hardly better; the house already had that dead, trapped feeling that long-closed places get.

'Gloomy place,' Maltby said.

'All it needs is some paint and a good cleaning. What do you want to see?'

Maltby groaned. 'I've been stuck with writing a description of it for the heirs. They mean to sell it. They don't understand how unbelievably sordid the neighbourhood is. I'm supposed to "evaluate" it. As if I'm some damned estate agent.' He sighed. 'I should look at everything and take notes, I suppose.' He showed a leather-bound notebook and a patent fountain pen.

Things were coming back that Denton had forgotten: he found he was thinking of the room upstairs whose proportions had seemed off somehow. His curiosity about the old man's death stirred. He said, 'You go ahead and look. I'm going up to the top floor.'

'You said you'd do it with me!'

He was scared, Denton thought. Not so much scared of the house as of the responsibility. 'Come on up with me, then. You can look into the rooms up there while I do something.'

'What?'

'Not your business.'

They trudged up the stairs, Maltby redder faced and breathing hard by the time they reached the top. Along with his other troubles, he was getting fat, Denton thought. He gave Maltby a little push towards the far end of the corridor and, taking the keys from his hand, said, 'Off you go.'

'The keys.'

'The rooms are open. I'll be right down there at the end.'

Maltby sighed and took out his notebook and began to write, presumably a description of the upper floor. Denton turned right and went to the room at the end, the room with the armoire where he'd found the wood shaving. He unlocked it and went in without looking back at Maltby. The room was as he remembered, and he stood in the doorway and stared at it and tried to remember why something had seemed off.

He looked at the armoire and remembered.

He stepped back into the corridor and looked down towards its closer end. He paced off that distance, then went back to the room and paced off the distance from the doorway to the wall against which the armoire stood.

The room was about four yards from doorway to wall. The corridor outside was eight yards from the doorway to the blind wall at the end.

He opened the armoire, as he had done on his first visit, and knelt, one of his knees cracking. The armoire's doors opened in the middle; the one on his left, open, blocked the light from the dirty window. Denton took out his flash-light, held it low, almost on the armoire's floor. Two small objects cast long shadows. He picked them up, turned off the light, took them to the window.

Wood shavings. Quite small ones, almost chips, one of them probably the one he had found and replaced the first time.

Dropping them into a pocket, he returned to the armoire and stepped inside, found it big enough to stand in, and rapped with his knuckles on the back. The piece was at least a couple of hundred years old, he supposed, solidly made. The wood was thick: even the interior was carved into panels. Could he try to move the piece alone? Probably not. Should he ask Maltby to help him? Anyway, if they were able to move the armoire, and he suspected that it would prove too heavy even for the two of them, would they find anything behind it?

Denton stepped out and closed the doors and tried to look behind the armoire, but it was tight to the wall. And unbudgeable, as he found when, after all, he tried to move it.

He stepped back and looked at the wall again. On its other side, he thought, was a space ten or a dozen feet wide and probably as long as this room—eighteen feet, more or less—to make up the longer dimension in the corridor. A space without a door, apparently.

Or was it?

He went out into the corridor again. Maltby had disappeared, probably into one of the other rooms. Denton pressed his face against the plaster, looked along the wall towards the corridor's end. Old plaster was always wavy, but fifteen or so feet down from the doorway this plaster became flat. Visibly different from the rest. He walked to the flatness, felt up and down, saw where there had once been an opening. Two faint joints in the moulded baseboard showed where, he thought, a doorway had been filled in. The workmanship was superb, the scarf joints almost invisible. And so, too, the plastering, which was in fact too good, for it was flat and smooth where the rest of the wall had undulations.

He stepped back. The wall had once been covered with a dark blue cloth, perhaps satin. Most of that was gone, revealing under it the remains of a stencilled pattern in terracotta and black. Where the doorway had been filled in, the new surface was identical to the old, even to the scraps of cloth and the faded, damaged painting. Again, the workmanship was superb.

Somebody was really skilled. And really wanted to hide something.

Maltby appeared at the far end of the corridor and waved. Denton raised a hand, his eyes on the wall. 'Depressing!' he heard Maltby call. 'What have you found?'

'Nothing.'

He went back into the room and closed the door behind him. He jingled the big ring of keys. Mysteries intrigued him; they also annoyed him. He wanted to take an axe to the wall next to the armoire. *Something* lay on the other side, if only a dead and empty space.

He stepped into the armoire again. Dumping the keys in a coat pocket, he felt over the panels of the back. They were hand planed; he could feel the slight unevennesses. He pushed on the panels, then on their corners. Nothing. He rapped.

He switched the flash-light on and trained it along the edges of the panels, then upward into the joint where a narrow moulding filled the corner between the armoire's back wall and its ceiling. The light showed him nothing. The searching fingers that came behind it felt a greater smoothness a foot from the left-hand wall; then the light, held at a different angle, showed a shininess there as if the spot had been polished. He switched the light off and ran his hands along the moulding to the right and found the same smoothness near the right-hand wall, and he put a hand on each of the smooth places and first lifted, then pressed in, and finally pushed sideways, and the moulding moved two inches to the right with a sound of scraping wood and a sudden *tunk*, and the centre panel of the wardrobe swung away from him.

A complex and delightful smell rushed towards him, made up of candle wax and wood and oil paint and cedar, incense and flowers, and, less delightful, dust and mice. Deep, velvety darkness opened before him. He stepped back, as if something was going to come out of it at him, and then fumbled for the flash-light and switched it on.

The pale light picked out first a stool and then a crude bench. Metal glittered: tools, a knife blade identifiable. Then colour: beyond the bench, something in a rich red, a hand. Then a torso and the red of blood.

He trained the light downwards. A step down of a few inches where the floor of the armoire ended would take him to the floor within. There, however, the floor almost glittered with white and black and red, some sort of tiling. Denton knelt and put his hand down and felt only a continuous surface; he shone the light again and looked close and saw that the tiles were only painted.

He stepped down into the darkness. He flashed the light around. Colour, figures, carving, woodwork gilded and polished, and overhead vaulting rafters and a ceiling painted like the sky. He swung the light lower and caught the glint of glass and recognised a shaped lamp, then another on the narrow space's far wall; he turned the light to the little bench and saw there a packet of sulphur matches and a single burnt match with its blackened head sticking out over the edge. He picked up the matches and, juggling his flash-light while he held the box, struck one—odd, he thought to himself, because he carried his own matches in a pocket—and held it near the glass shade and found the gas tap and turned it and heard the low hiss and saw the light come.

He went from lamp to lamp, six in all—two on each long wall, one at each end—and then stood in the middle of the space and marvelled, a man not attuned to art but sensitive to other men's skills. Here was a dazzling, a perhaps mad creation: a chapel in miniature that rose only a dozen feet in the air but that simulated greater height, not with tricks but with proportion and the evolution of vertical, carved oak beams into arches that met overhead.

A faceted oak beam ran up each corner, three more between them on each long wall. Between the beams were painted scenes that filled the spaces down to low, carved wainscoting. On the beams themselves were near-life-sized figures at floor level, one for each beam, and others at the figures' feet, and, climbing the beams, smaller figures, complete statues, a few as big as three feet tall, others less, some as little as a foot high, most of the small ones well up the beams so that they increased the sense of height.

Denton was not a churchgoer and not a Catholic, so he didn't recognise the big sculptures. It didn't take him long, however, to recognise the crucified figure at the far end of the chapel, rendered with gruesome frankness, and then the suffering, the scourged, the ridiculed major figures on the beams, and then the smaller figures grouped around them—Roman soldiers, Pharisees, taunters and torturers and challengers. And others—imps, demons. And grotesques, half animal. And children. Oddly, so many children.

The beams framed six major paintings on the long walls. Their skies joined the blue sky and puffy clouds of the ceiling at the top; below were distant cities or conical hilltops with roads winding down them, then rivers and forests and farms, men harvesting and women washing clothes, horses and cattle, a dog chasing a hare, a cat washing itself. There were summer and winter and autumn there. In the middle distance, people, especially children, ran, all of them running towards the bottoms of the paintings, where, dominating each one, a man was being tortured. By children.

The man and the children seemed to have been made to different scales, the man big, the children small.

He saw quickly that they were all the same man, as the Christs were all the same Christ. The tortures were different—a flaying alive, a roasting on a gridiron, an impaling—but, and it took him minutes of walking back and forth among the paintings to work it out, the two principal torturers were also always the same, a black-haired boy and a lighter-haired boy, unsmiling, hot eyed. They were naked, as the tortured man was. In one scene, they were garrotting the man with a rope, each holding an end and leaning back as if they were pulling in a tug of war, their faces contorted with effort and, perhaps, hatred. Their spread legs revealed their hairless groins, their pink, carefully painted sex.

'Oh, my God!'

Maltby was standing behind him in the entrance from the armoire. His mouth was open and he was staring into the space. 'What *is* this place?'

'Step inside and shut the door behind you.' In fact, Denton had closed it so as to study the portion of a painting on the back, but Maltby must have seen the light around the edges.

'But what *is* it?'

'I'd say it's the chapel of the Brotherhood of Saint Simeon Stylites.' Denton moved from the centre of the room to the little bench. He fingered the tools, a big lump of modelling wax stuck all over with dust and hairs, the half-finished *presepe* figure that was fixed in a carver's vice. 'And Fra Geraldo's workroom.'

'But it's—it's—*fantastic.*'

'I think that's exactly what it is.'

'But I say—are these old? They must be quite valuable. Oh, that picture there—that's disgusting.' Maltby looked away from a painting of a nude man having his guts pulled out with a hook. 'People shouldn't be allowed to paint things like that.'

Denton had wondered about the paintings' age, too, and now he saw that some distant figures were wearing clothes that could have been seen on the Naples streets that day. Others were recognisably of an earlier style, but no older than fifty years or so.

He had visited enough museums to have some rough idea of what different periods looked like, and these paintings, despite an overall feeling of antiquity—the conical mountains, the disparity in the size of figures, the conventional look of the rivers and roads—were contemporary. No Giotto here. He pointed out a carriage that could have been the one they had arrived in.

'But who could have done such a thing?'

'He was a painter. Also a sculptor.' Denton pointed to one of the major figures on the beams. 'Do you understand the sculptures?'

'Well, the big ones are the stations of the cross, of course— Christ on the way to Calvary, and so on. The little ones—quite disturbing. Grotesque. Gothic, wouldn't you say? Look at that one, a chap with a tail like a lizard and hands like claws. Fantastic. And the Roman soldier with a snout like a rhinoceros. Whatever does it mean, do you think?'

Denton was walking along a wall, studying a painting. Seeing it that close, he noticed that the paint was flaking; when he touched it, he felt a soft bubble, as if the paint were detaching itself from the plaster. He turned away and felt his foot strike something on the floor and bent to find a cat-o'-nine-tails. A moment's search with the flash-light revealed the painted tiles so worn there that the terrazzo showed through. 'He lay here and flogged himself.'

'You mustn't say things like that.'

'He told me he scourged himself. Didn't say for what. I think he whipped himself every night, from what he said.' He looked up at an angel who was hanging over him in the sky, wings spread, a look of bemusement on his or her face—impossible to tell which. A water stain ran across the face like a birthmark; paint had flaked from one wing as if it were moulting.

'But the angels didn't weep.'

The angel was looking down on the spot where he had found the whip.

Maltby said, 'I don't know what I can possibly say about this in my report. If I were to set this down, they'd think—They'd laugh at me. Anyway, one can't say things about peers of the realm.'

'Like what—that he whipped himself?'

'That he—' Maltby was whispering. 'That he had thoughts like *these*.'

Denton was looking at one of the tortured men. He was thinking that, yes, this one probably looked like Fra Geraldo at some much younger age; when he looked around at the others, he saw the face at different ages: the hair receded, grew grey; the muscles wasted. And after the one—apparently the youngest—that showed him with pubic hair and a penis and a scrotum, he lost the scrotum and then the penis, and the hair vanished.

As if he had been following Denton's thoughts, Maltby said, 'Some of them are just like that corpse. Really! I can't put that down in a report. An old man owning pictures like...you know!'

'I'd say they were self-portraits.'

'Oh!' Maltby sat down on the stool. 'This is too much for me. I'd say it's the straw that broke the camel's back, but this isn't a straw, it's a boulder! It makes me sick. I'm going to resign. I didn't join the Foreign Office to have to look at stuff like this.'

'Don't look at it.'

'I *have* to look at it! I have to write a report about it. First, I'm supposed to be an estate agent, and now I'm supposed to be an art expert! And to deal with pornography! I suppose it's nothing to you. You've seen it all. It isn't fair.'

'I wish you'd stop saying that.' Denton was touching the sculptures that surrounded Christ in his crown of thorns. Some of the cutting that had formed them had left flat planes that had not been sanded round, so that the figures, although scrupulously, sometimes shockingly, realistic, nonetheless proclaimed their nature as carvings. They were brilliant work, he thought; no two were alike; none was conventional, a mere type, a cliché. All were painted, even the smallest showing details of wrinkles and eyebrows and dirt. They were, in a sense, *presepe* figures of torment and suffering. And he saw, now that he really looked at them, that old spider webs, sagging with dust, joined them, almost shrouded some. He said, 'I agree that you shouldn't say too much about this room in your report.'

'I can't *lie*. Suppose somebody found out!'

'You can be strictly correct—so many paintings, so many stations of the cross, the carving bench, the figures. You don't have to be lurid about the subject of the paintings. You could say something like "painted in a mood of honest realism" or some such. Skip the nudity and the mutilation, say something like "not for the squeamish, and certainly not for ladies".' He thought of what Janet would say if she could hear him use 'ladies' that way. 'Probably be best to list them like a catalogue—"Six paintings of martyrdoms, the devils represented as young children". Nobody could argue with that.'

'I wish I had your gift. Say all that again, will you?' Maltby had his notebook out.

'We'll do that later. You've got to look at the rest of the house—you want to be honest, you said. You want to see it all.

Take these—' Denton pulled out the keys. 'You go on; I'll close up here.'

Maltby grasped the keys and stood, then hung there, looking down the room. 'How *could* he? Didn't he care what people would *say?*'

'I have an idea that this was between him and God.'

Maltby looked up. The angel looked down. Maybe something of the angel's lack of interest reached him. He said, 'But—how awful!' He walked slowly the length of the room, which seemed a great distance because of his slow, heavy walk, and he stood under the literal, cruel carving of the crucifixion. He said, 'He *meant* it—didn't he!' He turned around and looked at Denton.

'Yes. I think he saw himself on that cross, although that isn't his face.'

'Poor devil.' Maltby came slowly back, head down, hands behind him. 'Poor old devil.' He looked up at Denton. 'I have an awful thing to confess. I didn't think of him as a *man* before. I mean, in the morgue. When we talked about him. But—' He looked around him, turning a full circle to take in the whole madness of it. 'The poor old sod...'

Denton put a hand on his shoulder. 'How old are you, really?'

'What?' Maltby seemed to have trouble coming from some other place. 'I'm twenty.'

'Don't get your dander up—I mean this as a compliment: for twenty, that was a big thing to recognise.'

'People say I'm dense.'

'No, you're twenty. You go on downstairs. I'll finish up here.'

When Maltby was gone, Denton walked again around the room, turning the gas lamps off until he was back at the entrance and only one was burning. He wondered what he was going to do, or if in fact there was anything he could do. He was as sure as he was of anything that the old man had, indeed, created this room for himself and his God. It was not a work of art in the sense that it was intended to be seen by anyone else, and probably its purpose had lain in the making of it and not in any future—

the pictures, the carvings, the room. That it was the work of a wounded, perhaps a twisted, mind Denton accepted; he didn't accept Maltby's response that it was 'disgusting'. Yet Maltby had broken through his own conventional self to say 'poor old sod', and that was a triumph for Fra Geraldo's art. There must have been some of the same feeling in his making of it, some sense of pity—self-pity, but not what that term usually evokes—pity for sufferer and torturer both. And pity for the man who was seeking atonement up here in the hidden, closed space of his own mind.

Denton wondered if he should take something with him, had no idea what it would be. What did he want, a souvenir? He mentally sneered at that. A memento, a relic, a keepsake? He narrowed his eyes at the one painting he could see, now dim in the greenish gaslight. No, he wanted a record. Not Maltby's cobbled-up catalogue, but a thing detailed and specific.

To tell the story.

He pulled the armoire closed and slid the moulding back into place. How many times had the old man done this? At least once a day, surely more often when he was creating it. For forty-odd years. Denton stepped out of the armoire and closed its doors. He would have to come back with the keys to lock the door. He realised that he felt protective of the chapel, as if he had, by finding it, conspired in hiding it. But how long could it be hidden from the new owner, or from a buyer if he sold the Palazzo Minerva? And what business was it of Denton's?

Maltby was finishing the rooms on the floor below. He looked pained and weary, moving with his head bent and his eyes down. He shook his head when he saw Denton. 'Awful place. Just awful. No wonder he...'

They went down to the *piano nobile*. Maltby complained about the bathrooms, the dirt, the emptiness. 'And the neighbours! They're *peasants*! What was he doing living here? What was he *doing*?'

Denton looked again at the stairs where he had found the body. Again, there was no blood where he had expected to see it, except the small dark spot at the bottom where the head had lain.

'I suppose I'll be responsible for getting the place refurbished,' Maltby said at the bottom. 'I'll be expected to see it all put to rights and I don't even speak Italian. Find people to clean, find carpenters, find plumbers. It isn't f—' He caught himself.

Denton put out his hand for the keys. 'I have to lock that room.'

'My God, yes! Suppose somebody else saw it!' Maltby squared his jaw. 'I still have this floor to look at.'

Denton detached the brass key. 'I'll be right down. I think there's just kitchens and things down here.' He ran up the stairs, climbed to the top more slowly. He went into the room, opened the armoire, moved the moulding and stepped again into the chapel. He needed only his flash-light, could perhaps do what he wanted in the dark: he found the lump of modelling wax, a slightly soft, plastic stuff that reminded him of taffy-pulling, with the same greasiness. He used his pocket knife to cut off a chunk and pressed the key into it, then went out again and closed the back of the armoire, then its doors. Out in the corridor, he checked by window-light that the impression of the key was deep enough, then pulled the key loose and wrapped the soft wax in his pocket handkerchief with two calling cards to keep it flat. He locked the room and trotted down the stairs.

Outside, Maltby said, the key back on the ring and the ring in his hand, 'Look here—will you help me write this report? You've got the knack.'

Denton smiled. He imagined using the word 'knack' to Henry James. 'Bring me something—a draft. We'll go over it.'

'That's damned decent of you. You're the only decent chap I've run into in this place.' He jingled the keys and looked up at the sky, blue now with white clouds like the sky in the chapel. 'Do you really suppose he meant it to be himself in those paintings?'

Maltby, Denton thought, was a lot more perceptive than he seemed. 'I think so, yes.'

'Saw himself as being…ripped apart and skinned and—! Was he mad?'

Denton wondered how much to confide in Maltby. He said, 'He told me he was being haunted by the ghosts of children. They were trying to kill him, he said.'

'You mean it was *suicide?*' Maltby said this with almost a groan, as if it were personally hurtful. Well, he'd taken the wrong lesson from what Denton had said. Denton thought that perhaps that was just as well. He steered them to the *portiere*'s post and handed over the keys and another coin for future considerations and led Maltby out to the narrow street. They walked towards the brightness of the corner, a real street. Men watched them from the doorways of the *bassi*, smoking, lounging. Talk stopped as they went past. Women, too, were talking across the street above them, window to window; they, too, stopped, although there was some laughter. Denton looked up. Washing, strung from one side to the other, fluttered. At the top the sky was only a narrow band, like a ribbon laid on the black of the shadowed, shabby buildings.

'Appalling,' Maltby muttered.

'I kind of like it.'

'You can't.'

'A lot of the real swells actually live here—the counts and the princes and the old nobility—cheek by jowl with what you call the peasants. It's the middle class who hate the Lower City.'

'I must be middle-class, then.'

They walked to the Via Toledo and then along it, and instead of rushing to the consulate Maltby stopped with Denton at a baker's and had coffee and a pastry. He took out his notebook and went over the details of the Palazzo Minerva yet again. Denton wondered if the young man would ever get over his fear of doing everything wrong.

F̶ra Geraldo's chapel had re-charged his interest—changed his idea of the old man and therefore of his death. He felt as if he had peeled flesh and bone off the would-be monk's skull and looked into a heaving mass of maggots, into a hell of self-hatred and self-torment. Still, he understood no more of the death, although the symbolic violence of the chapel suggested that real violence might well have tracked the old man. He knew that he would try to make sense of it now—an old story with him, a sense of obligation to the unsolved.

He must make an effort to find the truth, Gianaculo and Donati and Maltby to the contrary. There was still 'no evidence' of unnatural death, at least not physical evidence; therefore, he must go elsewhere.

Would the old man speak to him from the Other Side? The idea was laughable without being comical. It made him want to spit.

Would a medium tell him how Fra Geraldo had died? Not a cat's chance. But—just in case. That was always the catch. *Just in case.* He had promised to visit Fanning's favourite medium, anyway.

❧ ❧ ❧

Fanning was staying at the Canterbury, a very English hotel on the Vomero that was designed to make the travelling Briton feel that he or she had come no farther than the city for which it was named. He had been there longer than Denton had been in the Casa Gialla, conducting his 'scientific research' on the Neapolitan mediums.

'I'm glad you've come to your senses about seeing Signora Palladino at last. She's absolutely the one,' he said to Denton after they had settled themselves in the hotel's writing room with tea. 'Not showy enough for your book, I suppose, but *authentic*. You *must* see her. And see her *first*. The rest are—' He sighed.

'You've tested her—*really* tested her?' Denton had done a lot of reading about spiritualism; he knew the lingo, at least, although he was a great sceptic.

'I'm happy to say that I approached Signora Palladino in the most objective kind of manner. I have observed her in three séances and interviewed her at some depth, and she is *absolutely* genuine. If yours were to be a more, mm, *scholarly* work, you would want to make her its *centrepiece*.'

'That would throw the thing out of balance.'

'She's the *only* one for whom I can vouch wholeheartedly. Some of the others are rather questionable. Not outright charlatans, I wouldn't say that—well, I wouldn't say it of all of them, although between you and me, far too many of them *are* charlatans and nothing else—but they are rather more *theatrical* than Palladino. One can't vouch for them scientifically. More your sort of thing, I suppose.' Fanning sat with his feet together on the figured carpet and his hands on his knees, as if he were a boy being examined by an adult. He held out a plate. 'They do butties rather well here.'

Denton took one, said, 'I don't want to sit through a lot of claptrap about flying banjos and spook voices. And I don't want to be told that my uncle's name is Charlie and he has a wart on his nose.'

Fanning chuckled and slapped his knees and poured them more tea. 'Let me warn you of something. All the Naples mediums know each other. Contrary to what you might think, they exchange information about clients and potential clients. You'd be astonished at what complete dossiers they build of even the most personal information. One has to be particularly careful—you've been in the press, and you're a well-known man, and they will all *seem* to be able to summon the most remarkable information about you, whether in automatic writing or slate writing or spirit voices. It's quite discouraging from a scientific point of view.' He rubbed his thumb and fingertips together to rid them of butter. 'We investigators are *very* sceptical men. But you won't be investigating, so I shan't bore you with details of controls and all that.'

Denton had read enough to know how the mediums operated. He said, 'But I want to know what I'm getting into. You insist that the séances be done in full light?'

'Oh, no.' Fanning tittered. 'Near-darkness is a condition of communication with the Other Side.'

'Why is that?'

'It simply *is*. If one's examining water vapour, one can't ask that it be done in a dry atmosphere.'

Denton didn't get that but let it pass. 'The medium still has her—or his—"cabinet" behind him? Or her?'

'Yes, yes, they require it.'

'But as I understand it, the "cabinet's" just a curtained-off space in the corner of a room. Nothing magical about it.'

'We're not talking about "magic," Mr Denton.'

'Well, I mean… There's nothing to suggest a telegraph line to the Other Side, or anything. It doesn't have special equipment, like a, mmm, spectral Marconi antenna or something.'

Fanning sighed. 'The *medium* is the "spectral antenna". Actually, the metaphor is quite a good one. We investigators are, as it were, testing a kind of Marconi apparatus. Does it really transmit to a distant spot? Does it really receive? Hmmm?'

'So the medium insists on having the "cabinet", although it gives her a convenient place to hide things—'

'Things are not hidden! We examine the cabinet with the utmost care before the séance. We examine each object in there!'

'The mandolin or ukulele or whatever it is.'

'Often a toy trumpet or a guitar, yes.'

'But you don't put anybody inside the cabinet during the séance.'

'No more than we'd put somebody inside the cage while trying to trap a tiger.'

Denton didn't see the aptness of that, either, so he tapped his lip and said, 'And you don't bolt the medium's little table to the floor or nail her sleeves to the table or anything like that.'

'Of course we don't!' Fanning looked shocked. 'The medium must be in a receptive state to enter the trance! How in the world could she be receptive if she were being treated like a convict?'

'Um. So then during the séance the dead "come through"?'

Fanning looked prim. 'Not in the way I think you mean. I have never personally sat in on a séance in which there were *scientifically verified* spirit voices. It's why I have such high hopes for you and Fra Geraldo—you and he have an affinity, and you can verify anything he says.' He made a little smile with closed lips. 'I am not to be taken in by *show*. One hears of—I have myself seen "spirit plasma," "ectoplasm," et cetera, but they were easily shown to be sham. I remain uncommitted on the subject of ectoplasm. I want to *test* ectoplasm under laboratory conditions. Not that I'm saying it doesn't exist, mind you—only that it isn't *proven*.' His little smile widened. 'I astonish you with my scepticism, don't I?'

'When you say that Signora Palladino's genuine, what proof do you have of her contact with the Other Side?'

'Physical manifestation.' Fanning put his cup and saucer aside. 'I wish I had my notes, but they've been sent to London for our report. Physical manifestation—sounds and the degravitation of an object.' He held up a finger. 'But a caveat concerning

Mrs Palladino! She *will* cheat if you let her. I think it's a game with her. She's absolutely genuine, as I said, but—she's like a child. She's a peasant. She'll cheat for the fun in it.'

'"Physical manifestations." The mandolin gets played?'

'A parlour guitar, actually. Yes. The guitar was *struck*.'

'Inside the cabinet.'

'Just so.'

'And when you say "degravitation", you mean—?'

'The movement of the table. Up and down, yes.'

'Signora Palladino couldn't have done it?'

'Impossible.'

It all sounded to Denton like a stage trick. Still, he said, 'I don't understand why dead folks—spirits, whatever—play the guitar and bump a table up and down. I mean, if they have a message, surely there are better ways to send it than whacking guitar strings.'

Fanning looked severe. 'Mr Denton! Do you think that if it were easy to penetrate the barrier between our world and the Other Side, the spirits would bother with tables and guitars? Of course they would not! But think of what they must do—the gulf between us and them that they must cross—the near-impossibility of it! The wonder is not that they don't play Sir Arthur Sullivan on the piano, but that they cause the guitar string to vibrate at all! Think of it— entities without physical existence crossing the barrier between life and death and managing to move a metal string in our world! It is a phenomenal accomplishment! It is as if we aimed a Marconi apparatus at the farthest star and received an answer!'

Denton scowled at Fanning's enthusiastic face. 'It'll be no good to either of us if Fra Geraldo decides to communicate by guitar.'

'If that is what he chooses to do at first, that is what we must let him do!' Fanning thrust a finger out, seemed to threaten Denton's great nose with it. 'The spirits are as delicate as maidens! They come veiled. You must understand: they are as fearful of us as we of them. Don't you see, don't you *see*, the monumental difficulty of sending a single word across the gulf of death?'

Denton said that he saw it, and he didn't see how hitting a guitar was any easier; and he said that he doubted such a thing would happen with him there, and he was tired, and he'd been chasing ghost stories for weeks, and he was frankly pretty sick of the gulf of death.

'I hope this doesn't mean that once again you will fail to sit with Signora Palladino.'

Denton sighed. 'No—no. I'm determined to do it now. No matter how—No matter what happens.' He wasn't going to tell Fanning about the chapel.

'I shall write to her at once, then. Tomorrow? You can make it tomorrow?'

'I suppose—I work every day—'

Fanning waved a hand at work. 'This is preeminent. I shall of course accompany you. She trusts me; it will help if I am there. Did I say she is a peasant? She is—a complete peasant. It is the source of her super-normal energy, I think—unspoiled by reason. She can be difficult. A bit of a *prima donna*. She's said she'll do no more séances, but she'll do one for me.' He got up and shook Denton's hand. 'You've made a wise decision.'

Denton sent for his hat and coat. While he was waiting, he said, 'I'll tell you the truth before we go into this: I want to know how Fra Geraldo died. That's my interest. And of course the medium, for my book.'

Fanning said sharply, 'There's some doubt about how he died? Mmm. That might sharpen his appetite for communicating.' He rubbed his hands. 'We shall see!'

Denton's things came, and he said as he pulled on his overcoat, 'Do you suppose they wear clothes like these on the Other Side, or does everybody stand around in the altogether? I ask because the people who tell me they see ghosts always seem to see them in their Sunday best. Or maybe their burial duds. It's the way they know they're from another century— the clothes.'

Fanning looked disgusted. It was not, he said, a question that could be scientifically answered.

The Haunted Martyr

Back in the Casa Gialla, he straightened things on his desk, glanced at a book, then stood and looked out into the vast court-yard. He felt like a sap for agreeing to go to Signora Palladino—it violated everything he believed about facts, death, the nature of the world. He snorted in disgust.

A woman was doing something to a grape vine on an arbour made of peeled saplings; she had to stand on tiptoe to reach it, frowning in concentration. Their own unweeded garden was empty, the gate closed; baking was over until the next holiday. He thought how much he would prefer to be writing about the life he saw out this window. It seemed a far more interesting subject than spooks and mediums: intersecting lives, contrasting levels of society—one of the old women who now and then appeared at a balcony, he'd been told, was a countess, living out her days in one room of what had been the family *palazzo*—love affairs and petty revenges—

Then he heard a voice say the most ominous words the meditative state can hear: 'Am I interrupting?' It was Harriet Guttmann, the comic sidekick of Janet's Lucy; she was, for once, serious, also unaccountably tentative for a normally boisterous young woman. 'I'm interrupting something, aren't I.' She made two syllables of 'aren't'.

'No, no—come in—' He didn't mean it, but what else could he say? He hadn't even known she was in the house. If she was, Lucy was. He was surprised that she had come to his workroom, surprised she even knew he existed away from Janet.

She more or less collapsed into his one armchair. 'I need a rest from being cheerful. They're going to *talk*. That means Luce will be all weepy and Janet will be Holy Mother.' She gave him a look that said that she wanted a response: she wanted his approval. *Good God, she's come to make friends.* She had a look of conspiracy, of the sort of secret-sharing small boys do with their first dirty jokes. In an instant, he guessed that she disliked Janet and knew that he disliked Lucy; she was looking for somebody to gossip with. She said, 'Oh, I'm just letting off steam. But those two don't *need* me. In fact they don't want me.' She grinned at him. 'Hard lines sometimes, being the homely one.'

It was the first time he'd been alone with her, the first time in fact he'd ever noticed her except as a rather painful emanation of Lucy. 'You're being kind of hard on yourself, aren't you?' he said in what he hoped was a kindly voice.

'Every pretty girl has a homely friend to set her off, Mr Denton. Lucy really is my dearest friend and I love her, but I know what I am.' She gave him the simplest smile he'd yet seen on her plump face. 'I'm so afraid I'm going to lose her to some Dago *lizard*. I think her mother's gone insane.' She scowled at him. 'Her mother's told Lucy she *has* to marry this *marchese* so she, Lucy's mother, I mean, can call herself the mother of an Italian title. Did I say he's proposed and Mama has accepted?'

This was news to Denton. 'Lucy seems young to marry.'

'Lucy's a child, a sweet, wonderful, loving child! And it isn't as if it's just anybody, it's a young man who looks to me as if he wears corsets and will make her life miserable. He'd shut her up in some horrible *palazzo* and have mistresses and affairs and be just *awful* to her!' Her look of conspiracy got more intense. Her voice had dropped almost to a whisper.

'Maybe he's a nice young man, regardless.' Denton wondered if Janet knew, if so what she had said. Janet was badly disposed to marriage on principle.

'He isn't a nice young man! He's a money-grubber who looks like Uriah Heep dipped in olive oil. And he's as poor as a church mouse, Janet says, and she got it from her friends at the university, who say he's one of the ungilded youth who hang around the *pensiones* and the theatres hoping to snag an heiress. Lucy told that to her mother, and she said Lucy shouldn't listen to gossip.'

'Janet doesn't gossip.'

'She says the *marchese*'s family are stony broke. They still live in an old *palazzo* near the Porta Capuana and can't afford to move to Monte di Dio like the rich ones.'

'Tell Lucy's mother that.'

She shook her shoulders and settled her well-padded rump deeper in the chair. 'I know my Lucy. She's one of the pampered jades of Asia—she'll do what her mother says because all her life she's been swaddled and coddled and taught not to say boo to a goose, and in the end she'll marry him and she'll be *miserable*. She thinks she's miserable now, but she doesn't know. She's just playacting at being miserable. Rather delicious to be the endangered heroine, but she doesn't *know*.'

Denton sat in his desk chair. 'You're a smart young woman.'

'I know a hawk from a handsaw. It's one of the benefits of being homely—what Emerson calls "compensation"—that you develop an eye and an ear.'

'And a brain?'

'Well, don't tell anybody. If they thought I had a brain, they'd have to get a new me from the factory.' She sighed. A little later, she left, and he thought, *Why aren't I writing a novel about the living—like Harriet Guttmann?* That evening, he asked Janet why she hadn't told him that Lucy Newcombe was being traded for a title. Janet said she thought he was too busy to care. And anyway, what business was it of his?

✿ ✿ ✿

Eusapia Palladino was a short, wide, busty woman with an immense pile of hair on her head and a masculine-looking face with a strong chin. The ghost of a moustache shadowed her upper lip. She looked nothing like Janet's Assunta, who was almost handsome, but he thought they had the same physicality, the same projection of a body whose physical strength was part sexual force. His late friend Hench-Rose would have called her a *jolie laide*, even if now a bit over the hill and going to fat.

Signora Palladino lived in a cluttered apartment near San Domenica Maggiore with a husband who seemed to vanish even as he was introducing himself. Work-worn, conventional looking, he seemed more depressed at having landed in the middle class, thanks to his wife, than pleased.

She had answered her own door; now, she served them a glass of not very good sweet wine, some bits of fried dough she said she had made herself.

'*Ecco.*' She had a harsh voice, almost crow-like. '"Texas Jack".' She laughed.

'You know who I am.'

She looked at DiNapoli, whom he'd brought to translate. Fanning was distressed; he said that she spoke some English and DiNapoli wasn't needed. However, from the beginning it looked as if she was going to be staunchly Italian today. When DiNapoli had translated what Denton had said, she laughed again, said something that DiNapoli translated as 'All the mediums know you'. He remembered what Fanning had said about their trading information. Did this mean that she would fabricate messages about Fra Geraldo? He said, 'But you don't know me.'

She shrugged, made a face. At that moment, she seemed rather jolly. 'I do and I don't.'

Fanning said, 'He would like to have a séance.'

She looked at him. She shook her head.

'He's willing to pay, of course.'

She burst out with something. DiNapoli said, 'She says she don't take money no more. She says any medium that takes money is a fake; they're all fakes, they all cheat. She don't cheat, so she don't take money.'

Denton leaned forward to cut Fanning off. 'But the "researchers" who have examined you say that—forgive me, signora—sometimes you do cheat.'

She began to count off on her fingers. 'Ox-ford! Pa-ris! *Un' isola privata! La Germania. Encora e encora e encora—!*'

DiNapoli murmured, 'She says all these places—'

'I understood. Those are all places where the investigators have tried to expose her.'

Palladino turned on Fanning and began to scold.

'She says he held her hands and her feet; he put his hands on her legs and—I ain't making this up, she said it—he felt her up.

He made her undress down to her, um, what you call that? Like a sort of nightgown women wear?'

'A shift? They don't wear them any more, do they?'

'Somet'ing, anyway. Other guys, they took her here in Napoli to some big hotel, put her in a room she never seen before, made her do her stuff there. She's sick of them and him and he can...she talks pretty rough, Mist' Denton. She talks kind of dirty. Anyways, she says never again. She been examined enough for the rest of her life.'

'Ask her how she's going to live if she isn't going to take money?'

'She says she got enough now.'

'So being a medium is over?' Denton felt relieved.

The woman leaned towards him. Her eyes had almost closed—in anger, he saw now. That harsh voice screamed at him. It was a voice he had heard a hundred times, the loud, hoarse shout of the Naples streets. He understood some of it: *'mai finite, mai, non è scelto mio, è un' possessione!'* It never ends; it isn't my choice; it is a possession! She screamed something more.

DiNapoli said, 'A demon, she says she got a demon.'

'Being a medium?'

She switched to English. 'You t'ink I choose it? You t'ink is all fake? Yes, I do tricks—I get...what is word—?' She screeched at DiNapoli, got his answer. 'Bor-èd! I make my fun at *idiote* who sit here and piss in their trousers when they cannot comprehend! *But it was never all tricks!* Some t'ings—' She waved her hands, wild-eyed now. 'I no do them. They do themselves! You think I *piacermi* to lose my own self?'

'You said "possession". Is this King John?' King John was the name of her 'spirit guide', according to Fanning.

'King-a John!' She all but spat. 'A name, so? People they want a name. I say, "King-a-John". *Idiote!*'

'But if you are "possessed", what possesses you?'

'Un demone.'

He looked at DiNapoli. 'A demon?'

She grasped his arm. '*Si, si,* a demon. He take me—he fill me up—' She grinned, the sexual joke clear.

'In the trance?'

'*Si.* In the trance, is very naughty sometimes.' She had shifted violently from the anger of a moment before to a sudden coarse flirtatiousness. 'I wake, I am—feel it in—' She looked at DiNapoli. '*C'è il demone nella fessa.*' She laughed.

DiNapoli blushed. 'She says, unh—she gets horny.'

Denton looked at her. She was smiling now, her head leaned on her left hand, her upper arm stretched along the back of her chair. She raised her other hand and, palm down, twitched a clitoral index finger at him.

Denton found that he was blushing, too.

She raised the hand and pointed at Denton and laughed, the laughter now deep and thick with sex. She looked at Fanning and put her tongue out, then at DiNapoli and muttered something that Denton couldn't follow.

'She says, send me and the other guy away, she show you. *Dio mio.*'

Then, as abruptly as she had plunged into the mood, she was out of it again. She stood suddenly and walked to a door, yanked it open. 'Come,' she said. '*Come.*' When Fanning stood, she said, 'Not you! You go fuck!' She waved Denton on, didn't object when he waved DiNapoli forward. She murmured something to DiNapoli and laughed. Fanning was still protesting when they walked out.

Beyond was an almost bare room. Several straight chairs and a small table were the only furniture. One corner had been curtained off with black cashmere.

The door closed behind DiNapoli. She had not come in with them. Denton heard her coarse shout top Fanning's murmurs, then footsteps. A door slammed. 'What's she up to?'

'She's crazy.'

'Well—strange, anyway—' He went to the black curtain. It was split in the middle, enclosed a triangle of space no more than three feet on a side. He parted the halves, looked in to see a round table hardly big enough to hold a good-sized vase, and, on the floor, a mandolin and a child's toy trumpet. 'The usual crap.' DiNapoli looked in. 'This is the magic stuff?'

'It isn't magic. Or so says the authority.'

He heard the door open and turned. Signora Palladino came in. She had done something with her hair, otherwise looked the same. He caught a hint of powerful perfume. She said, 'Sit.'

They pulled two of the chairs up to the table. She told them where to sit, then put a chair for herself at the end of the table with her back to the curtain. Denton sat on her left, DiNapoli on her right. She grasped a hand of each—tight in Denton's case—and put a foot under the feet of each. 'Control!' she said, and cackled. It was the word the psychic researchers used when they thought they had the medium's hands and feet neutralised.

'You're going to do a séance?' Denton said. 'You said you'd given them up.'

'Shhhhh!'

The room wasn't even dark: curtains had been pulled across the only window, but light spilled in at top and bottom, and Denton could clearly see both DiNapoli and Signora Palladino. When he leaned sideways to look under the table, there was plenty of light down there to see their feet, big male shoes with her smaller female ones on top of the toecaps.

'Ascolta!' Listen.

They waited. Two muffled knocks sounded, apparently from the table. Denton opened his mouth to speak; she shook her head. Three more knocks came. Then another. Then she laughed. 'Trick!' She cackled. 'Fake!' She took her hand away from his and raised it. 'Guarda!' Look. She moved her hand slowly in the air, and the black curtain billowed towards her as if a wind had blown it from behind.

She snickered. 'Trick. All tricks!' She took his hand again. 'Now—no trick—' She stared into the space between them. Her fingers moved within his hand. Her foot moved on his. A spasm passed over her shoulders, then another. She grunted. Her breathing got slower, then faster again, almost panting, with a hoarse vocalisation under it. Then it slowed again; her hands jerked; her foot pressed down on his almost painfully, as if she were becoming heavier, and then she groaned loudly and, her breathing now slower than a sleeper's, her head lolled to her right as she sank back in the chair.

Denton looked at DiNapoli. He was, probably unconsciously, drawing back from her as he might have done if she had been having an epileptic seizure; his face showed distaste and concern at the same time.

Her mouth opened. A deep male voice came from it. *'Fredo.'* Denton knew the word: cold.

'Fredo. Inverno.' Cold. Winter.

Then there was a silence of, he thought, at least two minutes. The time seemed long in the silent, rather stuffy room, long enough for him to become bored. He heard horses' hooves from outside and the distant sound of a bell. A fly buzzed against the window and stopped. It was as if they had been there all day, would have to stay there forever.

'Mi dispiace.' I am displeased.

Then, after a silence of perhaps another minute, the deep voice said, *'L'amore non c'è.'* Love—love what?

He waited. DiNapoli met his eyes, looked away; his face now seemed resentful, as if he had been made to watch something offensive. Suddenly, the deep voice from Palladino's mouth said severely, as if reprimanding them, *'Il poliziotto fa la commedia!'* Denton made nothing of it—somebody was making a comedy?

After another even longer silence, Palladino groaned and began to move in her chair, the movements not ones that women were supposed to make in public. Her hips and her torso squirmed; her thighs seemed to suffer electric shocks, and her feet left their shoes and moved against the men's shins; her heels drummed on the floor; once, a foot kicked the underside of the table. Her breathing became a hoarse panting again and then she woke, gripped their hands very hard, and looked around as if she didn't know where she was.

'*Eh?*' She looked at Denton and smiled. '*Il mio demone.*' She pulled herself up in the chair and took her hands away. '*Finito. Cosa' succedi?*'

DiNapoli appealed to Denton, then murmured to her in Neapolitan. When DiNapoli was done, she made a contemptuous sound and stood. 'You see? You like? What happens—I talk? King John comes?'

'Your voice was different. Like a man's.'

'*Ecco.*' She shrugged. 'Now you go. I am—*stanca*—ti-red? Yes. So. Some tricks, some real. You decide.' She made a shooing gesture with one hand. 'Go.' She meant it. The flirtatiousness was gone.

At the outer door, her husband was standing with a hand already on the big iron handle. When Denton stopped by him and began to reach into his coat for money, he heard her voice from the far end of the little corridor that ran through the rooms. 'No! No money! *Nien' di dinari, Carlo!*'

He opened the door, then closed it firmly behind them. Fanning, red-faced, was waiting in the corridor. Denton looked at him and shrugged.

Out on the narrow street, Denton said to DiNapoli, 'What do you think?'

'I t'ink she got some mouth on her.'

'What happened?' Fanning said angrily. Denton waved a hand at him, kept his eyes on DiNapoli. 'She said something to you I didn't follow—something about *fessa*—What's *fessa*?'

'It's, unh, what a lady got down, um—you know, where her legs—um—'

'Ah, that word! Is it Italian or Neapolitan?'

'Neapolitan. Naples peoples say "*'N la fessa della mama*" when they get mad.'

Denton understood that well enough.

Fanning demanded again to know what had happened. Denton gave it to him in brutal outline. Fanning seemed now like an interloper. Because she had shut him out, Denton thought. She was a woman of considerable power. Fanning said in a strangled voice, 'King John spoke? To *you*? Was it a message from the old man?' Denton didn't answer.

They walked a little and came out on the broader Via Anticaglia, which still ran along the route of the Greek *decumani* that had dominated the original city. Denton said to DiNapoli, 'What did you think of her "tricks"?'

'I t'ink maybe it's the husband. Or maybe a midget comes in under her skirts and sneaks around and knocks the table and gets in the black curtain. Or she got somet'ing she hits the table wit' up her sleeves or somewhere. Also in her hair—she got big enough hair to hide a kid.'

'What about the voice?'

DiNapoli looked embarrassed. 'That scared me.'

'It said something about the police.'

'The police!' Fanning cried.

'I don' like that kinda t'ing.'

'What did it mean?'

'I don' wanna... You mind, I don't talk about it?'

'Why?' Denton looked aside at him. 'You think it was meant for you!'

DiNapoli shrugged. Denton said, laughing, 'I thought it was about...something else.'

'What about the police?' Fanning insisted. 'What did he say about the police?'

'It wasn't for you, Fanning. I don't think she's going to call the *questura* on you because you copped a feel.'

'I dunno, Mist' Denton... The voice said *Il poliziotto fa la commedia*—the cop is doing a play. Like on the stage.' DiNapoli shook his head. 'She got all those tricks, and then she brung through a voice, and... Some t'ings you can't explain, you know?'

DiNapoli scuttled off on his own. His cynicism apparently wouldn't swallow a spirit voice that had seemed to speak to him about himself.

Denton pressed on towards home. He had forgotten Fanning.

'I demand to know what King John said!' Fanning burst out, beside him again.

Startled, Denton growled, 'Forget King John.'

'He came through! You must tell me! You must!'

'He didn't "come through". There's nothing to come through. For God's sake, Fanning. Drop it.'

'The spirit voice spoke! I demand to know what he said!'

'You heard DiNapoli.'

'But there was more. Wasn't there? There was more, I'm sure of it. Tell me!'

Denton stopped. He put a hand on Fanning's chest just below the knot of his necktie. 'There is no Other Side. There are no spirit voices. There is no communication with the dead.' He put his face close to Fanning's and said slowly, 'Grow up!'

He turned and strode away. This time, Fanning didn't come with him.

H̲e told Janet about the séance and Fanning and Palladino. She only half listened, he thought, although she perked up when he got to Palladino and *la fessa* and the demon. Most of it, however, rather bored her. He said, 'I hate myself for doing crap like that.'

'It's for your book.'

He hesitated. 'When she was in her trance, the masculine voice said, *"L'amore non c'è."*'

She frowned, translating it silently. '"There is no love"?'

'Is that it? More like "Love isn't in it", I think.'

'In what?'

He looked at her unhappily. He didn't remind her of what Fanning had said about the mediums' trading information: was it common knowledge that he and Janet were not equally in love? 'It also said something about the police.'

'They have police on the other side? Dear me.'

KENNETH CAMERON

'Something like "The policeman is playing". DiNapoli wouldn't talk about it. He thought it was meant for him because he's had trouble with the police.'

'Ah, but the other one about love, you thought that was for you.' She shook her head. 'Don't, Denton.'

He sighed. 'I don't seem to be able to help it.'

She took a cigarette from a little box he'd given her, a product of his prowls through the antiquities shops. 'It's all fakery, you know. If the dead wanted to communicate with us, why in the name of God would they speak in mysteries? Surely if Fra Geraldo wanted to tell you that there wasn't enough love in the world or some copper was on the take, he'd come right out and say so.'

'Fanning says getting through "the veil" is a monumental task. He has an answer for everything.'

'I'm sure it would be, if there were a veil and something that wanted to get through it.' She struck a Crown Vesta and held up the flame as if to demand his attention. 'On the other hand, the living put themselves fairly clearly: Assunta has asked me how she can stop having babies.' She shook her head. 'It was laughable, the two of us trying to talk about the body and reproduction. In Italian. But it's tragic, too. Apparently that ratty little husband of hers jumps her every night. She already has two kids.' She looked bereft. 'She can't afford a Dutch cap, of course. I told her about *la douche*, but she'll have to hide everything from him. Christ, men are awful!'

He fidgeted. He said, 'The medium's messages could be significant, even though they're fake.'

'For God's sake! I'm talking about somebody's life and you're talking about music-hall tricks!' She threw the cigarette into the fireplace. 'That's the way they do it! They invent "messages" that could mean anything. And why in the world would you suppose the dead know things that the living don't?'

'I wasn't thinking of that. I meant somebody could have put her up to it. Fanning says the mediums trade information all the time.'

'Fanning sounds a complete fool.' She got another cigarette. 'So do you, as a matter of fact. Why would anybody put gibberish in a medium's mouth?'

He muttered something about the book and left her. He went to a shop in the Galleria and bought a folding Kodak and a contraption that focused gas light with a parabolic mirror—he still wanted a record of Fra Geraldo's 'chapel'. The shop clerk tried to sell him magnesium flash powder and a thing that looked like a push-broom to fire it in, but Denton had seen one of those in use and had thought it was only one short step removed from setting off black-powder explosives. He didn't want to blow Fra Geraldo's chapel to smithereens; he simply wanted to take some pictures of it.

When he got back, she was dressing to go out. She said, 'I listened to you about your séance and the old man and the chapel full of tortures. The least you could do is listen to me about problems like Lucy and Assunta.'

'I do listen to you. You never said anything about Lucy.'

'Yes, but you don't—! I wish you were a woman sometimes; you'd understand.'

'Janet, I can't say things I don't believe. Or don't understand! I'm sorry about Assunta, but there are thousands of Assuntas here, old before their time, dead too soon from childbearing, slaves to their husbands. I know about it. But I can't do anything about it!'

'I see that.' She pulled a strap over a bare shoulder, looked at him. 'It isn't your fault. But that doesn't help.' She turned her back. 'As for Lucy, you've made it perfectly clear you don't like her.'

A maid brought in the mail. There was a stiff note from Fanning, saying that he'd decided to return to England and he regretted Denton's 'ignorant scepticism'. All in all, Denton thought it was the best news he'd get that day. Still, not wanting Janet to leave without his having done something to explain himself, he said, 'I've never had a chance to like Lucy. She seems a kid to me. But if I can help somehow, of course I will.'

She was putting on a hat. She eyed him with a hat-pin in her mouth. She said around it, 'I may hold you to that.' She took the pin out and put it through the hat and her hair without being able to see what she was doing. 'Promise?'

'Of course.'

She kissed him. 'She is a child, there's no getting around it. But—that mother of hers!'

❀ ❀ ❀

He got DiNapoli to take him to a locksmith—'somebody, you know, local, and not too inquisitive'—who worked in a *basso* a half-dozen streets away. The white-haired, bent man looked at the wax impression of the key to Fra Geraldo's chapel and asked a few questions (Were the two sides of the key the same? Was it a new lock? Not an American one, he hoped, by which Denton thought he meant a Yale). Of course he could make such a key. Today? Two *lire*. Tomorrow? One *lira*.

He went to the Palazzo Minerva next day, the folding camera and the key in his overcoat pocket and the lighting contraption under his arm. The *portiere* produced the keys when a *lira* was waved at him. He stared at the equipment and Denton said, '*La luce.*' When nothing dawned on the man's face, Denton said, '*Per l'evidenza.*'

'*Ah! L'evidenza!*'

Denton wondered if he was guilty of impersonating a policeman, remembered Palladino's murky statement about a policeman playing a comedy. Or had she—he, King John— meant somebody playing at being a policeman? Anyway, it was all nonsense; there was no King John.

He crossed to the big door and slipped inside. It was as if he were entering a just-opened tomb; the closed doors might have led to chambers where papyri lay.

In the chapel, he used his flash-light to fit rubber tubing over the gas nozzle of a lamp and dragged the little work table and then the stool into position in front of the first of the paintings. The camera went on the work table, the ball of softened wax helping to hold it in place; the contraption went on the stool, below and in front of it. He lit all the lamps, hoping that even their feeble glow would help.

He took five rolls of film, four of them of the paintings at different exposures up to as long as thirty seconds, as the shop assistant had advised, one each of some of the sculptures. He wished that he had brought more film: some urge made him want to photograph everything, as if it might vanish soon. He thought of this even while he saw the flaking paint and the mildew and, behind the sculptures, the dark brown stains left in the winters by cluster flies. Time's messages.

❀ ❀ ❀

The photographic prints of Fra Geraldo's chapel came back and were examined and put into a drawer. The carving of *Michele 'l ubriacon'* sat on his mantel. He studied both the carving and the photographs with a magnifier as if he expected them to speak, but they did not, or if they did, he didn't understand the language.

He worked. He went to other mediums, not for enlightenment but for usable stories. Walking back along the seafront from visiting one of them (one of Fanning's charlatans, as it turned out), he overtook Maltby, who was barely strolling, his hands joined behind him and his hat pushed low over his eyes. When Denton passed, he looked over and then said, 'Oh, Denton!'

'Mm, Maltby. I didn't recognise you from the back.'

Maltby looked at something off to the side and said, 'I wanted to talk to you about that peculiar room in the Palazzo Minerva, but they sent me away.'

'Where? Who sent you?'

'The consulate sent me away. Bari, to observe the naval manoeuvres. I know as much about naval manoeuvres as I do about playing the bagpipes. I explained that to them and they said it wouldn't matter, I was just an extra man because the

Italians expected a lot of show from us. The naval attaché was the real observer; I was just there to fill up an empty dinner suit and chat up the admirals' wives, which was fine if they spoke English, but they didn't. I was two days at sea. Desperately sick. Never even saw the Italian navy—rained the whole time, couldn't see the other end of the boat. I've just got back.' Maltby scowled. 'Desk was piled a foot deep, on the top a memorandum from my immediate superior saying the new Lord Easleigh's sending out a private detective and what was I doing about it? As if I'd been here the whole time! And he knows I was away! Most unfair.'

'A detective? What the hell for?' Denton felt personally offended, didn't understand why.

'It's all supposed to be my fault. Something I said in my report—simply was honest—you recommended it, straightforward, factual—something I'd said about you having doubts about the police report. It wasn't my fault!' He put his head down again and put his hands behind his back as if he were about to resume walking. 'I'm thinking of giving it all up.'

Denton realised again how very young Maltby was. He said, 'The first days in a job are always the toughest.' He was thinking, however, about a detective and the new Lord Easleigh and why his doubts had been taken so seriously. 'I don't get the detective.'

It was as if Maltby hadn't heard him. 'It was my mother had her heart set on me being a diplomat. My father'd as soon I was a policeman, which was what I rather fancied. Too late for that now, of course. She saw herself visiting me in Delhi. At the durbar with the Viceroy—that sort of thing. Not very realistic.' He pursed his mouth and stared at the pavement. 'Truth is, I'm no good at it. Might as well have drowned at sea, for all the use I was in Bari.' He sighed. 'I suppose I'd better introduce this detective to you.'

'Not on my account.'

'Oh, well, if you take that line—'

'No, no—'

Denton felt obscurely guilty, as if it were he who had sent Maltby off to the naval manoeuvres. No, it was because he'd disliked Maltby at first and been offhand with him, and then he had rather liked him, and now he found himself feeling sorry for him. Denton said, 'By all means introduce him. I suppose you mean he should quiz me about my doubts.' Maltby shook his head. 'That room! I couldn't get it out of my head, all the time on that infernal navy boat.' And then he said one of those things that made Denton like him for his odd sensitivity. 'I don't want to have to show it to the detective. Isn't that peculiar?'

The palm trees were blowing in the wind from the sea, their fronds rattling. The sky was a uniform, neutral grey, as if sun, stars, moon, even the blue, had been taken away. Close in, three fishing boats were bobbing in the chop, bow and then stern and bow again, as if they were hinged in the middle. Farther out, the bay merged with the sky. The palms rattled; the sea came in with a slap-slap-slap on the stones; the birds wheeled and made noises like squeaky carts. Maltby said. 'He'll be here next week.'

'I'll go with you when you show him the chapel, if you like.'

Maltby shook his hand. 'You go ahead now,' he said, as if he were the older man. 'You walk faster than I do. Lot to think about. Don't mind me. In the dumps. Bad company, I know. You trot along.'

Denton did. He walked quickly towards the Pizzofalcone, the Falcon's Beak, that cliff down which the Monte di Dio declines into the sea, and that resembled his own nose in profile. The air smelled of the water and of fish. The sky seemed to have turned everything grey, the buildings, the gulls, the palms. Denton paused where the Via Partenope begins and looked back; well behind him, Maltby's heavy figure was trudging along, beyond his right shoulder the pale shape of the island of Ischia, floating like a lump of rotting ice on the grey water. Denton thought of the terrible, to them at least, suffering of the young, most of it self-created: of his own at that age—married too young, in deep debt too young, trying to break the virgin crust of Iowa with an old plough and one horse—which he had survived, but with his youth pared away as if by a knife. So it would be with Maltby and

Janet's Lucy, he thought, who would outgrow their sufferings but sacrifice the sensitivity that made them possible.

❀ ❀ ❀

Janet was wearing one of her Pre-Raphaelite gowns; she was seated partly sideways on a Recamier couch that had come from the upstairs, her left arm over the high end, her long body and legs slanting down it, one foot on the floor, the other crossed over. The dress showed off her body. They had recovered from their argument about… What had it been about? Lucy and Assunta and his account of the visit to Palladino. He said, 'Let's go to bed.'

She shook her head. 'I've the guest in the house.'

'Oh, well… There are all sorts of things other people do.' He raised an eyebrow. 'Frank Harris told me about somebody who had himself tied up and was then told dirty stories by his mistress. It's all they ever did together.'

'A little hard on her. Well, that's the usual way, isn't it? You hear about most such stuff in a whorehouse. A lot of Englishmen have desires about the nursery—well-to-do ones, I mean—being spanked and having the girl dress up as Nurse, and so on. It suggests a real lack of a sense of humour.' She kissed his cheek. 'Unlike you. You have a healthy sexual appetite and enjoy it all even when you know it looks ridiculous. Plus you know how to give pleasure as well as take it.' She kissed him again. 'Thank God.' She leaned back. 'I shall give you a promissory note. Tell me about your day.'

'Today's medium was rubbish. Told me all sorts of things about myself he could have dug out of any newspaper. They must think I'm a complete idiot. Maybe I am.' He threw himself into a chair. 'I met Maltby on the way back. He's still brooding on Fra Geraldo's chapel.'

'Like you.'

'Well, it's a weird place.'

She said, 'Children as torturers, yes.'

'I think it has to be sexual.'

'That's new! Did you tell Maltby?'

'What else would it be? All that stuff about suffering martyrs, saints having their teeth pulled and their breasts cut off, it's all sexual, isn't it?'

'So Fra Geraldo was *sexually* fixed on children, was he? And they become torturers and he whips himself? And he talks to you about atoning? Not too difficult to see what he was about if you buy that, I suppose. A bit Yellow Book for your Mr Maltby, however. You make him seem a straightforward meat-and-potatoes man—lie down and spread your legs, dear.'

'You think he molested boys or he only thought about it?'

'Maltby? Oh, Fra Geraldo. Whipping himself could suggest either one. Or was he simply ashamed of dirty thoughts from long ago? That would be very English.'

'But it was children's *ghosts* he told me about. He'd *killed* children?'

'Rather a reach.'

'Well, you don't get ghosts without deaths.'

'But an adult is a dead child—no? Or a child who's gone away years ago is dead to you, isn't it? "Ghost" may be poetic licence. Or if you destroy a child's innocence, I suppose you could say that you've killed the child. And it becomes a ghost?'

He grunted. She lit a cigarette. She said, 'To spend forty years painting yourself as the victim of torture isn't entirely sane. And he did paint himself as the victim, isn't that it? Not pictures of himself buggering little boys behind the church organ.'

'The victim of a temptation that was also a torture? So it was all in his head?'

'Or in his paintbrush. It's like you when you're writing—you haven't done the awful things you write about, but they come out anyway; they're in there in some form, but they don't have to have really happened to cause you to spend a year or two writing a book. Maybe the poor man simply lusted for some child and has been punishing himself for it with his brush ever since.'

'Or he murdered two of them and buried them in the walls of the Palazzo Minerva. He was a damned good plasterer. And carpenter. And he liked to hide things. Even his paintings are sort of now-you-see-it-now-you-don't—proportions a little off, the far distance not quite right because it's so sharp. The angel on the ceiling may be sympathetic or it may be completely *blasé*.' He sighed. 'You've seen my photographs.' He inhaled heavily. 'Fra Geraldo's successor's sending out a private detective, Maltby says.'

'Whatever for?'

'Apparently to make sure the death was an accident. Sounds as if he's a little unsteady on his pins—maybe thinks his title's shaky. "Uneasy lies the head." God knows what the dick will tell him when he's seen that chapel. "Your predecessor was crazy as a loon."'

'And you, my dear, take the private detective as a personal insult. Am I right?'

They were silent. She smoked; he got up and took one of her cigarettes and lit it, standing at the window of the red room and looking down into the sere gardens. He said, 'Maybe an English private detective will find something I didn't. Maybe it needs fresh eyes.'

'You'll show him the chapel?'

He made a face. He got up and prowled the room. He said, 'I'm sick of the dead and spooks and mediums. They're all rubbish, no matter what DiNapoli says. Fra Geraldo was real. So is that chapel. Yes, I'll show it to the detective, or Maltby will. I can't pretend it's mine simply because I found it. Although I guess that's the way I feel.' When she didn't respond, he kissed her; she turned her cheek; he went out. His mind growled and grumbled like a sick stomach. Everything was in turmoil.

L'amore non c'è. Il poliziotto fa la commedia. Temptation as torture...

CHAPTER

15

When Maltby brought the English detective to the Casa Gialla, Rosa, the less frightened of the housemaids, appeared at Denton's workroom door with Maltby's calling card. He was downstairs; should he be allowed to come up? Denton was shuffling through papers, trying to find a note he'd written to himself, his workday nominally over.

'*Ma certo, certo!*' He thought the girl was an idiot, although mostly she was ignorant and frightened. She fled.

Several minutes later, Maltby and a cheerful-looking man in a rather loud plaid lounge suit came into the small sitting room. Maltby made the introductions, hardly needing to say that the stranger was the private detective. He looked as English as his suit and smiled while Maltby introduced him, then gave Denton a crushing handshake.

'Mr Denton, a real pleasure, sir.'

His name was Joseph Cherry. He seemed large, not tall but wide. He filled his gaudy suit quite amply, showing a good gut below the waistcoat and a big, round, red face above it, marked with a straight hairbrush moustache. His hands were like bunches of carrots, very hairy on the back; he had a roll of fat under his chin and another at the back of his neck. His eyes, however, were amused and sharp. He had one of those accents that bewildered Denton, this one presumably Birmingham because the next thing he said was that he was Brummie and far from home.

They sat and Denton had tea and sherry brought in. They made some meaningless talk about weather and London in winter and Cherry's struggles at the railway station when he arrived in Naples, which he turned into a comic tale of escape from brigands. When the tea was poured, the detective took a cup and blew on it and sipped. 'I used to be Sergeant Cherry,' he said. 'Birmingham coppers. Thought there was a good thing in the private detective line, tried it, found I was right.' He laughed, slapped a hand to his belly. 'It suits me.'

Maltby said gloomily, 'Mr Cherry's here to look at the stairs in the Palazzo Minerva.'

Cherry laughed again. 'Good deal more than the stairs, Mr Maltby!' He turned his amused, bright eyes on Denton to say something but then swung them over to the doorway. 'There's a dog if ever I saw one,' he said.

Sophie, Janet's now half-grown mutt from the Solfatara, wagged her way into the room. Denton called her name, meaning to put her out, but she sniffed Maltby's cuffs and at once went to Cherry and sniffed him up to the knee and then sat between his feet and let her head be scratched. 'She smells my dog,' Cherry said.

'I can put her out.'

'Not a bit of it. I like dogs.' And dogs seemed to like Cherry. Shortly, Sophie had her head on his knee and was making small half-whimpers that ended in a kind of growl. Cherry smiled. 'Some dogs purr like a cat, they do.' He put his face down towards the dog. 'Don't you—eh? Don't you, doggy? And what's your name? Well, you're a fine-looking doggy, yes, oh, yes, what a doggy, what a fine doggy…' He glanced up and, embarrassed, straightened. 'I'm a bit saft on dogs.'

Maltby looked severe. 'As I was saying, Mr Cherry's come to look at the stairs in the Palazzo Minerva.'

'And as I was saying, more than stairs, Mr Maltby.' Cherry nodded to Denton. 'I suggested we start with the stairs because of Mr Denton's comment as reported by you. Now, Mr Denton, I haven't come all this way to disagree with you—matter of fact, I think your observations were rightly made. I agree that there should ought to of been blood on those stairs. 'Course, strange things happen, as I'm sure you'll agree, but under the circumstances of an old man going arse over teacup as it were down a flight of stairs, I agree that there should ought to of been blood. We'll see.'

'Been kind of a long time,' Denton said.

Cherry put a finger beside his rather large nose and winked. 'There's more than one way to skin a cat, sir. What the human eye couldn't see before Christmas, modern science may reveal before Easter.' He chuckled and helped himself to a *biscotto*. 'Maltby here tells me there's ferocious little light on those stairs. I'll see to fixing that.'

'There's gas. You could use limelight, I suppose.'

'A battery light, Mr Denton—the newest thing. I'll go to limelight if I have to, but I think the battery light will do. Blind you at ten paces, it will.' He selected another *biscotto*, sampled it, eyed it, and said, 'I was a little surprised that the Naples police chaps didn't avail themselves of same. However, things are done differently here, I'm sure.' He sniffed and looked into the middle distance, an expression of complete innocence on his face.

Maltby squirmed. 'I told him that the Naples people were in my view pretty cursory and that the *Carabinieri* chap thought there was a lack of evidence.'

Cherry held up a large finger. 'Which is not to say there's no reason for us not to look things over again, Mr Maltby.' He tilted his head towards Denton. 'His Lordship wants everything above board. Now, you'll say he's young—seventeen is young to become a peer out of the blue, as it were—but he's no babbie, and I credit him for a lot of horse sense, if I can put it that way. I think he said to himself, "Here I am, all of a sudden in the House of Lords, I owe it to the man who came before to make sure his death was above board." And I say more power to him, although it's true I benefit from him saying it because I'm the one he's hired to do it—and I get a European holiday into the bargain.' He laughed.

'What exactly does the young lord think may have happened?'

'To be perfectly honest, he's afraid there might have been criminal involvement. We read things in the English newspapers, Mr Denton, would make your hair stand on its end. The criminal element in Italy is said to be fee-rocious.'

'The Camorra?'

Cherry shot a finger towards him, as if to say he'd got it in one.

'What would an old man who thought he was a monk have to do with the Camorra?'

'I don't think the young lord's thought that through, Mr Denton. But he knows his own mind! If there's been skulduggery or low dealing, he wants to know!'

'But there's no evidence of skulduggery or low dealing.'

'I believe, in fact, Mr Denton, that you're the one whose doubts put this bee in His Lordship's bonnet.'

'But nothing's come of it. No offence, Mr Cherry, but do you really expect to find something that everybody else has missed?'

Cherry laughed. He was sharing another *biscotto* with the dog, who was now half in his lap. 'Between you and me and the gatepost, no. I don't pretend to be one iota better than the average copper, even an Eye-talian one. What I hope to do is be able to set His new Lordship's mind at ease that everything's above board and the old man died of a very unfortunate accident.'

'So you intend to go over the whole house.'

'I do. Young Maltby tells me there's a remarkable room that you discovered, sir; I shall certainly want to see that. And the old man's lodging, and so on. I suppose you'll think I'm the nosy chap from Brum, but I assure you I mean to do this quick and neat and climb on my horse and ride home. And I apologise in advance for seeming to question what anybody did in this sad business. It's just a matter of making assurance doubly sure, as the Bard puts it.'

'You don't need to apologise for anything, Mr Cherry. What can I do?'

'You can come with me to the old fellow's house and show me about. Shan't ask more than that of you, I promise. And I'll be as quick as I can once we're there, so long as it squares with me doing a good job.' He grinned. 'Or as good as I'm able.'

'Whenever you like.'

'Maltby says you work mornings. I think an afternoon should do it. Tomorrow's too soon, I expect.'

Denton, actually rather eager to see the detective at work, said that tomorrow afternoon, late, would do. Cherry gave the dog a final scratching of affection, calling it Sweetie and Sweet Doggie, then stood and brushed dog hairs off his trousers; and they moved towards the door. Seeing them out, Denton learned that Cherry was staying at the Bristol, that he was afraid of getting a fatal disease while in Naples, and that he thought he would like to go to Pompeii in the morning 'so as to have something to tell my grown daughter when I'm home again'. Maltby looked pained but dutifully went away with the detective, who seemed to be his personal responsibility while he was in Naples.

❀ ❀ ❀

He told Janet about it while she opened the afternoon mail. He had got to a description of Sophie's behaviour, and, more to the point, Cherry's—'He's one of those men who can make absolute fools of themselves over an animal and not be embarrassed; he'd never make such noises to a woman in public—or even in private, I'll bet—' and he heard a sound from her like a muted sob.

He looked up at her. She had tears in her eyes. She was holding a letter, and the tears were starting shiny snail-tracks down her cheeks.

'Janet.'

She looked at him. 'Ruth Castle has cancer of the breast. She's known for two years and done nothing because she was afraid they'd cut her breasts off. She's dying.' She began to weep. 'She's so vain! She's so damned vain!'

Then suddenly she was out of her chair and throwing letters out of her way. 'I must go to London!'

'Janet—!'

She was at the door to the inner room. She paused, looked back at him, her expression angry, cheeks wet. 'I've been very good for weeks, Denton. It's your turn.'

He felt as if he'd been kicked. By 'very good', he knew, she meant that the time in Naples had been a pretence. A holiday. Now, she meant, she was going back to reality. Without him. And that was what he was supposed to be 'very good' about.

She was on her way to London that evening. Her last words to him at the railway station were, 'Don't let Lucy's life be ruined by her mother. With me not here... For me, Denton, if not for her.'

The next day was again warm, promising spring. Denton walked blindly to the Palazzo Minerva, stunned by her sudden leaving. He feared that she had been relieved to go—that she was tired of him. He thought unworthy thoughts: Had she been glad to go? Had she got Ruth Castle to write her the letter so she would have a reason for going? And that meanest of questions: was there somebody else?

He was surprised to find Inspector Gianaculo standing in a pool of late-winter sunshine, a crooked, slender cigar in his left hand. Gianaculo said something in English, Denton something in Italian; they found that they could communicate with a mixture of languages, Denton's Italian now the better of the two. When Denton said that he was surprised to find Gianaculo there, the fat man looked away and puffed on his cigar and said that the English consulate had informed the *questura* of the detective's visit as a courtesy. As Fra Geraldo's death had started as his case, he thought he would see what was going on. He shrugged. A minute later, Maltby arrived with Joseph Cherry. Then, to Denton's surprise, Capitano Donati sauntered in, gorgeous in a pale grey suit with a faintly lavender waistcoat, a thin cigar cocked in one side of his mouth like a battle flag. Maltby scowled and muttered to Denton, 'I felt I had to tell the *Carabinieri* about the detective, too. I'd no idea *he'd* come.'

The Palazzo Minerva felt as cold as if it had boxed winter up inside. Cherry shuddered as he stood at the foot of the stairs and said that it was as cold as your stepmother's breath. He looked upward. 'That's a mean staircase to come down head first!' He was carrying a small, scuffed suitcase, whose latches he now opened. 'My laboratory,' he said. He grinned. 'Customs gave me a little hell about it. Thought I might be an anarchist.' He chuckled, then looked at Gianaculo. 'I hope somebody will explain this to the inspector.'

Donati was happy to serve as translator. Gianaculo, who had watched the case being opened, was peering in at nested bottles and tins, not unlike a picnic set, and, on the inside of the lid, several sizes of brushes, two dental picks, and a scalpel, held in place by leather straps. Donati said to Gianaculo, *'Roba investigatoria. Non è cretino, questo tipo.'*

'What's that?' Maltby demanded.

Denton murmured, 'He said it's investigative stuff.'

Maltby looked suspiciously at Donati. Cherry, on the other hand, was holding up several items and saying in rather loud, carefully enunciated English, 'Brush! Scal-pel! Plas-ter of Pa-ris!' He took a wooden box that Maltby had been carrying for him, opened it, and took out the biggest flash-light that Denton had ever seen. Most of it was battery, he thought—a cube as big as a block of ice, above it on a metal hoop the lamp. Thin red wires led to the battery's terminals; on the lamp's front was a fresnel lens of the sort that was used on dark lanterns. 'Light!' Cherry said.

'La luce, si.' Gianaculo nodded. He finished his cigar and muttered in Italian to Denton, 'Am I deaf, he thinks?'

Cherry seemed to have decided to talk mostly to Donati. 'Tell the inspector that most of the stuff is just common sense— like here's a bit of soapy water to clean off surfaces and the like; that there's turps to wipe down paint or anything varnished. This here's a solution reacts with sulphur, useful to show up gunpowder of the old sort, black powder; useless on the new so-called smokeless stuff, unfortunately. Magnet for picking bits of metal out of dust.'

'The inspector wants to know if all British policemen carry such a case.'

Cherry laughed. 'I didn't put this together till after I left the force. And then it was done because of stuff I read and the like. Birmingham police weren't very daring—didn't accept finger-prints yet, though Scotland Yard do—and the French, o' course. But little by little, little by little.'

'The inspector wants to know when you're going to show us something.'

'Oh, now, sir!' Cherry looked unhappy. 'I may not find anything! But remember—negative evidence is evidence. I often have to remind folk of that. *Negative evidence is evidence.* When you've found nothing, Mr Denton, you've found something!'

Donati found that hard to translate, but when he'd got it, Gianaculo laughed and clapped Cherry on the shoulder and said, '*D'accordo—d'accordo!*'

Cherry, who was readying his lamp, smiled a little feebly. He raised the lamp. 'I'm going to look for blood.' He took a magnifying glass from the case, then put it in front of one eye and said to them, '"The game's afoot, Watson."' He laughed as if embarrassed, shrugged. Gianaculo looked at Denton for an explanation; he tried to translate, decided that humour was even harder to force through the veil of language than messages from the Other Side through the veil of death. He gave it up.

Cherry had shone his light on the bottom stair. He handed the light to Maltby and bent over. 'This dark spot at the bottom is of course the blood that everybody's noticed. We *know* that's blood. As for the rest...' He scraped up a little of the long-dried blood with the scalpel and put it into a glass tube of the sort that doctors carried pills in, then wrote on a paper label and dropped it into a rack in the suitcase. 'If I need more than six of those, I'm in trouble. That's all the bottles I've got.'

Cherry began to make his way up the staircase, slow step by slow step. He paused on the fourth, studied the stair with the magnifier, scraped with the scalpel and dropped the result into another phial, then drew a pencil line around the scraped square inch. He did the same on the seventh stair and again on one of the balusters that supported the handrail above. At the top, he went over the entire landing, pointing out to Maltby each place where he wanted light. Maltby sighed, groaned, rolled his eyes.

'E alora,' Gianaculo said while Cherry was down on his knees on the landing, 'cosa a trovato? Di sangue?'

Denton said that yes, he thought that Cherry had found blood in three places. 'Miracolo,' the inspector said in the voice of a man who does not believe in miracles.

Cherry came down the stairs with his head down, an index finger shoved against his moustache. He took off his overcoat and threw it down on his suitcase, followed it with his hat. 'Hot,' he said. He took the light from Maltby and turned it off.

'You found blood,' Denton said.

Cherry nodded. 'Three places. But damned little of it.'

Denton translated for the inspector: 'How do you know it's blood?'

Cherry said, 'I know blood when I see it. But I'll show you—there's a test, it isn't what you'd call reliable, because it reacts with some other stuff, too, but it *does* react with blood.' He selected a small bottle from his case, checked the label, and dipped in a sable brush from his collection in it. He stood over the large stain at the bottom of the stair. 'We know this is the real thing, right?' He knelt and painted a small area of the stain with the clear liquid from the bottle. A strong odour of acetic acid rose up. Where he had put the liquid, the surface bubbled and a pink froth appeared. 'That's what blood does.'

They crowded in and bent close. The inspector growled something that Denton did his best to put into English: 'What's the liquid?'

'Blessed if I know. Something and something in glacial acetic acid, if you know what that is. I don't do the chemistry, I'm sorry; I just do what works.' He went up several steps and sat next to the first place he had scraped and circled. They followed him. He shone his light and then dipped the brush and passed it over the small area. The old oak turned darker. A few bubbles rose along the lines of the grain, their surface shining faintly pink.

'*Del sangue,*' Gianaculo said. Blood.

Cherry gave the same demonstration at the other two places. Denton was most interested in the stain on the baluster, which was apparently a smear rather than drops or a puddle, suggesting a collision at speed. He looked up and down the staircase.

Cherry was watching him. He said, 'I make it that he fell as much sideways as down at the first, sir.'

'Yes, I can see that.' Denton pointed. 'Off the landing, maybe tried to catch himself—hit that post or whatever it is, which is as solid as a rock—then went on down. Face first?'

'No way to be sure, but I'd think he was on his back when he hit the bottom, if that's when the poor old chap broke his neck. Wouldn't have done it if he'd been face down, would he?'

'But he could have broken his neck when he hit the upright, the first thing he hit.'

'He could of, but Maltby reported that the contusion was on his forehead. I'm not a medico; I guess you could break your neck that way, but...' Cherry, who had been sitting on the step, got up, his knees cracking, the last few inches done slowly and as if painfully. 'We'll never know, sir.'

'You're satisfied, then?'

'I'm *not* satisfied, no, sir. I told you right off the reel, I agreed with you that there should ought to of been more blood.'

'You've found more blood.'

'Ye-e-e-s, but...'

As they went back down the stairs, Gianaculo murmured in Denton's ear, *'E di piu, è per certo il sangue umano?'* Denton thought it a good question: was it certain that what Cherry had found was human blood?

'I don't have a test for that, sir,' Cherry said. He was putting his tools away. 'If there is one, *I* don't know of it, which isn't saying much.'

'We should have found that blood ourselves,' Donati said.

'Don't go blaming yourself. There isn't enough light on those stairs to see the shine on your own shoes. No wonder the old chap fell. Any of us'd have missed it, sir. You didn't have a dark lantern or an electric torch that night, did you?'

Denton said, 'I had a pocket flash. Pretty feeble.'

'Well, then.' Cherry straightened, with the same noises and apparent pain. 'Let's have a look at the rest of the house.' He stared down at his suitcase. 'I'm not very pleased with the work *I've* done here, I don't mind saying. I'd hoped to find something that would tie it all up nicely and allow His Lordship to say, "Good, that's done, then." And I haven't.'

'I'd say you did pretty well.'

Cherry grunted. '"Pretty well's" a bit of a frost, isn't it?' He led the way upstairs. Denton followed along; partway up, he almost collided with Donati, who was pattering down and who smiled and whispered, 'WC,' and went on. Up Denton went. The rest were in Fra Geraldo's room, watching Cherry turn his light here and there. He got down on hands and knees to look under the bed.

Maltby looked around and whispered to Denton, 'Where's that poof Donati?'

'Call of nature.'

Maltby frowned, suddenly went past Denton and out the door. This, too, seemed to be a call of nature, but Denton thought it odd enough that he turned away from Cherry's performance and went as far as the door; then, hearing voices, he went to the balustrade overlooking the stairwell. He had stood here to look down at Gianaculo and the doctor the night that the old man had died. Now, looking down, he saw a foreshortened Donati standing next to Cherry's investigative kit, and, a step above him, Maltby. Maltby, his voice breaking like an adolescent's, said, 'That was not the act of a gentleman, sir!'

Denton heard Donati chuckle. The *capitano* stepped up and around Maltby, patting him on the shoulder as he did so, and, still chuckling, he came up the stairs, his cigar at a pleased angle. Denton pulled back but didn't try to hide, and Donati, coming to the top of the stairs, saw him and smiled and shrugged. '*La giovenezza,*' he said. He went into the room.

Denton moved to the top of the stairs. Maltby was coming up slowly, his face red. He looked up. He hissed, 'That Dago bastard stole some of the detective's chemical! And one of his phials!' He was breathing heavily when he came even with Denton. 'I've a mind to report him for theft.'

'I wouldn't.'

Maltby's eyes swivelled to Denton's face. Denton said, 'He's a captain of the *Carabinieri*. At the worst, he's hoping to steal a secret that the Birmingham police have and he doesn't. He's very scientific.'

'But it isn't *right!*'

'But it's very sensible. You catch more flies with sugar than with vinegar, Maltby—tell him it was a good idea and ask him to share the results with you. Might stand you in good stead if you become a copper.'

❀ ❀ ❀

Denton let Maltby take the others through the rooms. Four were too many for most of them because of their size; most were empty; none, except for the one in which the old man had slept, had any reason to interest them. Denton had prowled the corridor, then gone on upstairs, looking into rooms he had seen before, stopping finally in the one that had the dilapidated chair. It was at least a place to sit down.

The chair happened to be placed where it gave a pleasant view over rooftops towards the green heights above the coastal plain. The sun was slanting in over the house and brightening the walls facing him; it picked out the green of plants that somebody had put out on a roof. In the evening in summer, he thought, the last of the sunlight would just enter the room, then die, and the sky would darken to lavender and purple, showing pink and then orange before it went to brass and darkness. He closed his eyes, thinking of it.

He could hear the others coming up the stairs. He dreaded showing them the chapel. He wanted to escape it, to make some excuse. He felt he was betraying the old man. He pinched the bridge of his nose and then pressed on his eyeballs. It was no good trying to postpone it.

He tapped on the broad arm of the old chair. Head in hand, he looked down at it. For a chair without upholstery, it was quite comfortable. He picked at a gouge in the old wood's surface, then traced another, ran his finger around a large ink stain. The shape was not unlike South America. He had thought once of going to South America when he had been looking for a place to start over.

'Well, *this* is where you've been hiding.' It was Maltby. Gianaculo and Cherry were pushing into the doorway behind him.

'I was almost asleep. Are you ready to see the chapel?'

'Just doing these last rooms…' Cherry had come in, was looking around. 'No closets, no cupboards, not much to look into, is there?' He looked out of the window. 'They don't mind making a crazy quilt of their rooftops, do they?'

They looked quickly into the other rooms and Denton led the way to the last door. Without any show, he opened the armoire and moved the upper moulding.

'Bring your light.'

In that darkness, Cherry's big lamp was dazzling—blinding, as he had said. It moved over the nearby carving, picked out the work table, rested on a painting. Denton pushed past Cherry and stepped down into the chapel so as to light a gas lamp, then went from lamp to lamp until all six were lit.

'I'll leave you to it,' he said.

'You're not going to explain it?' Maltby cried.

'I think it explains itself.'

Gianaculo was still standing in the armoire, staring into the chapel. 'You knew this room?'

'I was in it before.'

Gianaculo was looking at something in the chapel, not at Denton. *'Ma che sorpresa!'*

'It was—' He didn't know the word for 'concealed'. He said, *'Segreto.'*

'Maybe, signore, you…need…warn me. Before.'

'The room was his—for praying. His *chiesa.'*

'Chiesa strana. But he was…*uomo strano.* He was—' Gianaculo shook his head and pushed past Denton into the chapel.

Denton went back to the room with the chair. He felt as if he had done something ugly. He again put his head in his hand and studied the chair-arm, and it was only after he had been sitting there like that for several minutes that he came out of his funk and asked himself why an antique chair should have a recent-looking stain of black ink on it. And it wasn't only the one stain: there were smaller ones on the arm, too, and at least one other on the chair's seat below the arm. He strained to that side. He could see black spots of ink on the floor.

He sat up. A chair in a room. The only chair in any room in the upper storeys of the house. Left by accident, or placed there because of…the view? Or the light? The chair stood where light from the window fell abundantly on the arm at which he had been looking. As if—

Denton took out his notebook and his fountain pen and pretended to write. Yes, the light was good. Yes, he was sitting properly to put the notebook where a spill could easily have stained the chair arm. Yes, this would have been a fine place to come late in the day to sit and to be quiet and perhaps to write.

Denton put away the notebook and the pen.

To write? They had found nothing in the house to suggest that Fra Geraldo had kept any records. Certainly, he had found nothing in the chapel, unless there was a secret hiding place in there. But if he had wanted to write in this room, would the old man have gone to the trouble of hiding his writing materials in the chapel, bringing them here and taking them back every time he wanted to write? Denton thought not. The chapel was... saturated. It was complete, over-complete; it was sufficient unto itself several times over. This room, on the other hand, was spare, insufficient, deliberately colourless. The chapel was a place in which to pursue madness. This was a place in which to pursue sanity. A place of darkness and a place of light.

He looked around the room. There was nothing, of course. He walked around the walls. He looked out of the window— nothing either above or below it in which to have hidden anything. He went to the door and looked at the room. There was nothing.

Except, of course, the chair.

He had finally to tip the chair on its back to find it. He knew Fra Geraldo's skill now, however, and so he knew that the smoothness, the slight darkening on the hand-planed underside of the seat, had been made by fingers, and pressure there now depressed the false bottom and allowed the board to tilt down to reveal, nested in their own compartments, two steel-nibbed pens, a bottle of black ink, and a ledger.

He stared at the ledger for seconds. He was reluctant to touch it. Janet had insisted to him that people had a right to their secrets; what they hide should be allowed to stay hidden. And to die with them. Yet—

He took the ledger out and closed the false bottom. He tilted the chair upright. Sat in it.

The ledger was one of those old ones that was tall and narrow and had been bound in three-quarter soft leather, the front and back mostly in marbled paper. The spine said only 'Ledger' and '1860'. Yet when he opened it at random, he saw a date in the year 1888, and the last entry—only two-thirds through the book, for Fra Geraldo had written little—was in December 1903: 'They have come back, their shrill voices. The imps. I will go mad.' It had been written three days before the old man had visited Denton to ask for his help.

On the first page, he had written, '11 June 1860. In this book, I mean to write of my depravity and the salvation I hope to find, for it is written that even the worst of us can be saved if only he repent. Gerald Sommers.'

Denton put his finger under the page to turn it, and he heard a voice calling his name.

'Mr Denton—sir! Are you there?'

Denton had time only to push the ledger inside his suit jacket and to stand, trying to hold his overcoat over his arm so as to hide the book. He started for the doorway as Cherry, red-faced, appeared in it.

'I was just coming out to, mmm, go to the WC downstairs.'

Cherry was shaking his head. 'That room! That room, sir! He was fair yampy, wasn't he, the old man!'

'I think he was unhappy, yes.'

'That's one way of putting it. I don't know what I'll tell His Lordship.'

Denton was edging towards the door. 'Tell him the truth. The truth is always best, Mr Cherry—excuse me—we'll talk in a minute—'

He fled down the stairs.

❀ ❀ ❀

They gathered outside in what was now the late-afternoon gloom of the courtyard, the surrounding buildings casting it into deep shadow. Maltby locked the huge door and, coming close to Denton, said, 'I'm done with this, thank God. Once I put Sergeant Buzzfuzz on the train tomorrow, I'm free of the entire mess.'

'Who's going to take care of the house?'

'Apparently His Lordship has passed it into the hands of an estate agent. I suppose I wasn't good enough for him.' He settled himself, like a wet bird shaking off water. 'I'm through with the whole business, anyway. I've given in my notice.'

'To the consulate?'

Maltby nodded. 'I don't know how I'll tell my mother. Perhaps I won't.' He strode away towards the *portiere*'s cage.

Cherry was standing by himself, his suitcase in both hands as if the added weight of the old man's dried blood were pulling him down. Gianaculo and Donati stood together, neither seeming comfortable, as if they were performing for each other.

Il poliziotto fa la commedia.

But which *poliziotto*? And why?

'We were speaking of the chapel,' Gianaculo said in Italian. 'What a madman!' Donati looked amused, his head turned upward, a thin stream of cigar smoke escaping his mouth.

Denton looked at Cherry. 'What do you think? The inspector says the old man was mad.'

Cherry shook his head. He looked almost ill, as if perhaps he had gone up and down too many stairs. 'Like stepping into a nightmare. I don't say he was mad—not *mad*—but he was certainly...' He shook his head again.

'Yes, I suppose he was.'

Denton led them out to the street.

The only benefit of Janet's leaving was that Lucy Newcombe no longer visited. Harriet Guttmann had given up coming, too. Denton took Janet's last words to him to mean that he was to 'do something' for Lucy only if asked; if she didn't appear, she couldn't ask.

He rattled around the emptiness of the Casa Gialla, had at least plenty of leisure to study the ledger from the Palazzo Minerva.

Fra Geraldo's ledger was written in a hand so small that Denton needed a magnifying glass, thinking of Cherry's 'The game's afoot, Watson!' as he ferreted one out of a still-unpacked box. Most of the writing was in English, but he found Greek, as well, the symbols recognisable to him as Greek but meaningless; now and then, a few words of Latin came in, as well. Latin was as opaque to him as Greek, but he did have a Latin-English dictionary, useful until then only in trying to puzzle out people like Havelock Ellis. He was able to decipher one word, *pecavi*— I sinned. It occurred often in the early pages, shortened then to P. In his first years in Naples, Gerald Sommers seemed to have sinned a good deal.

He had kept his record of sins and salvation by years, except for his first three years in Naples, which were summarised in a narrative of several pages at the beginning. That story was pretty much what Denton had expected, although presented with a self-flagellating contempt that he found overdone. In essence, what that early narrative said was that Sommers had used the English church choir as a means to recruit boys from the poorest families of Naples, and that, when he had found a suitable one— suitable to his tastes and his sexual needs, that is—he took the child over. He had succeeded with two of them, whom he called only E and M, because one was a foundling and one was a street kid—no families to buy off. Three other boys had had families and had made trouble; something from those scandals must have got back to the rector, because Sommers had been asked to leave the church. He had done so and had taken E and M with him, buying the Palazzo Minerva as a home. He had envisioned it as a resident singing school of the medieval sort, full of boys whom he could, Denton assumed, seduce or buy as he chose, although he seemed not to have gone beyond the two.

Sommers had been brutal about what he had done to E and M. The brutality may have been partly self-titillation, for once he had crossed through an account of sodomising M and inked in a thick, black P; another time, he had done the same to a description of E's buttocks and his hairless scrotum and had written *I am a miserable sinner, I am past forgiveness*. Some of his pleasures had amounted to torture, some to the sexual initiation of a child into things that might have destroyed a childhood. It was a vicious account, made not poignant but bitter by Denton's awareness of the chapel. Could a man who painted himself as a tormented martyr, even as a dying Christ, be said to have repented?

After seven months in the Palazzo Minerva, the two boys had tried to kill Sommers. They had almost succeeded. They had crept into his bedroom at night with a hammer and a sculptor's maul and beaten him unconscious; probably thinking him dead, they had run away. Sommers hadn't dared to go to the police. Patched up by his doctor, he had gone back to his house to find a man claiming to be E's father. There had apparently been a long wrangle, because E had been living on the streets, but finally Sommers had found it easiest to accept his tale and buy him off: he underwrote the family's emigration—E included—to Argentina. The other boy, the one he called M, did not come back—not then, at any rate.

Sommers had begun his record of repentance immediately after E and his family (if such they were; he had least attached himself to them) had left Naples. He recorded great hopes and abrupt falls, a recurring pattern of repentance and insistent sensuality. The letter P appeared often in those first years—for encounters with street boys, for experiments with prostitutes, for flirtations with other men. A code of sexual symbols appeared on the pages; Denton, knowing the real limitations on sex, thought he knew which meant oral, which anal, which vaginal. A stem with five lines shooting from it evaded him for several pages; then he realised it was a schematic of a hand. Masturbation.

It appeared after Sommers saw M on the street, M now an apparently homeless *scugnizzo* who ran off when he recognised his former singing master. The encounter brought some of Sommers' behaviour vividly back to him—P and the hand symbol.

He was painting portraits in those years, although his real life seemed to have been in his sexuality. In 1867, he wrote his first entry in Greek. A period of great hope followed, then the first return of P, but not of the hand. 'My thoughts, my thoughts!' he wrote. 'My thoughts are as evil as my deeds!' In 1870, he wrote another few sentences in Greek. Soon after, he started the chapel and gave up his career as a painter—'I lay my art at the feet of the dying Christ; I will become a penitent and a flagellant.' Fra Geraldo was born.

Denton rubbed his eyes and gave up for the night, wanting to talk to Janet about it, missing her clear, sometimes brutal mind. Missing her.

Next morning, he copied out the two Greek passages, a painful procedure because he had no sense of the symbols he was copying, and took them to a bookseller who dealt in classics. The man said he read Greek, *ma certo*, of course. In his forties, grey-haired where he was not balding, he wore thick eyeglasses that he pushed up on his forehead when he needed to see anything more than an arm's length away. He read Denton's copying, his nose almost touching the paper; he tut-tutted and wrinkled up his nose each time he found a mistake, but he was able to translate. The first said, *I cut the devil from my body with a sharp knife, first tying tight a string at the root; there was not so much blood as I feared. I went after to the physician for—*

The bookseller pushed his glasses up and looked at Denton. 'It says "for burning the devil's feet". What does this mean?'

'I think it means he cut off his *cazzo* and had the wound cauterised.'

The bookseller, who had told Denton that he believed himself a man of the world because he dealt also in pornography, paled and looked as if he might be sick. Denton asked him to translate the second passage.

He read it, his lips moving, and looked sicker. 'He went to his doctor to have his testicles cut off.' He pushed his glasses up again and almost shouted at Denton, 'What kind of book is this?'

Denton took the piece of paper from his fingers. 'An unhappy one.'

❁ ❁ ❁

Maltby and Cherry turned up at his house at midday. Cherry was leaving that evening, and Maltby apparently could think of nothing to do with him. Denton, annoyed but at the same time amused, took them off to a hole-in-the-wall that sold freshly baked *pizza* and various quick, fried things. Maltby was appalled, Cherry fearful; Denton said it was one of his favourite places and the food wouldn't poison them.

'They use *garlic*,' Cherry said.

'Absolutely.'

'Smelly stuff.'

'Live wildly, Mr Cherry—it's your only chance!'

Cherry ordered a slice of *pizza margherita* and stared at it when it came. 'If my daughter could see me now,' he murmured. Still, he ate it and pronounced it 'quite tasty, in its way' and drank a glass of decent red and said he preferred beer. Maltby sat with his arms folded and sulked.

They walked along the Rettifilo, Denton and Cherry side by side, Maltby dragging behind. Cherry asked about Denton's ghosts, seemed disappointed that he hadn't found any real ones. 'And the mediums and spirits?'

'All rubbish.' Denton thought of Palladino and the voice that had said, *L'amore non c'è*. 'Almost all, anyway.'

They passed the Galleria and crossed to the Caffè Gambrinus, where Denton offered them dessert. Both men perked up. Maltby's sulks seemed to retreat in the face of something filled with sweetened cheese; Cherry, his chin dripping chocolate, beamed.

They went down to the seafront and walked along by the Porto Militare. Ahead, Denton could see DiNapoli's friend the photographer, his huge camera like a fat insect on spindly legs. He was about to suggest that Maltby and Cherry have their pictures taken when Cherry banged himself on the chest with a hand and said, 'Damn me, I've lost my pocketbook!'

They both turned to him. Had his pocket been picked? When had he last had it? Cherry shut his eyes. 'By glory, I don't think I brought it. I think it's in the hotel. I've got to go back to my hotel.'

Denton said, 'It won't run away if it's there.'

'I have to know—you know how it is. It's the uncertainty of it, isn't it.' He pumped Denton's hand. 'If we don't meet again—a great pleasure—my apologies for that long performance yesterday—but that room!—yes, goodbye, goodbye—perhaps we'll meet in England one day—' And he was off, moving very quickly for such a big man.

'Does he know the way to his hotel?' Denton said.

'God, I hope so.' Maltby frowned, like a child trying to make an ugly face. 'Good riddance.'

'Well, look on the bright side—he's probably sick of you, too.' Denton clapped him on the back and led him towards the photographer, then stopped at the appropriate spot and let Spina photograph them. Maltby said he didn't like 'show' and he didn't like such 'middle-class seaside diversions' as having one's picture taken. Still, he seemed absorbed in the photograph of himself once he saw it.

Denton said to Spina in his crude but improving Italian, 'I thought I'd have another subject for you, but he ran off.'

Spina showed his few teeth and laughed. Decades of dealing with tourists had given him a rough English. 'Some peoples not *piace* the picture.' He shrugged. '*Non import*', I got his picture before. He was wit' somebody—his son. *Di Sardegna,* I t'ink. I never forget a face, *non mai, mai.*'

'Mr Spina, he's English. He's never been in Naples before.'

Spina shrugged. 'Maybe got a brother. Or a *doppio.*' Denton got 'double', *doppio,* from the context. 'They say we all got a *doppio* someplace.' He laughed, opening his terrible mouth. 'Cuts down the *soldi*, people got *doppi*—one photo do for two.'

Denton and Maltby walked on along the waterfront. Ahead and to their right, the Porto Commerciale stretched its long piers into the bay; masts and funnels clustered along them like trees. Maltby said, 'I've made a balls of everything here.'

'You'll get over it.'

'I've blotted my copybook. I'm finished.'

'Maltby, I've had thirty years more than you to learn things. D'you think that at twenty I wasn't in the same muddle as you?'

Maltby trudged along.

'Tell you what, when we get back to my house, I'll give you a card to give a friend of mine at New Scotland Yard. Maybe he can help you get into the coppers. How would that be?'

Maltby stared out through the gathered shipping as if his own boat had just gone down with all hands. 'I doubt they'll have me.'

Presumably, Cherry got on his train and left that night. Denton stayed up late in his workroom reading Fra Geraldo's diary.

After 1870, after his self-mutilation and his castration, Sommers' *pecavi* seemed to have been entirely of the mind, although no less real for him. He admitted that he had no control over his dreams, which he described with some of the same relish as his earlier accounts of abusing E and M. The erotic dreams were his sins; the tormented ones became the paintings in the chapel.

Sommers saw M more often on the street now, the event important enough that he put an M at the top of the page when they met. After he had settled into his Fra Geraldo persona and given up painting and begun going out among the poor, he began to seek M out. M was a young man by then, apparently a petty criminal. He spat once at Sommers, another time threatened him with a knife. Still, Sommers was able to befriend him after a fashion. On 11 January 1877, he wrote, 'I have atoned!' He had managed to bring M to the Palazzo Minerva, where he had fed him and washed his feet and made some sort of apology. M had been drunk, but Sommers hadn't cared. God had seen.

Then the self-whipping began. By the mid-eighties, he was bringing M into the house to do the whipping, although never that Denton could tell into the chapel, which Sommers always called 'the upper room', surely a monstrously arrogant appropriation. M was by then a drunkard; Sommers seemed not to care. His concern was with his own repentance. However, at some time before 1890 he saw that what he had done to the child might have caused the drunkenness of the adult; he welcomed this as a new cause for self-disgust.

For it was all, in the end, self. Perhaps, Denton thought, it could never be otherwise. *My* sin, *my* redemption. As love was always part ego, so perhaps was guilt, so prayer. We are prisoners of ourselves. By 1902, Sommers seemed to be coming to that conclusion himself. The chapel was finished; he was out all day among the poorest of Naples' poor; M had become simply a recurring opportunity for penitence, a ruin drinking himself to death. Sommers now wanted to do good distinct from his own salvation. He went to see 'the Av. F' about creating a foundation to help the *basso neve* in perpetuity. He did not write down how this was to work or what money was involved, but he did say 'all my wealth', and he added, 'That this will be to the detriment of my aristocratic title—vain folly!—and my line is of no consequence: I dedicate both to GOD.'

He began to hear 'the ghosts of the boys' only towards the end of 1903. He was a man with real physical fears, thus the more courageous for going into the most dangerous parts of the city alone. But the 'ghosts' were particularly terrifying—because they were ghosts or because they were children, therefore like the imps of the chapel? He had frightened himself, debased himself with scenes of torture—as Janet had said, he had suffered torture with his brush—and now did he think those scenes were coming to life? The ghosts had manifested themselves only as sounds, but they were sounds he had recognised at once: screams, squeals, laughter, singing. As if it were 1859 again and the choirboys had become fiends.

Fra Geraldo had received two actual threats. The first had been in 1885—a cat hanged on his front door. The second had been in early 1903—a pair of human hands found nailed to the floor of his bedroom. Sommers had written, 'I fear my Heavenly Father, not men. If they murder me for doing good, they win me time out of Hell.' He did not explain who 'they' were or why they might kill him for doing good.

Denton lay on his back in the dark. What had the inspector said—'a madman'? Perhaps. But not the mere eccentric he might have been thought. Mad, if he was mad, for a good reason, and in a disturbing way. And dead for a good reason, too?

❀ ❀ ❀

He slept badly, his dreams infected by Fra Geraldo's—Denton was no stranger to guilt, himself—and was glad when daylight showed through his curtains and he could leave his bed, although he felt as if some obscene bird had perched on his back. He felt used up. He made himself coffee on his spirit stove, then as he drank it studied the photographs of the old man's chapel. *Mad.* And were the two childish torturers the two choristers, M and E? And were the paintings portraits of them, as their victim was a portrait of Gerald Sommers?

He went out to his café. The day was blustery. He turned his overcoat collar up against the chill and sat outside, glad for once to escape the other customers. The owner brought him coffee and a finger-length of bread cut off a fresh loaf. He watched the women head for the cigarette factory. He watched the donkey carts. He drank more coffee and tried not to feel as if he had been embalmed. He would have walked off then, but Maltby came running towards him from a corner of the *piazza*, then walking, then trotting again; when he got close, he was red faced, breathing hard and fanning himself with his hat, but he managed to say, 'You must come! They're tearing out the chapel!' They looked at each other. Denton knew what he meant but made no sense of it. Stupidly, he said, 'Who?'

'Workmen. Come on, come along, they're tearing it to bits. It's awful. I couldn't believe it.'

They got into a carriage. Maltby explained that he'd gone to Denton's house and the maid, for a wonder, had explained where Denton had gone. The carriage horse tried to trot up the Via Toledo but the crowds were already too thick. People were walking in the street, all of them on the way to work, none very cheerful yet. They didn't want to make way for two swells in a carriage.

'Tell me again. Who's tearing out the chapel?'

'Workmen! The estate agent! I just happened to go by—I'm cleaning out my things from the consulate today; I don't know why I went there—that room!—to say goodbye after a fashion, though you'll laugh. There they were, and people starting to gather—you know what they're like here. I was stunned. I couldn't think what to do. So I came to get you.'

The people he'd seen gathering were now a crowd. Denton from the height of the carriage could look into the courtyard over their heads. It was as if some great event was about to happen, an execution or a miracle. The crowd was thin towards the street but denser as it got closer to the Palazzo Minerva. A donkey cart stood close to the house, already piled with smashed plaster and a few pieces of wood that jutted out like broken bones. The window farthest to the right on the top storey had been removed, and men in shirtsleeves were tipping out burlap sacks of plaster and lath. Denton recognised a piece of wainscoting as it fell and landed with an explosion of grey dust. By the donkey cart, two men were wrestling over something.

Denton got down with Maltby and went into the courtyard. A workman came to the window with one of the vertical beams of the chapel; it had been ripped from the wall, still encrusted with the little carvings that now looked like branches and galls, as if it were a diseased tree. The crowd cheered. They shouted. Denton caught the word for 'give'—give it to us, as if it were theirs and he was withholding it. He grinned and took a better grip of the beam and threw it forward; it sailed out and down, just missing two women, so eager were they to be where it landed. At once, the crowd fell on it. Denton saw a stonemason's hammer raised and then heard a hatchet's chop.

'They've gone mad,' Maltby said. He was hoarse. 'They're savages.'

It was a carnival; it was a mêlée. A man stumbled away from the crowd, in his hands most of one of the small carved figures; it had been broken off at the legs. Another man tried to snatch it; there were curses. Three women were fighting over something else, one falling to her knees and hugging it to her fat breasts; the other two struck and kicked her, but she fell on whatever it was she had and they couldn't roll her over.

Denton heard the crowd roar again. Part of another beam came down. From inside, he could hear the sounds of pounding, of ripping, of nails screaming as they were pulled out of the oak.

Maltby had tears running down his cheeks. 'Why?' he said. 'Why?'

Michele 'l ubriacon' came out of the dust and scuffling. His tongue was lolling, wriggling. He seemed to be trying to do some sort of dance around the woman on the ground. It became a pantomime of finding her, astonished, trying to help her rise, suffering the rejection of his help—what sense did it make? He began to sing 'God Save the Queen' in clear British English. Some of the crowd, unable to get into the shoving masses around the two beams, watched him and laughed. Women imitated his crude dance and raised their skirts at him, and he paraded forwards and backwards, thrusting his pelvis out and almost falling.

The donkey cart moved slowly out of the courtyard, an old man in a soft hat and no coat beating the animal with a heavy stick. Another that had been waiting in the street came in; more plaster and wood came down; the air became thick with dust.

The crowd got angry because no more figures were thrown to them.

At half after eight, a slick-looking young man who Maltby said was 'the estate agent's man' came out of the Palazzo Minerva and got up on a cart and announced something that Denton couldn't understand. Two clots of well-dressed men who had been lounging back against the buildings moved forward. They all seemed to know each other. The crowd fell back for them. The slick young man pointed up at the window.

The life-sized crucifix, feet first, was being pushed out. Denton thought they were going to throw it down, but they had it tied by the ends of the crosspiece and held it suspended just below the window. The crucified Christ looked down at the crowd with a pained frown.

'Autentico!' the slick young man was shouting. 'Veramente a l'originale! Fata per gli mani del' defunto Fra Geraldo! Chi mi dare mille lire? Mille? Mille? Cinque cento?'

'Christ, it's an auction.'

'It's a damned sacrilege!'

The first bid was twenty *lire*. Denton thought of bidding but wondered where he would ever put such a piece—and why. It went for a hundred and sixty. Christ was lowered on the ropes and one of the well-dressed men tried to carry it off but needed the help of the others, who laughed at him, so Christ was leaned against the Palazzo Minerva until the auction was over. Maltby said, 'I can't stand any more.' He looked at Denton, in his face a plea for something, and, not getting it, walked away.

Then came the stations of the cross. Some of the well-dressed men wanted them to be sold in lots. Some didn't. The slick young man sold them by threes. The first lot went for sixty *lire*, and some of the well-dressed men started to drift away. He sold them one at a time, for forty, twenty, twenty, seventeen *lire*. He sold a pair for fifty and the last three for forty, then a few of the larger carvings from the beams, the grotesques and the soldiers and the Jews, in a single lot. He jumped down from the cart. Well-dressed men were going in several directions, some with a half-life-sized figure of the tortured Christ or the sorrowing Christ in his arms. Several of them who had bought nothing helped to carry the crucifix, which disappeared around the corner, headed for the Via Toledo. Another sackful of broken plaster cascaded down the walls and landed more or less in the donkey cart. Men and women began to fight over whatever they could find in it.

Feeling his disgust like a coating of the filthy dust that had been stirred up by the feet of the mob—clothes, skin, eyes— Denton turned away and walked towards the narrow street. There, however, leaning in the shadow by the open gate, was Dottor Gianaculo. His small eyes looked dulled by the scene, as if he had consciously turned off some internal light. His fat face was slack and colourless in the shadow. He watched Denton approach but gave no greeting.

Denton said in his now rough-and-ready Italian, 'A displeasing spectacle.'

The policeman's eyes shifted to the crowd again. His shoulders moved with what might have been a belch, was perhaps some grunt of ironic comment. He said, speaking slowly so that Denton could follow, 'One of the *guardie* told me they were destroying the house.'

'Only the one room so far.'

The eyes turned back to Denton. 'I was here almost from the start.' He took something from his pocket—a triangle of plaster, a screaming mouth and chin painted on it. '*Memento mori.*'

Behind Denton, a louder scream rose above the noise of the crowd. It was a scream of rage, not pain. Denton turned. A woman was struggling with a ragged man; she had her hand in one of the pockets of his too-big overcoat. Denton recognised the coat and the brimless hat just as the struggle reached its climax: the woman tried to kick Michele and he clouted her in the head. She reeled back from him and fell and began to bellow. Michele turned to run and, seeing Denton, tried to stagger around him. Clutching something to his chest, he dodged, almost fell, and said in *Nnapulitan'*, his thick tongue like a snake in his toothless mouth, 'She was robbing me!'

Gianaculo, still leaning against the wall, said, 'She was—I saw it.' He sounded amused.

'There—there! He saw it!' Michele leered, put his tongue out. The woman, who had got up, was screaming at another woman, who was laughing at her.

Michele came closer to Denton. His sour smell reached Denton's nose, then the smell of wine. He grinned, waggled the tip of his tongue, and held up the thing the woman had tried to steal.

'Dièci lire,' he said.

It was another piece of plaster from one of the walls. Denton recognised the figures on it, the naked boys pulling on the rope to strangle the tortured man. Denton wanted it, but he thought it was obscene to pay ten *lire*—half a working man's weekly wage. 'One *lira*.'

'No, no!' Michele hugged it against his chest, said something in *Nnapulitan'* to the policeman, who chuckled. 'Ten. Eight!' He grinned and put out his tongue and then tapped the plaster triangle and said, 'It's me!' He waggled his tongue and widened his eyes.

Denton grabbed him. Michele instinctively pulled the plaster away, but Denton wasn't after the plaster; he put his big hand around Michele's left wrist and dragged him to the street. The drunkard began to howl, laughing as he did it, cackling and wailing as Denton pulled him down to the corner and across the adjoining street to a mean little café that had two rusted tables against its wall, one on each side of the doorway.

Denton pushed Michele down into a chipped wooden chair. *'Caffè!'* he shouted. *'Due caffè!'*

'No, no—*grappa*—*grappa*—!'

An ageing man appeared, coatless, tieless, but his collarless shirt buttoned up under a waistcoat. He looked at Michele with contempt, then at Denton, and seemed to make a decision. He raised his chin and disappeared.

'Grappa,' Michele said again.

Denton sat opposite him on a chair that seemed to have only three good legs. 'Shut up,' he said in English. He looked at Michele's eyes. 'How drunk are you?'

Michele did the tongue-and-eyes thing again and said in fair English, 'Not drunk enough. Give me six *lire*, I get truly drunk.'

'What did you mean, the painting is you?'

Michele tittered. 'I lie.'

'Why is it you?'

'I din't mean it. I sinned.' He giggled, then wagged his obscene tongue. 'Is jus' a little *scugnizzo*.'

'Who was torturing—hurting—Fra Geraldo. Did you hurt Fra Geraldo?'

Michele put the triangle of plaster down on the unsteady table, slowly turned it so Denton was seeing it right side up. Denton looked past him and saw Gianaculo leaning at the corner of the building, arms folded, face ironical.

Michele was wiping his hands on his greasy overcoat. The coffee came; he drank his in a gulp and shouted for grappa; Denton said no and told the man to bring another coffee. Michele howled, then slumped in his chair.

'Did you ever torture Fra Geraldo?'

He got a sly smile. 'I whip him sometimes.' He grinned and waggled his tongue. 'He like me to whip him. Also, he wash my feet. Ever' *Pasqua*, he wash my feet.' He opened his mouth wide and stuck his tongue out as if he were going to swallow something huge—Denton, the detective, the world. '"Inasmuch as you have done it unto the least of these..."' He giggled. 'I am the least of these.'

'When you were a *scugnizzo*—'

Michele hugged himself and rocked back and forth and shook his head quickly.

'—did you sing for Fra Geraldo?'

Michele stopped rocking and shaking his head and stared at the piece of plaster, still hugging himself. Suddenly, he put his head up and began to sing in English. 'God save our gracious queen—' His voice, roughened by alcohol and time, held none-theless a trace of sweetness, like a ghost of perfume left in an empty bottle.

'In the English church? Did you sing in the English church?' Michele frowned as if he didn't really know or couldn't remember. He turned away and stared into the street, his depraved face blank.

Denton took out a five-*lire* note and put it on top of the plaster. When Michele tried to snatch it away, he pulled it back and held on to it. 'There was another boy.'

'No.'

'Another boy.' He tapped the plaster, the painting of the two boys. 'His name began with E.'

Michele shook his head.

'Yes. E. What was his name? E—?'

Michele, never looking at Denton's eyes, stared at the plaster. He slowly put out his shaking right hand and touched the boys with his fingertips. 'Edouardo,' he whispered.

'Edouardo. What was his family name? Edouardo—?'

Michele was shaking his head very fast and murmuring, 'No, no.'

'You and Edouardo tried to kill Fra Geraldo.'

'No!'

'Have you seen Edouardo, Michele? Now, I mean—maybe in December, maybe when the *presepes* were for sale—maybe you took Edouardo to the old man's *palazzo* and sang as if you were boys again to frighten him—'

Michele burst into one of the Neapolitan street songs that he sang for coins, very loud, as if he wanted to drown out Denton's voice. Then, catching Denton off guard, he grabbed the five-*lire* note and ran into the street, where he stumbled and almost fell, then righted himself and ran off.

Gianaculo pushed himself off the wall, came to the table and sat in Michele's chair, keeping his hands off the table where Michele had touched it. He looked at Denton, their eyes holding, neither speaking. Finally, Gianaculo called for coffee and took out a box of cigarettes. He lit one and pushed the box and the matches across the table. Denton lit one, waited while the coffee was put down, said in fractured Italian, 'That was a terrible scene this morning. Fra Geraldo attracted violence, even when he was dead.'

Gianaculo said, his eyes slitted against the rising smoke, 'You still think the old man was killed.'

'It looks not.'

The *dottor* shook out the match and blew smoke out the side of his mouth. 'The English detective and his magic liquid? That's nice. Very modern.' He turned sideways to Denton and stared out into the street. He wore his hat at an angle, the brim turned up on one side, and Denton realised for the first time that Gianaculo was a vain man despite his fatness. Gianaculo said, 'I, too, think he was killed.'

'Why?'

'I do not like it that he fell down and broke his neck. It has a smell.'

'Did he have enemies?' He remembered that he had asked the question before.

Gianaculo was speaking Italian, but he spoke slowly and Denton got it. 'We all have enemies. The people on each side of the Palazzo Minerva, maybe. He used to shout at them because of their noise. He was always at them about the cesspool, which he said got into the wells, and of course he was right. Half the landlords of the Old City hated him because he was always at them about their buildings. Some of the great ones of the Church hated him because he practised poverty and charity and made them look like the fat-arsed hypocrites they are. The Church is always asking for money; Fra Geraldo was always giving it away. Yes, he had enemies. Would one of them kill him?' He shrugged.

'Maybe the Church hired the Camorra to do him in.'

Gianaculo grunted. 'The Church have their own *guappi* if they need them.' He looked into his cup, empty except for the thick mud at the bottom, and shouted for another. 'You know the old man was setting up a charity for when he was gone? Maybe he knew something was going to happen.'

Denton didn't want to reveal what he had learned from the old man's ledger. 'What kind of charity?'

'A clinic in each of the four worst *sezioni*, they say. Free food for the old. People to go around and teach sanitation in the *fondaci*.'

'That would take a lot of money.'

'He had a lot of money. So they say. He was a good old man, but he was crazy. All the money in Europe wouldn't change Naples.'

They sat until Gianaculo had finished his third coffee and then they walked towards the Via Toledo. Gianaculo put his arm through Denton's in the Italian manner. The *dottor* walked with his head back, his paunch forward, seeming to present himself to the world for admiration. He said, 'You interest yourself in some curious characters, signore.' They stopped at a corner. Gianaculo looked around with apparent pleasure. *'Che bella città.'* He began to steer Denton across the street, moving them both deftly around a pile of horse dung.

'I heard that Michele, but I did not understand the English. He sang for Fra Geraldo when he was a boy?'

'Michele had a special place with Fra Geraldo. Washing his feet, being beaten by him—"the least of these my brothers". He talked to me about—I don't know the word in Italian— atonement.' He tried to turn it into an Italian word. Gianaculo suggested several, none of which sounded right to Denton. At last, Gianaculo murmured, 'Ah, *espiazione, si—espiazione! Parole religioso. Ma certo.'* Expiation, yes—a religious word. But of course. For some reason, he chuckled. 'So he makes *espiazione* and debases himself to the worst human being he can find. Like Christ with the lepers. *Che pazzo.'* What a loony.

'He also carved *presepe* figures of Michele every Christmas. He was making a record of Michele's...I don't know how you say "to go downwards".'

Gianaculo took his arm again. 'You think Michele killed him?'

They came to the corner of the Via Toledo. Denton stopped there. He said, 'No, but I think Michele might know who did. I think that he thinks so, too.'

Gianaculo detached himself and looked up at the buildings opposite, his eyebrows raised. He tapped Denton on the chest. 'Not enough yet to go to the *magistrato*. But you tell me everything if it happens, yes?' He smiled his cynical, weary smile. 'Remember, signore, *I* am the detective.' He touched his hat-brim in salute and waddled off.

With Janet gone, the domestic economy of the Casa Gialla started a gentle crumbling, like damp plaster in an old house. The Wednesday lunches ended; the socialists and communists came no more. Assunta said that her husband had forbidden her to come any more to a house with only a man in it 'because of his honour'. Janet had left him written instructions to go on paying Assunta, so he supposed he would; however, he took the matter to DiNapoli for advice. DiNapoli's answer was to install an elderly woman as housekeeper. At once, Assunta's husband's honour was satisfied and she returned; however, Sirena, the more sluggish of the two housemaids, left because the housekeeper told her she didn't work hard enough.

DiNapoli became moody. Denton had explained why Janet had left, but DiNapoli seemed not to accept it. He seemed to take her going as a personal hurt. They all did, in fact.

❃ ❃ ❃

The rector of the English church was not English but Australian, and not a prissy country parson but a scarlet-nosed football fan. Denton wondered but didn't ask how he'd washed up in Naples, thought that perhaps 'washed up' said it all—some error somewhere behind him. Whatever his past, the Reverend Mr Porter tried hard to be cheerful, although the nose kept suggesting that he'd be even more cheerful if they could adjourn somewhere for a pint.

'Library? Yes, we've a library. Cheaper than Tauchnitz is what keeps it going. A Debrett's? Absolutely—it's the bible of a few of my parishioners, which isn't to say that the Bible isn't their bible, ha-ha. Fra Geraldo? Yes, I think I knew he was a duke or somewhat, but as he wasn't a parishioner I didn't pay much notice. He was Papist, wasn't he?'

Denton murmured that Fra Geraldo had once been choirmaster in this very church. 'His name's on the wall.'

'Really! Shows what you don't notice when you're thinking of Sunday dinner.' When Denton had pointed out the name, the rector said, 'Gerald Sommers, well, there you are. Long before my time. I've been here four years, so I'm still the new boy. Some of the older ones still call me Mr Semple, who was my predecessor. Can't get used to having an Aussie at the helm. Records? Records of the choir? Well, if the roaches and the mice and the wet rot have spared them, I suppose we might have records, but I don't know what sort of records we'd have kept of the choir. Children? We've had *boys* in the choir, if that's what you mean, sons of parishioners, you know—those high-pitched voices, can't say I much care for them, but many people do. If you mean records of *who* was in the choir, I suppose we keep something of that sort. Mrs Bridges would know. I'll just have a word with her—that's the library through there, the shelves against the wall under the window—and I'll find you in there with Debrett's, shall I?'

Denton made his way down a corridor all in brown, with varnished brown woodwork taking up most of the walls and worn brown boards underfoot. The library was really only the set of shelves he'd been pointed towards; otherwise, the room was given over to a huge typewriter on a table, two stacks of collection plates, pegs with assorted clothes hung on them—presumably the lost and found department—and a bicycle that he thought would be the rector's. One rather florid-faced Englishwoman, looking as if she'd been walking on the Downs, was standing by the shelves and said, 'Oh, hello,' as if they'd known each other for years.

'I'm looking for Debrett's,' he said.

'Second shelf.' She was reading standing up, perhaps trying to see if the book in hand was one she'd already read.

Denton glanced along the shelves, was surprised to see one of his own novels—but not surprised to see more of Mrs Gaskell's and Ouida's.

He took the Debrett's to the table by the typewriter and quickly found the Easleigh title. He made notes in his book—dates, names, children—without caring about the minor permutations of family that seemed to fascinate admirers of the aristocracy. To his surprise, Fra Geraldo had been only the fifth Lord Easleigh; the first had materialised from the cabinet of wealth at the end of the eighteenth century. Denton had thought that noble families all went back to the Conquest.

The woman who had been reading passed behind him and said, 'See you in church, I hope,' and swept out with a lot of noise of skirts.

The rector, having stood aside for her, veered in. 'Such records as we might have are in the tower. Apparently there's a trunk, maybe two, and old accounts and a lot of stuff are thrown in there when we finish with them. I'll give you the key if you want to climb up. Can't promise anything.'

'I'd also like to get more information about the Sommerses—the Easleighs, if that's what they're called.'

'No, they'd be the Sommerses; I think only the holder of the title is Easleigh. We don't pay much attention to any of that Down Under. Tell you who could, though—there's an old tyke I take communion to every week, as he can't get about any more. He's mad for the titles and their doings. Gets a couple of rags sent out from Blighty, all about them; has a pile of books. Go see him. Tell him I sent you. Nice old buffer, although don't tell him I said that. Actually gave me a brown ale instead of sherry, would you believe it—"Porter for Porter," he said. I could have wept in gratitude. In this job, you go out and about to a lot of old ladies and gents; the snake-piss they give you to drink would gag a platypus. Sir Martin Gort. Likes you to use the "sir". You go see him.' He wrote something on a card and put it down in front of Denton. 'Wave that at him; he'll know it's me. I suppose you want to make your ascension into the tower now?'

'No time like the present.'

'Wait until you see the stairs.'

The stairs, however, were merely narrow and steep; there wasn't enough of the tower to make them long, as well. Above was a small room reached through a trap; the stairs went on up to another trap and, presumably, a bell or bells. Denton stopped in the room, which held mostly cast-offs of congregations past—a few broken chairs, several large crates full of long-out-of-style clothes (perhaps the last stop for the lost and found department), several awnings, now raddled, that might have been a bad idea for the church windows in the Neapolitan summer.

Denton made his way to several trunks pushed together below a broken window through which birds evidently came and went: bird droppings were frequent. He knelt and opened a trunk and began to rummage through it. After twenty minutes, he knew he was in for a dirty afternoon; after an hour, his hands were grimy, his face taut with the feel of dust. He had been once through all three trunks, found nothing likely, was now methodically emptying them one at a time. He found old hymnals, old prayer books, old prize books ('Edwin Latham, Most Proficient in Memorisation, 1837') that the recipients either hadn't taken or had given back to the church, old plans and programmes for now-forgotten jumble sales and lawn parties. He found records of pledges to the church, of bequests, of gifts; he found records of moneys paid in pounds and francs, dating to well before Garibaldi. He found correspondence about prospective rectors and vicars. He found papers so mouse-chewed as to be nothing but a kind of damp lacework.

The second trunk was more of the same, filled out with old, rotted vestments. Somebody's boots had found their way there, very small in size and very out of fashion. Twelve issues of *Every Saturday*. A packet of brochures about the steamship route from Marseilles to Alexandria by way of Naples. That, oddly, was the first mention of Naples. The church, whatever its geography, was really in England.

Such choir records as there were he found in the third trunk in the backs of the vestrymen's accounts. The collections, counted and initialled by two sets of initials, were kept in the various coinages of their day, now and then with the intrusion of Spanish or German coins. Perhaps because the choir was considered an expenditure (the choirmaster's meagre stipend, gowns, music), the choir was put at the back of each ledger. Little was revealed to Denton that interested him until, raising small explosions of dust as he threw the books down in disgust, he found the volume that included Fra Geraldo's tenure as choirmaster.

And there he was: 'To Mr Sommers for music 9s/6d'. 'To Mr Sommers 12s/3d for the Christmas'. 'For Henson for singing Gt. Jehovah 1/2 crown'. And then there was an entry that quickened Denton's pulse and made him forget the dust: 'To Mr Sommers for housing the boys L1/11s/3d'.

Housing the boys? The choirboys? In the Palazzo Minerva—or hadn't he bought that yet?

Denton skimmed more and found nothing, looked at the next volume, then the one before. Nothing and nothing.

He returned to the first ledger and at last found, not in the section devoted to the choir, but under Irregular Employees and Labour, an entry for 'The Italian Boys, to have 6p each for each time they sing and 3p each per week that they rehearse, to include...' And there followed a list of names. Only two of them meant anything to Denton, but those jumped out at him: Michele

Esposito…Edouardo diToledano. Nonetheless, he copied all nine names into his notebook. Might DiNapoli be able to find them if they were still alive and in Naples?

'Bit smutty up there, I think,' Porter said when he came down the stairs. He was standing there as if he'd been waiting.

'I'm a little grubby. Still…'

'Found something? Oh, good! Never like to see a man labour in vain. Well, do go call on old Gort. You may not get anything out of it, but he will. And if you'd like to make a contribution to the foundation, there's a box by the door as you go out. Ah, that is generous. Good of you. Do come back. Come on Sunday! Come every Sunday—!'

His voice faded as Denton walked through the churchyard and back into the world of Naples.

❀ ❀ ❀

He gave the list of choirboys' names to DiNapoli and told him to try to find them or their families.

'Every other person in Naples got one of these names!'

'I thought you knew everybody. Look, DiNapoli, they were very poor, so you know where they must have come from.'

'Half them peoples, they got moved out by the *Risanamento*. These guys be fifty years old now, *older*, they're maybe dead. Maybe they emigrated. Maybe they don' wanna be found.'

'Find one. Just one.'

'You gimme a needle in a what-you-call-it—on a farm.'

'Haystack.'

'A pile of haystacks.' DiNapoli looked at the list. 'This one is *Michele 'l ubriacon'*, huh?'

'Yes.'

'Him I don't have to find, then.'

'I want to talk to him, though. I had him and then he ran away.'

'He moves around. I ain't seen him in a few days. I look.' DiNapoli said it without enthusiasm and went off with a sick man's posture. The only thing wrong with him, Denton thought, was Janet's absence. Well, he was suffering from it, too.

He had got something from his visit to the English church, but not enough. He needed to talk to the man who was 'mad for titles and their doings' and so sent a note to ask if he could come by the next day. The answer came first thing the next morning: Sir Martin Gort would be delighted to have him visit that afternoon.

In the same mail was a brief letter from Maltby. Denton winced when he read, 'By the time you get this, I shall have left Naples.' He remembered Maltby's look of appeal just before he had fled the dismantling of Fra Geraldo's chapel. He must have known then that he was leaving; he must have wanted some sort of goodbye. Denton had been too caught up in that spectacle to give him the chance.

'I wish to thank you for all the help you have given me,' Maltby had written. Denton winced again: what help? 'Thank you for everything, and I hope we will meet again under more propitious circumstances.' It was signed Frederick L. Maltby. Denton hadn't even learned his first name before.

It was not the happiest way to start the day. Maltby was a bit of a wart, but he had succeeded in making Denton feel guilty—a sin of omission. He walked to the flat of the man who knew all about the nobility with a sense of gloom.

Sir Martin Gort was a thin old man in a beautifully made grey frock coat, faintly wheezing as he sat in a hard armchair to receive Denton. An Italian maid who looked somewhat younger than he and as tough as a prison matron fussed over him and glared at Denton as if he had come on some evil errand, then vanished.

'Forgive me for not getting up,' the old man said. 'My legs, you know.' His hair had thinned to a baby-like sparseness, chalky white and a little yellow on the top. His gaunt cheeks were yellowing, too.

Denton made polite apologies and explanations, sat where he was directed, described his errand.

'Ah, the Sommerses. Yes, you mentioned them in your note.' Denton was relieved that the old man remembered it.

'The Sommerses,' he said again. 'I confess I never saw the fifth Lord Easleigh, though I believe he was long active in the poorer wards of the city. Certainly, he was in Naples long before me.' He shook his head. 'When I left India, I thought I would live in England, but I found London less familiar than Hyderabad. And I liked a warmer climate. Naples seemed to me about right. What is it about the Sommerses you'd like to know? Let me say, I don't trade in gossip, can't abide it, but I do take an interest in genealogy.'

'The family, really. The history.'

'Oh, yes.' The old man seemed to wiggle slightly. 'I do like aristocratic history. Well, the first one, you know, started as a regimental agent during the American War, made rather a packet. After the war, he put his money into slaving ships and made another packet! He was a great benefactor of the Tory party and so was given the title. A viscount by letters patent, I believe. The title has to do with the village where he was born, I think—Easleigh, in Sussex. Never been there. Nor have you, I dare say. Doesn't matter. He lived to a great age and so all but cheated his eldest of the title—the mother was a Desmond, I think the cadet branch, no distinction but said to have been remarkably pretty as a girl—where was I?'

'He lived to a great age.'

'Just so, he did. When he passed away, slaving had been banned, so the second earl went into the India trade. Not the best time for it; in fact, he had no head for money and so ran through a great deal of it—more than was good for the estate, if the rumour-mongers are to be believed. His passion was hunting—he was a regular with the Melton—and he did a good deal of coaching, and so on. Sometimes rather high spirited, I believe. He married an iron man's daughter, quite a good deal of money, and they say he went through that, too, although I don't know about such things.'

'The family was poor, then?'

'Oh, not poor as you might say *poor*, but for a viscount, perhaps so. I have always thought it dangerous to give inherited titles to such people—life peerages are so much wiser. I believe in the old families—the Spencers, the Devonshires—whose bloodline has been long established and who breed true. New money gives a certain vigour for a generation or two, and then—' He sighed.

'The Sommerses have gone downhill?'

'Well, the second Lord Easleigh was not wise. His son was a military man and hardly lived in England long enough to call it home, as I hear it. Killed in one of the Zulu Wars. Cetawayo's impis, I suppose. He had two sons; the second son was the chap who just died in Naples; he became the fifth in the line after his elder brother, who was the fourth, died unexpectedly in one of the cholera epidemics. This one—your one, I mean, the Naples monk or whatever he was—was as I understand it rather a radical, some sort of artist, and there were stories—I hate to retail stories; they're so unkind—that he had to leave England because of an indiscretion. Most unsuitable, if true. Bit of a black sheep, perhaps.'

'He never seems to have married.'

'I think not. At any rate, the title has gone to a—I just read about it in a court circular, really a kind of round-robin letter for those of us interested in genealogy; where is it?—oh, no matter, I remember the gist. The sixth Lord Easleigh is still a boy, it seems. Seventeen, I think. Not the happiest of stories: his mother was one of the daughters of the fourth Lord Easleigh—that is, the Naples one's elder brother, making her his niece—did I say he had three daughters—the fourth one, I mean? Well, he did, and not a brood mare in the lot. Not for sons, at any rate; they did produce a multitude of daughters, but what good is that to the title? I suppose it was a heritage from their mother, whose name I can't even recall. The new peer's mother—or her husband; I believe he is an engineer, as they are settled in Birmingham; it was one of those unfortunate marriages—one of them, anyway, was determined to produce an heir, as none of her sisters had, and so she kept on having children long after it was either wise or seemly for her to do so, and even after one of her sisters had a boy, she at last presented the world with this boy. He'd never have got the title, except his cousin—the boy born ahead of him to one of his mother's sisters and who should have inherited—was killed a few years ago in an accident on the steam underground. A cautionary tale, if one could take the meaning from it.'

'But there's no doubt about the succession?'

'I shouldn't think so. It's all quite simple and direct, as you've just heard.'

'And he inherits everything?'

The old man chuckled. '"Everything" of whatever there is left. Each child in each generation has had some money, of course; I think that the monk, the fifth, was probably on some sort of remittance, although I shouldn't say it, until he inherited. It won't be one of the great fortunes, I'm sure.' He chuckled again, apparently with satisfaction.

'He owned a *palazzo* here.'

'In a most insalubrious neighbourhood, I believe. The value cannot be great.'

'But I've been told that he had plans to endow a charity.'

'Oh, dear. Well, not to speak ill of the dead, but I should say he passed away just in time. I don't believe in noble titles' being passed on without the money to support them.'

'The fifth Lord Easleigh lived very modestly.'

'Yes, and let the title and whatever properties he owned in England go to rack and ruin, I'm sure. He should have been at home, minding his properties and fathering an heir! I have no patience with such men.'

Denton stayed long enough after that to drink a small glass of Madeira (he wasn't offered the brown ale—some judgement, he supposed, that the old man had made of his character). And to promise to call another time. The old man said that he had few callers and he liked a good chat. He never went out. Soon, Denton thought, he would go out for the last time, that one-way journey. He thanked him and left.

❋ ❋ ❋

Another afternoon, DiNapoli not available, he climbed the Gradino di Chiaia towards the upper town. He could go anywhere alone now, partly because he felt confident of the city, partly because of the sword stick, the blade polished as bright as a silver spoon and the mahogany smoothed and oiled. It went with him everywhere. It had been only slightly disheartening to him to learn that the local thugs and the petty *cammoristi* carried revolvers.

The stone steps passed between old buildings, the stairs really another alley, but one that happened to head towards the sky—laundry fluttered overhead; women sat outside doorways and gossiped, everything stopping as he passed by. At the top, the *gradino* opened into an irregular little stone *piazza*. Denton crossed it and headed for a far corner, hoping to find steps to carry him higher.

A cracked voice cried, 'Texas Jack!'

Denton turned. Eight or ten boys were clustered on the far side of the little *piazza* where there was a stone balustrade and a view towards Posillipo and a bit of sea. At the kids' centre was a little theatre the size of a steamer trunk, at its front a puppet Pulcinella in black mask and domino. He waved a stick and shouted again, 'Texas Jack! *Dio mio, uno* cowboy!'

The kids squealed.

Denton, amused, called, '*Buon' giorno, piccolino.*'

Pulcinella took great offence at being called 'little one'. He moved back and forth the width of his theatre; he put half his body outside it and shook his stick. He said something in *Nnapulitan'* that made the kids scream with laughter.

Denton walked towards the little theatre. The kids, suddenly unsure whether he was angry, parted for him. He went close to the stage but to the side, leaned towards the puppet and said, '*Piccolino, ma che naso!*' It was true, Pulcinella's black mask had a big nose on it.

The puppet was incensed. *'Naso—io? Naso!'* He turned to the kids. *'Guardi—guardi!'* He put his stick just under Denton's own huge nose. *'Il Pizzofalcone!'* The Pizzofalcone was a major—and noselike—landmark.

The kids loved it. While they laughed and shrieked and pointed, Denton leaned into the theatre and tried to see through the back curtain, behind which the puppeteer would be standing. He said, *'Beppe—è tu?'* He had pulled the name from the depths of his memory—the night in the cellar of the Casa Gialla, the little man who had worked the puppet of the lady ghost, the Scuttini boy trussed up to die.

The curtain parted a few centimetres. An eye appeared. *'Sì signore, sono qui.'*

Denton knew the voice, thought he had recognised it in Pulcinella's. It was indeed the little puppeteer he had caught in his cellar. He said, *'Non più dei mal'orme, eh.'* No more ghosts, eh?

The puppeteer started to say something, but Pulcinella whacked Denton on the upper arm with his baton and asked him what he was doing, putting his big nose into his house.

Denton said, his Italian beginning to fail him, that he was looking for Pulcinella's wife. This brought on more whacks, more words, more laughter. Pulcinella threatened him; Denton made a pistol of his finger and shot him. Pulcinella fell, mortally wounded, then sprang back up and blew Denton a kiss. Denton walked off, and the kids applauded and shouted, 'Texas Jack!', and women who had come out of their houses stared at him. He found the next flight of stairs and started up, smiling.

❁ ❁ ❁

He met Gianaculo at a café because the inspector had sent him a note. It was not a place that Denton knew, close to the *questura* with rather cold, brutal service that he thought might come from serving mostly cops. Gianaculo was at a small, not very clean table, a cup the size of a baby's fist in front of him. It was already empty and he was signalling for more. When Denton sat down, Gianaculo said, '*Michele 'l ubriacon*' is dead.'

Denton didn't try to hide his surprise and some other reaction—hurt? Resentment?

'Somebody found him on the beach at Cannavaciuolo.'

'Drowned?'

Gianaculo's fat shoulders shrugged; his waistcoat pulled up to reveal a little of his shirt. 'Drowned, drunk, who knows?'

Denton asked for coffee with grappa, perhaps reminded because of Michele. 'Why are you telling me?'

'You interest yourself in him.' Gianaculo gulped down his second tiny cup. 'You have DiNapoli looking for him.'

'Who told you?'

Gianaculo's eyes showed a possibly malicious satisfaction. 'DiNapoli, who else?' He smiled without parting his lips. 'DiNapoli has not told you he is a police informer? Mmmm. Well, DiNapoli is not so bad. You know he is a criminal?'

Frowning, Denton said, 'Was. In the *Stati Uniti. Deportato.* He told me.'

Gianaculo's mouth pulled down at the corners; the lower lip pushed up in the middle, as if to say, *Fancy his telling you!* Gianaculo said, 'You know he is a criminal; and you do not understand he is therefore an informer? I am so sorry, signore. Yes, little Vincenzo is one of ours. Do not think too badly of him—he has to make a living. We require that he come to the *questura* once a week because he is a criminal; as long as he is there, he might as well tell us what he knows.'

Denton felt choked. 'He informs on me and the signora?'

'What is there to tell? You are admirable people.' He patted Denton's arm. 'Do not be hard on DiNapoli. He reveres the lady. He has his own kind of honour.' He sat back and stared at nothing, and said, 'He looks for some other people for you, too.'

'Kids who were in the English church choir *molti anni fa*.' Long ago.

Gianaculo tipped his head back. 'Fra Geraldo again? Kids. His ghosts, eh?'

'I don't know.'

'You cannot leave it?'

'Can you?'

Gianaculo clapped his hands together as if they were the halves of a book. 'The *magistrato* says *fermata*.' Closed.

'Then why do you tell me about *Michele 'l ubriacon'*?'

Gianaculo smiled his fat, faintly oriental smile. He let his hands fall open again. He dropped some coins on the table. 'Tell me what you learn if DiNapoli finds any of the kids.'

'Was Michele killed?'

Gianaculo pushed out both lips. 'Michele was a walking corpse. You saw him. But maybe somebody helped him get where he was going.'

'Evidence?'

'The fish have the evidence.' He started to walk away and turned back. 'Did DiNapoli tell you he informs about you to the Scuttini, too?'

Denton stared. Gianaculo smiled, perhaps sadly, perhaps merely cynically. 'He does it to stay healthy, you know? If he doesn't, they break his hands. His hands, at least.'

❀ ❀ ❀

Without Janet, he slept strangely, some nights waking at midnight and lying there until morning, other nights sleeping at a depth that frightened him. The dog slept in his room, first on the floor and then on the bed. Old dreams came back, all that unresolved detritus of a life. One of the dreams was familiar and inevitable—his wife, a horse, her last walk to the meadow with the lye bottle. He didn't dream of trying to save her and failing, however; perhaps he had accepted his failure.

Some nights without Janet, he woke and got up, then prowled that part of the house, the red room and the corridors. The building was silent, without the creakings and whispers of a wooden house. He was the only one on that floor; the remaining housemaid had been moved upstairs by the housekeeper 'to keep an eye on her.' The dog trotted along behind him. He looked down into the gardens, all grey and black now in moonlight. He tried to read, gave it up, went back to bed and slipped almost unwillingly into something like sleep, brief dreams from which he jerked awake, only to sleep again and then dream at length.

He and Fra Geraldo were in the chapel. They were painting one of the panels, the old man working on a fore-ground figure at the bottom, Denton higher up, painting one of those vignettes in the middle distance. Denton was finishing a picture of a puppet booth. He had painted the *scugnizzi* who surrounded the booth, naked imps with gleeful, nasty little faces. He was working on the puppet in the little theatre's opening, a Pulcinella with the traditional black mask but a policeman's costume instead of the loose white smock. He and Fra Geraldo were talking in Italian while they painted. When he woke, however, it all dropped away and left nothing, like a wall that crumbled and gave a clear view of an ocean and sky that met in foggy greyness. He remembered something about speaking Italian, and then that, too, was gone.

It was still dark beyond the window. Denton got up, sipped a little water. What had he been dreaming? Something about Italian. The chapel; it came to him like the flash of a gun at night, almost vanished; he grasped it, held it. The chapel—the chapel—

Il poliziotto fa la commedia.

It was all a puppet show?

❀ ❀ ❀

His walks got longer, mostly without DiNapoli, who stayed away now and whom Denton no longer trusted because of what Gianaculo had told him. Denton wrote to Janet almost every day. She did not write to him.

Then DiNapoli told him that he'd found somebody who claimed to be one of Fra Geraldo's choirboys.

'"Claims"?'

'He looks too old. He's a old man. Plus you got the name Gianni Formoso; this guy's name's Giorgio.'

'Close enough.' But he was wondering if it was a fake, like so much else here—somebody seeing money in it. And he was wondering if DiNapoli had already told Gianaculo, and if so what Gianaculo would do. Could he trust Gianaculo? Could he trust DiNapoli, for that matter? Could he trust anybody?

'Dis guy, he works at the statue foundry in Orientale. He don't get home till seven and he says don' come to his work, they don' like it. He wants five *lire* to talk to you.'

'Tell him I'll come tomorrow night. Or he can come here.'

In fact, they met in an *enoteca* near San Giovanni del Mare that was as close to a Dickensian dive as Denton wanted to get. DiNapoli was nervous, said 'maybe they should have brought a couple strong guys wit' us'; Denton was less worried, carrying his sword stick, but wished he could have carried a gun as well. The place itself was all right inside—low ceilinged, dark, the only light three kerosene lanterns hung on nails driven into the cement between the rough stones of the walls. Wine barrels stood on trestles behind a bar of rough boards laid over sawhorses. There were some benches and stools, no tables.

Giorgio Formoso indeed looked older than Denton thought one of the choirboys should look, but people aged fast in the *vicoli* of the lower city. Formoso was bald, his scalp shiny and blotched; he had a big white moustache that drooped like Denton's but was stained with tobacco—he had a cheap cigar in his mouth and two more in the pocket of his short jacket. His nose was big, but round and not sharp like Denton's, a drinker's nose, perhaps, with one reddened eye to match, the other visible only as milky white under a drooping, scarred lid. He was drinking red wine from a thick-walled glass and had a half-empty carafe on the floor beside him.

Denton gave him the five *lire* and pulled over a stool, then another while DiNapoli was getting them wine. Denton looked around, met the stares of the other three customers, answering them look for look, theirs hostile, his neutral. He said, *'Buona sera.'* They didn't answer.

'They are all right,' Formoso said in Italian.

'Not pleased by strangers.'

Formoso shrugged. DiNapoli brought their wine and sat between them where he could translate. He'd warned Denton that Formoso spoke dialect, although the few words Denton had heard so far had been Italian.

Denton raised his glass, as if in a toast or greeting; Formoso simply looked at him with his good eye, head slightly turned. Denton drank. He said, 'You were one of the choirboys at the English church?'

Formoso nodded. He seemed to be rationing his words.

'What was the choirmaster like?'

Formoso shrugged. Denton said, 'Old? Young?'

'Young.'

'English?'

'Of course, of course.'

'Good to you?'

Formoso shrugged again.

Trying not to show his irritation, Denton said, 'Did you live with him?'

Formoso shook his head, drank off half the wine in his glass. 'This was a long time ago, signore. I was a little kid. You think I remember everything from when I was nine years old? Do you?'

'Where did you live?'

Formoso looked at the men near the bar, as if they might know where he had lived, then said, 'We lived in some rooms. Eight of us, with an old woman. She cooked and slapped us around. Sommers came every day and taught us.' He pronounced it So-mairss.

'Taught you what?'

'Singing, what else? Singing in English.' He put his head back and sang 'Nearer My God to Thee' in a surprisingly high voice, the English only slightly accented. 'That you don't forget.' Then he drank the rest of the wine from the glass and reached down for the carafe. 'The words meant nothing. He cared about the voice and the pronouncing, you know?' He poured himself more wine. 'I could have been singing about how great the devil is, for all I knew.'

'Did you sing in the church on Sundays?'

'Never.'

Denton was surprised. He said so. Formoso, who had not smiled yet and seemed likely never to smile, said, 'He told my father we would be a year learning.' He shrugged. He drank.

'What happened?'

'I don't remember. Sommers went away.'

Denton waited for more; nothing came. 'Why?'

Formoso shrugged.

'Was there trouble?'

'What trouble?'

'Did the boys make trouble?'

Formoso stared over Denton's shoulder. 'He was paying our fathers for us. My father said if I did not do well, if I was trouble, he would find real work for me. He meant he would sell me to one of the metal shops, they used boys and they died from the stuff they breathed, or they got burned. I knew he meant it. Anyway, we ate good; I remember that; the old woman smacked us around, but she was a good cook and sometimes we got meat. And he brought us cake sometimes. I remember that.'

'Then why did he go away?'

Formoso drank. He drank his mouth full and held the wine, puffing out his cheeks and his upper lip, then swallowed noisily. 'I was nine years old.'

'He took two boys with him. Edouardo and Michele.'

Formoso's eyes swung to meet Denton's, then went to DiNapoli. 'You already know these things, why do you ask me?'

'We know some things, not all things.'

'I don't know anything about that. But maybe...Edouardo and Michele.' He narrowed his good eye until it showed as little as the injured one. 'They were his favourites.'

'Did he touch them?'

Formoso went through the same look, first at Denton, then DiNapoli, and then he muttered something to DiNapoli in dialect. DiNapoli said, his voice weary, 'He wants more money.'

Denton handed over another five *lire*, then, when Formoso shook his head, five more. DiNapoli frowned.

'Did Sommers touch the boys?'

'I never—' Formoso puffed his cheeks and upper lip out, although there was no wine in his mouth. He looked miserable, then angry, as if memory had brought up something he didn't want to face—and couldn't talk about. 'There are things you forget. Some things, too, you did not understand back then.'

'Did he touch Michele and Edouardo?'

Formoso frowned and shook his head, as if that was something he didn't know.

'Then why did he go away?'

Formoso shook his head. 'How do I know? I didn't even know he'd gone away until a long time after. Something happened. Nobody talked about it, or I do not remember. Sometimes he would take one or two boys to the church so they could hear themselves sing there. One day, he came back—he had been there with Michele—and Sommers was mad, ugly. I think that was the day he shouted at us. Then one day, it must have been after that, they told us to go home.'

'Did the boys talk about what happened?'

Formoso poured himself more wine. 'Michele didn't talk. But I knew later, it was something about the priest at the English church.' He looked at Denton with one old, sin-weary eye. 'Now, I know what it was, I suppose. *You* know.' He looked at DiNapoli. 'You know.'

'And you all went home, and that was the end of it?'

'The priest came to our *basso* and said thank you, I remember. He paid my father some money—I didn't see that, but my father told me. My father beat the shit out of me and he said it was my fault and the priest had not paid enough. I don't know how much he got. I remember my father saying he was going to the English church to get more. I think the priest told my father not to say anything to other people, because that's what my father told me, to say nothing. He said if I talked about it he'd kill me because there would be no more money. I didn't know what he was talking about.' He shrugged.

'And the other boys?'

'I never saw them again, did I? We were from all over Naples, as far away as Torre Annunziata, Pozzuoli; how would we see each other? I saw one, what was his name—*Dio*, I lived with them a long time, it seemed like a long time then, and I can't remember the names. Anyway, one of them, a few times in the street; he lived in Vicaria, like me. But we didn't talk.'

'Where is he now?'

'How would I know? I haven't seen him in twenty years— thirty. Maybe he died. It's like I told you, it was over. We were kids, you know—a year later, we forgot, we were bigger, we were different. I was working by then.'

'In the metal shop?'

Formoso nodded. 'My father said it was my fault I wasn't at the singing school any more; he needed the money; he put me out to work.' He pulled his left arm out of his jacket and pushed up his shirtsleeve and showed a burn scar the length of the forearm, the swell of the muscle gone, only puckered skin remaining. He touched his bad eyelid.

Denton waited, thinking of what else to ask, and said finally, 'You know *Michele 'l ubriacon'*?'

'I know he was that Michele from the singing school, yes. I never talked to him afterward, though. Once, when he was a *scugnizzo*, I saw him, I waved or something and he ran away.' He was pulling down his sleeve, working his arm into the jacket. 'Michele was never right in the head, I do remember that. I think he was born peculiar. But he had a good voice, and he was a good-looking kid. *Pretty*, you know. But even before he started drinking, he was peculiar. He'd laugh at things weren't funny, and he'd say the wrong thing, like he was talking to somebody else. He was crazy.'

'And Edouardo?'

Formoso raised his carafe and looked into it, frowned to see it was almost empty. DiNapoli took it from him and poured his own wine in. Denton handed his glass over, and DiNapoli did the same with it. Neither of them had tasted the wine.

'Edouardo was...a *guappo*, you know? A tough guy. Little, but tough. Ten years old, tough. He hit the other kids a lot. He hit me, but I was big and I could hit him back. Edouardo had been on the street since he was four. Truly! He was one of those guys, even that young, you know—they know everything. He knew about girls, you know? He knew how to get on the right side of Sommers.'

'He was a foundling?'

Formoso paused, as if to think. 'No. It was Michele was from the foundling hospital; Edouardo was just from the streets. He had a family, but they didn't want him. I don't know how I know that.'

'So when Sommers went off, he took the two boys who had no families.'

'I suppose so.'

'And he came back to Naples—you know that? And he bought a house in Spagnuoli? And he had the two boys living with him for a while?'

'I didn't know that. I only knew later, lots later, that he was back. I didn't know anything about boys.' Formoso seemed frightened now, eager to separate himself from that knowledge. 'I saw him on the street, somebody said, "That's Fra Geraldo." I recognised him. But I didn't care. I remember, I recognised him but I couldn't think of his name. Later, the name came to me, but—so? Why would I care?' He sounded defensive.

'So Fra Geraldo never came to see you? Never visited your father? Didn't pay any money?'

Formoso looked away towards the door. It was made of the same rough boards as the bar, held loosely by an old-fashioned thumb latch, and the wind was causing it to open almost an inch and rattle the latch. Cold air blew across the dirt floor. Formoso said in a musing voice, 'My father got some money sometimes. Not a lot. I don't where he got it. Mostly, he played the lottery with it.'

Denton had little more to ask. He did mention the police, which made Formoso indignant: why would the police have anything to do with the singing school? Denton didn't know what the police had been like back then—1857, 1858, Italy not yet unified, the corrupt Bourbons still trying to hold on to Naples. He gave Formoso another five *lire*, to DiNapoli's disgust, and left.

Outside, he walked into the guttering light of a small shrine, the candle flames thin and streaming in the wind, and looked back at the *enoteca*. Two of the men who had been standing at the bar came out and looked at them. Denton slid the sword a foot out of the stick and let them see the shine of the metal.

'I don' think they mean nothing,' DiNapoli said.

'Just helping them be certain that's what they mean.'

They walked towards the brighter lights of the Strada del Duomo, where Denton turned left to go home. DiNapoli was going another way and said goodnight. After he had gone, Denton could hear him singing, the clear tenor voice offering one of those sentimental Neapolitan songs to the night. Denton listened, then turned towards home. DiNapoli had taught him a word, *sfiducia*, distrust, and now Denton found himself applying it to DiNapoli himself. They saw each other less with Janet not there, and something had come faintly between them, perhaps nothing more than Denton's own cynicism. Yet he found he felt *sfiducia* towards DiNapoli. Maybe it was only the spying. But he couldn't resist walking that ugly cat, suspicion, back to the beginning: it had been DiNapoli who had found him in the Galleria, not the other way around. Suppose it had been deliberate? Suppose the Casa Gialla, the puppet-ghost, the dying boy in the cellar, had all been part of a scheme? But it was ridiculous: there was no way anybody could have predicted that Denton would find the boy or that he would go to Scuttini or even that he would stay in the Casa Gialla. And none of it had anything to do with Fra Geraldo, who had come to Denton at the *pensione* before the DiNapoli and the Casa Gialla and Scuttini and Gianaculo had even entered his life.

And who would be behind such a crazy plan? Naples, like all of Italy, loved conspiracies, but they were usually no more real than the ghosts, this one least of all. No, his *sfiducia* was absurd: DiNapoli was a petty informer, both to the police and the Scuttini, but he was loyal to Janet and, Denton hoped, to him. Hoped.

CHAPTER

20

Two evenings later, sitting in the red room because it was more comfortable than his own and because, he supposed, it gave him some sense of Janet, he heard muffled sounds downstairs and the thud of the door. It was late—he was filling time until he went out to eat, and doing that only to fill more time—and he knew nobody who would call then. It was likely DiNapoli, he thought, but when the maid appeared and curtsied, she handed him a calling card with 'Harriet Guttmann' embossed on it and, written below in very black pencil and underlined twice, *I must see you!!!!!* Harriet Guttmann, Lucy Newcombe's plump friend, now as vanished as Lucy herself since Janet had gone away.

He had learned the Italian for *Show him up*, so he said those words, the feminine escaping him. He half expected to see Lucy, as well, but realised that if Harriet's visit was worth five exclamation marks it was probably about Lucy, and she had likely come alone.

And he was right. Pink-cheeked as if she had been running, Harriet appeared in the doorway and, for the first time since he had met her at the *pensione*, seemed to be without words. He was standing by then; he said, to cover what seemed to be confusion—maybe she was still flustered by Janet's absence, thus being along in the house with him (what would her mother say?)—'Miss Guttmann, how good to see you. Do sit down. Won't you take your cloak off?'

The maid was hovering behind her. Harriet lurched into the room and waved at the girl to go away, and when, after a frightened glance at Denton, the maid had fled, Harriet closed the door with something like a slam and, leaning back against it, said, 'You must help us!'

'Of course—Miss Guttmann—what is it?'

'Oh, Mr Denton, it's Lucy! It's the awful *marchese*—her mother has *engaged* her to the brute. They've signed papers! With a notary!'

'I doubt he's a brute, Miss Guttmann. Do sit down—'

'If he marries her against her will, he's a brute. She'll die of it!' She was tearing at the ribbons that held her hat to her head. 'They'll lock her up in some antiquated *palazzo* and they'll be horrible to her and she'll *die*.' She threw herself into a chair and started to weep. He offered her wine; she refused with a disgust that would have been justified by his offering her dog's piss and said between sobs, 'I can't stay. I'm supposed to be at the opera—I *was* at the opera and I ran out during the overture—It's all awful!'

'Lucy only has to say "no". You don't need my help for that. She's as capable as I am of telling her mother and the *marchese* to go suck eggs.'

'But she *can't*! She's soft; she's...nice! She doesn't want anybody to feel bad *ever*. She's really very sweet and very kind, but she doesn't have, you know—*spine*.' She pulled a handkerchief from a sleeve and snuffled and sniffled and alternately balled the handkerchief and pulled it flat over a knee.

'Miss Guttmann, it really isn't my business to interfere in. Anyway, what can I do?'

'You can go to your friend the Camorra man! He could fix it in a twinkling. They can fix anything.'

'"My" Camorra man?'

'It wasn't my idea; it was Mrs Striker's. She said it one day. Before she left. She said you had done a favour for a bigwig in the Camorra and you could put a stop to it in a second.'

Denton wanted to say, *Damn Mrs Striker!*, which he didn't mean, but he thought that the 'Camorra man' wasn't Janet's business, and then saw that it was, because she was the one who'd charmed him. Still, the idea of going to Scuttini was loathsome. 'Maybe Lucy needs to grow herself a spine.'

'She can't! And it's worse since Mrs Striker left!' Harriet had tears in her eyes again. 'Can you keep a secret, Mr Denton? Promise me it will be a secret! I shouldn't tell you but I must, and Lucy would be broken hearted if she knew you knew, but—She's in *love*, Mr Denton. Back in the States. She has an *understanding* with somebody.' Her wet, rather cow-like eyes appealed to him.

'"Somebody".'

'A young man. In Rochester. He's quite young—well, older than Lucy by several years—and he's got a good job at his father's business and he'll own it one day, so he'll be a good husband. Oh, I know it doesn't sound much! But it's what Lucy wants. Lucy isn't a very modern woman, Mr Denton. I know you don't think much of her; she doesn't have ambitions and she doesn't want to be terrifically cultured or anything like that—my goodness, she didn't even want to leave Rochester to come to Italy!—but she's a good, sweet girl and if she's allowed to marry her young man, she'll have a lovely wedding and her father will build them a fine house on East Avenue and her husband will love her and *it will be all she ever wants*. Don't you see?'

Denton let his voice become very dry. 'You're asking me to do something extraordinary for a very ordinary, dull, uninteresting young woman, is that it? What could be more sensible?'

Harriet gripped her hands together as if she were trying to crush the balled handkerchief between her palms. 'If she marries the *marchese* she will *suffer*!'

'She'll suffer regardless. That's life, Miss Guttmann.'

'No, no, she'll be protected if she marries her young man. *Please!*' She was weeping again.

He thought of Janet's observation that Harriet's affection for Lucy went beyond friendship. Well, perhaps—but to her credit, Harriet didn't want to save Lucy for herself.

Harriet said, her voice suddenly flat, 'It isn't as if I were asking for some huge thing.'

'What are you asking for, then?'

'Only for you to go to the Camorra man and ask him to call the *marchese* off. It's nothing! Janet said it would be nothing!'

Denton looked at her for some time and then got up and walked around the room, stopping at the window to stare out, then turning back and coming to her. 'Do you understand what this "nothing" means, Miss Guttmann?'

'It doesn't mean anything.'

'But it does—for me and for you. Do you know what "dining with the devil" means?'

'Of course, but—'

'Do you understand that Scuttini is the devil?'

'I'm sure he's quite a bad man, and quite low and awful, but—'

'Every dishonest *soldo* that changes hands in Naples helps to make Scuttini and his ilk richer. Every woman Lucy's age who goes into prostitution—don't gasp, Miss Guttmann, I'm sure you know the word—helps to make him richer. Every man and woman who bet five *soldi* a week on the "little game"—*and always lose*—help to make Scuttini rich. But more to the point— you and me—do you know what it means if we ask him to save Lucy? It means that we—and Lucy—profit from his power, and it means we are just as guilty as he is.'

'We won't have done anything wrong!'

'You mean we can wash our hands and turn away. *You* can, I think, for now, but maybe when you're older you'll see you didn't in fact get away clean. Nor will Lucy see it, and I doubt that she'll ever have either the courage or the brain to see at what price she'd have bought her "happiness".'

'If it will save Lucy, I'd do a deal with the devil himself!'
'Sell your integrity for a flibbertigibbet? Then you're a fool.'
'All right, I'm a fool!' She was angry now and she dared to
show it. She stood to face him, as any young woman would who
had watched such a scene played in melodrama. 'Will you do it
or won't you?'

He certainly didn't want Lucy's gratitude, nor Harriet's
for the matter of that. Yet he knew that he must do it, because
she had put him in a box from which he could escape only by
compromising himself or by seeming, even to himself, to be a
prig. And Janet's last words had been 'For me, Denton, if not for
her.' He said, 'I'll need to shop for a long spoon.'

'Oh—!' She clapped her hands together, the effect lost
because the handkerchief came between them. He thought for
an instant she was going to rush across the room and kiss him;
he saw her think of it, want to do it, and then stop herself. She
said, 'I have to be back before the second act starts!' and she ran
for the door.

❀ ❀ ❀

He didn't take DiNapoli with him to see Doro Scuttini. Not that
he couldn't have used him to translate, but—*la sfiducia.*

Scuttini lived in one of the tall buildings on the boundary
where Mercato met Vicaria, an area impacted with people since
the *Risanamento.* From the outside, Scuttini's building was no
different from the *fondaci*, dark, austere, ugly. Inside, however,
was another matter. Two middle-aged tough types met him in
the entry, which carried the ugliness of the outside into the interior, so that anyone looking in would see only another warren of
poverty.

Once on the stairways, however, he found that everything
was better, cleaner, brighter. Windows had been opened on an
interior courtyard larger than the dark, chimney-like holes of the
real *fondaci*; light and fresh air came in. Above the *primo piano*,
the stairs were carpeted.

The two mugs led him to a hallway, also carpeted, men and women lounging in doorways as if it were a *vico*, studying him with interest and perhaps amusement. They went through a doorway that Denton thought would lead to an apartment, but it took them to another stairway with still better carpet and bigger windows. Hefty men in dark suits, tieless, stood at the top and bottom; the bulges in their jackets were guns, he thought. A double shotgun leaned in a corner at the top.

There was a door, then a kind of foyer, yet two more *guappi* waiting. One of them opened Denton's jacket and felt around his waist and under his arms and took his stick away. Denton was led into a large, high-ceilinged apartment crowded with furnishings in what even Denton, who claimed no taste, knew was bad taste. One of the *guappi* took his hat and coat and pointed unnecessarily at the *compare*.

Scuttini was sitting on a horsehair sofa big enough, had it been supplied with four sets of oars, to have crossed to Capri on. He was dressed like a businessman—tight grey suit, well-filled waistcoat, thick silk necktie—but he hadn't shaved. He didn't get up, but nodded as Denton crossed the room towards him and patted a place beside him on the slippery horsehair.

'You will understand today well enough what I say in Italian? You don't bring your little man?' That was his greeting. He waved a hand at the *guappi* and said something and they all waited until a tall, cadaverous man in a black suit was brought in. He stood next to Scuttini and, when needed, translated into both Italian and English.

Denton sat down, regretted doing so because he couldn't see Scuttini's eyes. He moved to an armchair opposite, and Scuttini frowned. He glanced at the two men who had remained in the big room with them, as if he were checking to make sure he had not lost face.

'I wish to ask something,' Denton said.

Scuttini nodded. 'I owe you.' He said it rather grudgingly.

'That is why I can ask you. How is your grandson?'

Scuttini raised his chin. 'Well. He is living on one of my farms in Apuglia. I thought to get him away from bad influences.' As if to himself, he said, 'He is young and foolish. You like your house?'

'We like it.'

'You got my gift of wine?'

'We did, and wrote to thank you.'

'I can send you more.'

'No, thank you.'

Scuttini had no smile to wipe away as a sign of annoyance; he instead raised his chin again and looked at Denton the way a buffalo looks at something it is thinking of pounding into dust. 'The signora has left the house, I hear.'

From DiNapoli. 'She has gone to London.'

'She will come back?'

'A friend is dying there.'

Scuttini breathed heavily, as if he had something wrong with his lungs. He said, 'You got yourself a friend in the police.' Had DiNapoli told him about Gianaculo? Or did Gianaculo have a direct conduit of his own to Scuttini?

'Not a friend. An—' He didn't know the word for 'acquaintance'.

'I have many friends in the police. The police are useful.' Scuttini looked around the cluttered, ugly room as if he had lost something in it. His next question, however, made it clear what he was looking for: 'What do you want?' He made it sound brutal.

'There is a *marchese* who wants to marry a young American girl.'

'The Marchese Rocca-Scutare, yes. A fine match.'

'You knew of this already?'

Scuttini smiled. 'This is a time of marriages. My grandson, the one you know, is in fact going to marry the youngest daughter of the *Avocato* Spinoso—the one who owns your house. The one who owned the house when it was being used for smuggling, and my grandson was left, but for you, to die there.'

'*Avocato* Spinoso didn't tell me he knew your grandson.'

'He didn't at that time.'

'They are in love?'

Scuttini grinned. '*L'amore non c'è.*'

Denton searched his frog's face for any sign that he knew that Denton had heard the words before. There was nothing. It would have been easy to believe that Scuttini knew what Palladino's voice had said to him, even that Scuttini had prompted her to say the words, but there was nothing. As if Scuttini, too, were only an ignorant voice.

Scuttini, apparently unaware of Denton's interest, said, 'The happy couple have never met. But it will be a good marriage. As I told the *Avocato* Spinoso, it will bind our two families together. He was so happy, he cried.' Scuttini chuckled.

Denton waited for the laughter to stop. He said, 'I want you to tell the *marchese* to withdraw his proposal of marriage to the American girl.'

Scuttini's smile vanished. He folded his hands over his gut. He was not pleased, the posture seemed to say, but he was a reasonable man who would listen to sense. 'You do not like him?'

'He wants her money only.'

'The Rocca-Scutares have many debts. Many, many debts. It is the duty of the *marchese* to pay those debts.'

'The girl has not enough money.'

'Her father is a millionaire! My friends in Rochester, New York, say he owns a big factory.'

'If he owns it, he owns it with the banks. If he has a million dollars, he is not going to give them to his daughter. Look, Scuttini—the father is an American businessman; he has a hard head. Americans do not give big dowries. He would give his daughter a new house in Rochester and a few thousand dollars— not nearly enough to save the Rocca-Scutares.'

Scuttini frowned. 'He does not love the girl?'

'He is an American businessman; he loves his business more. He will expect her husband to support her. Believe me, he will not pay the debts of the Rocca-Scutares.'

Scuttini again looked around the room and came back to Denton's face. They stared at each other for several seconds. Scuttini unclasped his hands and shifted his position on the sofa. He said in a lower voice, as if things were now confidential and they were getting serious, 'The moneylenders have the Rocca-Scutares by the balls. You understand—balls? If the *marchese* does not marry well, the moneylenders will lose their money. And then *I* will lose money. You understand? That cannot be.'

'I want the marriage stopped.'

'Maybe the father will give her enough to pay five *soldi* on the *lira*.'

'You do not understand me. You said you owe me a life. I want the marriage *stopped*.'

Scuttini folded his arms and looked at his brilliantly polished shoes. 'The *marchese* has no other woman to marry. He is not much, between the two of us—very little to him.' He waggled his fingers: the *marchese* was a butterfly. 'He is not going to find another rich woman in time.' He breathed heavily. 'The Rocca-Scutares are about done. They need new blood, new strength—new money. If they do not get those things, then I will have to—the moneylenders will have to—take their *palazzo*. They will be on the street.'

'That is not my business.'

'But it is mine! I respect these old families. I respect their titles. They are a tie to our glorious past. However, they cannot be allowed to cost me money.' He sighed. 'You insist the marriage must be stopped.'

Denton nodded.

'You understand that I disapprove?'

Denton nodded again.

'You understand that if I do the thing, you and I are even?'

'I will be happy, signore, not to have you indebted to me.'

Scuttini narrowed his eyes and gave Denton what must have been intended as a hard look. Denton knew hard looks, had seen them before, and he gave back an expressionless face as reply. He hoped, nonetheless, that Scuttini's idea of obligation wouldn't end before Denton got to the street; he didn't want to be beaten up on the stairs as a parting reminder of a new status.

Scuttini's hoarse breathing was the only sound for some seconds, and then he said, 'Even seizing their *palazzo*, I will lose money.' He sounded more plaintive than angry. 'You are a hard man, signore. I saw it when you were at my farm. I knew it from that fine woman's story of your shooting four men. You know, I had thought maybe you and she would join my family. But you are too hard. Eh?'

'I have a family, signore.'

'You have yourself.' Scuttini nodded rapidly, held up a finger. 'In Naples, one is not enough. This is not the Wild West. But I will not turn against you. For that fine woman's sake, I will not think my honour has been challenged by what you say.' He stood, went to a small tambour table and opened it. Stooping, he said, 'Even though you are costing me money.' He took out a bottle and two tiny glasses. 'If I was young, maybe I would be angry. But I am not.' He poured a small amount of clear liquid into each glass. 'You do not like me, signore. Maybe I do not like you, either, but I respect you. Or maybe I do like you.' He gave Denton one of the glasses. 'We drink to tell each other that we understand. I will stop the marriage; you will ask me for no more.' He tipped his glass into his mouth. Denton did the same; it was like fire. The *compare* looked at one of the men by the door and moved his head to the side. Moments later, Denton was headed down the stairs.

It was, he thought, as satisfactory as he could have hoped. He felt emptied, rather humiliated, as he supposed he was meant to; however, none of the tough types tried to beat him up. He resisted feeling dirtied, as it was a dirty world and he was hardly virginally clean himself. He would have felt better if Janet had been at home to talk to about it; her gratitude—would it have been gratitude, or relief, or mere acceptance?—would have been an antidote to Scuttini's 'honour'.

All that waited for him at home, however, were the dog and the afternoon mail. Nothing from Janet: she had been gone long enough for a letter to reach him—a dozen letters, in fact—but he knew now she would not write. If Ruth Castle was really dying, was really in the final stages of life, she would be completely absorbed. Naples would have been left behind like a cloak she had dropped at the railway station.

Among the bills and trivial letters and circulars, however, was another from Atkins, this one full of the latest successes of the recording business. Also included was a clipping from one of the nob magazines Atkins affected, usually passed on from some butler friend in a high-class house. Atkins, a declared leveller, nonetheless maintained a contradictory fascination for what he called 'our betters', especially the titled ones, and usually knew which lord had married which lady and who was third cousin to both of them: he could have had mutually profitable conversations with Sir Martin Gort.

The clipping was on shiny paper and included a photograph of a vapid-looking, long-haired boy, under the heading 'Lord Easleigh to Give Maiden Speech in Autumn'.

Denton had kept Atkins abreast of the events that had rolled out from Fra Geraldo's visit to the *pensione*. Atkins was now responding in kind. The text with the photo was drivel, except the fact that the young lord—he was seventeen, as Gort had said—had taken a flat at the Albany 'after having lived previously with his parents, Mr and Mrs Arthur Murie, in Birmingham'.

Couldn't wait to leave, Denton thought.

He looked at the photograph again. The face was rather feminine, perhaps only as a result of residual little-boy fat in the cheeks and rather full lips. The eyes promised nothing; perhaps that was in the nature of studio photography. The hair was what you saw, in fact, even more than the face; it was all but ringleted, shoulder length. Denton couldn't avoid a nasty thought about Fra Geraldo and boys and what he might have made of this one at ten years old.

He put the photograph of the young Lord Easleigh on the mantel with the piece of broken plaster he had got from Michele *'l ubriacon'* and the *presepe* carving of him. He stared for a while, then got out the photos of Fra Geraldo's chapel and stared at them and wondered what to make of it all.

❀ ❀ ❀

Two mornings later, he had a note from Harriet Guttmann:

Dear, dear Mr Denton,

You have done it! O thank you, thank you, thank you!!!!! The miracle has come to pass because of you. Lucy is beyond happiness—'twere bliss now to be alive!!! How shall we thank you, good Mr Denton, dear Mr Denton! The marchese has entirely gone off. He came to see Mother Newcombe yesterday with a long face and he wanted to beg off from his proposal because he has found he has a fatal illness, he said, and he begged her not to go to law as it would cause acute pain and he will be dead before the Italian courts can have decided anything. Mrs N. was hacked beyond belief and had a complete fit! She said indeed she would go to law &c. &c., but after the poor young man (for I may call him that now the danger's past) had fled, and she had spent at least two hours on the war path, she and Lucy had a long talk and for the first time I think that our L spoke her mind, though I am sure in the nicest and sweetest way. The upshot is that they are returning to Rochester at once and my mother and I are going to Baden-Baden, as Mother despises Naples and stayed here only because Mrs N is her friend.

Oh, dear Mr D, I fear I shall not see you again before we go. May I write to you? Will you write to me? Our conversations have meant a great deal to me!!! You cannot understand the effect your experience and wisdom have on a young girl just starting out on life's journey! I do hope and pray you will agree to correspond and that I may even hope to see you again before I start in September at the University of Rochester.

Ever your friend, Harriet Guttmann

PS. Letters will reach me at Thomas Cook's, Baden-Baden, until further notice. Letters will always reach me at 19 Genesee Street, Canandaigua, NY, USA. Until we meet again, H. G.

Denton laughed. Whatever else Harriet might be, she was cheerful, and she had the effect right then of cheering him. Gloomy enough already, he had been dropped down a dark well by his meeting with Scuttini. Harriet's account, besides cheering him up, also made him for the first time a little sorry for the *marchese*. He thought of the scene that must have taken place in the Rocca-Scutare *palazzo*, the lot of them sitting or standing in an unfurnished drawing room as the young man explained that the marriage to the rich *americana* was off and they were all going to be put out into the street. It pleased his American egalitarianism, but then he felt briefly sad and had to tell himself again that they seemed to have brought it on themselves.

And so Lucy was not to suffer, after all. Rather, she would continue to be cosseted and pampered and would become, in an American fashion, a new kind of Rocca-Scutare, wealthy, snobbish, narrow, smug, perhaps the matriarch of another clan that would in its time, after she was gone and couldn't know, run through the money and be out on the street with the rest of the world. Had she done anything to deserve such special favour, such happiness? he wondered. Why Lucy and not Harriet? Or why Lucy and not Assunta or the housemaid or any of the thousands of women in Naples who worked and suffered and endured?

He did his morning work and went out because the day was pleasant, clean smelling and bright with a sky overhead that shaded from hard blue to a soft green over the bay. He felt better

KENNETH CAMERON

when he had walked, as if something had been settled—an illusion, of course.

Coming along the corridor towards his rooms, however, he heard a soft scraping sound that he thought was the sliding of a drawer. He went more quietly and turned into the doorway of his workroom, and he found DiNapoli there where he shouldn't have been; worse, he had the photos of the chapel in his hands.

'What are you doing in here?' Denton was honestly surprised, also instantly angry.

'The girl—Rosa—she said to wait in here—'

'She can't have done.'

'They was cleaning the parlour; she put me in here.'

Denton snatched the photographs from him, his anger rising. 'Where did you get these?'

'They was on the desk.'

'They weren't on the desk! They were put away.'

'They were on the desk, I'm telling you! What you t'ink, I'm gonna steal them?' DiNapoli looked like a child about to be scolded.

Denton threw the photos into a drawer. 'Don't lie to me. What were you going to do, take them to your pal Scuttini? Or the *questura*?'

'Mist' Denton, what're you saying?'

'You spy on us for Scuttini; you spy on us for Gianaculo; what should I believe? I heard you open the drawer as I came down the corridor! You're a snitch and a sneak!'

DiNapoli made a sound as if he had been physically hurt, and he said, 'I didn't sneak,' in a strangled voice, and in an instant he was out the door. Denton ran after him, telling him to wait, Denton as abruptly remorseful as he had been enraged.

DiNapoli looked up at him from the foot of the stairs. 'I don't come here no more. I come for *her*, and she ain't here. I don't come no more for you.'

The front door slammed.

Denton told himself he had done the right thing and knew he had not. DiNapoli was a petty crook; DiNapoli *had* opened the desk drawer; DiNapoli *had* spied. But Denton knew he had done a shameful thing worse than anything DiNapoli had done. He, a man with everything, had been deliberately cruel, and maybe deliberately unjust, to a man who had nothing and who couldn't fight back. Perhaps DiNapoli wasn't Janet's 'innocent', but if he was guilty, it was of something petty and venal. DiNapoli had been earning a few *soldi* to stay alive; Denton had been a bully.

He roamed the rooms, tried to read, was grateful when Rosa said that somebody wanted to see him. He hoped it was DiNapoli and ran to the head of the stairs, but to his surprise it was Spina, the photographer from the Via Santa Lucia. Over his shoulder, Denton saw the huge camera in the lower hall, the tripod folded, a crude wooden dolly under it to move it through the streets.

'I tell DiNapoli I got something for you but he wouldn' bring it.' Spina held out a photograph. 'The *inglese* I said I remembered.'

'What *inglese*?'

'He was wit' you and the other *inglese* but he went away. I never forget a face. Remember?'

Denton didn't remember, then recalled something about Cherry, the detective. Maltby had been there, too. Cherry had had to leave them for some reason—his wallet. Did Spina mean the English detective?

He turned the photo so he could see it right side up. It was the usual Spina scene—the Via Santa Lucia, a bit of the Pizzofalcone, the Castel dell'Ovo in the background. In the foreground, a man in rather too-formal clothes was standing awkwardly, held in place by a smaller man whom Denton took to be a guide. His left arm was raised partway, as if he were gesturing at Spina and saying something like 'Smile'. But the subject wasn't smiling; he looked thoroughly angry, in fact. In the next instant, Denton thought, he might have shaken the guide off and perhaps turned and marched the other way. But no matter, Denton didn't know him. It certainly wasn't Cherry.

'I don't get it,' Denton said. 'I don't know—'

Spina pointed to two figures in the background. 'I don't mean them ones in front! These two—the guy from Sardegna and his boy.'

Denton saw a face that might have been familiar. But not one he could put a name to; his impulse was to tell Spina that it had nothing to do with him.

Before he could speak, Spina said, 'The guy that run off that day, that's him there.' He jabbed at the photograph. He seemed to mean another figure, one with the face blurred by motion.

Denton and Spina were still standing at the top of the stairs; the light was bad there, the air cold. Denton tried to see the figure Spina meant, couldn't make it out in the poor light without his reading glasses. He led Spina along the corridors to his workroom, where he slid open a drawer and took out the magnifying glass. He leaned close and saw blurred figures swim up towards him like fish rising to a crumb. Behind the shoulder of the photo's real subject were several people who hadn't had any idea they were being photographed. One, the one a little smeared by movement, was thick and dark, a middle-aged man in a soft hat and dark lounge suit, the face not quite clear but recalling one Denton knew.

He remembered. He and Maltby and the English detective had been walking along the Via Santa Lucia and Cherry had had to leave them. And then Denton had had the conversation with Spina; yes, he remembered now. Spina had said something about having photographed Cherry before.

But Denton's real attention was not on the dark, blurred man who might have been Cherry. It was focused instead on the young man with him, who was smaller and slender and had abundant, curly light-coloured hair.

It was the new Lord Easleigh.

To make sure, Denton looked up at the clipping on his mantel. 'When did you take this picture, Spina?'

The photographer stared at his photograph. 'I got it in a— what's the word?—*credenza*—like, to put t'ings in—?'

'Closet? Cupboard? Does it matter?'

'If it's in there, I don't take it just yesterday, understand?' He tapped the photograph. 'This one I don' take yesterday.'

'How old? Last year? Five years ago?'

'No, no—not so old as that. These photograph, they start to—what you say?—*fa giallo*—'

'Yellow?'

'Yeah, pretty quick. You t'ink I can do some kind of permanent work under that cloth, in the back of the camera? No. My photographs is to take home, you show the family, the friends, then you put away. I ain't Michelangelo, make picture for the ages, signore.'

'Last year, then?'

Spina looked at the photograph again. 'There's a woman got a fur collar. So it was maybe cold. The man who should have bought the picture but didn't—I think he was German; the Germans are tight—he's got an overcoat. So it was winter, maybe. And that's Parillo's carriage there—see? The one coming towards me? He's got the feather decorations on his horse. So maybe near Christmas, but I don't think it's Christmas yet because I don't see the lights in the park.'

'This last Christmas?'

'Yeah, yeah, this last Christmas, or the picture would be all *giallo*.'

Denton straightened and looked out over the bay. Absently, he took coins from his coat pocket and gave them to Spina.

The new Lord Easleigh had been in Naples in December. Fra Geraldo had died in December.

Maybe the private detective, Cherry, had been with him.

I have to go to London.

CHAPTER

21

It had been almost spring in Naples; in London, it was winter. The city seemed dour and strange to him, the people speaking a language that sounded harsh, their movements sluggish and graceless. The streets were crowded with motor cars and motor buses and closed carriages and horse-drawn omnibuses, and the smell was like a gas, manure and urine and motor exhaust.

He had been three full days on the way, one night spent in a sleeping car and one in Paris, then the day getting to Calais and across the Channel and up to London. Fatigue stabbed into his shoulders and pinched the muscles of his back. Looking out of the carriage that took him from Victoria, he wondered what he was doing there. The sky was overcast, the late afternoon light like the absolute end of day. Who were these unsmiling crowds who marched so relentlessly along the pavements? Who were these unhappy souls who rode the omnibuses, staring straight ahead, never moving? He felt like a visitor from another planet. When the cab driver had spoken to him in an East London accent, Denton had stared at him and wondered what to say—In what language?

It was the City of the Dreadful Night, into which he had been thrown as if from another dimension.

Yet he recognised landmarks, streets, shop signs; he knew his own street when they turned into it, recognised the welcoming front of the Lamb. And his own house just before it, set back behind an iron gate that needed painting. And standing there in a short black jacket and striped waistcoat and dark trousers, Atkins, smiling as if he'd just given birth, behind him in the doorway his huge black dog.

'Well, well.' Denton got down from the cab rather creakily, stiff from days of travel. 'Back sooner than we thought, eh?' He patted Atkins on the shoulder. He felt suddenly embarrassed, unwilling to show emotion. 'You look well.'

Atkins had been saying at the same time, 'Welcome home, welcome home!' in a voice too cheery by far, taking Denton's one suitcase from the cab driver's hands and boosting it inside the gate. 'Go on in, go on in, General, you're home, I'll handle this!' As if he, too, felt embarrassment.

Denton tried to pay the driver as Atkins was doing the same thing; there was confusion, and then Atkins picked up the suitcase and humped it into the house, bending sideways under the weight because he was a small man. Denton came behind him, closing the gate and then the front door, abruptly glad to be back in the familiar downstairs hall with nothing to relieve its drabness but the two horrible paintings of Scottish cows. The dog was sniffing Denton's trousers. Atkins was dragging and thumping his way up the stairs with the case; Denton hurried behind and lifted some of the weight, to Atkins' disgust. 'Who's the master here and who the man?' he demanded at the top.

'Neither of us. You're a capitalist now, aren't you?'

'Bit of a story about that. Leave off, Colonel, let me do my work.'

'Oh, put that damned suitcase down. You're not a servant any more!' Atkins was by then halfway down the long room that served Denton as sitting room and parlour; at the far end were the stairs to his bedroom. He turned. 'Matter of fact, General, I am. Or will be if you'll take me back.'

'What about the recording business?'

Atkins cleared his throat. He looked profoundly embarrassed. 'I left the business for, ah, mmm, reasons of an ethical nature. I'd like to apply formally to take up my old position with you, if that's possible, sir. If you don't have somebody else. If you're not just glad to—'

Denton had come striding down the room to embrace him. 'My God, you don't need to ask! Yes, and yes!' He stood back, holding Atkins at arm's length as if he might try to get away. 'What the hell happened?'

'Could I wait to tell you about it? It's very fresh, and, er, not very flattering to my business judgement. May I say, instead, Colonel, that I'm pleased as Punch to be in your service again.' He eyed Denton. 'At the old wage.'

'The old wage, of course.' Denton was grinning. 'I'm sorry about the recording business, but—'

Atkins was pulling at Denton's overcoat. 'No use to cry, Sarah! Chuck yourself out of that coat and hat and I'll put them where they belong before you fling them at the nearest piece of furniture. And don't you take that suitcase upstairs; that's my job! You hungry? 'Course you are. You fancy a drop of sherry? It's the right time of day. Whisky, brandy—?' Atkins raised his eyebrows.

'What I fancy is tea.'

'Tea! Oh, I suppose I could do tea. If you really *want* tea.'

Seeing that tea had been the wrong answer, Denton said with a smile, 'Sherry?'

'There you are.' Atkins headed for a small table near the fireplace that had been crowded against the wall by Denton's easy chair; he lifted a decanter, peered into it, got two small glasses. 'Thought I'd be asked to join you,' he said.

'Won't you join me?'

'I will, thanks very much.' Atkins poured, handed a glass to Denton.

'How's Mrs Striker?'

Atkins took a deep breath. 'I never see her. Never here.' Janet owned the house behind, the gardens connected through a door in the wall. 'She's living at Westerley Street, is the word I get. Hasn't been home except the day she arrived, and then only to tell the Cohans she wouldn't be staying.' The Cohans were the couple who lived in her half-basement and took care of the house.

Denton frowned and turned away. He had hoped to see Janet at once. The gloom he had felt crossing London returned; he tried to shake it off by saying, 'I'm sure she'll want to see me.'

Atkins rolled his eyes. 'You just got here; don't you want to sit down with your pipe and slippers and say it's good to be home? Be it ever so humble and so on? Tell me traveller's tales till I can't keep my eyes open?'

He threw himself into his chair. 'I don't have any tales. Let's hear yours—what happened to the recording business? Last I heard, you were on the way to being a millionaire, and then—'

Atkins made a face. 'Can't you wait?' He sighed. 'If I say that I came into the office last Saturday and found my partners making a recording called "What Mabel Did with the Postman on Saturday Afternoon", will you get a whiff of what happened?' He sipped again. 'There's my friend Shelm and some "actress" who was really a tart from over the way, and perfect for the role as all she had to say was "oooooh" and "eeeeeeeh". Also some words I never expected to hear on a wax recording, but some people have no sense of propriety. Could have knocked me over with a feather duster. Here I thought we had a nice little company for the making of comic songs and monologues, doing quite nicely, thank you, and behind my back they're making stuff to sell under the counter in pubs and tobacconists. I was hurt— deeply hurt! *And* worried about the police.'

'And the business went bust?'

'Not at all. My part of the business went bust! I went straight to my legal adviser, got a letter sent saying that because of the making of recordings not consonant with our contract and offensive to me, I was withdrawing, etc., etc. And I did. Thirty-six hours after I heard Mabel and the postman doing the dirty, I was out of the lodge of capitalist strivers and one of the mass of the unemployed.'

'Your partners didn't object?'

'They were delighted. One less piece of the pie to be cut. Also, they thought I was an obstacle to growth—me! And the whole company was my idea!'

'Well, I'm sorry.'

'Don't be, for my sake! I've other irons in the fire. More than one way to skin the cat. In the meantime, welcome home, thanks for having me back, all's well that ends well, and pip-pip. Now may I carry that case upstairs?'

'*Can* you carry that case upstairs?'

'Oh, ha-ha, Italy hasn't changed you a bit.' Atkins picked up the suitcase as if he intended to toss it through the large window at the end of the room, then swayed around the newel post and headed up the stairs. The dog came behind, panting as if he were trying to make it up the Matterhorn. Denton waited for the sound of falling but heard Atkins make it to the top, cross to Denton's bedroom, and drop the suitcase with a crash that made the house shake.

A huge pile of mail sat on a table near his chair. Anything important had already been sent on to him in Naples; knowing what was left was dross, Denton started quickly through it. When Atkins appeared again, he said, 'You might as well have thrown this lot out.'

'Then you'd have asked me where was so-and-so and it'd have been all my fault. Anyway, I wasn't in your employ when most of that lot arrived, so I'm not liable. You eating in or out?'

'I thought I'd go out.'

'First night home after seven weeks in an Italian cesspit, and you're going out? I could have something brought over from the Lamb.'

'I thought I'd stop by Westerley Street.' He hoped Janet would go somewhere to eat with him.

Atkins watched him flip through envelopes with a finger, piling them against his left thumb. He said, 'What brought you back, anyway? Not to pry, of course. The lady, is it?'

Denton stopped, kept his finger in the stack to mark his place. 'Something came up about a man who died in Naples.'

'Oh, no. Oh, no, Captain—not somebody else you think was murdered!'

'As a matter of fact, yes.'

'Oh, I knew it. You could go to Timbuctoo and they'd murder somebody for you, just to make you feel at home. What is it this time, some Dago with a knife in his belly?'

'An old Englishman, actually. "Dago" isn't a nice word.'

'I didn't mean it to be nice, but I apologise if it turns out you're Italian.'

'I'm not, but I like them. *And* their food.'

'No accounting for tastes.'

Denton flipped more envelopes against his thumb and at last came to the end of the pile. 'Toss them all out,' he said.

Atkins took the stack. 'You taking the motor car?' he said. He seemed apprehensive.

'Good God, I'd forgotten I own one. Is it still in one piece?' He'd allowed Atkins to drive it while he was gone.

'It, mmm, had an encounter with a dray in Oxford Street. Functions like a well-made watch but has a bit of a dent.'

'How could you have hit a dray?'

'Didn't hit a dray; the dray hit us! And, mmm, I wasn't driving. An error of judgement on my part. I admit it. Thinking with my heart at the time, not my head.'

'A woman? You let some woman drive my motor-car?'

Atkins tipped his chin up and turned away, his hands full of the letters. 'I'll tell you about it another time, shall I?' He went down the room and then took the stairs to his own quarters.

Denton strode after him and bellowed down the stairs, 'How bad is it?' The dog, as if he, too, expected an answer from the lower depths, sat on Denton's foot and stared down.

Atkins' voice floated up from somewhere below. 'If you hadn't surprised me by coming home, you'd never of known. A pal of mine is knocking out the ding on Monday next.'

Denton stared down the dark stairs. He thought about his ridiculous little car, which had three seats, the third one backward-facing and intended for the dog. He laughed. He scratched the dog's head, causing the dog to throw himself to the floor and expose his privates. Atkins' face appeared at the bottom of the stairs. 'You seducing my dog?'

'I think he's seducing me.'

'He's pleased to see you. Asked about you every day.'

Denton stopped scratching, and the dog rolled on his side, sighed, and went to sleep. Denton went back to his chair and sat, thinking about Janet. Janet loved her house; it was astonishing that she wasn't living in it. He supposed that Ruth Castle must be very near death. It was trivial, even mean minded, but he thought that in that case Janet wouldn't want to go to dinner with him.

In time, Atkins came up and asked if he wanted dinner clothes laid out.

'I'll just go the way I am.'

'You most certainly will not. You're wearing travelling clothes!'

'Well, I've been travelling.'

'And you look it! I'll draw you a bath and unpack your case. I suppose you didn't bring the good dinner suit back with you, oh, no. What's left here to wear will do for the Café Royal and the like, but stay out of the Criterion, will you? I know people there.'

'Do you know, I haven't thought much about clothes for weeks?'

'Yes, but you were among *Italians*, General. This is London.'

So it was. Gloomy, noisy, smelly London, where in the morning he'd have business with the police.

❀ ❀ ❀

Westerley Street was a quiet, short row of good but not palatial houses put up in the eighteenth century. Ruth Castle's brothel had become so famous, however, that the name of the whole had come to stand for the part: say 'Westerley Street' to a cab driver and he would take you to Mrs Castle's.

Denton had been a patron off and on until he met Janet. Ruth Castle had been a mentor of sorts to Janet, a sometime adviser to Denton, particularly where Janet was concerned. Pretty even in middle age, Ruth Castle had become increasingly alcoholic, a bottle of champagne always at hand as she held court in Westerley Street, surrounded by often powerful men and the much younger women they picked out from her stock. A kind of social club as well as a whorehouse, the place, always slightly shabby in Denton's time, had from late in the afternoon until early morning shone with electric light and flattered the ear with soft music. Denton never understood what the neighbours made of it—cabs coming and going, men strolling in and out—but he knew that Ruth Castle paid the police and made generous contributions in the borough, and a former pugilist named Fred Oldaston maintained decorum at the door and inside—with his fists, if he had to.

Now, however, in the early darkness of a winter evening, the house was the darkest and the quietest on the street. Denton thought the cab had brought him to the wrong place, but of course the driver knew what he was doing: when Denton had said, 'Westerley Street,' the driver had said, 'No good, sir—closed up.' But he had brought Denton here when he insisted, and now Denton saw that it was indeed closed. The windows were dark, only a dim light showing behind a curtain on the second floor. The music was silenced. The gas lamps that framed the front door were unlit. No black crape, however, had been hung on the pillars, so Ruth Castle was still alive.

Denton paid the man, who said he'd be happy to wait, and knew another place Denton could go that was almost as good, but Denton waved him on. He went up the familiar steps, remembering that he had not so long before been shot in the back only a few yards away. He tried to look into a window next to the door, saw nothing but his own reflected scowl.

He pulled the bell. Nothing happened, and after thirty seconds he pulled it again. Some sound reached him, perhaps a door closing, then footsteps. When the door opened, he expected to see either Fred Oldaston or Janet, but the woman whose face appeared in the opening was a stranger—heavy featured, stern, beyond middle age, with piled-up hair that reminded him of Eusapia Palladino. The woman said, 'The house is closed.'

'I know that. I haven't come for... I want to see Mrs Striker. I was told she's staying here.'

'There's illness in the house. Serious illness.'

'Will you take a message to Mrs Striker, please.'

'Mrs Striker's resting. She's not to be disturbed.'

'I believe she would want to see me.' Would she?

The woman put her head out a little farther. 'Is your name Dunton?'

'Denton.' He reached for his card case, wished he'd started by offering a card, but the woman pulled her head back into the house and closed the door. It made Denton instantly angry, too angry, fatigue and frustration combining; he yanked on the bell-pull. He was ready to haul on it again when the door opened a few inches and an envelope appeared, long, blunt fingers holding it. A couple of feet above it but back in the shadow of the interior, the same face looked at him. 'She left this for you.'

He took the envelope but put his other hand flat on the door so it wouldn't close. 'How is Mrs Castle?'

'She's dying, isn't she? Nurse says tonight or tomorrow.'

She tried to shut the door; he pushed against it. 'Where's Fred Oldaston?'

'Let go. No reason for him now, is there?'

'I want to see Mrs Striker!'

'She's resting, I told you. Leave off pushing on that door, or I'll have the police.'

'When will I be able to see her?'

But the woman must have put her shoulder to the door, because it closed with a soft thud, and he heard bolts being thrown on the other side. He looked up and down the street, as if to see if he had been caught in a shameful moment; except for a small man with a dog the length of the street away, he saw nobody. It was getting on for the dinner hour. People would be in their houses.

He walked down the steps and turned on the pavement to look at the house, as if he might see Janet looking down from an upper window, like the mad wife in a novel. But the place had closed in on itself, and, except for the open shutters, it was lifeless.

He walked down towards Marylebone Road and wandered until he found a chop house, which he made the mistake of going into. He ordered a sort of supper, which proved to be as bad as English food's reputation in Italy. He read her letter, which was short and unemotional and, he thought, exhausted: 'Please don't try to see me, I'm not seeing anybody. Ruth is dying. I can think of nothing else. We shall talk when this is over'.

He decided to drink his supper and pushed the greasy plate away.

In the morning, hung over and repentant, he went to New Scotland Yard. Detective Inspector Donald Munro was an acquaintance of several years, a massive man with a limp from a household accident and a perpetual sense of indebtedness to Denton for having helped to get him out of a paper-pushing office and back into the CID. A Canadian, Munro had been in the London police for thirty years but still sounded as if he came from somewhere else—another affinity with Denton.

'I got your cable.' Munro had greeted him as if they had last seen each other the day before, had immediately sat down again behind his scarred desk. Around them, a dozen other men were trying to do the CID's business, several of them shouting into telephones at the far end of the huge room. 'What are you on about now?'

'A death in Naples. I thought you might be able to help.'

'How's Mrs Striker?'

'Ruth Castle's dying. She's with her.'

'I heard about Mrs Castle. Rather changes the face of London, doesn't it? What's a retired cop in Brum got to do with a death in Naples?' Denton had asked about Cherry in his cable.

Denton rubbed the bone just above his enormous nose; the headache seemed to have taken root there. 'A question of evidence.'

'Hmph. Naturally, you've stuck your big nose in.'

'That's more or less what Atkins said.'

'Well, he's right. It sticks so far out in front of you it's always getting into things it shouldn't. You're going to trip over it one of these days. You a bit the worse for wear this morning?'

'Just tired.'

'If you say so.' Munro opened a drawer, swore when it stuck, and took out a piece of paper. 'I got a reply from Brum police. Yes, Joseph Cherry was a sergeant, retired seven years ago, still collects his pension and is believed to be living with a married daughter. That do it for you?'

'No photo, I suppose.'

'No, no photo, you didn't ask for a photo! Anyway, no time to get it here since you sent me your message. You want me to ask for a photo?' He sounded exasperated.

Denton shook his head, a movement that made the headache seem to sway within his skull like the clapper in a bell. 'But he's still alive.'

'Seems to be—I'd take "believed to be living with a married daughter" to mean something like that.'

'But they didn't say he's a private detective.'

'No, they didn't. Didn't say he isn't, either. Would you like to let me know what this is about?'

'Don't want to take up your time.'

Munro laughed. 'You should have thought of that when you sent the cable. I've got a quarter of an hour to spare, thanks to a butcher who's confessed he's the one went in the next-door window and stole nine pounds eleven from the till. I'm going to get us each a cup of tea, which I can tell you need, and then you can tell me your tale and I'll tell you whether my time's been wasted or not.' He went off, pivoting his bulk around the corners of desks and between people with the grace of a younger and lighter man. When he put the tea on the desk, Denton was sitting with his head in his hands; Munro said, 'I put lots of sugar in yours. What you need is sherry and a raw egg, but I don't have that.'

'I wish you hadn't mentioned sherry.'

'Actually, you probably are tired. Just got here yesterday, didn't you? Well, drink your tea. Tea makes the world come right—even CID canteen tea. All right, what's this about a Birmingham cop who's involved in something in Italy?'

Denton told him about the private detective who had shown up in Naples. He described the death of Fra Geraldo, the lack of evidence, Cherry's finding of the blood on the stairs. Munro was frowning. 'What?' Denton said.

'He had a chemical that brought up bloodstains?'

'So he said.'

'Bit fanciful.'

'Not a procedure you use?'

'Not a procedure I ever even heard of. Which doesn't mean it couldn't be in use in Brum, but Brum isn't exactly the centre of new police methods, is it? On the other hand, it's a big city for chemicals, and somebody could have invented something.'

'He had a bright light, too. I'd looked by gaslight, and not much of that. And before you ask me, yes, the Naples coppers missed it, too—but they had the same light that I did.'

'Bit careless, were they?'

Denton frowned. 'They have a different system. A magistrate came in—he's really the one runs the investigation. I think he'd made up his mind that it was an accident. The magistrate closed the case.'

'"Death by misadventure".'

'I don't know the Italian for that.'

Munro looked into his tea. He said, 'So an old man who may be cuckoo comes to you and says that ghosts are trying to kill him, and when you go to listen to his tale of woe, he's dead. The coppers come and say, "Right, he's dead, he fell downstairs." Then a private detective comes from Birmingham—*Birmingham*—and uses a big light and says, "Oho, here's blood." Then he works a little magic with his fizz-water and everybody says—what does everybody say?'

'In a nutshell, the blood on the stairs shows that he hit in several places on the way down, so he wasn't thrown, so it's an accident.'

'We've a couple of crowners would have the hide off me for a conclusion like that.'

'I kept it simple.'

'You kept it stupid. All right, you sent me a cable asking about the detective with the magic holy water, so I gather you're bothered by him and you want to know if he's a twister. Eh?'

'Something like that.'

'But a twister for what? What's his fiddle? Who sent him, anyway?'

'The new Lord Easleigh.'

'Who said so?'

'Maltby. Kid from the consulate. I gave him your name, by the way. Did he ever show up?'

'Practically as he stepped off the train. Actually looks like a not-bad prospect for the next intake. I sent him to Recruitment.'

'I should let him know I'm here. Although he's a pain in the neck. I suppose he went back to Essex, or Sussex, or whatever it is.'

'Told me he was going on a course in criminal law. Very eager.'

'Hmph. Oh well.'

'Recruitment will know where he is.' Munro scribbled something on a slip of paper, pushed it over. 'Give them this.'

Denton grimaced, winced.

'Where was I? The private detective. You think he's a con. Why are you suspicious?'

Denton told him about Spina's photograph. Munro sat with his big hands clasped around his china mug as if to warm them—or perhaps actually to warm them, for it was cold in the CID room—and his jaw set, staring at Denton. When Denton was done, he said, 'So now you have a photo of the new Lord What's-his-name.'

'In Naples.'

'Can you swear it's him?'

'Of course not.'

'And the detective—he's there, too, although it may not be him at all?'

'That's about right.'

'Cripes, Denton, I wish I had your time and money to throw about on trains and travel. Must be nice, being a swell. "Oh, this is a bit curious, I think I'll take a three-day trip to chat with my old pal Munro about it."'

'It's more than curiosity.'

'It's you being you. You got suspicious the night the old man died, and you don't let go. I know you. Not that you don't get results.' Munro slurped his tea. 'All right, I agree with you that the magic potion sounds a bit wide. And what's it supposed to mean if the new Lord Muck-a-muck had his picture taken in Naples?'

'That he was there when the old man died.'

'You know that for a fact? You got a date on the photo? Signed by young Lord Piss-pants—"Here I am in Naples on eleventh December last"?'

'No, the date's unsure. The photographer said that—'

'You told me what the photographer said. Put that in the witness box, counsel for the defence would have the jury laughing in fifteen seconds. And what's the rest of it? An overcoat and a horse? No birds carrying sprigs of holly to show it's Christmas?'

'They don't have holly in Naples.'

Munro extended his arms along the desk. 'Here's what we do: I'll ask Brum for more on the detective, what's his name again?—Cherry. Photo if one can be had, if not try to get them to send somebody to ask ex-sergeant Cherry if he's been to Naples recently. I'll also poke around and see if any of CID's younger sparks know anything about bringing up bloodstains. There's always the chance it really is a new technique and the old farts like me haven't heard about it. What I suggest you do is get some sleep.'

Denton raised his head, looked at Munro with pained eyes. 'As long as you're volunteering, there's something else you can do.' Munro groaned. 'There was another fellow who'd have inherited the title, but he was killed a year or so ago. Some sort of accident in the underground. I'd like to be sure it was an accident.'

Munro groaned again. 'That's all you have—"another fellow", "some sort of accident"?' He pointed a finger. 'You find me the name, the date, the place, chapter and verse, and I'll have a look. Otherwise, now you really are asking me to waste CID's time.'

'Even if it's a London crime and not a Naples one?'

'What are you saying? That a lad of fifteen or sixteen kills somebody because he stands in the way of his inheritance, then waits a year, then nips off to Naples and kills the incumbent, then comes back and hires a Birmingham tec to splash some fluid on the stairs for no good reason that I can see? You should go into music hall; you'd get more laughs than Dan Leno.'

Denton drank the rest of his tea and thought that it might corrode his already abused stomach. He leaned back, sighed, tipped his hat forward to shield his eyes. 'Know what the Camorra is?' he said.

'Oh, cripes, a secret society! We had them on the docks five years ago. The Black Hand. Don't tell me the young milord is one of them, as well.'

'The Naples detective said that the Camorra had reason to hate the old man.'

'That's fine, and it makes a lot more sense than a kid in London. But why in that case are you here? You should be telling all this to somebody at whatever they call the Yard in Naples.'

'The *questura*. But I think it would be the magistrate I'd have to talk to. Anyway, the detective didn't think it looked like the Camorra's work.'

Munro pushed his cup away. 'And your time's up. You go home and try to pull this together. Get me chapter and verse on the man who died here; I'll see what hare that starts. Go home, Denton. Get your man to make you a raw egg in sherry.'

'Do I really look that bad?'

'If I was a medico, I'd put you in hospital. I'll see what else I can pry out of Birmingham. *Go home.*'

'That's not as easy as it sounds.' He got directions to Recruitment, showed Munro's note, got a London address for Maltby. He wondered why he was doing it: the thought of seeing Maltby just then caused physical pain. On the other hand, Maltby had seen a lot more of Cherry.

Nonetheless, he made it home, and after eating a breakfast of eggs and bacon and fried bread—he hadn't been able to face food earlier, and sherry sounded revolting—he went out to the British Museum. The walk was barely long enough to give him needed air, but it and three headache powders made life tolerable; soon, he was seated at a table in the reading room, poring over an index to *The Times.* Realising at last that he couldn't go blindly flailing about looking for accidents in the underground, he got a copy of Debrett's and dug out the name of the now dead heir. Harold Northcote, an elder cousin to the current peer.

Northcote, Harold, produced a brief obituary, and that only because he had been the presumptive heir to a title. He had been in his late thirties, as early a child as the eventual heir had been a late one, a clerk in the Foreign Office, son of the second daughter of the fourth earl. At least the obituary gave an approximate date of death. From that, Denton was able to move to the actual newspapers. He found in one of them what he wanted.

TRAGIC EVENT IN HAMMERSMITH
Underground Death
An Heir to the Title of Easleigh Falls under Train

Trains beyond Hammersmith on the Hammersmith and City Line were stopped this afternoon at twenty minutes after two when a man fell to his death from the westbound platform of Hammersmith station. The unfortunate victim, Harold Northcote of Fulham Park, was seen to approach the platform's edge as a train became visible in the tunnel that gave entry to the station. 'He was there one moment and then he was gone the next,' said an eyewitness to the tragedy.

Mr Northcote, a Junior Clerk in the office of the Foreign Secretary, was a nephew of Lord Easleigh and his presumptive heir. He is succeeded by his mother, his father, and four sisters.

The directors of the Hammersmith and City Line insist that all safety measures were rigorously enforced. An investigation is to be anticipated.

He copied out the article and posted it to Munro on his way home. There, he found a telegram from Janet:

RUTH DIED LATE MORNING STOP
ARRANGEMENTS PRIVATE STOP MUCH TO
DO STOP JANET

He wondered what 'arrangements private' meant. That he was not to involve himself? But he had a lingering affection for Ruth Castle. And he was Janet's lover. Of course he would involve himself.

CHAPTER

22

The funeral, perhaps oddly, was to be late in the morning of the next day at Old St Pancras. He learned of it only from Atkins, who had got it from the Cohans. No notice appeared in the newspapers. Denton wondered how the hundreds, perhaps thousands, of Mrs Castle's loyal clients would learn of it. The answer was, of course, that they would not. Janet didn't want them to know. Would anybody at all appear at the church? Well, he would, and he supposed that Fred Oldaston would, and, if Janet had been in touch with them, many of the women who had worked for Ruth and aged into respectability and often marriage. His late friend Sir Hector Hench-Rose would have gone, had he known of it— or would he? He had been a regular patron, but he had also had a very upright, in fact narrow-minded, wife.

He had sent Maltby a note to say that he was in London for a few days. He didn't care whether he got a reply. Maybe the young man had found, once in London, that he was glad to be rid of him. At any rate, he thought he'd done the right thing; if Maltby let the ball drop, that was his affair.

He also sent a telegram to the new Lord Easleigh, asking if he might call on him. Easleigh's case was different from Maltby's: if he didn't reply, Denton would think something was up.

Despite his hangover, Denton had thought seriously of going to Birmingham. Spina's photograph nagged at him. If the blurred face was really Cherry's, and the photographer was anywhere near right about the date, then Cherry had been a good deal less than forthcoming—at best. And if the other face was really that of the new Lord Easleigh, then something was very wrong. He supposed that Cherry and the young milord could have been in Naples sometime in the autumn quite innocently, but if so, why hadn't Cherry mentioned it? On the contrary, he'd been almost a caricature of the first-time visitor, hopeless in the language, puzzled by the food.

Of course, it was likely that the blurred face wasn't Cherry's at all, and if the other one could be proven to belong to the new Lord Easleigh, was he therefore culpable? He might argue that he was free to travel if he liked, that he had had a distant cousin in Fra Geraldo and had wanted to see him. If Fra Geraldo's diary didn't mention him—and it did not, Denton knew—neither did it mention any other details of his life; the diary was a record of contrition, not trivial events. A visit from a distant nephew could have gone unmentioned, could have involved nothing but a mutually embarrassing few minutes in the cold entry of the Palazzo Minerva.

If Denton went to Birmingham, he told himself, he could confront Joseph Cherry and make sure he was the man who had turned up in Naples. If he was, Denton could ask him about the photograph. Birmingham was only a few hours away by train; he could go up and back in a day. But it was too late that day, and the next was the funeral. Maybe the day after. Or maybe by then Munro would have more information for him.

The truth was, the toxic effect of alcohol had left him unfit for much of anything. He rarely drank too much any more; when he did, he remembered why he had stopped. Hangovers of a certain intensity were worse than the symptoms of the influenza. What he really wanted to do after he left Munro was go back to bed.

And so he did.

He woke about five in the afternoon. He felt better, still a little light headed but no longer as if he might lurch if he tried to walk. He got up, pulled on an ancient dressing gown over his trousers and shirt and went downstairs. Atkins was straightening things in the sitting room. He looked up as Denton came down the stairs, raised his eyebrows but said nothing.

'I overdid it,' Denton said.

'Effects of travel, I'm sure.'

'I'm going to the funeral tomorrow. Do I have clothes?'

'Same outfit you wore for Sir Hector's. You only wore it the once.'

'Lay it out, will you? Make sure it's pressed and all that.' Denton fell into his armchair. 'Any sign of Mrs Striker at her house?'

'Nor hide nor hair.'

'I suppose she's staying on at Westerley Street. Lot to do. I should send flowers.'

Atkins, who had been bent over with a whisk broom, straightened and said, 'I think maybe you ought to consider that gentlemen aren't welcome at this occasion, General.'

'Gentlemen were her speciality.'

'All the same, pardon me, they ain't Mrs Striker's, and she's paying the fiddler. I'd go easy, if I was you.'

'Approach the church with caution, prepared to flee?'

'You know her better than I do.'

Denton lay back and closed his eyes. Atkins went on whisking, then ran a carpet sweeper, muttering something about the dirt people made when they'd only been in the house twenty-four hours. Denton opened one eye.

'Sit a minute.'

'Now what've I done?'

'I want to tell you about the death in Naples. You help me to think.'

'You always tell me my ideas are rubbish.'

'That's how you help me.'

Uncomplimentary as that was, it seemed to satisfy Atkins. Telling him what had happened, trying to put in everything in order, Denton found himself seeing it more clearly himself. Atkins was naturally conservative, and at first he pooh-poohed the notion of a murder. Later, told about the chapel and the ledger, he said that Fra Geraldo sounded like a rum old loony but not one worth murdering. He dismissed out of hand the photograph that seemed to show the young Lord Easleigh: Denton was seeing things. His conclusion, after an hour's talk, was that Denton should let sleeping dogs lie, and with that he went off to make what he called 'a proper tea', meaning his idea of a three-course meal.

Later, a knock on the door produced a hand-delivered note from the new Lord Easleigh: he would be delighted to see Mr Denton tomorrow afternoon and looked forward to meeting a man about whom he had heard so much good from his private detective, Mr Cherry.

❀ ❀ ❀

When Atkins came up with a loaded tea tray, Rupert panting behind him, he brought with him a load of questions. As he set up two folding tables and laid out food, he shot them at Denton like somewhat sarcastic bullets.

'Now, this new Lord Hoo-ha, you say you see his face in a photo, you're off on a wild hare to London because you think you've proof he was in Naples. What's the point?'

'He came to Naples and killed the old man.'

'Oh, of course—he wants to be the Gay Lord Quex and can't wait another year or two.'

'He's seventeen. That age wants things right now. Can't wait.'

'My hat! He'd be daft to risk it when he's got a sure thing not too far away.'

'Ever tried telling that to a seventeen-year-old who has some girl ready to fall on her back for him?'

'Oh, ha-ha, I don't see the relevance of that. Don't try to come over me with tricky arguments.'

Atkins, the pot and cups and dishes he had brought with him set out, went back the length of the room and opened a door opposite the Dresden stove—the dumb-waiter. He hauled on the cable, inhaled, and came back with a single large tray with half a dozen dishes on a white cloth. He began to put those on flat surfaces around Denton. 'Tinned smoked trout, courtesy of the late Sir Hector, bless him. Boiled eggs, had them made up in the icebox, devilled them with a bit of curry. Cinnamon toast—leave the cloth on to keep the heat in, if you please. Bread and butter, very thick, very well buttered. Pickled cockles, not everybody's cup of tea, but mine. Sliced ham. Eccles cake. Bit of Scottish shortbread, comes in a tin from the Army and Navy—not too bad. Gooseberry conserve. Hepburn's Best Military Chutney. Pound cake with—where is it? Aha, in the gravy boat, couldn't find anything else—custard. Jam tart.' He looked severe. 'That's all there is!'

'How many of us did you plan to feed?'

'I thought this chat we're having would take a while. And there's Rupert.' Rupert was the dog.

Atkins cracked open a linen serviette, dropped it with a flourish on Denton's lap, then got one for himself and sat. 'Tuck in, General, tuck in, you've been a soldier—you never know when your next chance to eat will come. All right, back to your murder that wasn't a murder—who else?'

Denton told him about Scuttini and the Camorra; Atkins' view was that they'd have strangled him and thrown him into the tunnels under the house and nobody would have been the wiser.

'The boys, then. E and M—the choirboys who tried to kill him, at least according to the ledger.'

'For buggering their bums? Well, yes, if he said they tried to kill him once, I suppose they might try again. But that was when—back in the age of Napoleon?' He gave Rupert a triangle of shortbread.

'Eighteen sixty or thereabouts.'

'Pardon my untutored maths, Major, but I make that to be forty-four years. They've waited all this time?'

'They had to mature. They had to let their hatred grow. It fermented in their minds, soured, exploded.'

'Sounds like cheap champagne. The mind goes all fizzy, then pop! I thought you were the one read all the psychology, not me. I'd say from my layman's point of view that's rubbish, but then I haven't read the latest by Herr Doktor Poop-Fartlebee.' Atkins was eating large pieces of smoked trout on buttered bread. 'Anyway, you said that "M" was a drunkard who could hardly put one foot in front of the other.'

'He could have been temporarily sober.'

'And he said, "Oh, I'll get my old pal 'E' and have another go at murdering old Geraldo." Where's "E" been all these years, by the way?'

'Maybe he emigrated and came back, and it was he got in touch with Michele, fed him full of the old grievances, got him sober.'

'Just happened to be able to creep into the old man's *palazzo*, pretend to be ghosts by imitating kids having their backsides split.'

'Might have had a key. He and Michele had lived there, you know. Could have stolen a key then and kept it.'

'For forty-four years? Love a duck, you've a high opinion of the human capacity for devilment! Though I'll grant you one point: somebody that had been that mistreated as a kid and had made himself some money and become somebody might just want to get back at his persecutor. Put the seal on his being a man, eh? Show he can't be buggered any more? Think about it.'

'I have thought about it. Was the smoked trout good?'

'Capital. I offered you some. Try the cockles. All right, I'll concede a lurid possibility for "E" and "M", but I think it's far-fetched. And there goes your argument for the photograph and the young lord—if it's "E" and "M" grown middle-aged, where's Lord Boyishness?'

'I don't know.'

'Meaning that you admit that idea is thinner than Irish soup.'

Denton was eating a devilled egg and feeling better. How he wished he'd had Atkins back when Fra Geraldo had died! He said, 'Then there's that spirit message about the policeman.'

'You mean a spook voice from a so-called medium you wouldn't trust to give you a correct message from the telephone, much less the great beyond? Come off it. The spirit voice is a fiddle, nothing but a deliberately mysterious sentence that came out of a medium's mouth; she might as well have said, *The dressmaker is playing cricket.*'

'"The cop is doing a play." Meaning the cop is acting a part.'

'Which cop?'

Denton shrugged and ladled custard over pound cake. 'Then there's the old man's money. Everybody wants money, Sergeant.'

'Was there money? You're sure of that? Thought you told me somebody said the family had run through the money.'

'He didn't know for sure. Anyway, there's the title. People would kill for a title, a lot of them.' He thought of Mrs Newcombe, who would have destroyed her daughter's life for a title.

'They say they would, maybe. Hard to believe when you come to it. Try the Eccles cake—rather good.' He woke Rupert to give him a piece.

'And that would explain the photograph—that the face in the picture is the young lord, and the blurry one is the detective, who's "acting a play".'

'And where did that photograph come from, I ask you. You say it came from some seaside artiste, but in fact *he* was brought to you by this Dago who forced himself on you from the very beginning—eh? Eh?' Atkins was waving a cockle pick at him.

'Don't say "Dago". DiNapoli didn't force himself on me. Anyway, that was before I ever heard of Fra Geraldo. No, wait— it was just *after* the old man came to the pension to ask me for help.'

'Aha! So the Dago had followed the old man to your place; like everybody in Italy, he knows Texas Jack and his doings, so he follows you and attaches himself to you like a limpet. Then when he's done the old fellow in, he's in a perfect position to influence your every move. He translates for you! You don't know what people are really saying; he could be feeding you the whole Munchausen line! He's in with the Camorra fellow—you said so yourself. He's the one brings you the photographer. He's your evil genius, Colonel. Playing Dago Svengali to your Trilby.'

'I should never encourage you to go to the theatre.'

'Have some jam cake.'

'Mrs Striker thinks that DiNapoli is one of the world's innocents.'

'No offence to the lady, and I concede she has a wide knowledge of the world, but I think she missed a beat with this one. He sounds a thoroughly tricky sort. A man can smile and smile and be et cetera. Criminal past, into all manner of skulduggery, lives by his wits—at best shifty, Colonel, and could be lots worse.'

'Why in the world would he murder Fra Geraldo?'

'He was one of the choirboys. Or he's working for that Camorra. Or…some reason we haven't even thought of. I'll get the cheese.'

Denton looked around at the ruin of their tea. He shouted towards the stairs, 'And more of those Scottish biscuits, while you're at it.' Rupert looked startled.

❀ ❀ ❀

He slept deeply, woke with an idea in his head and no memory of dreams: *I was a fool to come to London.*

It was as if he'd thought it through overnight and now the idea was clear and entirely decided. Fra Geraldo, the photograph, the theatrical policeman, Cherry—it was all nonsense. What had he been thinking of?

He faced an obvious truth: he'd come back to see Janet. The rest was self-deception.

He pulled on a long robe, in which he felt like somebody in a bad play but which he needed because the house was infernally cold. He washed in cold water, finding no hot in the pipe; downstairs, he prowled his sitting room, looking for heat, finally started a fire in the grate and then boiled water on his spirit stove and made tea. He thought how quickly habits changed—in Naples, he would have been walking to his café—and wondered if thinking, the mind, changed in parallel, as they said in the electrical sciences: did he now think differently about the old man's death because he was in London? It was true, Fra Geraldo seemed distant; the Palazzo Minerva was somewhat hard to visualise; the chapel seemed to have diminished. Was Naples a play, London reality? Or was Naples play, London work?

It was not yet seven. Atkins seemed still to be asleep. The first mail had come through the slot before he heard Atkins letting Rupert out into the back garden. Denton got the mail, was coming up the stairs with it, not looking where he was going but reading the envelopes instead, when he almost ran into Atkins in the upper doorway.

'Watchwhereyergoan!' Atkins growled, swaying back into the sitting room. 'Cripes, it's you, Major, what're you doing out of bed?'

'Full of pep. The house is like an ice cave—what happened to our Dresden stove?' The enormous porcelain thing filled an alcove near the stairs; it had been supposed to be the heater for all the upper floors.

'Oh, cripes.' Atkins looked chagrined. He had not shaved yet, was wearing a robe so old the nap of the velour had been worn down to woof and warp. 'With you not here, I got out of the habit of lighting it. I'm heated from the furnace.' Denton had tried having a furnace put in, a disaster for the house except for Atkins' quarters and the draper's shop in the ground-floor front.

'And no hot water.'

'Well, I said I forgot, didn't I? I'll do it, I'll do it—' He scuttled up the room towards the stove.

Denton had hoped for something from Janet. Even one of her telegrams would have given solace, but there was nothing.

Among the bills, however, was an envelope with writing he didn't recognise; on the back it said 'F. Maltby' and the address in Maida Vale Denton had got from Scotland Yard's Recruitment Division.

'Dear Mr Denton,' the note inside said, 'It was very good of you to write to me. I am well. Your friend Inspector Munro helped me and I think I will be joining the police force come September. May I call on you this afternoon? I have something to tell you. I am taking a course in criminal law and will be in your neighbourhood. Very sincerely yours, Frederick A. Maltby.'

A visit that afternoon? That was unwelcome. Ruth Castle's funeral would be this morning; he wanted time with Janet—of course, she would be grieving, he'd have to be available to her—and then, in a day or two, they'd head back to Naples. It was important to him to get her back there. They'd been *happy* there. Hadn't they?

'I think that the truth is I came back to London out of homesickness,' he said to Atkins, who seemed to have got flames going in the porcelain stove and was huddling over the open door with his ratty robe pulled tight around his throat.

'Better than some daft murder,' Atkins said. 'No offence intended.'

'I wanted to see Mrs Striker, is the truth.'

'Funeral today. So then it's off to Italy again, is it?'

Denton had come down to the alcove where he kept the spirit stove. 'I certainly hope so. Tea?' he offered.

Atkins looked exasperated. 'That's my function, General!'

Denton heard a muffled bark. Atkins headed for his stairs. 'Cripes, I forgot Rupert. Everybody's up too bleeding early today!' He stamped down the stairs, and a few seconds later Denton heard the back door being opened. When, half an hour later, Atkins appeared, he was shaved and dressed in a clean high collar and shirt, black alpaca jacket and waistcoat and cinder-grey trousers; the Dresden stove was putting out more heat than a chameleon; and hot water flowed from Denton's tap. He spent a while looking out his rear window into Janet's garden and the blank windows of her house, then dressed in the black clothes that Atkins had laid out and went down to the sitting room to find a black silk hat, black gloves, ebony walking stick and black overcoat waiting.

'I'll be back by one. I'm not going to the graveside.'

'Hope you're not the only one there, if you don't mind me saying. The line she was in, people fall off easily.'

'Nonsense, there'll be huge crowds. Ruth Castle was an institution.' He held up Maltby's note. 'A young man may come by. Maltby. If he's here before I am, stick him up here and give him something to read. He's all right.'

'Did I say he wasn't? Never so much as set eyes on him.'

'He gives the wrong impression sometimes.' Denton pulled on the overcoat and put the top hat on his head. He detested top hats. 'I look like a suburban undertaker.'

'You look exactly the way you ought to look. Very respectable, if I may say so.'

Denton studied the man in the mirror—the dangling grey moustache, the lined face, the peculiar hat that seemed to rest on the tops of his ears, the too-correct overcoat and gloves. 'Texas Jack,' he said with some sarcasm.

❀ ❀ ❀

Old St Pancras Church was an easy walk away, only across Euston Road and along Pancras Road. Denton took it quickly, his long legs eating up the pavement as the ebony stick rapped in tempo. Pancras Road was a thoroughfare for wagons and lorries delivering and picking up goods at the freight stations, and it was noisy with hooves and motors; it seemed hostile, as if not made for human beings, yet Old St Pancras Church, even from a distance, looked like something in a village, its grey stones soft among the greens of elms and the old churchyard—a watercolour in a surround of steel engraving. Nearing it, Denton saw that a sizeable crowd was milling about the door; closer still, he saw that most of the crowd were women. Turning in at the gate, he realised that he was in fact the only man.

Some of the women turned to look at him. Their talk, which had been low, murmurous, fell off to a few voices nearest the church. All in blacks and purples and whites, they seemed to fit with the old stones. Many had their faces veiled. Of the faces he could see, Denton recognised none. These were not the 'girls' of Ruth Castle's most recent crew; they would have moved to other houses as soon as she closed hers, perhaps had been sent by her while she could still manage as part of an informal rotation that kept new faces in the good houses of the big cities. The women he saw now were all older, some with grey hair, many looking middle-class and comfortably heavy.

Uneasy with their stares, Denton took a turn in the church-yard, pretended to study a few of the stones. When he turned back, he saw another male figure entering the gate; he felt an impulse to rush to him but tamped it down because it was nobody he knew. The man was old, small, bent. Less than a minute later, another man came in behind three more women. Denton recognised him.

'Fred,' he said as he hurried closer. They shook hands. Fred Oldaston had been her muscle, always a fixture at the door in a dinner suit; now, he looked uncomfortable in black serge and a black bowler, a mourning band on his arm. He said, 'Damned glad to see you. I thought I was going to be the only one with danglers here.'

Denton nodded at the old man. 'Who's he?'

Oldaston squinted where Denton had indicated with his chin. 'I think he used to come in to do the drains. Fancy him coming to her funeral.'

'I thought the place would be full of her old clients.'

Oldaston laughed. 'It's one thing to go to her house, another to tip your hat to her on the street. They won't come.'

Denton looked at the women, who were beginning to straggle into the church. 'I don't feel very welcome.'

'I wasn't sure, m'self. May not be, in fact. Mrs Striker sent me packing the day she arrived. Nothing personal, her and me always got along, but she said she didn't want any men in the house. We'll see if that goes for the church as well.' Oldaston moved towards the church door. Several women hurried in, as if to get away from him, and, even though two of them spoke to him—they must all have known him, Denton supposed—they didn't smile or drop back to talk with him.

Oldaston stopped just short of the door, apparently to let all the women go in first. He turned with a chastened smile and said to Denton, 'Thought I'd let them all get up front, slip into a back pew.' He nodded at somebody behind Denton; Denton turned and saw the old man. He nodded; the old man nodded back and said, 'Nice day. Sad time. Always good to me, she was. Paid on time, unlike some as thought they was better.'

The last of the women disappeared through the door. Oldaston said, 'Well,' and shrugged himself into his clothes but didn't move forward. Denton, annoyed at the notion that he should hang back and creep in like a poor relation, stepped around him and, planting the cane firmly as if to claim the ground under it, strode through the door.

Janet was standing a few feet inside, her back to the sanctuary doors as if she were guarding them. She looked, he thought, dreadful, as drawn and hollow eyed as when she had had typhus. Her dress looked too big for her, perhaps was borrowed; her hair had been caught up any old how, with strands escaping down her neck. Never attractive in hats, she wore one that perched too far back on her head and looked as if it might fall off.

'Janet,' he said. He was smiling, happy at last to see her. He moved forward to say something conventional about Ruth Castle's death.

'What are you doing here?' Her voice was like an angry man's.

Behind him, he heard Fred Oldaston suck in his breath. Denton said, 'I've come because of Ruth—Janet, she was—'

'Go away. *Go away!*'

At that moment, he knew, she hated him. He felt his face go hot, then his neck and shoulders, and anger surged up through his body with the blood. At that moment, too, he hated her.

He turned, knocking into Fred Oldaston, who was already backing out the door; behind him, the old man was standing on tiptoe, trying to see in. Denton stumbled, gave Oldaston a shove to the side and brushed past the old man as he rushed from the church. The old man said something; Oldaston muttered a curse, but Denton was already almost to the gate. He hurtled through, his face flaming, and turned and almost ran along the pavement towards Euston Road.

The bitch! he thought. *Those bitches! They could have told us. They could have let us know it was a twat party! They have telephones, some of them; Janet sends telegrams like they're confetti, she could have done that. A whore's trick, a fucking bloody whore's trick on the men! Fucking congregation of cunts—!*

He could feel the snarl that was on his lips. The cane reached out as if he were trying to stab something, and it hit the pavement with a harsh crack. On Euston Road, people got out of his way; one woman, clearly frightened, cowered against a lamp-post with an arm raised to protect herself. On and on he went, cursing, infuriated, muttering to himself, devouring the small streets below Euston Road and racing at last along Coram Gardens and across Guilford Road and into Lamb's Conduit Street.

Reaching his own house, he didn't ring for Atkins but shoved his key into the lock as if he were disembowelling an enemy. He slammed the door behind him; the whole house shuddered. Atkins' surprised face appeared. Denton was already taking the stairs two at a time.

'I say—General—'

'Shut up!'

He tore open the upstairs door and then slammed it behind him even harder than he had the front, hoping it would break, hoping *something* would break. He raised the stick over his head and threw it down the long room, where it crashed against a wall and then the floor and bounced; there was a sound of breaking glass. Denton ripped off the overcoat and threw it at the grate, then took the hat and smashed it as hard as he could to the floor. When it settled, apparently still in good condition, he kicked it, followed it, and stamped on it. He stamped on it again to make sure it was crushed, then did it once more because his anger was still at red heat. Then he had to stand in the middle of his sitting room and look around to see what else he could smash.

His eyes met Maltby's. The young man had been standing by the window behind him. Aware that he'd been noticed, Maltby said, 'Uh, uh, I'll leave. Just leaving.'

'No, stay!' Some dreg of courtesy, perhaps nothing more than shared maleness after all those women, asserted itself. Maltby had shaved off his whiskers, looked young and vulnerable; the sight steadied Denton. 'No.' He started for the stairs. 'I'll be right down—change these God-awful clothes—' From the stair, he shouted, 'Don't go!'

In his bedroom, he tore the clothes off, saying to himself, *Never again. She said she'd been good, well, she doesn't know how good I've been, at her beck and call, always, always doing what she wants, fucking when she wants, sleeping with her when I'm allowed, living where she wants, putting up with her goddam insipid girls! I'm through with it. Harnessed to her minge and made to gee and haw like an ox! No more! By Christ, she can spend the rest of her life with women! I'll sell this house; let her keep hers. I'll go back to Naples. Live in Naples. Or the States—!*

He pounded down the stairs, dressed now in a dark sack suit with the first necktie he'd seen on the rack, brown brogues that Atkins would disapprove of, but he didn't care. Coming down into the sitting room, he saw Maltby precisely where he'd left him, but the funeral hat and coat and stick were gone; some broken glass lay below the dumb-waiter door, shoved there, he thought, by Atkins' foot. He said, 'I'm sorry for the performance. I've had a shock.'

Maltby waved a hand weakly. 'I'm sure—quite all right. I didn't notice.'

Denton barked out a harsh laugh. 'Have you gone blind and deaf, Maltby?' He grabbed the whisky decanter from the table beside his chair and poured a glass, drank it off, and poured another. 'Want some?'

'No, thank you. I really must go.'

'Stay!' Denton put the glass down on the mantel and rubbed his forehead. He found that he cared what Maltby thought. Why was that? 'I'm sorry. Something happened.' He flashed a rueful smile. 'It isn't you.' He pulled the bell, which he normally hated to do, hated the idea of summoning a human being with a bell. Atkins appeared at the top of his own stairs as if he'd been waiting. Denton said as gently as he could manage, 'Please pack up my things. I'm going back to Naples tonight.'

Atkins looked at him, waited for three seconds as if hoping for more instructions, and went up the stairs towards Denton's bedroom.

Thinking aloud, Denton said, 'I'll have to send a note to Lord Easleigh to tell him I'm not coming.' He looked at Maltby, said, 'I was supposed to see Lord Easleigh this afternoon. Waste of time.' He turned away. 'Most things are a waste of time.' He took a sip of the whisky, rubbed his forehead again. 'You wanted to see me.'

'It doesn't matter.'

'It must matter, or you wouldn't have written.'

'I, uh—it's nothing. Just a little thing. You've got other things on your mind.'

Denton laughed unpleasantly. 'You could say that. Well, I'd like to get those things *off* my mind. I hear you're joining the police.'

'Yes. That was one of the things I wanted to tell you. To express my thanks.'

Denton waved a hand without looking at him.

'I'm taking a course at University College in criminal law. Sitting in, that is. Came in too late to take the whole course, but they're letting me sit in. Thought it might...' His voice ran down; he forced it into life again. 'Help me.'

'Good idea. Shows the right spirit.' Denton turned towards him. His own face, he knew, was probably frightening; certainly, Maltby looked frightened. 'You'll make a good copper.'

Maltby flushed, shook his head. He hesitated, looked at Denton again. 'The other thing...'

'Yes?'

'It isn't anything much, maybe nothing, but I thought you'd be...' Again his voice ran down. This time, he hardly managed to drag it back to a whisper. 'Interested.'

Denton sipped the whisky. He was trying to drive Janet out of his mind. He had thought Maltby could help, but Maltby was being no more distracting than Atkins, who was bumping about softly in the bedroom overhead. He said wearily, 'I'm interested, yes, tell me.'

'It's about that private detective. Cherry?'

Denton had to think about who Cherry was. All of that seemed so distant. Like people he had known in his childhood. Cherry. Yes. And the old man and DiNapoli. That name caused him a twinge of shame. 'Yes. Cherry?'

'Well, you remember that Dago poof from the *Carabinieri*? Donati? Rather childish ass, very full of himself—'

'Yes, yes.'

'Well, you'll remember I caught him stealing from the private detective's case. He took one of his glass phials and some of his bloodstain fluid. I told you at the time—when we were in the house—'

'I remember.' He controlled his irritation. Maltby was proving a trial.

'Well, I just had a letter from him—Donati. It came by way of the consulate. I suppose he was trying to butter me up so's I wouldn't tell anybody what he'd done. As if I would. He's had Cherry's fluid analysed and he shared the results with me— because, he *said*, he thought the British authorities should know the facts. The long and the short of it is, Cherry's fluid is no good.'

Denton raised his head. Finally, Maltby had got to him. Janet receded.

'That's what the analysis showed—the claim that he could find hidden bloodstains just isn't in it. Imagine! Unless somehow he believed it himself. People are remarkable when it comes to their own hobby-horses. He was convincing, I thought. Didn't you? It just shows you what sort of world it is. He seemed such a respectable sort of fellow—rather low-class and certainly uncul-tured, but trustworthy, didn't you think? And why would he invite us all to see something that's no good? Why such a show?'

'How does Donati know it was no good?'

'He had the fluid analysed. I told you. He says it's nothing but a mixture of water and common vinegar and permanganate something-or-other. Donati said his people tried it on bloodstains and it did nothing. *Nothing*. They did some sort of analysis in a laboratory; I don't understand that stuff, couldn't stand chem-istry except for the set I got once for Christmas, then it was fun making smells and so on, but I didn't know what I was doing. Donati says you could make the foamy reaction if you poured the fluid on common soda, but they couldn't make anything turn pink with it. The only way it could be done, according to Donati, who has a very cynical mind, I think, is if you performed some sort of sleight of hand and sprinkled soda and a bit of red dye where you poured the fluid, but I'm sure Cherry didn't do that because we were watching the whole time. Weren't we?'

Janet had vanished. Denton was staring at Maltby as if he meant to kill him. 'If Cherry's fluid was a sham, there weren't any bloodstains on the stairs!'

'Well, exactly. What a cheap trick—just, suppose, to inflate our idea of him. I expect people to behave honourably, but really—'

But Denton had walked away from him and was rattling the hook of the telephone that leaned from the wall next to the dumb-waiter. He shouted a number into the mouthpiece and then pointed at Maltby and bellowed, 'Don't you go away!'

Denton waited. He fidgeted. He pounded twice on the wall. A rough voice shouted from the earpiece, 'CID, Plackett here!'

'Give me Munro! Inspector Munro! Can you hear me?'

'They can hear you in bloody China.' Denton heard the voice calling for Munro. He pictured the big, noisy, swirling CID room, Munro's desk at the far end from the telephones. The first voice said, 'Coming,' and then he waited some more, and then Munro was there, sounding irritated.

'It's Denton.'

'Well?'

'That man, Cherry. You said you'd check again with Birmingham—'

'Well, I haven't. Don't get your dander up; there's other cases than yours. And lots more important.'

Denton's anger flared, displaced from Janet to Munro. He stepped back from it, made himself at least seem quiet. 'What about the death in the underground? I sent you the details.'

'Nothing yet. No time, Denton. Cripes, man, it's only been hours.'

'Right. Well, anything you hear—'

'Right, right—when I've a minute—you're in a long queue.'

When Denton turned from the telephone, Atkins was coming down with his bag. Atkins said, 'Lower hall?'

'Yes. Atkins!'

'Sir?'

'It's nothing to do with you. It was…her.'

'I *know* that, sir.' But he didn't seem mollified.

Denton strode back to Maltby, who started to say something, but Denton stopped him by putting a finger in his face. 'If Cherry's fluid was a try-on, then so was Cherry himself.'

'Oh, but, see here—'

But Denton wasn't listening. He went to the mantel and addressed the amber fluid in the glass that sat there. 'If Cherry's a sell, then what was the plan? To make it appear that the old man had hit his head as he fell? Where does that get us?'

'I thought all this was over and done with.'

'Where it gets us is that if he fell and rolled or bounced like a ball, then he probably wasn't thrown. But either way, there wasn't a lot of blood. Even Cherry's magic liquid couldn't produce a *lot* of blood.' Denton looked at his watch. 'What are you doing from now until four o'clock?'

'Oh.' Maltby shrugged. He looked embarrassed. 'I often walk about at this time. Look at the shops. Things.' He frowned. 'I don't have many friends yet in London.'

'Good. You up to spending two hours with me?'

'Oh.' Maltby blushed, apparently with pleasure, or at least satisfaction. 'Where are we going?'

'The Albany.' Denton picked the glass from the mantel and threw the contents into the grate. He put the glass down and went to the box that held his ancient derringer, took it out and put it into his jacket pocket; it felt comfortable there after weeks of absence. 'Wait here.'

He went down the stairs to Atkins' quarters, calling ahead because he knew he was going where he wasn't much wanted. Rupert appeared, then Atkins; neither looked pleased.

'I'm going out.' That at least didn't seem to displease Atkins. 'How are you fixed for a soft cap and an old scarf?'

'What's on, General?'

'Going to a masquerade.'

Atkins eyed him. He pushed out his lips as if he were going to kiss something—not Denton—and raised his eyebrows and went into his sitting room. 'Have a seat.' He disappeared, Rupert behind him. Minutes later, he was back with a small Gladstone bag, much scuffed. 'Sending this stuff to the Salvation Army, but you're welcome to go through it. Please don't throw any of it out.'

'Sorry about all that. She—'

'Don't tell me.'

'No, it's better you know. She made it pretty clear we're... She didn't want me around.'

'Figured it was something like that. Nevertheless, you don't want to go off the handle, General.'

'I already have.'

He was going through the handbag. He selected a cloth cap and a stained trilby. 'No scarf.'

'I ain't the Old Curiosity Shop. What's wrong with your own?'

'Not ratty enough.'

'Oh, but mine would be. Flattering.' Atkins went to his bedroom and came back with a length of dark cloth that hung from his hand like a dead snake. 'Ratty enough?'

'It'll have to be.'

'Rupert likes to chew on it. Might smell a bit doggy.'

Denton took it and thanked him and started for the stairs. Atkins said, 'General?'

'Well?'

'She's one in ten thousand.'

He stopped. 'Not today, she isn't.' He went on up.

He draped the scarf around Maltby's neck and put the cloth cap on his head, which Maltby ducked to escape, but Denton insisted. He tucked the ends of the scarf into Maltby's jacket. 'Cigarette,' he said.

'I don't indulge. Very bad for the wind.'

Denton got a cigarette from a box on his table and broke it in half and stuck an end in Maltby's mouth. He stepped back. 'Slouch.'

'What?'

'Slouch. Look unhappy.'

This was never hard for Maltby. Denton looked him over. 'You'll do.' He went upstairs and got one of his own old overcoats. 'Put that stuff in your pockets for now. Don't lose the cigarette.'

'What's all this about?'

'The game's afoot, as our pal Cherry put it.'

❀ ❀ ❀

They watched the two entrances of the Albany for more than an hour, Denton at a peephole behind a first-storey window on Piccadilly, and Maltby in the less likely Burlington Gardens. Maltby had been put in the shadow of a pillar by an empty house where a leafless plane tree gave a little cover; he was wearing the cap and scarf and half-cigarette. He objected that he was sure he looked foolish.

'You're practising police work, aren't you? Think of yourself as an undercover narc. Hop to it.'

Denton had tried moving back and forth between the entrance to Burlington Arcade and the Albany wearing Atkins' old hat and his own old overcoat. Policemen twice tried to move him on, but each time he took them to the art dealer Geddys in the Arcade and got his assurance that Denton was a respectable person. After the second time, the always irascible Geddys said he was tired of Denton's bothering him.

'"Allus movin' on,"' Denton said.

'What's that?'

'It's the police keep bringing me to you, not my choice.'

It was then that Geddys telephoned a friend across Piccadilly and got permission for Denton to sit on a hard chair behind the little door that allowed a tailor to put examples of his work— best gentlemen's suitings, by appointment—on display one storey above the street.

When they were only ten minutes away from the appointment with Lord Easleigh, Denton walked around to Burlington Gardens and told Maltby to pack it in.

'But I just *saw* him. I couldn't leave my post to tell you, but I saw him—Cherry!'

'He didn't recognise you? What did he look like?'

'Like somebody's gent's gent—black jacket, striped pants, bowler. He went into the Albany and he hasn't come out. Not my way, anyway.'

Denton took off Maltby's cap and scarf and dropped the cigarette in the gutter, then led the way to Geddys' shop, where they had left their own outer clothes. Geddys—small-goateed, twist-backed—gave one of his malevolent looks when Denton said he wanted to leave the soft cap and other old clothes there.

'This isn't a rubbish tip; it's an art shop!'

'I told you, if you accommodated us, I'd let you buy my Scottish cows at a good price.'

'They're a drug on the market.'

'Maybe I'll *give* you the cows.'

As they walked down Piccadilly towards the front entrance to the Albany, Maltby said, 'I saw you put a gun in your pocket. Is there going to be trouble?'

'Habit. I'm not *looking* for trouble, if that's what you mean.' He glanced at the young man's puckered face. 'If you want to get out of it, now's the time.'

The old man who served as Cerberus at the main gate to the Albany was the same one whom Denton remembered from a couple of years before. He didn't remember Denton. He checked a list and said that, yes, Lord Easleigh was expecting him, but not the other gentleman, so would they please *both* sign the book? Denton, who had seen at least a dozen people go by the old man's booth while he apparently napped, said nothing.

Inside, Maltby said, 'Funny place.'

'Very tony. Doesn't look it, I know, but it is. Men only.' He thought bitterly that it might suit him now. 'Not a block of flats at all—more like a small street.'

Maltby said, 'Undercover work is boring.'

'The better crime novelists don't tell you about that part.'

Number 12C was on the second floor of a small detached building. Denton went ahead. At the top of the stairs, he murmured to Maltby, 'Let me do the talking.'

'You already told me!'

'No inventions—no inspirations. Just think of yourself as a plodding, silent, apprentice copper. And witness.'

He twisted the bell set into the middle of the door. Almost too quickly, the door opened, apparently pulled with a lot of force from inside. The young Lord Easleigh himself appeared in the opening, mouth open, face rather red. He wore a somewhat startling afternoon suit of a blue that Atkins wouldn't have approved. His long hair, ringletted, hung almost to his shoulders. He looked about fourteen.

'Mr Denton, to see Lord Easleigh.'

'Phh! Oh, of course. I'm Paul Murie—Easleigh, that is. My man is off today. Answering the door myself. Rather—rather...' He seemed unable to say rather what.

Denton was studying the face, trying to find the black-and-white image in Spina's photograph. Was it really the same? Maybe, from a certain angle...

'This is my friend, Mr Maltby. He's on leave from the Naples consulate. I thought you might like to chat with him, too. He made the arrangements for you, I think—' Denton was moving them into the flat, Easleigh backing away from him as if being pushed by an invisible wave that Denton threw up in front of himself.

'Oh, yes—ah—yes…' Easleigh managed to free himself by turning around and striding ahead into a sitting room. 'I've just moved in. Not finished—rather a mess, in fact. I'm thinking of having a cosy corner over there…' His voice trailed off. He was gesturing towards a corner where several pasteboard boxes were piled.

Otherwise, the sitting room was crowded with new-looking furniture of the heavy, machine-carved sort that filled middle-class houses all over England. Denton was thinking again that Easleigh was very young, also that he was not very lordly. His accent was the same as Cherry's, indubitably Brum; he was a too-young, middle-class kid snatched from the jaws of respectability by the accident of inheritance.

'An *Oriental* cosy corner,' the very young man said. He now seemed to see Maltby for the first time and, after staring at him for a second or two, shot out a hand. 'I'm Easleigh.' His earlier nervousness was somewhat damped. 'Thanks for taking care of things in Naples.'

Maltby shook his hand, muttered something about it's being his job.

'Still, good of you. Awful good.' He reddened. *'Awfully* good.' He looked around the room as if somebody with more experience and better manners might be there to tell him what to do next. 'Shall we sit down?' He seemed uncertain where, although the room had chairs for at least a dozen.

'Yes, please. Good.'

They all sat. Denton took his time looking around. 'Very pleasant room.' In fact he thought it was one of the ugliest places he'd ever been in. He saw a fireplace, three doors stained almost black, a blizzard of framed photographs and chromos that almost managed to hide the chintz-patterned red and brown wallpaper, and a melodeon that rose up one wall like a siege engine. 'Do you play?' Denton said.

'What? Oh, that. No.' Easleigh was very red again. 'But I mean to learn.' After a silence, he said to Maltby, 'You like music?'

Maltby looked at Denton as if asking permission to speak and muttered, 'Not so much.'

Easleigh crossed, uncrossed and recrossed his legs the other way. 'Me neither.' Again, he looked around. 'I suppose I could offer you some sherry...'

Denton had been wondering how long the young man could go on thinking of things to say. The answer seemed to be that he couldn't go on much longer: his silences were getting thicker. This suited Denton; on the other hand, he'd have to come to business before Easleigh got silent for so long that he threw them out. Or would he never have the courage to do that? Denton said, 'Perhaps you'd like to ask us about your cousin.'

Easleigh looked dumbstruck.

'The fifth Lord Easleigh. Your predecessor.'

'Oh. Um. Ye-e-e-s, well...'

A silence fell. From another room, a thud came, as if a shoe had been dropped. Easleigh jerked and said too loudly, 'The moving man! Still moving me in. Clumsy fellows.'

Denton waited for another thud but nothing came. He said, 'Mr Maltby could tell you about the investigator you sent to Naples, for example.'

Easleigh, mouth open, stared at him. 'Oh, yes.'

'You hired him.'

'Yes.' He jerked upright again and said, as if suddenly in a hurry, 'I hired him in Birmingham before I moved down here. He came very highly recommended, a former member of the Brum police. First-class fellow. Up-to-date methods. I thought it wise to have my own investigation done because of the reputation of the Naples police.' The last sentence seemed to come from something long memorised, like the phrases mouthed by a politician after too long on the stump.

'We admired his work. Didn't we, Maltby.'

'Everybody did. First-rate.'

Easleigh tried to smile. He seemed relieved but stayed bright red. 'Yes, first-rate.' He cleared his throat. 'He set your mind at rest, then, Mr Denton.'

'My mind?'

'You expressed doubts. Mr Maltby said so in his report, which was sent to me.'

'Oh, those doubts. Yes, of course. Set at rest, yes, of course.'

'Oh, good. Good.' Easleigh managed to smile. He looked at a hideous ormolu clock that sat on the mantel like a toad. 'I have to go out by and by...'

'Yes, and we must be going soon. Soon.' Denton smiled at him. Easleigh's eyes swivelled away and swung here and there as if they had slipped their moorings. 'Anything else we can tell you?'

'No... No...' Easleigh uncrossed his legs and, after another look at the clock, planted his feet as if he meant to stand.

'Have you ever been to Naples yourself, Lord Easleigh?'

'*Me?* No!' Easleigh lay back in his chair, then slumped and looked from Denton to Maltby and back.

'I thought you might have been. Having a relative there.'

'I was in school!'

'On holiday, I meant.'

'No! We didn't know him at all. He never wrote. Out of touch. No, I've never been out of England. Hardly out of Brum. Ever.'

'But Mr Cherry had been there before?'

'Cherry?'

'The investigator.'

'Why would you think a thing like that?'

'I thought you might have hired him because of prior experience.'

'I didn't. I mean, I did, but in England. No, he'd never been there. He told me. He said it was an awful place. He couldn't wait to get back. Why would you ever think he'd been down there at all?'

Denton took Spina's photograph from an inner pocket of his suit jacket and offered it to the young man. 'This photograph seems to show both you and Mr Cherry in Naples. We know it's Naples because of the castle in the background—rather a landmark. You probably remember having it taken.'

The young man's voice became a shriek. 'I don't! I was never there!' A terrible look took hold of his face, haunted and fearful. He turned his head a fraction, and Denton suddenly had a dizzying sense of recognition, as if a moment from a dream had flashed on his consciousness. This was not dream, however, but memory: a young man in near-darkness, that same turn of the head and, although the face was obscured, somehow the same expression. Where had it been? And then he remembered: the first night he had gone to Fra Geraldo's, the night that he had found the old man's body, he had stopped in the darkness of a *vico* to ask directions, and he had been aware of somebody young in the shadows.

And then another memory emerged more sluggishly, like some amphibian hauling itself from the ooze. He had asked directions from a man while the young one waited. He had thought the man was somebody from the street. And of course the man had in fact been Cherry.

Shaken, Denton said huskily, 'I'm afraid you *were* there. I saw you. And you saw me.'

'No, I didn't—I didn't—!' The boy began to weep.

Denton raised his voice. 'And you saw me, too, Mr Cherry!'

Maltby looked utterly flummoxed. Easleigh's half-stifled sobs went on. A footstep sounded from beyond one of the doors and then the door opened, and Cherry came in. He was smiling hugely. He was wearing a valet's clothes—alpaca jacket, dark waistcoat, grey trousers—and he was carrying a tray covered with a white cloth and several dishes.

'Here we are, then, here we are! I was out. Did you offer the gentlemen sherry, my lord? Sherry—did you?'

The boy snuffled back his tears, nodded.

'And what did they say? I don't see any sherry glasses put out. *Did* you gentlemen want sherry?'

Maltby managed to say no and then burst out with, 'You're not a detective at all!'

'Oh, but I am, sir. The same Joe Cherry, ex of the Brum police, been a private tec these several years. When His Lordship here ascended to the title, as it were, his father thought it best to get him some protection, so I was taken on. The role of val-it suits, you see—a kind of disguise. But I couldn't introduce myself that way in Naples, could I—how'd it have seemed if I'd said, "I'm His Lordship's val-it, come to investigate the poor old man's death?"'

He smiled at them. Denton said, 'You're a sham, Cherry. You're no more a detective than I am. Your fluid for finding bloodstains was a dodge—it wouldn't find bloodstains in a slaughterhouse.'

Cherry was standing by a hideous sideboard; he had opened a drawer and was taking out small rectangles of white cloth. 'I thought you gentlemen would need serviettes.' He looked up and smiled. 'Why ever would you think that solution, which you saw show up bloodstains with your own eyes, wasn't what I said it was?'

Maltby jumped in ahead of Denton. 'Donati had it analysed! It's water and vinegar and *stuff.*'

Denton said, 'I saw you the night you two killed the old man.'

The boy shrieked, 'I didn't!'

'The two of you threw him down the stairs! But he was already dead, wasn't he, Cherry? Or should I say Signore diToledano?'

Cherry's smile lost its force but lingered. 'You made that up, about seeing us. We was never there.'

'I've a photograph that shows both of you.'

'For certain, sir? Absolute identification? I don't think that can be. Well, I know it can't be, don't I, because we wasn't there.' His smile reasserted itself.

'It's the photo next to His Lordship. You're welcome to look at it.' Denton reached into the inner pocket of his jacket and took out one of the photographs of the chapel. 'That's you, too. As a kid. I've got a witness who can identify you in that one. Michele wasn't the only one of the choirboys still around. And the photographer will identify you in the other one, and that will place you in Naples at the right time.'

'Cock and bull. One of your romances, if you don't mind me saying so, Mr Denton.'

'This boy won't last half an hour in a police room, Cherry. They'll break him like a cheap toothpick.'

Cherry finished what he had been transferring from the drawer to the tray. He looked at the new Lord Easleigh. He nodded once, apparently to himself. His right hand, which had been doing something in the drawer, came out with a shiny revolver. He said, 'You're fly, Mr Denton—cuter than I thought.' He jerked a hand towards the boy, the gesture suddenly violent and rude. 'Denton's got a gun in his side pocket. Get it!'

'He won't live to tell the tale if he tries,' Denton said.

'You move so much as a pinky and I'll shoot your thick friend.' Cherry-diToledano pointed the pistol at Maltby and took a step towards him. 'I mean it.'

'A shot will bring half of London.'

'My arse. You could shoot off six-pounders in here and nobody'd twig. It's live and let live in this poof alley.' His voice became harsh. 'Get the gun!' he shouted at the boy, and Denton saw who the real master was.

Easleigh sidled towards him as if Denton were a dog that might bite. Denton looked at Maltby, who was looking into the barrel of Cherry's pistol. Cherry could hardly miss at that distance; Denton would then have time to charge at him, he thought, but the derringer would be deep in his pocket and might snag on the lining. Cherry might even have time to shoot Maltby and then get one shot at Denton; the idea didn't dismay him, especially because he thought that Cherry's pistol was a cheap .22 calibre of the kind made for cyclists. They were turned out by the thousands in Belgium, larded with fake engraving, probably less accurate than his derringer at anything more than five feet. Denton didn't fancy getting shot, however, even with a .22, although he knew from his experience in the American West that one shot from a .22 wouldn't put a big man. Although it would hurt like hell.

'Get his pistol!' Cherry shouted again, and he took another half-step towards Maltby; he was now in a good spot to shoot Maltby in an eye.

Denton raised his right arm and allowed the boy's trembling hand to slide into his jacket pocket. A few seconds later, he felt the weight of the derringer leave his side.

'Give it me,' Cherry growled.

Instead, Easleigh looked at the thing in his shaking fingers. He held it in both hands, then laboriously pulled back both hammers. Denton heard the click. He said, 'There's no safety on that thing; be careful.'

'Shut your mouth,' Cherry said. 'I'm sick of you.'

'How did you kill him? You broke his neck, didn't you?'

'The both of us, yes.'

'I didn't!' the boy cried.

Cherry laughed. 'You held him while I twisted, boy; to the law, you might as well of done it all yourself. Give me that gun.'

'But you killed Harold Northcote by yourself,' Denton said.

'Cousin Harry?' the boy squealed. 'He didn't!'

'I think he did.' He looked at the older man. 'You pushed him in front of the underground train, didn't you?'

Cherry shook his head. 'Fly, very fly. You should of stayed out of it, Denton. Now it'll cost you and your chick your last breath.'

The boy was agitated. 'You never said anything about Cousin Harry,' he cried. He looked at Denton. 'Harry was killed in the underground.'

'And then Cherry came to you and said you could be the new Lord Easleigh with just one more push.'

Cherry laughed again. 'Me, was it! Yes, I come to him, but *he* was the one would do anything to get out of Brum! *He* was the one that said it wasn't fair for an old fart to go on living while he wanted to *live*!'

'I didn't—I didn't—'

'You did, you sad little squit. You'd have sold your soul for ten quid if anybody'd offered.' He looked at Denton. 'He even had half a scheme for topping Mum and Dad, only he hadn't the spunk. If I hadn't dropped into his life, he'd still be rubbing himself up in the jakes and drinking his ma's eau de colo-nee for his idea of a spree.' He turned his head towards the boy. 'You're a useless little nit, ain't you, my lord?'

'You ruined my life,' the boy moaned.

'Yes, I did, and good on me! Because now I'm getting some of my own back for what was done to me. For my use, you'll do just as well as *him*. I've been a long time about it, but I've got Lord Easleigh by the balls, and you're going to lick my tool and let me up your arse just the way he did me.' His eyes shifted to Denton. 'And you ain't going to stop me, Texas Jack.'

Denton heard a roar of outrage and saw Maltby charge. Cherry's gun went off; then a howl of pain and another gunshot came at almost the same time and both Maltby and Cherry were down, and the thick, acrid smoke of black powder spread in the room. Easleigh was standing with the derringer stuck out in front of him, his eyes wide, smoke lingering at the end of one of the short barrels.

Denton leaped across the room and kicked Cherry, who was down on his right elbow and forearm, blood staining his white shirt high up near the right side of his neck. He went down on his back and tried to raise the little pistol; Denton whacked it aside with his left hand, then twisted it from his fingers as another shot from it ripped into a wall.

Denton turned to Maltby, who was sitting with his back against a chair. He had spread his right hand over his chest as if he were about to take an oath. His eyes met Denton's. He looked surprised and insulted. The bullet had hit him somewhere up near the collarbone.

The young Lord Easleigh screamed, 'He ruined my life.'

Denton looked up. The young man still had the derringer. He was pointing it at Cherry, and as Denton watched, he took a step to move closer, raising the derringer as he moved. Unlike the .22, the derringer fired a big slug of metal, and another bullet from it might kill Cherry.

Denton wanted Cherry to live. He said, rising, 'Don't do it, boy.'

'He's trash. He's a criminal.' He raised the little gun.

Denton moved almost between them, the .22 visible but not pointing at him. 'Don't do it. If you do, I'll have to shoot you. Leave him for the police.'

'No! No—he's evil, he's bad. I'm going to hang because of him. Because of *him*!'

'No. You're young—a good lawyer—' He stepped right between them. If Easleigh fired now, he'd hit Denton. Denton held out his hand. 'Give me the gun.'

The boy stared at him. His face was contorted with fear and with something that might have been triumph. He almost whispered, 'There's nothing left.' He raised his voice again to a cry of pain. 'He ruined my life!' He put the muzzle against his chest, and Denton was not fast enough to stop him from pulling the trigger. He touched the wrist as the gun went off; the boy's hand slammed against his fingers, and black smoke billowed back as if it had been exhaled from the falling body, and then Easleigh was on his back. Denton leaned forward. Easleigh went into sudden convulsions. His legs kicked; his back arched. Blood spurted from his chest, then fell to swelling right above his heart. Denton heard the boy's feet thumping on the floor.

'Help! Help!' Denton had his head out a window. 'Police! There's been a shooting!' He looked down through the bare branches of a tree. An elderly man with a dog was looking up at him angrily. 'Get a policeman! There's been a shooting!'

'In the Albany?'

'Please—a policeman. And a doctor. A man's dying.'

Farther off, a young man was running towards them. A window came up across the lane. Denton shouted again, 'Police! A shooting!' and the elderly man tried to hurry in one direction as the younger one sprinted off in another.

Denton looked down at Maltby. Cold air poured in through the open window. Maltby looked up at him with that same affronted expression he so often wore. He took his hand away from his wound and looked at the blood on it, then up at Denton again. 'This is my best suit.'

❈ ❈ ❈

The noise in the CID room was muted because the hour was late. The shootings at the Albany had engaged, even amused, the detectives for part of the afternoon; now, most of them had gone off to a last duty or the pub or home. Munro, who looked as if he wanted to be heading home himself and who should have been, was still at his desk, Denton opposite him.

'The boy died. He was alive when they got him to hospital, but the medicos couldn't save him. Sorry.'

Denton, slumped in a hard chair with his hands in his trousers pockets, tried to shrug. 'He said his life was ruined. Kids are damned stupid.' He had been two hours at Division, explaining over and over what had happened.

'He'd have got at most a year or two. Get him a good barrister—he'd inherited some money, hadn't he?—he'd have been all right.'

'At seventeen, you don't see it that way. "Life" means the next six months.'

Munro made a sound that might have been agreement. He put the paper aside. 'You're satisfied this "Cherry" is one of the kids who sang in Naples?'

'Edouardo diToledano.'

Munro nodded. 'I got on to Birmingham by phone and gave them that name. Waiting to hear from them.'

'Anything new on Maltby?'

Munro was looking at a pencilled sheet somebody had brought him. 'As right as you or me. A .22 up high, they took the slug out like you'd pick a gooseberry—it was right there against the bone. Cracked the bone, of course.'

'We knew that much at three o'clock.'

'Well, nobody's shot him again since. He'll be fine. Sort of thing looks good on the police application—"Victim of shooting while trying to prevent a crime". We may have to give him a medal.'

'I'll go see him. It could be argued that he saved my life.'

'You mean you could have done it better without him.'

Denton shook his head. 'I mean I'd rather have taken that chance myself. He's just a kid.' He eyed Munro from under his brows. 'Make a good cop, Munro.'

Munro folded his arms and sighed. 'I'd be home now if this hadn't happened. It'd been a quiet day until I was told there'd been a shooting at the Albany. Then I find it's three shootings. Then I find it's you.' He swivelled his neck and arched his back to stretch it. 'I suppose I'll get stuck with telling the Naples coppers about it. Lot of fun that'll be, trying to explain it to a crowd of Dagos.'

'Just the same fun it'll be for them, trying to understand you.' Denton looked moodily into the nearly empty room; his thoughts were turning again to Janet and his anger. 'That boy's room looked like the last act of *Hamlet*. At least nobody wanted to charge me with the shootings.'

'Actually, they thought about it. It was your derringer, after all. And you admitted to having the .22 in your pocket when the coppers arrived. However, you seem to have weaselled your way out of it.'

'I didn't even have to call my solicitor this time. The law is a wondrous thing.'

They sat in silence for a long minute. Munro said, 'You interested in supper? It's going to be a long evening.'

'I think I'd best go home. There are some things that—'

A telephone rang at the far end of the room. Both men waited. Somebody shouted Munro's name and he got up, saying in a satisfied tone, 'About time.' He went off. Denton stared at his own boots. He would go home, he thought, and, painful as it would be, confront Janet. She had to be made to understand that she had wronged him. Humiliated him, although that was the least of it. *She done him wrong.* They had been going wrong for months; he had fooled himself into believing that they hadn't. The fault was his as well as hers, but what had happened at the church was unforgivable; if it meant the end of their relationship, then—

'The boys in Brum.' Munro was falling back into his chair. 'They actually got off their arses and did something. Sent a detective, an actual detective and not a bluecoat, out to see the real J. Cherry. Turns out Cherry collared an Edward diToledano twenty-two years ago for assault and robbery. DiToledano had almost killed a householder with a bludgeon. Brum jury took that seriously. Twenty years' hard labour, reduced to seventeen and a bit for being a good lad. Maybe explains how Cherry speaks English with a Brum accent.'

'How'd he get to Birmingham?'

'No idea. Coppers are checking. Maybe we'll find out from the man himself—he's got a hole in his side, but it isn't mortal. All doped with morphine at the moment.'

'He'll hang.'

'He will if we can lay the steam underground death to his account, but unless he admits it—which he won't—I doubt we'll even go to court with it. I've got somebody checking to see if he was one of the witnesses, maybe used a different name. He must have been right there if he pushed the chap off the platform. From what you say, he has the ballocks to've given information that it was an accident and he saw the whole thing.'

'He'll hang in Italy if not here.'

'Let's hope so. But it's a God-awful process, them being foreigners. You sure you have him dead to rights on the old man's death?'

Denton nodded.

'It's one thing to be sure, and another to have proof.'

'I saw the two of them the night they did it. It was dark; and defence counsel would make hash of it, maybe, but it's a point.

Second, there's Spina, the photographer; he'll remember Cherry. Third, there's the cock-and-bull story of him being a detective and showing us his chemical, which was a complete swindle. Then there's the morgue doctor, who would testify that the old man's neck was broken with a twisting motion, and the lack of blood that points to him being dead when he went down the stairs. And finally, there's me and Maltby, who heard Cherry as much as admit he and the boy murdered the old man.'

'"As much as".'

Denton dismissed the scepticism with an angry hand. 'Once they've searched Easleigh's flat, they'll come up with more. I think there'll be a photo showing Cherry and the boy in Naples—in the photo I had, it looks as if Cherry is pointing towards the photographer. I think he was dragging Easleigh along to have their picture taken together. He wanted it as proof they'd been there. More power over the kid.'

'Self-incrimination?'

'I don't think he cared about that. He cared about making the boy helpless. The way he'd been helpless. It's all about revenge, Munro. It's Naples—when you're helpless, the only justice you believe in is revenge. My guess is that if he could have, he'd have cut the old man's cock and balls off and stuffed them into his mouth after he killed him, but they weren't there to be cut off.'

'Forty-five years is a long time to bear a grudge.'

'As the old man wrote in his diary—his diary of his sins and his penitence—"It is a carnal sin to take childhood away from a child". That's what he'd done to diToledano. And to that poor drunken bastard Michele, who was also killed by diToledano, I suppose, but they'll never prove it. Or give a damn.'

He uncoiled himself from the chair and stood, moving as if his weight had doubled, as perhaps it had: he was heavy with anger and hurt and the anticipation of what would happen with Janet. 'I'm heading home.'

'Lucky man.'

'I don't think so.'

❋ ❋ ❋

Denton's house felt cold and alien. His suitcase waited inside the front door, as if the house wanted him gone; over it, Atkins had draped an overcoat and placed a hat that he judged, Denton supposed, proper for travelling.

Denton called to Atkins. The cold house's silence announced its emptiness. He looked at his watch. If he was to catch his train for Paris, he should leave.

He went upstairs and, still wearing his overcoat, went to his bedroom; there, as he expected, were fresh clothes laid out for the journey. Denton looked at them, touched them as if they were objects he didn't understand, perhaps gifts from the so far hidden residents of the house. He looked at his watch again. He went down to Atkins' floor, where Rupert, taking up most of the little sitting room by lying on his side, raised his head, looked at him and dropped his head again with an audible thud. Denton stepped over him and went out into the back garden, then across it to the door in the garden wall. The door was locked. He had no key: that had been their arrangement.

His rage flared again and he raced through his house and, hatless, out to the pavement and around and up her street, took her front steps two at a time and pounded on the door. Only a dim light was burning inside, something from an inner room. He leaned back and looked up, could see no lights on the floors above. He pounded on the door again.

'Nobody home,' a voice said from below. Denton looked over the railing. A one-eyed face looked up at him, light flooding from a door behind him.

'Cohan!' It was the former boxer who lived down there with his wife.

'Oh, it's you. Thought you'd gone off to Italy.'

'Where is she?'

'Gone.' The eye looked up at him. As if grudging the information, Cohan said, 'She didn't say where. Not sure she *knew* where. She was here for maybe an hour, but she went away.'

'When?'

'Late in the afternoon.'

Denton swore and screwed his body around to put his watch in the light. She had been gone for several hours. He said, 'Let me in.' The eye looked at him, thought about it, disappeared. A full minute later, the front door opened. He went through her house in a kind of frenzy, found everything there except, he thought, her most severe clothes, the clothes she wore for business, for the university. The gaudy dresses she wore at home were still in her closet. Nothing that she might have cared for—books, music, mementoes—was missing. If she were truly gone, she had taken nothing of herself, of the self that he knew. As if, perhaps, leaving him, she had left part of herself as well.

He ran out of the house and got a horse cab to Westerley Street. The house there was locked, the curtains drawn. Black crape hung on the door. In a downstairs window was a sign: *To Let*. He knocked and knocked.

Nothing.

He found another cab and went back to her house and wandered through it and thought he was going to do something terrible and stupid, throw something down the stairs or put a fist through a window or a wall. His earlier rage had rotted into something softer and self-pitying. He tried to play a few notes on her piano, walked again, stopped at a window with his face in his hands. Scenarios of the future without her careened through his mind: back to casual affairs or the whorehouse, long bouts of loneliness and inertia, back to heavy drinking. He would sell his house, maybe go back to America. Or he would go looking for her. Or he would give up writing and lose himself in exhausting work. Farming again.

He looked at his watch. He had missed the boat train.

His mood changed again, still black but now angry again.

It was all a way of saying, How could she do this to me? He said it to himself in each of the rooms, and at last he heard the *me*.

It made him croak out a laugh. *The great me.* It made him groan; it made him ashamed; it made him feel weak in the knees. If this was all about *me*, what was all that shit about love? He wasn't nineteen: love wasn't a search for a mirror.

It was as if the end of love affected only one of two. Yet she must be feeling something, too: relief, misery, joy, along with the grief over Ruth Castle, which must be entirely real and perhaps all-encompassing. He had to face the likelihood—no, the fact; he had been confronted with it for days—that she loved Ruth Castle. Perhaps her *great me* was being entirely spent on grief. Perhaps she felt nothing for him yet. And when she did?

He sat at her desk, surrounded with the neatly arranged residue of her university life—books, papers, pens, her inkwell. One pen lay at an angle, as if it had been thrown aside. The cover of the inkwell was open. One pigeonhole in the rank above the writing surface looked untidy, writing paper from which a sheet or sheets had been pulled, drawing out others an inch. He looked to see what she had been doing, found nothing, and looked in the wastebasket on the floor. A crumpled paper, balled small as if in anger, lay there.

He opened the paper on the desk's green leather surface.

It was a letter—to him.

'I am leaving you—when you read this, I shall be gone. I can't bear the weight of what you call your love for me any more. I do not want to be loved. I want to be somewhere by myself and look at a different world.

'I know you will be hurt by this—*and this is part of the burden of being loved.* I don't want to be able to hurt you. You or anybody.

'For God's sake find yourself some woman who wants your love. Barring that, find yourself a whore who is a better liar than I am.'

She hadn't signed her name. Nor had she sent it, of course. Because she had thought better of it? Or because she had thought worse?

The bitterness of her last sentence made him sick. Then he saw that it could be read two ways: find yourself a whore who will lie about what she feels and thinks; or find yourself a whore who can hide her own crippled self. Read either way, it was terrible.

He walked into the little parlour, white and pale grey with bits of her bright colours, and went to the front window, sightless, heedless.

A cab was standing at the kerb. She was just stepping down from it.

He ran to the door and wrenched it open. She was looking in her handbag to pay the driver, but when she heard Denton she looked up and, seeing him, squared her shoulders and stared at him. What was it she was expecting? His rage? His violence? Certainly he shouldn't have been standing on her doorstep. The cab driver looked from one of them to the other, his expression saying that he understood that something was up and he wanted to leave before it overflowed on him. On his *great me*.

She gave the driver money and came a couple of steps towards Denton. She said, 'I was going away. I got as far as Victoria.'

The cab driver went past her with her luggage, only two bags, and stood at the bottom of the steps and raised the bags a few inches to show Denton that it was his turn to take them. Denton went down and took a bag in each hand. Janet flushed. She went past him, pulling her skirt aside so it wouldn't brush him. This was not the way she had thought her return would go, he guessed.

He went in behind her and dropped the bags in the peculiar little entry—lozenge-shaped in the rear because of the fireplaces behind the wall on each side—and followed her into the parlour. She hadn't taken off her awful hat but stood there as if she were meaning to go away again.

He said, 'I didn't mean to…be here when—I didn't think you'd come back.' He was babbling. 'I read the letter. In your wastepaper basket. I shouldn't have—'

'I sent you a nicer one in the post. You'll have it tomorrow.' She had great courage: she looked him in the eye, her back straight, made no apology. 'The first one was too cruel.'

'Some of it.'

'I meant for you not to follow me. It's been awful these last weeks. I thought I wanted to get away from you, but at Victoria, I knew it was wrong. I was sitting in the train. All that banging of doors. Like the end of the world. I couldn't do it.'

Her eyes were crystalline with tears. Not for him, he thought, but for the implacable situation, from which there was no running away.

'You love Ruth Castle,' he said.

Her head went back; there was the same straightening of her spine he had seen at the kerb when she had seen him in the doorway and known she would have to deal with him. 'I loved Ruth *once*. She was all I had. My anchor. Then I found she was shallow, and she drank too much, and I had to leave her.' She winced. He could have said, *As you left me*, but he didn't. She gave him time to say it or something worse and then said almost defiantly, 'When she was dying, I loved her again. I'm sorry, Denton.' Her face was haggard with, he realised, grief.

His rage had killed itself on that rock, his *great me*. Seeing her through the window, he had felt it revive, but it had gone for good now. 'You've told me over and over you didn't know what love is.'

'I was wrong. Or I lied.'

'I love you.'

Her face toughened, tightened; he knew the look. 'Before, with Ruth—we were *lovers*. Do you understand?'

'Was it all—with me—was that what you meant by a whore who was a better liar than you?'

'Oh, God! That was stupid; it's why I tore it up. No, I meant…you deserve better. You shouldn't have read it.'

He felt himself flush, embarrassed, humiliated, having to know and humiliated because he had to know and couldn't find the words.

She understood without his saying it. 'Oh, the sex, you mean?' she said. 'No, it was real. No. I hadn't been with anybody since Ruth's house, and it was like…discovering something impossible, like a lost city or an ocean. I was genuine with you, Denton, but *I loved Ruth*.' Her face softened. 'You can't change the past. You can't improve me.'

'I don't want to improve you. I want you as you are.'

She came closer to him but stayed more than an arm's length away. Her eyes were still shiny; so were his, he supposed. She tried to smile, then shook her head.

'I'm going back to Naples,' he said. 'I'd be gone now, but I missed the train.' He added, as if it would explain everything, 'I have to apologise to DiNapoli.' He swallowed, found it difficult. His voice was hoarse as he said, 'Come with me.'

She smiled, not very happily.

So they stood, she in travelling clothes and a hat, he with his hair messed from his rage, looking into each other's tears. They knew what we learn with difficulty: this is an imperfect world and we are imperfect creatures, and the great emotions that bring us our happiest moments always bring pain in their luggage. We are surrounded with the ghosts of our own imperfection.

He moved towards her.